Riding Shotgun

Riding Shotgun

Paul Schaefer

Edited by Wendy Weckwerth
Cover by Kevin Cannon

ISBN 13: 978-1-59298-700-9
Library of Congress Catalog Number: 2016919515
Printed in the United States of America
First Printing: 2017
21 20 19 18 17 5 4 3 2 1

Interior design by Athena Currier

Beaver's Pond Press, Inc.
7108 Ohms Lane
Edina, MN 55439–2129

(952) 829-8818
www.BeaversPondPress.com

For

Tonnelli,

Enjoy the Ride!

thank you,

Paul Schrader

4-17-18

This book is dedicated to Trudi, Bronwyn and Josh,
the architects of my fortunate life.

Chapter 1

Mary had pulled out onto Highway 1 in pouring rain. They were barely onto the highway when the other car spun out of control and slammed into them.

The rest was vague. Mike yelling, pulling her out of the car. Ominous hissing from their little Nissan, half wrapped up in a chain link fence. Mary thoroughly soaked. Blinding ambulance lights. An ER, Mary in a bed, Mike next to her. A young doctor (Latina?) telling her that she was lucky, the side airbag had probably saved her life. Just a mild concussion and a couple broken ribs. And a vivid seat-belt bruise. Mike had one too.

Later, they'd laughed as they compared bruises. They hadn't laughed when their daughter Emma made inquiries about the other driver. The woman had suffered a serious concussion and a broken limb or two. Leading Mike to conclude they were done driving small cars. And that's how Mary's trip began.

"Who knows how long we've got left, Mary, but from now on, we're going to be ultra safe in some big machine, OK?"

And who knew then how little time Mike had left? About two years, with his final three months not much of a life at all.

Back in Pasadena after their accident, Mary and Mike rented a large SUV of some kind, all white and kind of threatening, as they decided on their new vehicle. While it seemed that half of Los Angeles was now driving SUVs, during their trial rental they agreed that they weren't going to join the four-wheel-drive-to-go-to-the-grocery-store set. It didn't make sense, and it wasn't who they were. Nor were they going to buy a new car. Never had, as Mike insisted that buying a new car was a big waste of money.

"You lose ten grand as soon as you pull out of the lot. Let somebody else eat that, and we'll buy their leftovers," he'd argued.

An argument Mary agreed with, more or less, because she simply wanted to get on with it. Get another car, and stop driving that awful rental.

But as often happened with the Finnegans, the plot thickened. As in, Mike coming home with a camel hair sport coat from the Goodwill. That being the only store he cared to shop in, mostly looking for old jazz LPs. And yes, he'd found some gems over the years. Oscar Peterson. A lot of Coltrane. Too much Miles, if you asked Mary. But a camel hair sport coat?

"Mike. A sport coat? Camel hair?"

"Yup. It was only two fifty. Two dollars and half a buck. And look what great shape it's in. But the real reason I got it? Solidarity. With the Arabs." He grinned his elfin smile.

"OK. I know you can't blow your nose without it being political. But explain this one."

"Simple. Ever since 9/11, the Arabs have been everybody's favorite group to hate. Even when it's been Muslims who aren't Arabs—like the Afghanis—most Americans just think 'raghead.' Bad guys. Deport 'em. Beat 'em up. Oh, and invade their countries. So . . . Arabs. Camels. Used to smoke 'em. Lawrence of Arabia. A camel hair sport coat. Least I can do." He grinned again.

Mary laughed. Mike's impeccable logic. And later, hanging the coat up, knowing he'd never wear it, she noticed an envelope in the inside pocket. Sitting on their bed, she opened it and two three-by-five color photos fell out. Both showed an older white man standing proudly next to a very large car, maroon, with one of those faux leather roofs. The sort of auto they'd often made fun of—gas guzzler, tank, road hog.

That evening, sipping their gin and tonics in the new sun porch Mike had built, they puzzled over the photos. "Haven't a clue about the guy. But the car? It's a Lincoln Town Car. Late '80s. The kind the big shots on Wall Street use. Hate to say it, but they're actually pretty decent. Old man's ride. Think I saw an ad for one at the hardware store."

"You paid attention to it?"

"I did. This pic makes me think I might just go check it out."

Which, the next day, they did. Mary was along reluctantly, hoping to stay Mike's purchasing hand. But to no avail, because in talking to the elderly woman selling the car, it became clear that the Lincoln was *the* car—the one in the photos. Yes, she'd given away her deceased husband's clothing to the Goodwill. Yes, the photo from the jacket was him. No, she didn't want it back. And yes, of course, they could take the car for a test drive.

Stepping away from the Lincoln after driving it, Mike told Mary, sotto voce, that the purchase was inevitable.

"Hey. I buy the jacket. You find the pics. There's the guy, there's the car, I see an ad, and it's the freakin' car in the photos. The auto gods, Mary, have given a very strong nod in our direction. I'm gonna make her an offer she can't refuse."

Which was exactly the price the widow was asking. They brought a money order to her that afternoon, and Mike drove the great beast home.

Daughter Emma had much to say as soon as they drove the thing down to Silver Lake to show her. "Those are Republican cars, Mom. For old white guys who love to tell about getting to shake Ronnie Reagan's hand at some golf course. Someplace that probably excludes blacks, Latinos, and women. And look at the size of it. It's a g-d dreadnaught."

"Well, dear, your dad is indeed an old white guy. But a Reaganite? Remember how he used to spit out the car window every time he heard his name? Dreadnaught, though. That's a good name. That's what we'll call it."

The Dreadnaught. Eventually it would haul Mary halfway across the country to visit her sister.

Chapter 2

In Garberville, a town in redwood country far north of Los Angeles, Chet Adams called his daughter Joni and asked her to come out and see him.

"Why, Dad? I don't have any money, honest."

"I know. Neither do I, so we're even. But that's what I want to talk to you about—money! Maybe a way to get some, so come on out and bring some milk and bread and peanut butter, will you?"

"Ugh, I knew it. Want me to pick up some steaks and some beer, while I'm at it?"

"Yeah, that'd be great!" her moocher dad replied eagerly.

Slamming her cell phone down on the passenger seat, Joni barely made the stoplight in front of her. And of course there was a cop, one of Geeville's finest, at the intersection. As he looked her over slowly, she saw it was her favorite officer, Walt Samuelson. Sammy the Shit, everyone called him. It was a mystery that no one had offed him by now, since he had pissed on so many people.

"Let's see," she thought as she drummed her nails on the wheel. "How many times has that fucker stopped me, and how many times has he hit on me? Hey, same number!"

The first two or three times, back when she had just started to drive at sixteen, Joni had dutifully told her dad about it. Bad idea, she quickly learned, because Chet had a wicked temper. A temper that now forced him to live out in the hills, out by the growers, where ostensibly the law couldn't find him. Truth was, however, no one wanted to find him, not even that prick Sammy. Way too much trouble for way too little return. Even Joni didn't want to know where he was. But she did know, and suffered accordingly, she thought as she pulled into the gas station convenience store. Actually, she'd even considered turning him in herself once. Someone had said something about reward money. But she couldn't do it.

She remembered too clearly her grandmother Eunice's admonition. "Sorry, honey, but he's your father. The one and only. You don't get to pick your parents. I know he loves you, he just finds it hard to tell you. I mean, even your crazy mom loved you, in her own weird way."

"Yeah. Then why'd she split, leaving you to raise me?"

"I don't know. Probably had something to do with this shitty little town, I'd guess. She never liked it here," Eunice explained as she tugged at a sleeve in one of her endless, but futile, attempts to hide the ugly track marks on her arms. A ragged history written right there on her skin of her lifelong battle with heroin.

"Hey, Joni, how's your doper granny?" the assholes at school would taunt.

"Fuck you. And fuck your whole family too," was her usual witty retort. One that had gotten her smacked around more than once. And right here, clerking at the checkout, was one of the former smackers, LuAnn Jacobs.

Their childhood feuds long gone, LuAnn asked, "Hey, Joni, party tonight?"

"Not sure," Joni dumped her purchases on the counter. "Maybe something going on at the Hood, the room near the office?" she guessed, referring to a local low-rent motel, the Robin Hood. "How's your kid?"

"Juanita," LuAnn asked, pulling a picture off the wall behind her and handing it to Joni. "Look at her smile. A beauty girl, huh?"

"Wow, yeah, she's great. You're lucky," Joni lied.

"Be a lot luckier if her bastard old man, Juan, had hung around!" the cashier scanned Joni's food.

"Yeah, I suppose," Joni replied sympathetically, retrieving her change and grabbing her dad's groceries. She hurried out with a "see you" over her shoulder, thinking with relief as she started the car and moved back onto the highway, "God at least I didn't do that. A kid, for chrissake!"

Kids, actually. They were all over town. The woods was full of the little brats. Half, maybe more, of the girls in her small graduating class now had kids. And all, like her, not even twenty-five yet. Man, how dumb, Joni thought. Even the ones who were married, or had stayed married, had to devote their lives—lives they hadn't even started to live—to little kids. Yuck!

These and other thoughts scrambled in Joni's head as she took the increasingly crappy roads to her father's hideout, a miserable little two-room cabin so deep in the forest that sunlight seemed never to touch it. Hence the moss and 'shrooms on the logs outside, and the damp and mold on the inside. And then there was Chet himself. Also mossy, damp, and 'shroomy. Always making her uncomfortable with his overlong hugs and his comments about how great she looked.

"Hey, cut it out," she'd had to tell him more than once. "You're my dad, and fathers just aren't supposed to be checking out their daughters!"

"Ease up, little girl," he'd say with his hands in the air in mock surrender. "I'm not messin' with you. Just admiring the product of my loins."

And truth was, he'd never really molested her, he was just a little too affectionate. Hugged her a little too hard and little too long. Yuck, again, she thought as she finally turned onto the logging road that was the last lousy leg of the trip, and a challenge in any weather, but especially miserable after a rain like yesterday's. She slip-slided her ancient Civic—with its odometer that had given out at 263,000 miles—up to the cabin.

Grocery bag in hand, she knocked several times before Chet came to the door. Looming in the tiny entrance, all six feet four of him, albeit increasingly stooped, despite barely scratching forty-five. The result, she thought, of his very hard life. The booze, the pills, the coke, and the smokes—dope and ciggies, one of which was in his mouth as he let her in.

"Hey, what happened to your no-smoking deal?" she asked as she kept the bag of groceries in her arms to ward off a hug.

"Hey your own self, little girl," Chet said as he sized up the bags. "One thing at a time, like they say in AA. I haven't done hard drugs now for probably five years. And I'm making a real effort, me and Cherie, to cut back on the booze. Having no money helps that, but the smokes? Don't think I can do it. Not just yet, anyway." He pointedly put his cigarette into the small wood stove in the corner.

"Whatever, Dad. Anyway, here's your groceries." Grateful that he hadn't yet tried to hug her, she escaped into the tiny kitchen and put the stuff into his fridge, which was propane operated since the cabin was off the grid.

"Makes it tougher to find me," he'd say. "No electric bills to trace."

"Right, Dad, but what about that cell phone?" Joni had asked when he moved here.

"No *problema*, it's in Cherie's name, her account. She just lets me use it."

Joni had learned not to pursue Chet's logic about hiding out, and the various parties, the law and otherwise, pursuing him. His rampant paranoia. None of it made much sense so best thing was to stay away from it, from him. And especially from the awful Cherie, with her chain smoking, her nasty little dogs, and her enormous breasts, on which the woman always displayed some gigantic piece of cheap jewelry and her gold-chained glasses, calling attention to what was already too obvious.

Looking over her shoulder into the fridge, Chet asked, "So where's the beer and the steak?"

"Yeah, sorry. What I brought just about tapped me out, and I don't get paid until Friday," she heard herself explaining, even though she knew she should feel no obligation to him whatsoever.

"OK, OK. Sit down, and take a look at this," handing her a letter. A very official-looking letter, addressed to him at Cherie's address. His last "official residence," as he called it.

Quickly scanning the letter, and looking again at the name of the firm on the envelope, Joni asked, "Isn't Rochester where Grandma was from, in Minnesota?"

"Yeah, it's where she grew up, before she split and came to sunny Cal."

"This says they want you to get in touch with them regarding some kind of estate, right?" Joni asked as she stood with the letter in her hand.

"Yeah, but I'm actually totally suspicious. Might be a fancy trap, the FBI could easy get some lawyers to put together a letter like that. Draw me out, I show up in Minnesota, if I even get that far, and bingo! They got me, right?" Chet walked to the door and peered out to see if maybe Joni had been followed.

"Not right, Dad. Jesus, now you say you've got the FBI on your ass. Really? You really think that?"

"Doesn't matter what *I* think. It's what *they* think! They hold all the freakin' cards, baby girl. And me, I got the joker!" Chet turned to the window and continued scanning the trees around his place.

"So you mentioned money on the phone. Isn't that what estates are about? Money? I mean maybe this is simply—like they're sort of saying here—that your grandfather, a guy you never met, died and has left you some serious bread, Dad. Think about it!" Joni pleaded. "I mean, what if it's a lot, a whole lot, of money? Shit, Dad. You could buy yourself a piece of land in say, Canada, or Mexico, where they'd never find you."

"Maybe . . . ," Chet said as he wrapped his orangutan arms tightly around his upper chest and started slowly rocking back and forth. "Or," he grimaced, showing max teeth, "maybe they grab me, and I find myself on a nice piece of land surrounded by a bunch of guys in stripes. Know what I mean?"

Joni threw her head back in disgust. "Well, I think you should go check it out. Get there, look around a little, reconnoiter. You know. If you smell cops, you split. If not . . . go in and collect your bundle."

"Or not," Chet replied seriously. "Who knows if there is any money at all? Ever hear of estate sales? Somebody dies and the family sells the furniture, dishes, maybe an old Buick, whatever. Not necessarily money, though." Chet looked outside the cabin again.

"OK, so let's say there's lots of spendy stuff. You sell it! Have you talked to Cherie about this?" Joni was, as usual, exasperated with her father's crazy illogic.

"No, she was half in the bag when she brought it," he admitted. "And I'm sure she's forgotten about it. So I didn't tell her. Not going to. Just you." Chet propped up against a dusty log wall.

"Fine, but what can I do, Dad? Except recommend that you see a headshrinker about your paranoia! FBI, Jesus!" Joni was getting ready to split.

"Hey, you never know. And that's the whole thing with these bastards. Keep me guessin' until one day I go out to take a piss. Bam, they got me. Adios, Chet. Rock-breakin' motherfucker! But I got an idea, OK?"

"What?"

"Easy, you go out there instead of me! Bring the letter, tell them I'm indisposed, or whatever, and see what's going on. You know Eunice had a brother? I think he was in Nam. She didn't know much, but once in a sober while she'd call an old girlfriend of hers back there to check up on her family. I know her mother died, a long time ago. So if the brother is still there, still alive, maybe he'd help you figure this shit out. Not sure, but I think their dad might have been a doc. Real bread, you know?"

"Right, I show up and make a claim on stuff the brother would get if nobody shows," Joni paused at the door. "Why would he help?"

"Hey, now who's paranoid?" Chet accused. "Maybe he's a decent guy, has a nice place you can stay. Maybe a nice family, cousins for you. You've always wanted more family than just me and Eunice."

"Wow, Dad. I can see it now. Thanksgiving in a month or so, there I am at the long table. Huge turkey, bunch of little blond kids sitting politely, the wifey in her apron, and my uncle—no actually, *your* uncle—at the head of the table, head bowed in prayer. 'Please, Lord, welcome this young sinner into your heart.' Yahduh, yahduh!"

"Whoa, girl," Chet put a tentative hand on his daughter's arm. "Give it a break! Give *me* a break! Just go, will you, and see what's up. Please?"

"Prob'ly not, Daddio. Too far, too weird, too expensive." She had the door open now.

"OK. Just think about it, will you?" he pleaded. "I'll call you in a couple of days. Can't let something like this go on too long, you know." He let go of her arm.

"All right, Pops, gotta go now." Giving him a hurried hug, she fled the cabin and drove back to Geeville as fast as she could. Which was fast, considering her tiny, ancient Honda, because she was a good driver and loved to speed. Had gotten too many tickets because of her heavy foot. Had to take a stupid night class in order to keep her license. Big, fat old guy, had two huge bellies, one below the other. He ran the stupid "class" about driving safe as he sat on his desk and bored them to tears. Dude actually tried to hit on her. Disgusting. Led him on a little until she passed the class, and kept her license. Then told him to go fuck his ridiculous fat self! A great moment watching the hate boil up in his toady face!

Back in town, she went home to her crappy little apartment, changed into her stupid uniform, and then walked to work at the Best Western where she was a "housekeeping associate." Something she loved to tell people, with a leer, when they asked what she did.

"Housekeeping associate, man!" she'd say.

"What's that?"

"What do you think, man? A freakin' maid! Only thing I 'associate' with is a vacuum cleaner."

Although truth told, she actually worked all over the place in one of the biggest buildings in Garberville, a huge place. X number of rooms, she never remembered the number. Whoops, "suites!" So much space, bigger than her apartment, for two people, mostly couples, to spend a night in.

People came to a motel for what, really? To sleep, maybe to fuck. Eat the "free" breakfast. Little kids loading their plates with muffins larger than them. Old people, way overweight, stuffing themselves like it was their last meal. She saw this because she often served, if that's what it could be called, at the breakfasts pouring coffee, keeping the gravy boat filled, hauling in the very white scrambled eggs. White eggs, white people. Ninety-five percent of them, anyway. She could count on two hands the number of blacks she'd seen there. Some Hispanics and Asians, but not many. Lots of Germans—white, very white and always trying to talk to her, asking about the redwoods and so on.

Redwoods, deadwoods. What did she care about trees? Too many here in Geeville, she thought. Always foggy, damp, gloomy. What in the hell Eunice had seen in this place she did not know. But, of course, what Eunice had seen was a great place to hide out. From Chet's abusive father, bad Grandpa Adams, long dead everyone supposed. Hide from her dealers down in Los Angeles, from her heroin habit, who knew what else. And now, Joni thought, I'm stuck here. Thanks, Grandma. Thanks a lot! But hey, maybe I *should* look up that letter. Be one way to get the hell out of Dodge!

Chapter 3

Mary loved her little Pasadena bungalow. Built in the 1920s with a certain Arts and Crafts heritage, the house had, yes, character. Visitors had often praised the craftsmanship evident in the open redwood rafters and the built-in oak and stained-glass cabinets. Then Mike loved to tell them that it had been assembled from a kit, delivered by the Ready-Cut Bungalow Company. The cabinets too.

"Factory-made, the whole damn thing," he said, grinning, pointing out that much more authentic specimens could be seen in northern Pasadena in the area preserved as Bungalow Heaven.

Kit or not, Mary was proud of their home, especially the landscaping and gardens that graced it. The plants, including a great variety of both shrub and climbing roses, the pink Sweet Surrender being her favorite, all kinds of native succulents, several variations of rhododendrons, and a lovely raised bed filled with many kinds of herbs. Almost all of the greenery Mary had gotten free in her career as a landscaper. Clients tired of or had too much of this or that, so she took them. Transforming, over the years, a boring little property into a spectacular one often visited by local photographers and commented on by passersby. If she liked them, they got a tour. If not, they got a nod.

Yes, she loved her home, but now, with Mike gone, it was hard, too hard, to stay. Most of their almost sixty years of marriage had been there, so every single thing—from their coffee mugs to a certain afternoon light that lit the lovely tile floor Mike had laid in the sunroom—reminded her. Not so much of Mike, but of them, their life together. Now over.

God, she was lonely. And the thought of staying here with the ghost of their marriage hovering everywhere was frightening. It would be easy, like one of her widowed neighbors, to start her gin and tonics at lunch and continue them until she staggered to her empty bed. Or she could smoke marijuana every day, all day. She and Mike had smoked Mary Jane off and on for years, but never a lot. Too expensive. But now, with her medical marijuana card, it was cheap and plentiful. And powerful. Yikes! Walk around her yard in a haze until she fell and broke a hip in a classic oldster ending? Nope. Come on, old lady, you're smarter, tougher than that. What you're going to do instead is take that quintessential American medicine, a road trip. Drive the Dreadnaught across country to see Theresa. Her sister in Minnesota.

Thinking about it as she ate her favorite supper of beans, tortillas, and salsa, Mary began to get a little excited. A little. Unlike Mike, big excitement wasn't her M.O. Any obstacles? Emma, of course, would be dead-set against the idea. But hey, it was just a car trip. She wasn't one of those grandmas about to set a new record for flying airplanes or climbing some mountain, then going on the news to brag about it. Just an old lady driving cross-country in a pretty safe part of the world.

After supper, Mary called her friend Janet and invited her to breakfast at the great little Cuban place in Silver Lake, Cha Cha Cha.

"I'm planning a trip, Janet. To see my sister in Minnesota."

"That's a good idea. You need to get away for a while. Flying?"

"No. Driving. And that's what I need to talk to you about."

"Driving? Really? OK, pick me up at nine, please."

Next morning, Mary took more time than usual selecting what to wear. Janet was an aging clotheshorse, one who really believed that the clothes didn't necessarily make the woman, but neglect of them lessened the woman. And the man, for that matter.

"Once we came off the African plains, my dear," Janet had said more than once, "and started to wear things, it was only a short evolutionary stroll to having those things become meaningful, so those who don't care about how they dress are, to my mind, not fully human." Her friend smiled when she said it, but Mary knew she meant it.

Clothes. Mary had little time for the whole appearance thing. Maybe because she had always looked OK? Maybe even cute, but never a beauty. True, she was never bedeviled by bad teeth or thin hair or weight. In fact, now at eighty, many people thought she was still in her sixties, even with her heavily wrinkled skin, won in hard combat with the California sun over many landscaping years. Let's see . . . some black cotton slacks, a Mexican blouse, and her Bjorn clogs. She did care about shoes because her feet had started to trouble her about the same time that menopause arrived, a long time ago, and clogs were her favorite part of her wardrobe.

As Mary pulled the Lincoln out onto the street on yet another sunny L.A. morning she thought aloud, "Some rain would be nice!" How many times had she said that? Too many, with too few results.

While she drove, she deliberately became conscious of being at the wheel. It took work, as driving was usually something you did more or less automatically. But with all the anxiety Emma would have about Mary's trip, she decided she needed to start paying attention, make sure she was totally on the ball. Rather, on the road!

Let's see, no speeding up to make the yellow. When stopped, watch the rearview for the car that might brake too late and hit her. She had been rear-ended twice. The first time, she never even saw the perp, who backed madly, screechingly away, swerved wildly around her and sped off, through the red light. The second time, just a year before they got the Lincoln, the person who hit her actually backed up, parked his car, and then came up to apologize and give her his insurance data. In L.A.! Imagine! He was an older Indian gentleman, perfect English but with that lovely Hindi lilt to his speech. What was his name? Chatterjee? Bannerpree? Decent man, anyway, especially in the hit-and-run capital of America.

At Janet's house, in a Pasadena neighborhood a little more upscale than Mary's, her friend left the stoop and strolled, part of her class act, to the car, ducking a bit as she entered. For years they'd put up with the comments about them being Mutt and Jeff, as Mary was five one to Janet's five ten. There seemed to be more tall women around now, but when Janet was growing up she was unusual. And rather than hide it, she flaunted her height with her elegant clothes, and that saunter.

"Janet, have you ever *run* somewhere, or even been in a real hurry?"

"Of course. Running I can't remember doing except in high school. We had to in gym, which I hated. And in a hurry? Compared to James, I'm an Olympic sprinter."

Janet's husband James was a beanpole of a man, the kind of person who when he sat, did so in sections, knees bent, butt carefully down part way, torso tilted forward, and then the grand finale. But he did have a bad back. Had it for years, and needed to be careful. Slow and careful hardly began to describe James, a man who habitually polished his silverware before eating, whether at home, in a restaurant, or at Mary's house.

"Don't take offense," Janet told Mary years ago, "he does it everywhere."

And Mary had eventually relaxed about it, even when Mike, to bug her, would polish his spoon and fork too. "Shine it all you want, Mike, you'll never be anywhere as tall as James."

"How is the professor?" Mary asked Janet.

"He's fine, down to just one class now. He should have gotten out years ago, but I think he's not sure what he'll do if he doesn't have at least one class to prepare for."

"But isn't it that French lit course he's been teaching for eons? What's to prepare?"

"Oh no," Janet bemoaned. "James has always revamped his courses each time he teaches. No yellowed note cards for him. It's bothered me over the years, all the time he puts into his teaching, but I think he's right. I had way too many stale classes in high school and college. I was always so disappointed because I loved learning, and then found out that many of my teachers actually didn't. I bet neither Emma nor Carlos serve stale bread in their classes. And speaking of Emma, James has heard that her particular brand of political fire has been bothering some of the bureaubirds at City. I mean what if the right-wing politicos hear of it and cut funding to the college?"

"They shouldn't worry," Mary noted. "If funds are cut, the administrators and deans will keep their jobs, and get raises, and each time a full-time faculty member like James retires, they'll just hire some more adjuncts to 'temporarily' fill in. Low pay, no bennies, no standing. Emma doesn't care, because she's got all the money and bennies she needs from the high school."

"Please, my dear," Janet sighed. "Let's just move on to this trip you're thinking about."

Before Mary could answer, they arrived at Cha Cha Cha, which they both loved, for despite its plastic palm fronds, sickly cacti, and thatch-covered patio with bugs, the food was wonderful, the service was fine but not obsequious, and it was dependable. It had been here for well over twenty years, a restaurant record in trendy L.A., and in that time the menu had scarcely changed.

Sitting on the patio, they stopped talking long enough to order, in deference to the waiter. They usually split something because the portions were so large, but it was late and they were both very hungry so they ordered separately. God, the food: jerked chicken omelets, black beans and rice, banana French toast, fried plantains, fresh fruit sections on every plate, deliciously crusty, warm bread, and coffee strong enough to peel the paint off Mary's Lincoln. Eating in silence, they glanced at each other with grins of approval, until finally Janet, pausing with her coffee, asked again, "OK, dear friend, what's up?"

Cleaning chicken from her teeth with a toothpick, Mary sighed, "Well, it's not really a big deal, but then maybe it is. Simply, I plan to take a cross-country car trip in the Dreadnaught, of course, to visit my sister. Theresa. The one who fled Chicago like me, but ended up on a farm in Minnesota? Even though we're close, and we talk quite a bit," Mary continued, "she's only been here once, for Mike's memorial. And we only visited her and her now long-dead husband once, years ago. We had a great visit. Mike wasn't much interested in the corn and the animals, but he loved the machinery part of it. We even talked briefly about moving to the country ourselves on the way back, but that idea lasted about half an hour. We had our jobs, our friends, like you and James, our whole life was here. Now, with Mike gone, I don't feel as anchored, and I'm lonely. Very. So I'm going to see Theresa. And I want to do it with one last great road trip. Killing two things with one stone, really."

"What do you mean, killing *two* things?"

"Well, I want to see Theresa, and her farm. I've always thought about that place—the animals, her gardens, the trees, the view. Of course I could take the train. Amtrak makes a stop in Winona, where she lives, or a plane. Theresa's son could pick me up at the airport. So, obviously Emma would want me to do that."

"Do what?"

"Take the train or the plane. The plane preferably, as by her lights, I'm probably least at risk that way. On the train, you know, a gang of flag-waving Tea Partiers saying nasty things about Mexicans could get on, I would yell at them, they'd harass me, and we'd all get thrown off the train in Fargo or some desolate place like that."

"Fargo. My God! Remember that movie?" Janet grinned.

"Who could forget it? The body in the wood chipper. I've used those, you know, so I paid close attention in case I'd need to chip someone up one day!"

They both laughed. "So, why the car trip then?"

"OK, here it is. You know how much I miss Mike. Terribly. Will until I'm gone. So the trip is . . . what would James call it in French? *Un homage* to Mike. He loved to travel, especially by car, and he loved that car. But he never got any further than Monterey in it before he got sick. I know it sounds silly, but the Dreadnaught seems to demand, every time I'm in it, that I take a long trip, for Mike. And for me. One last major jaunt before they take my license away."

Janet reached across the table and covered Mary's hand. "I know you miss him. God, I hope I go before James. I can't imagine life without his cranky ranting. It's a pain in the butt, but silence would be much worse. And the car? I get that. I really do. I have clothes, some not worn for years, that demand things from me. Wear me! Give me away! Take my picture! Get this spot of olive oil off me, for goodness sake! So what can I tell you but do it. Do it, of course. However, my dear . . . ."

"However what?" Mary demanded.

"I do think Emma should be worried," Janet admitted. "Bad things happen to good people on America's highways every day, and with the economy in the trash can—there's desperation afoot. Hey, I like that line. There's desperation afoot." An amateur poet, Janet paused to take a pen out of her purse and write the line down in a small notebook.

"Yes, that's a great line. Anyway, I'm going to take the trip, so I guess I just take the risk and do it the way I really want to. Right?"

"Not entirely," Janet cautioned. "If you're going to drive across the country, you'll have to take certain measures. To reduce the risk. You go out in a boat, you bring a life jacket. Your car is a boat, a land yacht, really, and you will need a life preserver. This will shock you, but I've got an idea. Kind of crazy, and it actually might work. In fact, as soon as I heard about your idea I thought this up." Janet put her hand to her mouth. "Whoops, guess I blew it!"

"So you knew about my trip *before* I told you?" Mary was more amused than angry.

"Emma called me," Janet admitted with a guilty smile. "She called last week and told me you were up to something, and she figured it was this. The trip. So she asked me to dissuade you, talk you into taking a plane. I said I'd think about it, which I did. James and I talked about it too. Ultimately both of us sided with you. Not against Emma, necessarily, but certainly in favor of you taking your monster car wherever you want. So, let's let go of my little deception, and focus on my big idea, OK?"

"Fine. Full speed ahead. What do you have?"

"In my sewing room, where I design and sew all the fabulous garments that line my closets and fill you with envy," Janet smirked, "maybe you remember, I have two or three mannequins. They're useful, of course, but strangely comforting as well, silent but friendly sentinels who listen to me gripe about a botched hem, or complain about James and his rants, and especially, allow me to pour out all my anxieties about the kids. It's not that I actually talk to them, but I do mutter when I work, and I like to think they really hear me, unlike most people who at best only hear part of what you're trying to say. I imagine the mannequins take it in and change it to suit their notions. They have a totally accurate record of my mutterings, so if I could push their playback buttons they could repeat my life's most intimate moments of reflection. Of course, there is the very large problem of my not knowing mannequinese, their language," Janet laughed.

"So," Mary pushed, "you talk to your mannequins, so it's fine if I talk to my car. But what's your big idea?"

"Of course, my big idea. But you know, I have to say, for far too long we assumed humans were the only ones with language, tools, culture, and so on. Then Jane Goodall goes off and finds out chimps make tools, talk to each other, and have a cultured, learned society. Then it's other apes, dolphins and whales, mammals in general, birds. Even plants. So I've always wondered, why wouldn't inanimate objects talk in some fashion too?" Janet's sidetrack was wearing Mary out.

"How about because they're inanimate? Without life?"

"But what did Disney and his cohort do," Janet persisted. "Right here in sunny southern Cal? They animated knives and forks and spoons, brooms, books, and cars. Putting on the screen ideas that have been around since the beginning of time, I'd bet. Excalibur, Arthur's famous sword? Animated. Dorothy's Tin Man? Animated. Kids have no problem at all with the idea. That's why they're scared to go to bed at night, because the stuff in their room frightens them. And it's no good telling them it's just a chair, because to them the chair is alive!"

"Sure," Mary conceded. "I took an anthropology course at Pasadena City years ago. The teacher told us that for the precivilized folks, everything was animated, from arrowheads to cooking pots to the stones they used to weigh down their fishing nets. That's why they were so careful not to be cutting down every tree in sight too, because for them trees were full of spirits who could help or harm you."

"Yes, well, as a former Catholic, you remember the 'host' piece of bread *becomes* the 'body of Christ' as the priest puts it in your pious mouth." Janet held up the imaginary wafer.

"Right, and the wine too," Mary added. "The fancy Catholic word for it is transubstantiation."

"OK, enough about that. Now that we have *substantiated* that my notion about the mannequins listening to me isn't so weird, here's my idea." Janet gave a nervous laugh. "We take my male mannequin, paint a face on it, dress him up, put him in a decent hat, and buckle him into the Dreadnaught's passenger seat!"

"Riding shotgun?" Mary asked, using one of Mike's phrases.

"Yes, riding shotgun!" Janet pumped her fist. "And that's a great way to put it, because that's his job, to make people think you have a man riding with you, which will considerably decrease anybody's idea of taking advantage of the old lady in her Lincoln."

"Janet. You're crazy. Seriously nuts. So naturally, I'll do it. It'll make Emma hit the ceiling, but honestly that might be half the fun!"

So the two friends began to plan the passenger's disguise, and by the time Mary dropped Janet off at her house, they'd made plans to start the project in earnest.

"Y'know, Mary, this is great," Janet said as she climbed out of the car. "I feel like we're in high school, doing something slightly forbidden. And, boy, I needed a fun project. I mean how many blouses can a woman make without turning into one herself?"

Chapter 4

THERESA, "TEE" TO HER LATE HUSBAND TONY and her sister Mary, awoke later than usual, at seven. Turning, she snuggled for a moment, covers over her head, hoping once again that when she died she would simply go to sleep and not wake up. After telling that wish several times over the past year to her son Rusty, he chided her for being morbid.

"When do your kids begin to chide you?" she wondered as she dressed slowly, hampered by her arthritis. Even as children, did they start looking forward to the role reversal? Rusty, she had to admit, rarely gave her much grief. Unlike his wife Carmen, who Theresa regretfully a long time ago dubbed a nag. She was a beautiful, talented woman, but she couldn't stop harassing people. Including me, Theresa thought as she headed from the bathroom to the kitchen with her daily dose of pills.

She tuned to public radio's classical music station, her favorite. The station came from Rochester, home of the Mayo Clinic, the source of her pile of morning pills. Synthroid for her thyroid, lisinopril for blood pressure, simvastatin for cholesterol, and half an aspirin just to keep her blood nicely thinned. She had taken almost no medications when she was younger, but age—she was eighty-two—caught up with her. Still, there were many people much younger than her who took twice as many or more meds every day of their adult lives!

Tony, her husband, used to say the entire country was overmedicated. "Heck. If everybody had as much to do as farmers, they wouldn't need to take all those drugs. America is overweight and depressed because people are sitting on their asses bored out of their minds!"

Theresa had disagreed with him. "Yes, right, like there are no fat farmers? No depressed ones? How about the ones who hang themselves in their hayloft or beat up their cattle or their wives? Are they the exceptions?"

"Point taken, Tee," he'd conceded, "but, of course, farmers are depressed with ag policy ruining farming and all of rural America."

How much she missed those exchanges even after all these years. Whoops, a tiny tear. "Stop it!"

She put coffee water on and headed to the barn, followed by Mose, her white German shepherd, almost as arthritic as she was. Old lady. Old dog. Both had slowed considerably over the years, but still loved going to the barn in the morning.

Even in January, twenty below and blizzard winds whipping the snow into a frenzy, going to the barn was an unparalleled pleasure. There was the building itself, of course, and then the knowledge she'd gained over the years about its construction, something she'd known nothing about when she'd moved here.

Growing up in her white, working-class Chicago neighborhood on the South Side she'd simply assumed buildings. Her house, schools, the church, even the big structures downtown. They were just there, always had been there, and maybe always would be. She didn't think about them at all. They were seamless aside from doors and windows. As a child, she just thought God had simply plopped her house and all other buildings down according to some divine plan and moved on to wars and more important things. When she was old enough to play Monopoly with her brother and sister to get through their endlessly boring summers, she occasionally thought maybe God had created Chicago, and her house and neighborhood, as his own great Monopoly game.

"But then who would he play with?" her brother Konrad would challenge.

"I don't know. Jesus, maybe, or Moses. How about the saints?" she'd point out.

"Well, it must be Saint Theresa then, right?" the know-it-all would taunt.

Now, as an old lady, she still wasn't entirely sure if God wasn't just playing Monopoly with this crazy world, but she did know that He hadn't had much of a role in constructing the buildings on her farm.

"I'm sure a prayer or two was said by the carpenters though, don't you think?" Konrad, a newly minted priest at the time, had said on his first visit to the farm.

"No doubt, *father*," Theresa had replied, exaggerating his pious title. "But let me tell you something about these buildings," she continued in earnest, leading him to the barn as she started her soliloquy on rural architecture.

"This, Father Konrad, is called a basement barn, because the whole first floor on three sides is built underground. They did that because it kept the barn warmer in the winter, and cooler in the summer."

Leading him around the barn's perimeter, she'd pointed, "See how the entire south side is open, so the cattle can get out into the cow yard, and we can get manure out and feed in? And the top floor, almost thirty feet to the peak, is for hay. See that rail up there, and that fork thing hanging from it? That's a hayfork, which before the war would be dropped down outside of that huge door there onto a hay wagon, it would be set to grab the hay, and then be pulled up into the barn. Then it would be drawn along the track to a particular spot, the forks would be opened and the hay released by a trip rope right onto the floor into a pile. Then, over the winter, they hand-forked it to the basement level through that trapdoor. We still store our bales up there and throw them down through the trapdoor."

Bemused at first, Konrad had let her talk on, but soon actually seemed to enjoy his sister's knowledge. Standing in the hayloft, she pointed out the massive beams, thirty feet of solid tree trunk in the east-west direction, oak and elm and ash logs cut right here on the farm. The beams showed the marks from adze and axe that removed the bark and shaped the ends where they joined those running the fifty-foot north-south length of the building.

"This is called post-and-beam construction. The whole thing relies on mass to hold it up," Theresa explained. "Massive beams, huge posts and those two-foot-thick limestone walls in the basement."

Later at breakfast, and much to Tony's amusement, Theresa continued her brother's education.

"Now this house, Konrad, is what's called stick built, no posts or beams," she lectured. "Just lots of boards nailed together in a way that makes the house stand, although in a heavy wind I swear it sways. Of course, all the lumber came from this farm, cut down the road at somebody's sawmill. The two exceptions are the shingles and the siding, which are both made of cedar imported all the way from Washington State. When we've torn off some siding you can see a marking with the mill name on it. It all came here by train, then by wagon up from Winona. And it was all done by hand, Konrad. No electric saws or drills. Just men with handsaws, axes, hammers, and nails. Can you imagine?"

"So," Konrad asked partly in jest, "this wasn't part of God's Monopoly game, I take it?"

"How do I know? You're the priest."

Her long-dead brother the priest, she reflected as she entered the barn. Why were men, especially the ones you loved, so fragile, she lamented.

In Father Konrad's case, the pack of unfiltered Camels he smoked daily may have been a factor. Plenty of brandy too. And, God, he must have been lonely. Just like in that sad song by The Beatles, "Father McKenzie . . . darning his socks in the night when there's nobody there." And now here she was, lonely too.

"But we get used to it, don't we, Mose?" Theresa patted the dog, who was busy devouring a pile of chicken manure he'd discovered. "Ah, your morning meds."

In the barn, Theresa counted her goats. A dozen does, one buck, and fifteen kids. All there. She was locking them up at night now because she'd been hearing coyotes a lot closer to the house and barn than usual. Or at least she thought they were closer. But then she was a worrier, always had been.

Tony would say, "Tee, every once in a while if things are going too well, I figure I better invent a problem just so you have something to worry about."

And sure enough, he'd given her the biggest problem of all. He'd died!

"Dead, you lovely man. Dead!" She smiled ruefully at how often she still thought about him, about their lives together.

True enough, she was a bona fide worrier, but at least a disciplined one who never allowed her anxieties to actually overcome her. No pills, counselors, nail biting, or indigestion. Just an ever-present cloud off in the corner, looming larger some days than others, ensuring she kept a wary eye. Just part of who she was.

She let the goats out into their yard, threw a bale of hay out into the feeder, checked the water buckets for raisin-like goat turds, and called Mose to follow her to the chicken coop.

Whereas, according to tax records, the house and barn had come into being in the 1870s, the chicken coop had been built much later, probably in the 1920s. Like the house, it was stick- built, settled on a much-patched concrete foundation that canted radically to the south. When the cement was poured, the builders had put lots of odd bits of metal farm detritus into it for strength, so bits and pieces of old horse machinery, water pipe, windmill scaffolding and twisted bolts were sticking out at random inside the building. When Rusty was little and sent to collect the eggs, he'd often worried his mother by being gone too long. So she'd hurry down to see if a rooster had assaulted her offspring, only to find him sitting on the floor, right in the dirty straw, tracing the outlines of the odd metal bits in the foundation, the eggs next to him in their basket. Nowadays they'd have some label for that behavior and urge her to medicate him.

Mose followed Theresa into the coop in search of more chicken droppings for breakfast. Urban visitors were always grossed out seeing the various Kozlowski dogs over the years eating chicken, goat, and even cat manure. In addition to being disgusted, they worried about the animal's health.

"That can't be any good for them, Tee," her friend and soft-hearted dog rescuer Abby would say. In fact, she still said it, after all these years of being a dog owner herself. What was that Simon and Garfunkel song, "Still Crazy after All These Years"? So Theresa patiently reminded folks that dogs, like wolves, coyotes, and foxes, were scavengers. Just like us. We're all capable of eating pretty much anything and thriving on it.

"But we, and dogs, are carnivores, not poop eaters," Abby would protest.

At which point Tony, unable to restrain himself, would join in, "Come on, Ab, you know as well as I do that anybody who works in a factory, or a big corporation, or the military, or even a schoolteacher like you, eats a large ration of crap every day. That's what's great about being a farmer. I just walk in it and spread it, I don't have to eat it!"

"And," Theresa would add to Abby or any other animal lover worried about the treatment of the farm pets, "look how long our dogs live here on the farm. Far longer than your average pet, and all while eating nasty, tasty chunks of long-dead deer, squirrels, and raccoons, not to mention chicken and fish bones, lots of grass, and the occasional veggie. You can't tell me you think your dogs are living better when they eat all the processed crap out of a can, packed with preservatives and no identifiable meat?"

In fact, Theresa loved to tell the story of their Rottweiler, Roscoe, who lived to a ripe old twelve, which was a long time for a Rott. When he was about a year old, very big but still a pup, she'd been picking raspberries, and when she filled a container, she put it on the lawn at the edge of the berry patch. After her third box disappeared, she looked over at the dog and noticed bits of green cardboard sticking to his jaws. He'd been eating the berries, boxes and all!

Some years later, some beautiful, big cantaloupes she'd planted in the garden were disappearing just as they got ripe, one after the other.

"Coons," she thought, until she saw Roscoe devouring the remains of a melon he'd hauled some distance to a hidden spot in the yard. That same dog, weighing in at a solid one hundred forty pounds, would take a rotten egg very carefully in his monster jaws, look over his shoulder to see if he'd been caught, then retreat to a safe place to eat his treat in private, shell and all.

As she left the chicken coop, she thought more about her architecture lessons for Konrad, or anyone else interested in her outbuildings. "See how the roofs on the barn and the chicken coop are in two pieces? The top at about a forty-five and then the lower section almost straight down? That's called a gambrel roof, built to shed rain and especially snow."

This morning, the six hens and one rooster rushed inside the coop from their fenced yard to see what she'd brought them, which most days was kitchen scraps of rotting veggies, old bread, or spoiled meat. Compost in. Eggs out. A great exchange. Chickens were scavengers too, wholly omnivorous, making them marvelously adapted to human needs. Many times she'd told visitors, to their horror, that if she fell down and couldn't get up from the chicken coop floor, eventually the flock would just start devouring her, starting with her eyes.

And the goats too seemed to eat almost everything—but they were ruminants, so no meat, of course.

"Cud chewers," Theresa said of them, "but also thinkers, turning ideas over in their mind," she imagined. Wasn't it Thoreau who called Persia, now Iran, a "ruminant nation"? How about a children's book, *Gertrude the Goat, the Ruminating Ruminant?* How many thoughts does a good goat have while chewing her cud in the morning?

Theresa's goats, a meat breed called Boers, of South African origin, were used by the Departments of Natural Resources in many states for clearing brushy acres. They devoured any plant material in sight—thorns, thistles, vines—leaving behind a landscape ready for a park. But goats had also devoured much of the Eastern Mediterranean and North Africa, leaving not parks, but deserts. You couldn't blame them, though, they were simply doing what their masters wanted.

More than once, Theresa's precious landscaping around the house and farm buildings had come under goatly assault when they got out, happily devouring a lovely and expensive mugho pine or a swath of Asian lilies.

Theresa collected four eggs, including a cracked one for Mose. Then up to the house for breakfast of coffee strong enough to wrinkle tin and a fried egg on homemade sourdough, slathered with fresh pesto she made yesterday from basil in her garden. All in the presence of lovely morning sunlight cast on one corner of her kitchen cabinets. Cabinets made of cherry by Rusty. Rusty, who had tried twice to attend Winona State with no success, much to her distress at the time. It had been less of a worry for Tony, who reminded her that skill and intelligence did not necessarily reside only at the university. In fact, often the opposite was true.

"Just remember all the beautiful stained-glass windows my father made, Tee, with never a day of schooling past the sixth grade," Tony would remind her. "And Curt Wandmacher? He knows more than the vet about cattle, a lot more, and I bet he never even made it to the sixth grade! And how about some of the other teachers at your school, with their high IQs but they can't open the hood on their own cars?"

"I know, I know, but college isn't just about book learning, it's also about attitudes, a certain kind of consciousness."

"Right," he'd fire back. "Like all those highly educated leaders who run companies into the ground, drag our country into war after war, and pass legislation that only benefits the rich?"

Happily for everyone, Rusty had gone to the vo-tech in Rochester to learn carpentry. He only stayed one year before he went to work for a local contractor and turned his love of woodworking into a career as a cabinetmaker. First he apprenticed himself to a shop in Winona, then not long after opened his own business. Now he was one of the most sought-after cabinetmakers in the region.

And recently Rusty had expanded his talent for woodworking into sculpting. "Just fooling around," he'd say, despite the fact that many of his pieces resided in galleries and mansions. Some could also be found in the homes of friends and family who'd been lucky enough to be given a piece. Like the lovely plinth standing four feet tall on its granite base in Theresa's living room, where it glowed in the morning sun. It was made of red elm. Graced with broad swathes of striking, dark-red grain, the wood was harvested right here on the farm. When he'd just started out, Rusty had also made his parents' kitchen table, also from red elm, which Tony had cherished as a daily tribute to his son's skills.

"Show me a professor that can make something that beautiful, Tee," Tony would demand, in defense of his son's lack of degrees. "Shoot, if he'd gotten his BA, he'd probably be selling insurance or running a store!"

As she looked at the plinth, Theresa thought about how rare red elm was now, due to so-called Dutch elm disease. The misnomer actually referred to an imported Asian beetle that devoured both white and red elms, virtually eliminating them from the Midwest starting back in the 1970s. Now there was the emerald ash borer to worry about, a glistening pest threatening yet another important native wood. And how about buckthorn, the ornamental shrub from Asia now threatening woodlands throughout the Midwest, consuming thousands of acres of understory and preventing native species from flourishing? Were the Asians getting back at us for all of our depredations in their lands?

With the help of Rusty and her friend Luther, Theresa was successful in keeping buckthorn out of her woods, but the rich doctor who owned the adjacent vacation McMansion was doing little or nothing about it on his land, so she was forced to remain vigilant on her fence lines. Several years ago she'd gone to see him about the problem, likening the woodland invader to a cancer to appeal to his medical senses, but to little avail. He was politely concerned, and did indeed hire a local man to grub out some of the buckthorn one spring, but since then he'd done nothing, wholly fulfilling many rural residents' beliefs that absentee landowners were adding to the ruination of the heartland.

As she sipped her coffee, absentmindedly rubbing Mose's head, and looking at the sun-filled plinth, Theresa's thoughts of woods and farmland brought her back to the ever-present subject of Tony. Their lives had been so intertwined that it was hard to think of many things that didn't remind her of him. She'd been lucky to meet and marry such a tender, considerate farmer who wasn't so caught up in his animal husbandry that he didn't make an effort at being a patient husband as well.

And then after Tony died, there was her friend Luther. She and Lute were still close today, but without the bedroom entanglements anymore, which seemed fine for both of them. He had moved into their neighborhood in the late 1970s, a strange figure from the start. Extremely tall and rail thin, he sported a lengthy blonde ponytail, and wore what appeared to be castoff military garb. It turned out the pieces of uniform were actually his own, kept after returning from combat in Vietnam, an experience he rarely mentioned.

He'd eventually shared a bit of his story with Tony on a dark evening while they drank a lot of beer. His unusual appearance accompanied odd behavior. Dangerous even, to some. He'd bought an old, rundown, nineteenth-century farm. No road to speak of into the place, no electricity, and no running water, what locals called "water in the wall." The house was decrepit at best, and while it eventually became evident that Luther had the skills to make repairs, he initially did little to fix up the place.

In truth, he was a skilled carpenter and mechanic, could install and maintain electricity, and even do some plumbing, but his lack of fix-it-up motivation caused people to mutter that he was "living there like some goddamn hermit."

Lute was clearly moody, and would rant at the drop of a hat, usually directing his anger at the U.S. government. Those leanings were what led to his reputation as a dangerous man. One evening, not long after he bought his place, he was inadvisably in a Winona bar where he heard a couple of men complaining about what a shame it was that America "hadn't had the balls to crush those fucking gooks once and for all." Bystanders reported that Luther had spoken up to mildly disagree at first, but when he was called a "goddamn commie cocksucker," he'd waded into them, leaving the place a shambles and the instigators requiring hospital care.

When the sheriff found out Luther was a combat vet, he only kept him in jail overnight. In the morning, he made him agree to pay for the damage to the bar and to not enter the place again, and then set him free.

Gradually Tony and Theresa learned not only that Luther didn't agree with the war, but that like many others, he suffered from post-traumatic stress disorder, or PTSD. Lute wasn't interested in pills or therapy at the VA to tame his nightmares, but he had discovered he could greatly reduce their grip by working. Like a horse. He worked so hard, that despite the strong misgivings of his neighbors, he earned local approval through sweat equity.

"I don't care what you say," men would argue as they waited at the feed mill, "that boy can work! He's a goddamn working fool!" A funny turn of phrase that was truly a compliment.

"Took me years to hear it about myself," Tony would say to Theresa when they talked about their odd neighbor. "And I'm sure some are still withholding judgment."

Eventually, Lute became a regular dinner guest at Tony and Theresa's table. At first Theresa kept the moody man at a distance, but she eventually came to admire him.

"You're a born caretaker, Tee," Tony said, "and he clearly needs that."

Theresa could also see that beneath the long hair, beard, and general scruffiness was a handsome man, although she never acted on this observation until a couple of years after Tony died. Luther had been over for one of his regular suppers when she started to weep. He comforted her, and was surprisingly good at it, then one thing led to another.

Of course, Theresa did worry about what people would think, so she and Luther were discreet and never went anywhere together. But eventually Rusty figured out what was up, and in his quiet way let her know he approved. After all, he'd often worked with Luther when he was younger, and they were friends of a sort.

And at school, a couple of Theresa's friends had asked nonchalantly if that "neighbor of hers, what's his name?" was able to lend a hand at the farm now that Tony was gone. Their meaning was all too clear, but she didn't give them any fodder for gossip.

Luther was not only helpful around the farm, but the man could also play the piano. Years ago Theresa had tried to interest Rusty in playing, without much success. She herself played often, but not very well. When Tony was alive, and Luther would visit, he never even looked at the instrument. But one day when Luther was over after Tony died, he simply sat down at the old upright and played.

It was a Shaw, built in 1898, Theresa knew because some long-ago tuner had ferreted out the date and left a note penciled with it inside for future owners. With its age, the piano suited the farm, which was of a similar, albeit slightly older, vintage. Its beautiful butternut woodwork also suited the house, falling in line with Rusty's handmade cabinets and table. Despite a major rebuild some years back, the piano's sound was less than perfect, and required regular tuning by a man from Winona.

"You know, Theresa," the tuner reminded her, "this isn't Carnegie Hall, and your wood heat and cold walls aren't ideal for a piano. I'd have to live here to keep it tuned."

So it was especially wonderful that Luther could make the old piano sing. He knew many of her classical favorites by heart. Mozart, Bach, Beethoven. Many of their concertos and sonatas. Bizet, Brahms, Dvořák, Chopin, the nocturnes and scherzos. The Russians, Prokofiev, Tchaikovsky, Rimsky-Korsakov, and most importantly for the piano, Rachmaninoff, the preludes and elegies. And things he didn't know, he could sight-read at a glance, going from page to piano, creating lovely sounds in a moment. To hear these pieces right in her living room often brought tears to Theresa's eyes and she would urge him to play more.

His musical talent was another odd piece to fit into the puzzle of Luther's life. It turned out he'd grown up in Rochester, the son of a Mayo Clinic doctor, taking piano lessons for years.

"Why don't you have a piano in your house?" Theresa asked him.

"I don't know, I really don't. I guess I actually never thought of it. And anyway, it's nice that you have one that I can play here for you."

And so he did, for many years now. And over time, Theresa herself stopped playing. Why struggle to do something so poorly, she thought, when there's someone else here who can do it so well?

The piano playing got her to thinking about what she *did* do well. What would be said about her when she died? Who knew? And should she really care? A modest person, she wasn't falsely so. She did moderately well academically at her Catholic high school in Chicago, and improved markedly when she went to the College of St. Teresa in Winona. Perhaps finally being on her own at college gave her the discipline she lacked as a younger student. At St. Teresa's, compared to many of her classmates, she was an exemplary student. Even in subjects she cared little for, such as math, she did well, and in her chosen field of English, she excelled. She always loved to read, but in college began to enjoy writing as well, so much so that by her second year she became editor of the college newspaper. That, in addition to carrying a full course load and working as a part-time nanny for a local Catholic family.

And when she married Tony and moved to the farm, she discovered she also had an untapped capacity for working hard physically.

As her mind continued to wander, Theresa drifted off for a late-morning nap thinking about the teaching job she took to stay here. Mose curled up next to her and woke her briefly when his leg jerked in his sleep. Maybe, she thought sleepily, it was an omen?

Chapter 5

The day after their breakfast at Cha Cha Cha, Mary met Janet at her house.

"I've thought about it, Janet, and you know I'm really not sure about your idea of the mannequin."

"It's a simple if inconvenient truth, Mary, that having a man in the car makes you safer."

"A man, maybe, but a mannequin?"

"Well, you could run an ad in *The Reader*: 'Elderly lady seeks traveling companion, male, for cross-country journey.'"

"Very funny. This is L.A. Just imagine the responses I'd get, thank you not." Mary grasped her coffee mug. "So, how about this? I just go by myself. I'm alone anyway, so why not just admit it and stop the silliness? A mannequin companion? Please."

"Mary. You know Emma's not going to let you go by yourself. This idea might placate her a little."

"Emma Dilemma? Worried about her old mother driving alone cross-country? You have to be kidding, Janet. But OK, you win. What can I lose but my self-respect? I'll try the mannequin. Put it in the car. Drive around. See if the police stop me."

"Last I heard, my dear, there was no law against riding around with a mannequin."

Of the two male mannequins in Janet's sewing room, one seemed too young, but the other was rather ageless, suitable for transforming into Mary's elderly companion. They started with a mustache, and a slight five-o'clock shadow.

"Hey, I don't want to be riding with the ghost of Nixon," Mary grimaced. For clothing, she'd brought some of Mike's shirts, jackets, and hats. Yes, Mary had saved a few of his things, and now was glad she had, especially the camel hair sport coat, the details of which she shared with a delighted Janet.

"Solidarity with the Arabs! How like him. But are you OK with making this thing into Mike, or his facsimile?"

"Yes, actually. I'll need somebody to talk to, and I know almost exactly what Mike's response would have been to anything I said. Of course, it would really piss him off that he can't respond. But I'll be fair and respond for him. As long as I win when there's a disagreement," Mary grinned ruefully. "Do you think it's spooky or weird?"

"Maybe, dear. I don't know. Nor do I care. Your car, your trip, your life, and no harm done to anyone, so have at it. However, if when you come back you have him installed in the living room, and set a place for him at your breakfast table? Then we'll have to have a chat, don't you think?"

They spent most of a day experimenting with Mike the Mannequin's appearance, first in the house, then out in the car, with him firmly seat-belted into the passenger seat. They took turns walking past the car, both sides, close up, then at some distance, to see how he looked. Once, Janet walked right up to the passenger window and knocked on the glass, then pronounced herself satisfied that even a cop might just conclude the old guy was having a nap.

"But remember, if you get stopped," she warned, "put his head back. And I'd do the same when you go into a rest stop or gas station. No one is going to want to get up close and personal with some old man snoozing in his Lincoln. Or at least I hope not!"

Satisfied with their creation, the friends finally relaxed and went to a nearby Vietnamese place for a late lunch. Janet had her usual mock duck, while Mary tried yet another of the marvelous soups. Something filled with pieces of tripe, tiny quail eggs, jalapeno peppers, cilantro, onions, and noodles.

"You know it's not fair," Mary noted, "we go over there and devastate their country, and in return we get to eat their incredible food. When we first moved here, Mike and I thought Mexican food was the be-all of eating. Spicy, healthy, totally different, and much better than most of the food we ate as kids. My mother, I've told you, cooked German American fare. Pork, cabbage, sauerkraut. Bread. And lots of potatoes. Pretty boring. But then when the Vietnamese came here and we tried their food—my God—the best we'd ever eaten!"

"Yes, and now there's Thai, and Cambodian, and Korean. Chinese and Japanese have always been here, but I can't say I ever enjoyed either of those as much as this. And isn't it odd that we used to think that the height of good cuisine was French? With Julia Child and her TV show? I told you that when James and I were in France a couple of years ago, we had only one really good meal, and that was in an Arab restaurant."

"Who knew? Carlos, you know, likes to cook. Lucky for Emma, who does not. Recently he's started making Asian dishes. He tells about the first few times he went into the Asian grocery he shops at. He'd be standing in line and these tiny women would ask him, 'you got Asian wife?' as if it was unbelievable to them that a man would be cooking."

"Yes, the whole gender and cooking thing. The stereotypes are thick in the kitchen," Janet pointed out. "Men can only cook outside, while drinking vast amounts of beer—unless they're gay, of course, when supposedly they love to cook. But the great chefs, and food critics, are almost all men. You know there's so much difference with ethnicity, but I can't think of a single culture where men are traditionally expected to cook in the home. The Irish? Not a problem because Irish women don't cook either, at least nothing most of us want to eat. German men? Too busy engineering stuff! The Scandinavians? Same thing. Italians or Greeks? Men don't know where the kitchen is because if they go into it, they'll lose their masculinity. So hooray for Carlos. Crushing the stereotype."

The friends ate for a few minutes in silence, soaking in the complex flavors.

"Speaking of French food," Janet pushed her empty dish away. "Didn't your grandson Andres work in that fancy French place?"

"He did," Mary replied. "And he came home with great stories about how the Mexican cooks were so tough that the little Jewish guy who owned the place was afraid to go into the kitchen. The cooks yelled at each other, yelled at the waiters, and leered at the waitresses, but the food was wonderful, and everything they did in the back never surfaced in the front. So the customers thought the place was nice and quiet. Very plush and expensive, so they probably assumed that the chef and his assistants were all recently over from Paris, and if there were any Mexicans in the back they were washing dishes and peeling carrots. Cuernavaca, the new Paris!"

"Wasn't that the place where the owner was bothering the waitresses?"

"It was. And worse yet, his wife was pregnant. She'd often come by for coffee and a croissant. Andres was only seventeen, but he went into the man's office one night and warned him to lay off—maybe that's not the best word—the waitresses. The man was furious, but he stopped. Emma and Carlos were very proud of him. So were Mike and I!"

"When James started teaching," Janet remembered. "Several of his colleagues made it a point of honor to sleep with as many undergrads as they could. And they boasted about it. In fact, one of them started a rumor that James might be gay just because he *didn't* hit on his students. But a lot of that has changed, hasn't it?"

"I think it was incremental. A woman here. A group of women there. Attorneys smelling big money going after harassers," Mary said. "So what about Minnesota? Are you absolutely sure you won't go with me to see my sister? I bet we'd have a great time."

"We probably would. But there are two reasons not to. One, I get carsick if we drive outside of L.A., really sick. And two, I promised James I'd take a major trip with him this year. He's worried we're getting too old to travel, so we have to do it while we still can."

"OK, I remember about the car sickness. I used to get that when I was little. And your trip? Where are you going?"

"Oh, we don't know yet. He's always wanted to go to Peru, to see Machu Picchu, the Inca ruins. That's fine, but I'd rather do something more resort-ish. Sun, martinis, snacks on the beach, that kind of thing. Totally bourgeois, I know, but I don't care. I think James would probably like the same thing, but he can't fess up to it. He thinks we have to do something more academic, more respectable. Anyway, we have to hurry up and decide. I'm hoping we can go at the end of the year so we can miss Christmas, which you know I hate."

"Yeah, I'm not crazy about it either anymore," Mary confessed. "Let's see, I don't believe in Jesus so I don't need to celebrate his fake birthday. I hate all the Christmas-consumerism crap, and there are already displays up in stores. And without Mike . . . ."

"I know. I'm so sorry, Mary. You can't exactly put the mannequin next to your Christmas tree." Janet squeezed her friend's hand.

"God, Janet, I just can't seem to get used to him being gone. What am I going to do?"

"Take this trip, for starters. Who knows? You might even decide to spend Christmas with your sister. Theresa, right?"

"Yes. But I call her Tee."

"What's she like?"

"Well, I don't have an absolutely clear picture. Although her visit for Mike's memorial helped us get back in touch somewhat. I mean, we've talked on the phone for years, of course, but that's not the same as seeing someone regularly."

"And?" Janet pressed.

"And . . . we're quite different. All the way back to when we were girls, she was always more obedient, quieter, and more careful than me. But we usually got along. I don't know." Mary shook her head.

"I talked a little with her at the memorial," Janet noted, "and she did seem pretty quiet. But I have to say, she also seemed pretty resolute—living by herself all these years on that farm out in the middle of nowhere. How long has she been alone?"

"It's been about twenty years since Tony died."

"Wasn't some gruesome farm accident thing, I hope?"

"No. Just a heart attack. Fell down and died outside his barn one morning. She found him and wondered if she'd gotten there sooner, she maybe could have saved him, but the doctors said no, he'd died instantly. When Mike was dying, there were plenty of times, I'm ashamed to say, I wished the same had happened to him. Zap. Just gone, no bedpans, no Depends, vomiting, the whole mess. I sure as the devil wasn't cut out to be a nurse." Mary grimaced.

"Nonsense. You did a fine job. I'm not at all sure I could do the same for James, which is why I hope and pray that I go first, preferably on some warm beach after several cocktails. But back to your trip. When do you take off? You better get going before Emma pours sand in your gas tank."

"Let's see," Mary sipped her tea. "today's the fifteenth. I think I'll go day after tomorrow. I'm going over to Emma's for dinner tonight, so I'll bring "Mike" along for them to see. Hopefully my safety plan, our plan, will calm her down a bit."

Outside the restaurant, the two friends embraced in the very bright sun. Janet, suddenly a bit tearful, held her friend at arm's length. "I know absolutely that you're going to have a splendid trip. Say hello to your sister for me, and keep your cell phone charged."

"You bet," Mary promised. "I'll see you in a couple of weeks, full of news from Lake Wobegon."

Janet watched as Mary drove off with Mike the Mannequin rigidly attentive beside her. Would she herself be willing to drive around with that thing? Probably not.

Chapter 6

As Theresa nodded off for her morning nap, Luther Rasmussen was hooking an old manure spreader up to his new tractor to haul wood. He considered the tractor an indulgence, the result of a sizable inheritance he'd received after his father's death.

Lars Rasmussen was someone Luther had never gotten along with. The noted Mayo surgeon had worked his way up from an impoverished childhood into the status and wealth of a position at one of the world's most famous medical facilities. There, he served many wealthy and powerful clients, including some of the Saudi royal family, and once, to Luther's chagrin, Henry Kissinger.

Recognizing a rant developing, Luther tried to relax his mind as he loaded tools into his makeshift trailer. Chainsaws, fuel, oil, wrench, axe, wedges, and his marvelous new Peavey log lifter. His delight in the new tool, its grand utility, helped to quell his anger, but not quite.

His ongoing diatribe changed little over the years. Most wars, including "his," the invasion of Vietnam, were brought about by elite white men who had never been in the military, let alone in combat. Almost always a function of domestic politics, these battles were waged on other countries' soil, where Americans caused incalculable harm to millions of people.

And rarely did America's warmongers ever pay for their misdeeds. They rode in limos to fancy restaurants, went to the opera, had affairs with beautiful women, chatted with presidents over breakfast, and filled their bank accounts with dirty millions.

Money that Luther thought should burn their hands as they tried to spend it. Money that should scream at them with the voices of dying children as they tried to withdraw it from their accounts.

But for the men who started the wars where other people suffered, there was no retribution, not a bit of it. Instead they often lived in a steady stream of lionization, fawned over by the sycophantic media. Then finally there'd be a grand funeral, celebrating their supposed success right into the grave. No wonder so many vets went crazy.

Why, he wondered for the thousandth time, did no one ever go after these guys? Why did no grieving father, his son killed in a senseless war, take up his deer rifle and go to one of the public functions where one of these "leaders" appeared and off him? Why had no PTSD-plagued vet, unable to sleep, work, or sustain a decent relationship, simply take one of the SOBs out instead of murdering his wife or committing suicide?

Why did the crazy mass murderers take out their rage on school children and fast-food patrons instead of the elite and powerful men driving the country into the ground for their own gain? Like the CEOs with their ill-gotten billions, who were never attacked by the poor drones who lost their job, house, and maybe even family to the poor management of those at the helm?

Luther couldn't begin to understand why the peons hurt one another or themselves, and never the kings of commerce or lords of war who were truly to blame for their plight. And he himself, big talker, why hadn't he? He'd thought often enough about going postal. Cutting his hair, shaving his beard, buying a suit, packing a bag full of weapons and stalking the likes of Kissinger. Walking up to him as he reached for the limo door one morning and shooting him in the face.

Now he needed to take a deep breath, absorb the peace and solitude around him in the woods and bring his heart rate down before he started the chainsaw. Back in the early "daze" after the war, he'd almost headed down the path of violent destruction for himself and others. But instead, he'd begun anchoring himself, making himself well, as soon as he'd gotten to this farm. This piece of land and its decrepit buildings, which he loved at first sight, eased his heart every day.

Calming, he could finally start the chainsaw and spend the day doing one of his favorite things, heading into the lovely stand of trees in front of him to make wood. Wood to heat his house and sell to people in Winona for their cozy fireplaces. When he drove to town in the winter, he imagined the smoke he saw coming from the rows of chimneys was a product of his own hard labor.

Luther loved everything about making wood. Cutting, hauling, stacking, and splitting. Fall, the time to do it, was his favorite season. Summer was too busy, never a moment to rest from his gardens and the farmers' markets where he sold his produce. Spring was wonderful, at first. But then too soon planting took over. And winter was initially peaceful, but then grew boring, driving him into his workshop to make just about anything to keep busy.

But fall offered perfect temperatures. Weeds were frost-dead and out of the way. Leaves were stunning in their multicolored hues, so captivating that even the urbanites left their TV-lit homes to drive down the river and soak in the color.

There was also peace in the fall woods. Yes, the chainsaw was noisy, and dangerous. But when you shut it off, perfection! Pour coffee from the thermos, light up a cigarette, or a joint, and then sip, inhale, exhale. Then tighten and sharpen the chain on the saw, fuel it up, and cut more wood.

Jesus, he took such pleasure in simply knowing the species of every tree and shrub in his small twelve-acre woods. He knew this tiny forest like the back of his own hand, more than once correcting the DNR forester who came to check on the status of his managed forest, a state program for which he got a tax break.

"No, that's a red elm, not a piss elm," he'd point out quietly.

"Are you sure?" the college-educated forester would ask, peering up into the canopy. "How can you tell?"

"The bark is just a little different," Luther would explain as he broke a piece off for inspection. "More rough, see? And the cross section—notice how it's red all the way through. Now look at the same section on a white elm. See? It's kinda white."

Red elm, one of his favorites, was now mostly eliminated by Dutch elm disease. It was great wood for his woodstove, full of clinkers that kept the heat all night. It was also ideal for fence posts, as it was strongly water resistant. Only thing better was white oak. And when you sawed it into timbers, four by six or six by six, it made raised beds for his garden that lasted for years.

And lumber? He'd replaced all the rotting trim on windows and doors of his house with red elm, with its beautiful grain and deep, rich, color. Most people thought it was oak, but knowledgeable folks like Rusty, Theresa's son, knew the difference. And now his ash trees were also threatened. With emerald ash borer, another goddamn bug. Still, he had plenty of red oak, a good wood for lumber and heating, its acorns keeping the squirrels well fed all winter. And lots of cottonwoods, the largest trees on the farm, no good for firewood or lumber, but great for shade. He had one next to his house that was well over a hundred years old, its southern location perfect for keeping the place cool all summer. And, every year Baltimore orioles built a tiny nest up near the top of the tree, swaying in the wind up there a hundred feet or more. That the nests survived most winters was a testimony to the birds' skills.

And there were many smaller trees and shrubs in his woody catalog. The beautiful ironwood, which rarely got big enough to use for anything. Three pagoda dogwoods he transplanted to his yard for their lovely branching effect. Valuable black walnuts he'd planted all over his woods and in the yard. Females, so they yielded plenty of nuts in the fall. Some for Theresa to make wonderful cookies. The bulk for the squirrels.

No native evergreens except for red cedar, a scrub tree the lumber of which was a stark, bloody red, useful for closets and clothes chests as a moth repellent. A couple Kentucky coffee trees he'd planted by the house—not natives but flourishing, very slowly so, with their odd and intriguing branching. The seeds of the females were used by settlers down south too poor to buy coffee, so they ground the beans into a bitter brew, something he'd not tried. The forester told him about a very large specimen across the river in Perrot State Park in Wisconsin, probably accidently rooted there by Native Americans who had used the dried beans as gambling chips.

"Who couldn't appreciate trees?" he wondered as his woodpile grew.

The vast and ancient forests of North America had fallen to European settlers. All that white pine used to build sturdy houses and wonderful barns, most of which were now either gone or falling into decay. It depressed Luther to drive around the countryside and see these wonderful buildings abandoned. So foolish, so wasteful. He took such pleasure from his own farmstead's buildings, and the fine materials and workmanship that went into building them.

He'd read a book that called the American suburbs the single greatest waste of resources the planet had ever seen. What if the Europeans had taken some lessons from the Native Americans about how to live when they arrived here? Luther imagined America would be a wonderfully different place.

In the drone of the chainsaw, his mind wandered as the sawdust flew around him. If the settlers had followed in the footsteps of the Native Americans and charted a different course, he puzzled. Then his father likely wouldn't have been a doctor, and probably never met his mother, and . . . . "Stop!" Luther found himself suddenly standing in the quiet woods, the chainsaw idle in his hand. When his mind began to spin, he had gotten in the habit of saying *stop* out loud as a way to break his often bitter trance. This time he startled himself enough to let go of the saw's trigger. Nothing good ever came of the rants. Just anger and disgust. All a waste, certain to spoil his afternoon. He knew the geology of his brain included some volcanic detritus from his PTSD eruptions. The trick was to control them.

Luckily he had begun reading alternative lifestyle magazines like the *Whole Earth Catalog*, *Mother Earth News*, and *Organic Gardening* before he went to Nam. He kept their messages as a beacon while he was there, which led him to buy this place when he got out. A place that needed so much work that he'd had little time to indulge his anxieties.

Wasn't that a large part of the problem today anyway? Too much self-indulgence? Even the poor overindulged. And the rich? Jesus! Remember when McCain, the great war hero, was running for president? Silly guy didn't even know how many houses he owned. Even the members of the French court probably knew how many villas and palaces they owned as they ascended the guillotine!

After filling his wood hauler, Luther finished his coffee, lit a joint, and peered up at the small red squirrel who was nattering at him. "Relax, dude. I'm about to leave."

Early on, Luther had hunted and eaten plenty of squirrels. They were plentiful, and tasty. But then he'd stopped hunting, for no particular reason beyond the obvious baggage attached to killing stuff. Now he only brought out his gun for feral cats, which decimated the bird and rabbit populations. Even they were on the wane, thanks to the coyotes, which killed and ate cats with gusto. Last week, a young guy had stopped by and asked if he could run down a coyote he'd chased onto Luther's land.

"Nope," Luther had answered simply.

Totally surprised, the eager tracker had demanded, "Why not?"

"Because I've got nothing against coyotes. I actually kind of like them, that's why," Luther responded, watching the wary look come over the hunter's features. Pissed off, the young man simply turned on his heel and stalked to his truck, then spun his tires leaving the yard.

"Fuck you too," Luther thought with a chuckle. These were the same punks who wanted to hunt wolves, and then work their way through the entire endangered species list for the sport of it. These guys would shoot robins if they could.

When Luther bitched about it to his ancient neighbor John Moe, the old farmer had said, "Those are people from town mostly, with boring jobs, who watch too much tellyvision and think 'cause they have a gun it means they're badass. They think they'll be called to save the country from the bad guys. John Waynes. You heard it here first, those SOBs are gonna lobby for a permit to shoot people someday, and that day isn't far off!"

Luther didn't doubt it, although he sincerely hoped it wouldn't start until he was pushing up daisies, or heirloom veggies. His smoke finished, he lingered to enjoy the lovely sound of a distant train whistle, thinking that its echo through the woods was just about as perfect a music as could be.

As the sound drifted away he cranked up his little blue New Holland tractor and headed back up to the house to unload the wood he'd cut. The warm autumn sun poured through the leaves overhead, dappling his tractor with spots of light. It made him want to stop, lie down, and take a nap in the tall grass on the edge of the woods. He'd done it before, but knew he'd wake up cold and stiff with a desperate need to piss.

At the woodpile, he unloaded logs twenty-two inches long into cords roughly four by eight in width and length, all stacked on wooden pallets, braced at the ends with steel posts. The larger pieces he added to an already formidable pile stacked next to his splitter, the next chore.

In early years on the farm, with no electricity and just the windmill for water, Luther tried to live like someone in the nineteenth century. Had to have a vehicle, of course, but otherwise he did as much hand labor as possible, including sawing logs with a variety of old handsaws he bought at auctions. But it only took one winter of not enough wood—in a bitter cold with the water in his jugs frozen in the kitchen every morning—for him to give in to a chainsaw.

Now he had two, a small one for limbing, and a larger one for felling trees and cutting them into logs. Not that he actually felled many trees. He mostly relied on the wind and decay to do that dangerous work. For three or four years, he'd also split wood by hand, with a maul. But as his gardens grew he had less time for woods work, so he bought and now used a much more efficient engine-driven splitter.

As Luther unloaded the trailer, he was energized by the pride of knowing every piece of wood in the pile. Putting a piece in his stove in

January, he'd know what kind of wood it was, how well it would heat, and usually where he'd cut it on the farm. Disdaining the accumulation of traditional wealth, he had to admit he was a kind of a Croesus, delighting in how much wood he had. "Like money in the bank," John Moe said.

John and his brother Donald, ages eighty-five and eighty-six respectfully, spent their summers cutting, baling, and storing thousands of small, square bales of hay. Most farmers had long ago moved to big round bales that they left lining fields like some sort of Hay Henge. But not John and Donald. And it turned out that many people, including Theresa, still wanted the smaller bales because they were easier to transport and store.

So the Moes sold their bales easily every year, even in a tight economy. And in the winter, when Luther had all his wood cut and mostly split and stacked, the brothers kept busy cutting vast quantities of firewood, not in stove lengths, but in longer measures suitable for outdoor wood burners. Many rural and even some suburban homes now had exterior furnaces that could burn any kind of wood—and burn the wood green, which unfortunately creates vast amounts of dirty smoke—and lower heating bills. Cutting wood gave the Moe brothers plenty of work, which Luther thought was probably keeping them healthy and alive.

In the house Luther's dog, Azteca, was lying in a patch of sun on the kitchen floor. He reached to pet her and realized that if he didn't help her outside, she'd end up lying in a puddle of piss. He got the aging beast to her feet, rear legs scarcely functional, and guided her outside where she peed immediately then almost fell over.

"What are we going to do, girl?" Of course he knew the answer, but he was procrastinating in mind and spirit. Before winter he needed to take her to the woods and put a kindly bullet in her brain. Before winter, because he would want to bury her right away. The alternative possibility of his beloved dog lying in the top of the barn all winter was too depressing. What would it be like if his neighbors had to keep their dead kin laying around the house, in the cellar, the granary, or the barn all winter waiting for the ground to thaw, instead of handing them over to the funeral home? John Moe had no children, but his brother Donald had several, including a ne'er-do-well son whose poor farming skills and various excesses had cost his frugal, hardworking parents much grief.

What if when Donald passed that son of a bitch Georgie-boy had to keep his father well frozen in the seat of his favorite tractor all winter long as a ritual obligation, a necessary penance? Now there's a notion! Luther chuckled to himself, thinking he should share this clever thought with Theresa tonight during their weekly dinner. She might be slightly shocked, but also amused at yet another outrageous notion from her friend.

Theresa still went to Mass, for reasons he couldn't quite fathom. He knew she was at least mildly critical of the Catholic Church as a failed institution—the pedophiles, the misogyny, the vast wealth accumulated over millennia, the deeply hypocritical homophobia. But still she went to church. Why? She said she loved the Mass and seeing the families and their children who attended her church. It seemed it was more about community and tradition than faith, but what did he, a rank unbeliever, know?

"Luther," she'd said more than once, "at my age I get to be self-indulgent. The building, the windows with that glorious light streaming through them? I love it. So I go, I sit there in peace. I scarcely listen anymore to the words that are spoken. I've heard them all before. I don't bother to be critical. I just feast on the people, the movements, the hymns, leaving my pew to get the host. I never take the wine! And the choir? What can I say? It's a wonderful sound those people make. And then, when it's over and people I've known for years, their kids, their grandkids, greet me with real warmth, and ask after me? I don't know? Isn't that what we're supposed to do? How we're supposed to be? A community?"

His response was always the same. "We don't need an institution for that. Especially one as corrupt as the Catholic Church. Why can't we just get together around something we have in common like farming, or food, or music and do it on our own? No priests, popes, pastors, or politicians, with their vested interests. Hey, did you like that? *Vested? Vestments?* I recommend less church, and more auctions—now there's a place for community."

And so it went, their odd romance and not-so-odd friendship, developing over the years. Unlike Theresa, Tony, her dead husband, had been no fan of the Catholic Church, or any church. He'd been raised by devout parents who were always afraid of offending their priest, or any priest. While Luther's anticlerical arguments were mostly intellectual and political, Tony's were personal. He had known the church up close and hated it, which made Theresa's regular attendance all the more hard to figure.

As he got ready to head over to her house for dinner Luther thought about the very important topic he wanted to talk about with her. The letter. The one sitting on the kitchen table that had arrived yesterday from Rochester. It was from his late father's attorney, the one who'd handled the estate and made a very substantial deposit in Luther's bank account that led to his new tractor, new wood splitter, and that Peavey. It would also soon be funding a replacement pickup because his old F-150 was flapping in the breeze, big rust holes everywhere. But the letter that came this time wasn't about money, or not directly anyway.

After feeding Azteca her scant supper laced with expensive canine painkillers, Luther showered, enjoying the marvelous luxury of water in the wall, as his elder neighbors called running water. In Vietnam, showers had been rare, and his memory was of being dirty the entire time he was there. When he returned, he'd deliberately dealt himself a no-shower hand by buying this place, which had no running water, just a windmill with a cistern and a hand pump. He'd had to haul water five or ten gallons at a time the hundred or so yards from pump to house in buckets and plastic jugs.

It hadn't done him any harm the first years, but then he'd succumbed to the modern era. He'd had an underground electric line brought in, and soon after put a submersible pump down about five hundred feet, connected it to a pipe and pump above ground to send water right into his cellar. Then he'd installed his own plumbing. Man, the electric lights were nice, but the water was better. Hot water right out of the showerhead, instead of from a pot on his woodstove. Each time he showered, he felt spoiled.

Clean shirt and pants, roughly combed hair and beard, and into the pickup Luther went with the letter and some late tomatoes from the garden. Black from Tula, a Russian variety. It was probably the ugliest tomato he'd ever seen, very hard to sell because it looked so misshapen, and scarcely red, but it tasted wonderful. What was the adage about appearances belying interiors? He couldn't remember it, if he'd ever known it all. And the notion of tomatoes from Russia? Who'd have known?

Chapter 7

As she punched the time clock in the staff lounge, really just a tiny break room with a Coke machine, Joni knew she was a little late and would have to take shit from Bess. Bess the Bitch, as she was known by the staff. In the meantime, she went up to the second floor, grabbed a cleaning cart, and started opening doors. It was after eleven, checkout time, so everyone should be gone unless they were staying a second night or more, in which case there should be a Do Not Disturb sign.

Not that over the years she hadn't opened a door and walked in on people screwing. One time they were on the floor. And once there was this guy, a loner, who just stood there in the nude, wanting her to look at his tiny unit. Ugh! And then there was the great-looking, somewhat older couple, driving a very expensive Porsche, who propositioned her. Joni was outside having a cigarette and the woman, a really stunning blonde, joined her, chatting about this or that. Then she simply came out and asked if Joni wanted to have a threesome with her and her husband.

"You're awfully pretty, you know. Lovely in fact," the woman said casually. "So we'd like you to join us, nothing too weird, no pain. Bet you'll like it. And there'll be one-fifty—cash, of course—for you when we leave."

Joni had almost done it, was real close. The money was great, and she was curious. Others around town had talked about threesomes, and a former loser boyfriend kept bugging her to join him and some older woman. She'd scoffed at the notion, but still . . . . Finishing her cigarette, however, Joni had thanked the woman, told her she wasn't offended, but just wasn't ready to try something like that.

"Don't wait too long, honey," the woman had said with just a touch of bitterness. Later, she watched them get into their beautiful car, listening as they drove away to the sweet rumble of that mighty engine.

"Maybe if they'd offered to let me drive that Porsche, I'd have agreed," Joni thought, smiling to herself.

Cleaning a particularly nasty toilet bowl, Joni wondered why she hadn't taken that chance, or others.

Like the wealthy lawyer in town who'd offered her a gig in his office, despite the fact that she wasn't a secretary. She actually wasn't great on computers at all, and she realized he wanted to screw her, plain and simple. Would probably be better than cleaning these shitty toilets, she thought now.

Now there was this thing from her dad, from Eunice's past. Maybe money, who knew? But certainly something different. She'd never really been anywhere. And why not? Because she'd been taking care of Eunice. But her grandma had been dead for some time. And Chet, her dad? Joni was definitely not staying here to take care of him or his horrible girlfriend, Cherie, who liked to pretend that Joni was her daughter too. Yuck!

Why was she still here in this shitty little town then? Friends? Not really. She knew a lot of people. It was a small town so you couldn't really help it, but she wasn't close to anyone and never had been. Boyfriend? She'd been with a couple of guys, total losers. The kind of men, boys really, who boasted to their friends that she gave head. Babies, idiots! So, why not go out there, to Minnesota, and see what the letter meant? What was the worst that could happen?

The day progressed, more toilet bowls, sheets with stains, masses of wet towels, "I luv you" scrawled in lipstick on a bathroom mirror. A pile of matches on a sink where someone was smoking something. She began to think, even get a little excited, about really leaving this crappy job, this crappy town. Let's see, she thought. She had about four hundred dollars in the bank, which was good enough.

Back in her apartment, Joni was still steaming from her encounter with Bess about being a little late. The bitch! A bitter woman who delighted in yelling at the women who worked "under" her. But hey, Joni brightened, tomorrow she'd quit. Be done cleaning other people's shit and taking more shit from Bess.

And her stuff? She'd never been a hoarder, so it should be easy. Let's see. Don't wear that sweater, same with those shoes, finished that book—all to the Goodwill. She could easily pack the belongings she wanted into the Honda. And the car? Old, a million miles, even smoking a little when she started it in the morning, and the tires were a little funky. Well . . . nothing to do about it but pray to the car gods. Whoever the hell they were. She'd do it! Get the hell out of here, and do something for once! Going through her things, Joni put on music. *Nirvana: Unplugged in New York*. A favorite. Cobain was a junkie, like her grandma. Killed himself. That was stupid. All that fame. All that money. And he offed himself?

Joni turned down the sound and called her dad, who answered right away. Sounding sober, thankfully. She told him that she'd thought about the letter from Minnesota, and would go.

"Yeah, Dad, I'll go. Fact, I'll drive up right now and get the letter, OK?" She didn't even bother to get out of her maid's uniform, just drove straight up to the cabin.

As she was leaving, her father's last words were, of course, a request. "Hey, honey," he said sweetly, which caused Joni to raise her eyebrows in suspicion. "You know I looked at a map and you're headed to Rochester, which is real close to Red Wing, Minnesota. They make those sweet work boots there, you know, and mine are about shot. Couldn't begin to buy boots like that here, but I bet you can get like a factory discount or something if you buy them there. So, uh, I'm a size 13D. Here, I wrote it down. Irish Setters, OK?"

"Sure, Dad," she barely hid her disdain. *Hey, honey,* she thought as she turned away, *would you mind driving across country for me to collect my inheritance so I can spend it all on booze while I hide from the cops? I don't have a reliable vehicle to loan you, and I can't pay for any of the gas, food or expenses on the trip, but while you're there, can you pick me up a pair of expensive boots?* What an asshole!

She practically leapt off the porch and into the Honda, driving too fast in the rain, on muddy gravel, most of the way into Geeville. She suddenly couldn't wait another minute to hit the road and leave all of this shit behind. Getting to her apartment, she packed what she wanted in the car. Some clothes, stuff from the bathroom, and all of her CDs. Then she added a few treasured books; a couple of photos, including one of Eunice when she was still young and pretty; a blanket, the ugly afghan Eunice had crocheted in her many attempts at sobriety; and a pillow and sleeping bag. No spendy motel stays for her! Finally, she added a flashlight, a pad of paper and some pens, and her phone charger.

In the morning, Joni headed first to the motel for the pleasure of telling Bess in person that she quit. The woman freaked out, of course, and told her she couldn't, that she had to give two-week's notice.

"Oh shit, I forgot! Sorry, Bess," Joni answered, her voice dripping with sarcasm. "What's the penalty, are you gonna send the deputies after me? 'Please come with us, ma'am. You're wanted back at the Best Western, I mean the Burst Cistern!'" She knew that would piss off Bess. She hated that nickname even more than Worst Western, Joni's favorite handle for the place.

"I'll tell you what the goddamn penalty is, miss smartass!" Bess spit out, angry and red-faced. "You'll never work in this town again!"

"Oh please say it's true. Please! 'Cause if things go right, I'll never *be* in this shitty little town again," Joni folded her hands in a mock plea. Storming out, she almost, almost, felt sorry for poor old Bess, stuck here forever thinking her crappy job was somehow important.

Joni went to the bank, drawing out the four hundred cash in tens and twenties, and leaving fifty-seven bucks to draw on if needed, not realizing her checks would be worthless out of town. Back in the apartment, she wrote a note to her landlady, apologizing for leaving without giving notice.

One last look around and she was in the car. A quick stop at the goofy Kum & Go station at the edge of town to gas up. When she went inside to pay and grab a candy bar, she chatted for a minute with the checkout guy Reggie, who had adored her since high school. She liked him too, he was one of the few sweet men she knew. But she'd never been able to take him seriously since he was a few bricks shy of a full load. Funny, but just right, that he was the last person she was going to talk to in Geeville.

As she got back into her car, she thought back to the incident that had put her on Reggie's radar. In high school the usual jock assholes were messing with him one day at the bus stop, giving him shit. They'd all known each other their entire lives, and even when they teased Reggie back in grade school, they'd known he was a bit damaged and totally harmless.

But those guys couldn't help themselves; cruelty was a sport for them, the kind of punks who probably tortured puppies. So Joni had gotten furious, a nice, righteous fury because that time it wasn't about her. It was somebody else they were fucking with.

Sick of their shit, Joni walked up to the older boys and started calling them the whole gamut of names she'd heard from Chet and Eunice growing up—assholes, motherfuckers, shit-eating dog humpers. Surprised, the bullies stopped for a minute before they turned on her, throwing her bag and pushing her down, then turning back to beat up Reggie, who had foolishly waded in to help her.

Some adult, probably a parent, saw the fracas and came over to yell at them, not particularly caring about what happened to Joni or Reggie, just angry there was fighting. After they got to school, one of the worst offenders, a real prick named Evan Register, had grabbed Joni by the arm and warned her, "This ain't over, bitch. And say hello to your doper gran for me, will you?"

And she had been enough afraid of him that she foolishly told Chet what had happened and about Evan's warning. So a couple of nights later, Chet, head full of coke with a whiskey chaser, confronted Evan at the local Purple Cow ice-cream hangout, grabbing the stocky kid and smashing his head repeatedly against the side mirror of a nearby car. Hurt him pretty bad, and it would have been worse if the cops hadn't shown up and hauled Chet away.

They sent him off for a month or two, but with work release privileges during the daytime. It was bad, but Joni had to admit those assholes never even looked at her or Reggie again. Never! So maybe sometimes violence was the only answer? The trouble with Chet was, it was usually his first response. Her dad, a *first responder*. Ha!

Before pulling out of the station, Joni anchored the little bobblehead toy she'd bought from Reggie to the middle of her dash. What was the name of those boots Chet wanted? Red Wing?

"OK, Mr. Red Wing," she said aloud to the figure as she pulled out of town, "Let's roll."

Chapter 8

The day after dinner at Emma's house, Mary spent preparing for her trip. The next morning, she got up quite early and left Los Angeles with her mannequin companion anchored firmly beside her.

"Well, Mike," she said as she pulled away from her house, "here we go, our last great adventure! Take the 210 east to La Verne, stay on it and grab the 15 north to Barstow, then on to Vegas, our first stop."

Mary had promised Emma and Carlos she would take only major routes all the way to the northland. No sight-seeing. No two-laners. Just drive straight there and call along the way, every night and more if needed.

"Heck," Carlos said, "you get into any trouble, I'll hop on my motorcycle and be there pronto!"

"No way, Jose," Mary told Mike as she remembered Carlos's offer. "I'm definitely not going to need help. I won't get into any trouble."

As she entered the freeway, traffic scarcely moving even at seven a.m., she thought maybe she'd be lucky if she simply escaped L.A. today, never mind made it to Vegas.

"Where in the hell are all these people going?" Mike used to wonder.

"Hey, Mike," she'd reply, "where are *we* going?"

"Yeah, I know," he'd nod, "but still . . . ."

As she drove, Mary reviewed the recent dinner with her family. The good meal Carlos had made. They'd laughed as they remembered how suspicious Mike had been about the vegetables Carlos bought from the Asian groceries. Where were they from? How had they been grown? Had there been maybe the legendary night soil of human excrement involved in growing them? Working in produce his whole life, he'd seen the quality of many things sold at the supermarkets where he worked go downhill, so you couldn't blame him.

Emma had talked about some research she'd been doing for the class she taught at City College. Mary remembered her describing a couple of brothers named Magón who'd been active in the Mexican revolution against Díaz at the turn of the twentieth century. Emma was very excited about them because when they were exiled to the U.S., they met the famous anarchist Emma Goldman, her namesake. Mary thought about the difference between her daughter and Carlos when it came to radical politics, or any politics. Emma was a confirmed radical, a virulent critic of inequality and injustice anywhere, anytime, but especially here in the U.S. While Carlos cared about justice and shared many of his wife's beliefs, he read little about politics and didn't really do anything that could be termed political, radical or not. As the difference had become apparent to Mike, he'd wonder aloud time and again how it was that a full-blooded Mexican could spend so little time worrying about the vast number of misdeeds that had been done to his people over the centuries, and still today.

"But, Mike," Carlos would say with a gentle chuckle, "Emma has it covered for both of us. She gets up in the middle of the night to look things up and write them down. Me, I sleep like a baby."

Mike soon realized what a good man Carlos was, even if he wasn't politically active, and in some ways perfect for Emma. If she'd married a firebrand like herself, she probably would've ended up in jail long-term, as opposed to the few hours she'd been in for her various protests.

"So, Mike," Mary asked her very sober companion as she crept along the packed freeway. "Are we ever going to get out of this traffic, my favorite part of L.A.?"

Despite driving in this kind of traffic almost every day, Mike had never ceased wondering at the stupidity of it. "No one could have devised a more foolish and wasteful transportation system if they'd tried," he'd said time and again of the packed lanes, never one to mind repeating himself.

And she had always agreed, especially since on most days she got stuck on the freeways going to and from work. Which is why she'd taken a pay and prestige cut to work at a nursery near their house, for a commute that required only a brief jaunt through city streets. The owners there, a two-generation family, had been difficult people, she recalled with a grimace. Worried, suspicious, always hovering even though it was clear from her first day that she was overqualified for the job. She was the superior plants-man in the place, or plants-woman. But given the vagaries of a small business, either poised on the brink of losing it all, or if you were successful, being hounded into selling to a larger outfit, she understood their anxiety. Their son, Spencer, was pleasant and made it clear that as soon as he graduated from college he was out of there. It was going to break his grandmother's heart, because he was clearly the brightest of the lot, but that was why he was leaving—he was too bright to hold on for years, waiting to take over the little business.

Spencer and Mary had become pals right away, and they secretly made gentle fun of the rest of the family. The overweight and very domineering granny, Arlene, who owned the business, her husband having fled to the grave years before. God, Mary remembered the muumuus the woman wore daily, huge tents of fabric covered with multicolored flowers that bore no resemblance to any living plant. In a nursery, for God's sake!

Arlene's henpecked son Clarence, harassed daily until he bled by both his mother and his wife, a tiny Colombian woman, Eva, who always dressed in black and was as formidable in her own crazy way as her mother-in-law. The two women were constantly locked in silent battle, fighting for control of the little business. Unfortunately, they all lived in two tiny houses right on the property. The old lady lived, of course, in the nicer one with her two nasty, snuffling Pekinese pups.

The other was home to Clarence and Eva (who favored being called Evita, not knowing the connection to the former fascist queen of

Argentina) and their two children, Spencer and his sad twin Susan. Susan was a young woman who harbored all the family's anxieties, in spades. Hey, Mary smiled, *spades*. In a nursery!

For the first several months Mary worked there, she knew the girl was keeping tabs on her. Was Mary working? Was she taking too long a coffee or lunch break? How was she treating the customers? Did she really know all she pretended to about plants? And worst of all, Susan often followed Mary out to her car on some shallow pretense or another to see, Mary knew, if she was taking anything home. Which, of course, Mary never did.

Unlike other nurseries where she'd worked, where it was common to take stuff home that was damaged, or too large, or all the things that happened to plants that made them unsalable but still useful. Kind of like Mike did with produce. The joke in their house was that if they ever ate truly fresh produce, besides what came from their own garden, they'd probably get sick. Much of her lovely perennial garden at home was populated with plants discarded from nurseries where Mary had worked. But at her final place of employment, Green Acres (what an awful name!), she took nothing home. Not a pebble.

Oh well, she'd only had to work there for four years before she retired. By that time, they'd actually come to like her and very much depend on her. They'd even ordered in bad Chinese takeout for lunch on her last day and sent her off with an only slightly damaged cactus as a going-away gift. A cactus that was now thriving, she thought with satisfaction. And out of loyalty, which was her style, after she retired Mary bought all of her nursery items from them, taking time to go into the yard and talk to the Mexican landscapers she'd worked with.

Those guys had a sense of humor, or they couldn't have stomached all the crap they took from that family. Especially from Evita, who let them know daily that Colombia was a far superior country to Mexico, and that she herself came from a middle-class family who had once owned a store! A store, imagine that! Mary smiled at the memory.

Fuhgettaboudit. Mary thought for a moment her hitherto silent companion had just said something in his best Queens accent.

"OK, OK, Mike. I get it," she told her silent companion. "Stop dwelling on the silly past. But I have to tell you, that Evita really pissed me off. And Arlene, Our Lady of the Muumuus?!" Mary gestured in disgust to the mannequin.

But here finally was the turnoff to Barstow and points north. Pretty straightforward, as she expected the entire trip to be. Relaxing into the drive, Mary began to wonder what her sister Theresa was like now, after so many years. Did she garden? Mary thought she did. How could she not in such a wonderfully abundant part of the country? She remembered the time she and Mike had driven out there, staying with Theresa for about a week, then heading on down the Mississippi to St. Louis, where they'd turned back west. En route, they'd stayed as much as possible right along the river, and were struck primarily by two things: how beautiful the country was and how poor most of the towns seemed to be, squalid even.

Even Hannibal, Mark Twain's birthplace, was a shabby little place. Why, they wondered, the great disparity between what was a lovely and probably quite fertile country, running right alongside one of the grandest and most famous rivers in the world, and the low-rent appearance of the many little villages and towns along the way?

Mike, for once, didn't have a ready answer, but he did say, "When you've got poor people, shabby housing, and lots of bars in the middle of what should be abundance, somebody's getting screwed. Just like the immigrants working the fields in California, shitty housing, lousy sanitation, low incomes, but the fields are full of wonderful veggies, citrus, and grapes—and the owners are living in gated mansions."

Well, Mary thought, I wonder what Theresa would have to say about that? And her sister's health? "Pretty good aside from arthritis." That's what she'd said in one of their most recent conversations. Had it in her hands just like Mary, the result of years of hard work apparently. Thank goodness it wasn't the inflamed, wholly debilitating kind—rheumatoid.

Nope, the sisters both just had plain, old, worn-out joints, which was beginning to show up in her old landscaper's knees too. Mary's plan was to take some ibuprofen once in a while, but otherwise ignore it and get on with the day.

Mary remembered that her sister still attended Mass. Would Theresa ask her to go to church with her? And if so, would Mary go?

And did she cook? Of course! Their mother had done a good job of schooling them in the limited basics of German American food. Not very exciting, but Mary still loved spareribs with sauerkraut and mashed potatoes. Theresa would probably make that. And schnitzel, made from pork, not veal. In fact, Mary wondered, were they still allowed to raise veal in America? Theresa would know.

And she probably made various goat dishes, of course, because she raised them, Mary thought as she remembered the goat curry Carlos had made last night. Always good food there, at Emma's, and when she got to Theresa's too no doubt. But likely not much in between on the road, she knew. America's freeways were places to gas up and go, she thought, reaching over to get some raisins from the container on the seat next to mannequin Mike.

"Raisins, Mike?" she offered. "Lots of iron, dear husband."

Traffic had thinned out immediately once Theresa left the 210. Now it was more semis and smaller commercial vehicles, along with the usual retinue of RVs, something she and Mike had never owned. She had mentioned maybe getting one once or twice, but Mike's response was so caustic she always gave it up right away.

"Nomads?" he'd snort. "Gimme a break! Look at the ridiculous names. *Prowler* for something forty feet long and ten feet high. *Cougar* for the same thing with two huge bump-outs. That's a big cat, all right, gonna jump right off the freeway and grab you. Only thing that's going to grab is about a hundred gallons of gasoline. Here we are, running out of oil and burning up the planet, and these guys are in a giant *Dune Chaser* burning through the fossil fuel. My ass! Get that ten tons of steel and plastic out in the sand, it's gonna stay there. Forever! The

Martians will find it and figure it must have been part of some kind of cult—which it is!"

Looking at the ridiculous things, many of them towing some other vehicle behind them—a car, SUV, or even a small truck—Mary had to agree with Mike's disdain. Besides, it took forever to pass them, especially with the Lincoln, which wasn't exactly a sprinter. But Mike had to eat some crow when they got the Lincoln, which got about twenty-one miles per gallon, nothing to brag about. Slightly down, but never out, Mike would respond to his Dreadnaught critics by suggesting that because it was old it was less of an environmental pig than a new car. Even the much-vaunted Prius that Emma and some of her friends drove. Why? Because the energy required to build a new car, no matter how great a mileage it got, took years of gas savings to justify, whereas old cars, even some of the monsters from the 1970s, were easier on the environment because they're already built, saving vast tons of steel and plastic and the energy needed to build a new car.

James, Janet's husband, who was very proud of his Prius, took issue with Mike, although he agreed that reuse and recycling were better for the environment, "OK, Mike," he'd say. "You drive your Dreadnaught, but I think you should wear some kind of pimp hat when you're at the wheel!"

Blah, blah, blah. Many times over their many years, Mike had tried her patience by taking umbrage at almost anything and everything. They'd just be sitting quietly reading and all of a sudden he'd say, "Listen to this, Mary," and read a passage about how the English had been exporting grain from Ireland during the great potato famine when millions of Irish either died or fled the island, his voice rising and face flushing with anger as he read.

"Mike," she'd remind him, "that happened a hundred and fifty years ago!"

Then he'd expound on how that amount of time was nothing, and that wounds from such an outrage took centuries, maybe longer, to heal, going on and on whether or not anyone was listening.

Everything was political with Mike—or moral, or whatever the right word was for his indignation at all of the inequality and injustice in the world. And L.A. was a fount of both, vast mansions in the upper reaches and ghetto conditions down in places like Compton.

"Ah but, Mike, what I wouldn't give for a good gripe from you right now. Instead, guess I'll listen to . . . ," She looked at the titles on one of the tapes Andres had made for her. "Chopin, Piano Works, Elisabeth Leonskaja. Great." He'd made the tapes because that's what the Lincoln had, an in-dash tape player—no CDs, iPods, or any of that modern stuff. And there were none in music stores anymore or even thrift stores. Lots of old LPs, but no tapes. Why? Who knew?

Driving and listening, her thoughts drifted to her childhood. Both she and Theresa had taken piano lessons at St. Francis, the Catholic elementary school they'd attended. Their teacher, an ancient, cranky nun, hadn't hesitated to rap their knuckles, the famous Catholic-school punishment, for hands that drooped over the keys and similar infractions of posture and piano stance. It left Mary with the impression that playing the piano was mostly about how you held your hands and how straight you sat on the bench rather than making beautiful sounds. Their parents, marginal as the household economy had been, had even bought them a piano, an upright as old, or older, than the nun. And they had dutifully practiced every day after school, and after Mass on Sundays. But the three, or was it four, years of lessons never really took. Sure, Mary could read music, meaning that at some low level she could play the piano—but barely, truth be told. Did Theresa have a piano? She wondered, not remembering if there'd been one in the house the time she was there.

Why hadn't their piano lessons taken hold? Let's see—lack of talent and no innate musical gift in either of the girls. Lack of application? No, they'd been very good about practicing, as painful as it often was. They were dutiful girls, and realized what a sacrifice their parents were making by paying for the lessons and buying the piano.

But there was another possibility, one she'd discussed with Janet, who played with real skill. And that was that the only music in the house was their piano playing. They didn't have a Victrola and the 78s to play on it. And no favorite music programs, just news and ballgames. Their parents read, played cards, did various things at church, but no music. Konrad had a trumpet, and took lessons for a year or two, but the screeching he made while practicing drove the whole family crazy.

So it was soon abandoned in favor of Mary's much-applauded (by her parents) rendition of "The Toreador Song" from *Carmen* or the barcarolle from *The Tales of Hoffman*. Over and over and over again while their friends were at the skating rink, or the movies, Mary played. Once the girls were out of the house—off to college for Theresa, work then marriage for Mary—the piano was left behind. But here she was as an adult enjoying, immensely, someone who could really play the piano. Chopin late at night, with a glass of wine, could make her weep. With sadness? Sure, but more really, with just a great emotional surge. Music did that. The roots were probably in the gene pool, but also in those lessons and all that practicing. So in a very, very roundabout way, her parents' investment had paid off!

"Well, crack my knuckles," Mary said aloud.

Coming into Barstow, one enormous truck stop, she needed to pee and thought she might as well get gas. Let's see, she thought, punch the Pay Inside button, remember where the gas cap is, and fill it up. The station was hot, noisy, and reeking of gas and diesel. The whole scene with people filling their vehicles, hurrying into the station, hurrying out, nobody talking to anyone, could have been right out of a science-fiction story, she thought as she filled up. *Star Wars*? Maybe. William Gibson? Ursula Le Guin, her favorite sci-fi author, was less materialist, much more subtle, than those. This scene was good for Mary to see, however, she thought with some guilt—it was probably much more like most of America than her safe little slice of Pasadena.

And inside the station, where the smell of diesel was replaced by that of fried food, the pandemonium was, if possible, even greater. Even though she was pretty sure she knew what was going on, she still had to pause to orient herself. A huge space, filled with vast quantities of . . . what?

Magazines over there, more of them than you imagined existed. Food aisles with candy galore, chips aplenty, small cans of soup and stew and beans and, God forbid, Vienna sausages. Ugh, she thought they'd been outlawed. An aisle of oil, windshield washer fluid, and other auto sundries. Another aisle of communication gear, including CB radios—really, still? And over to the left, a deli, the source of the food odors with trays of fried chicken, potato salad, Jell-O salad, baked beans, fried fish, tacos, and more, all under heat lights that gave the food a surreal glow. More science fiction!

"Fictive food," she thought as she grinned to herself, finally spotting the ladies room. She headed in, peed, and commented on the heat to a fellow sufferer, probably an RV wife. As she left, she realized that even in the restroom the thing that was bothering her most was the incredible din from the awful music—should you even call it that—enveloping the entire store. When, she wondered as she picked up a Mars Bar on the way to the checkout line, had they started to play music in almost all public places? Awful music, usually. In fact, she and Mike had long made it a point never to eat at a restaurant that played background music, even good music. Not to mention having a TV on! Well, OK, they went with Carlos and Emma to some Mexican places where mariachis strolled around in their gigantic hats, but that was different, it was live music.

She remembered that once or twice Mike had even asked the waitress or waiter to please turn off the music. "It doesn't look to me like anybody's listening," he would say. They were always shocked. Some did turn it off, though. Some refused, and so they'd just leave. Here she just had to endure long enough to pay. The man in front of her was so huge, with a cowboy hat and boots, that he blocked her view of the cash register. She darted over to another empty register and paid the person beyond the counter with her credit card, escaping as fast as she could to the outside. Was that person a man or a woman? She was even more uncertain about his or her ethnicity—Asian, Mexican, Tongan?

As she crossed the lot, she looked up to see an older Mexican man, also cowboy-hatted, standing by her car. "Dis your auto, lady?" he asked as she approached.

"*Sí.* Yes, it is. Why? *¿Por qué?*" she responded, very uncertain.

"Well I jus' wanna tell you that your old man in there, he ain' lookin' too good. You gotta leave the window open when is so hot. *Muy caliente.*" He pushed his hat back on his head and wiped his very wrinkled brow to emphasize his point.

"Oh, thank you, you're right. *Muchas gracias. Gracias,*" Mary nodded as she unlocked the car and shut the door quickly behind her.

Thankfully the man hobbled off to an ancient pickup at the next row of pumps.

"Well, *mi amor,* sorry about that," Mary apologized to the mannequin, laughing nervously as she carefully pulled out of the enormous station.

Back on Highway 15, which would take her all the way to Vegas, Mary forgot to turn on the tape player as she reviewed the recent stop. Let's see, she thought, be sure to leave the window on Mike's side open a bit, but try to pull into more obscure spots when you gas up. She had to admit being a bit flustered at the enormity of the place, inside and out. At home, after all, she usually went only to one gas station, a comparatively small one for L.A. The kind that had only four pumps because it was actually also a garage, the one she and Mike had gone to for years when they needed advice or repairs.

The original owner, Jerry something or other, had been a white guy. Then a couple of Mexican brothers had bought it, followed by a Vietnamese man whose English was very hard to understand at best. And now it belonged to two brothers (or was it three?) again. They were from Iran. But throughout the years the owners had all kept the same name, Jerry's Gas and Garage.

And even though the pumps were all supposed to be self-service, someone from the garage always came out and pumped her gas and washed her windshield, or sometimes all the windows. The cost of the gas, Mike had pointed out, was a little bit more, but so what? You bought their gas so that when they worked on your car, they knew you as a loyal customer. That kind of loyalty was something both she and Mike, and now Emma and Carlos, felt was very important.

She used to say, with Mike's emphatic agreement, "Just because it's an impersonal economy, with a price on everything, including love—doesn't mean we shouldn't fight it as often as we can. Try to overcome it with kindness, recognition, support, and especially loyalty." Her little speech against the impersonal bent of recent times.

You couldn't, shouldn't in fact, be loyal to Wal-Mart, or Target, or Safeway, despite all the public relations humbug about your being a loyal customer. Or "guest," God forbid! But you could be loyal to particular people who worked there. And more especially, try to do business with the small, independent places strewn by the struggling hundreds of thousands all over L.A.

Thinking about kindness, Mary remembered with a flash of anger the popular bumper sticker some years back that encouraged "random acts of kindness." What crap! Kindness, genuine regard for someone else, is anything but random. Now the stock market that the radio reported on by the hour, that was random for God's sake! But kindness? Kindness is deliberate, thoughtful, careful, considered. Not random.

All of Mary's career as landscaper had been founded on efforts to overcome the impersonal nature of the marketplace. By treating the people she served as human beings first and customers second. Same for Mary's coworkers and employers, where she could. And most of them responded in kind, more or less. Although truth be told, the higher folks were on the food chain, the less inclined they were to reciprocate. Like the person—whoa, buddy—in the monster SUV who just about took her fender off as he swerved in front of her. Let's see, Mary glanced at her speedometer, she was going seventy-five, so he must be doing ninety, at least, and it appeared he couldn't care less about silly things like turn signals.

"Of course," Mike had said. "When you have a lot of money, a real lot, you're always worried that someone is nice to you because they want your money. And people don't tend to get huge sums of money without hurting someone along the way, or a lot of people. Maybe you didn't do it, but your grandpa, or your uncle did. Whenever there's a huge bank account, bodies are buried underneath it, believe me! Those kinds of folks would rather deal with most everybody as a commodity. A waiter is worth X. A pretty waitress, X-plus. A gardener, like you, is worth Y."

Well, he was probably right, but she had worked for some wealthy homeowners who were decent, treated her right, respected her skill. But Mike always painted with the widest possible brush. "Didn't you?" she asked the mannequin.

And then she thought of the old Hispanic man who had been concerned about Mike. If *she* was distressed entering that enormous gas station, what about all the people who had come to California as immigrants from remote rural areas? Immigrants from Mexico, Central and South America, China, Laos, Vietnam, and Africa. How had these folks managed, she wondered? How *did* they manage?

Learning a new language must be daunting enough, but learning a new culture? Well some of it must involve plain, old luck, and now she realized she herself was heading to the world capital of luck: Las Vegas. Or as Mike called it, "Lost Vegas," but then he had often called their hometown "Lost Angeles" too.

Mary suddenly remembered a tape Andres had included for her with music from a waiter he worked with at the restaurant where he bussed tables. Where was it? Here. The man's name was Josh something, and the tape was simply a compilation of his songs. Most of them weren't exactly Mary's cup of tea, but it seemed appropriate to play the one titled "Vegas" as she headed into Sin City. As she popped the tape in she fast-forwarded to the song and actually turned the volume up to give her strength for the sensory overload she knew was coming. The singer's voice offered up the plaintive, compelling tune:

Joe and Marie went to Vegas to try their hand at the cards
Said "hey, mister"
How do you play this?
Oh, kids, it ain't hard!
"First I'll take your heart
Then I'll take your soul"

And he said this
As his eyes flashed black
As this young couple
Gave all that they had
He said, "Y'all come back!"
You see all that glitters ain't gold
Sometimes you play the fool . . .
And if you go to Vegas
Don't lose your cool!
'Bout five hours
From the heart of L.A.
Lays a land
No man should play
But they do!
Goddamn but they do!
Take my kids
Please take my wife
Here's the keys
To my home
And the deed to my life
'Cause I'm stayin'
Goddamn but I'm stayin'!
See all that glitters ain't gold
Sometimes you play the fool
And if you go to Vegas
Don't lose your cool!
Don't lose your cool!
Don't lose your cool!

She loved that song, not sure why, as she was wholly unlikely to lose her cool. But she'd certainly known people who had gambled their lives away.

But then capitalism, Mary thought, was nothing but one big gamble. The difference being that the world-class players on Wall Street and in the corporate boardrooms ran almost no risk in their gambling because the taxpayers always bailed them out. The little guys lost their jobs and their houses, maybe their families, and certainly their dignity. She always thought the difference between Vegas and Wall Street was simply that Vegas had more lights, while Wall Street had more suits.

Or different suits, she thought with a smile as she remembered Liberace's glittering ensembles. Must be where they got the term "well suited," she pondered as she began looking for a motel. Could get a suite, she thought. Did you have to be well suited to rent a suite? And was it appropriate to eat sweets in a suite?

Clearly she needed a break from the road.

Although it was very early in the afternoon, Mary decided to stop for the night. "All that glitters, sometimes you play the fool," the lines from the song going over and over in her head as she drove down Las Vegas Boulevard right through the glittering center of the city. The lights were blazing in full sun at The Venetian, The Palazzo, The Sahara—whoops, that one is closed and under deconstruction—the aptly-named Stratosphere, with its tower turning slowly in the bright sky, the gaudy Golden Circle and Mon Bel Ami wedding chapels. She continued past the block-long line of people waiting to get into a pawn shop.

She finally reached Fremont and took a right into the lesser casinos and steadily smaller motels, some of which were clearly "residential" and looked, frankly, dangerous. Now don't be a snob. But don't be a fool either, she thought as she looked for the right place. No motorcycles, broken RVs, or cars up on blocks in the courtyard, for a start. Also, old as they are, the signs should be properly hung, not drooping radically down one side. No broken windows, that's a good sign. *Star* seemed a common motel moniker here: Star Motel, Desert Star, Vegas Star. Then the Alicia, the Monterey.

When she reached what seemed the end of the motel line, or at least when she'd seen enough, she turned around and retraced her route, going more slowly and carefully this time. She was thinking that the farther back she went toward the Boulevard, the better the places she might find. She finally stopped at the Winter Star, which had no cars in the courtyard and seemed clean enough, and frankly, she was tired of looking.

Parking the Lincoln in the covered area by the office, she went in to ring the bell and was immediately enveloped by a strong, familiar odor. Trying to focus her tired mind on the smell, she thought of Carlos, her last meal with Emma . . . Curry! That was the smell. Not unpleasant, but unusual for a motel.

A door behind the registration desk opened and a very dark-skinned man came out, not black or Native American, maybe Latino? But as soon as he spoke, Mary remembered the so-called Patel Motels, the vast network of older motels owned throughout the country by people from India. Recalling a trip with Mike through northern New Mexico where they saw signs proclaiming "American-owned" on signs, they discovered local white motel owners were trying to distinguish themselves from the new East Indian proprietors. Of course, she and Mike had stayed at the Indian-owned places!

The man behind the counter greeted her in that familiar sing-songy voice she associated with people from South Asia.

"Yes. And you will be having a room? For the night? Or do you stay awhile, please?" he asked her with a smile.

"Just for the night, thank you," Mary replied.

"OK. Do you like to be closer to the street, or more quiet, over in the corner?" he inquired. "If you stay right by the office, you can come in and play our machines."

At this Mary looked up and realized that the small room was filled with what were probably slot machines and video games, all well lit and some routinely giving off odd sounds. Odd to her, anyway.

"In the corner, please," was her tired request. "I'm sorry, but I don't gamble, so I won't be using the machines."

"Lady," he said as he picked out a key for her. "You are in the capital city of gambling, you should try."

"No thanks. And how much will a single be, please?"

The owner glanced out the window as he replied. "A single at this season is only $35. But . . . ," he looked nervously out at the Lincoln again, and then back at her. "You must want a double, and that is $50!"

"No, there's just me. A single is all I'll need," Mary insisted.

Silent for a moment, the man turned from the counter suddenly, saying, "Excuse me, please, lady," and went into the room he had emerged from. Mary then heard the sound of raised voices.

"Come on," Mary thought. "What's the problem? Whatever it is, I'm simply not going to be forced into paying the higher rate. As tired as I am, I'll just go to the next place."

Just then the man came out again, followed by a young woman of startling beauty. A teen movie star, Mary thought absently.

"Hello," the girl greeted her in perfect English. "My uncle tells me there is some misunderstanding about a room?"

"Yes. I want a single, and he's telling me I have to have a double," Mary was beginning to be annoyed. "So there is clearly some misunderstanding. A single is all I need, please."

"Yes, I understand," the girl continued. "But my uncle says you have someone with you? Your husband, perhaps? The man in your car," she said pointing to the Lincoln.

Mary froze. Laugh? Or cry? Neither? She was truly flummoxed and too tired to respond quickly. Her clever ruse had been so easily discovered when she wasn't paying attention. Nice going, Mary. Giving up, she dove in with the truth. "I'm sorry. That man in the car is not a real person. He, it, is just a mannequin. You know, like they have in clothing stores? He's not a real person. Honestly."

The young girl and her uncle exchanged glances, unsure themselves of what to do with this revelation.

"Please, just come outside and take a look."

They followed her outside, tentatively approaching the passenger side of the car as Mary opened the door and gave her quiet companion a slight nudge, which of course generated no response.

"See?" she proclaimed earnestly.

At this, the uncle couldn't restrain himself. He asked, his voice even more sing-songy, "But, lady, why are you having him with you? What are you doing, please?"

But before she could answer, the young girl clapped her hands in delight, proclaiming with a grin, "I bet I know! He's there to make people think you have someone with you. A man to keep you safe! Am I right?"

Much relieved, Mary almost hugged the girl. "Yes, you're a clever girl, very clever. I'm not a crazy old lady, or not that crazy. My family was worried about me traveling across the country by myself, so a friend and I put the mannequin in the car so it would look like I'm not alone. We dressed him, made up his face, and put the seatbelt tight around him, so he won't fall over. I promise, when I go to my room tonight, he stays in the car."

"Very funny," the girl said with a brilliant smile. "Like an Alfred Hitchcock movie, right?"

As they all headed back in to the front desk, Mary handed over her credit card, and asked the girl, "How do you know about Hitchcock? His movies are from my time. That's quite a while ago."

"Oh, I'm taking a class on the American cinema. I plan to be a screenwriter, maybe even a director of films."

"Really?" Mary furrowed her brow. "But, forgive me, you're really beautiful. Why aren't you thinking about acting, like everyone else?

With perfect aplomb, the girl agreed, "Yes, I know I'm pretty. My auntie says I should go back to India and become a star in Bollywood. Do you know about Bollywood?"

"Yes, India's movie industry, right?"

"Yes, we watch as many movies from India as ones from the real Hollywood because my auntie and uncle are more comfortable with Hindi than with English," the girl explained.

"OK. So, why not acting then?" Mary probed.

"That's easy. Pretty only lasts so long, you know. And even if you're very smart, people tend to look down on you as not too bright *because* you're pretty. Not fair, but true, right? I mean look at all the lovely and very talented women you see in movies, once, twice, a few times. Then never again, or only in stuff way below their level. Sure, a few get parts, like Meryl Streep, but she's not even that pretty!"

"Yes, I know," Mary agreed. "My daughter is good-looking and very smart, so she's had to deal with that double standard. Even now, as a teacher, some of her students make the mistake of thinking that because she's attractive they won't have to work as hard in her classes."

"Oh, she's a teacher. We value teachers in my family. Both in India and here in the States. I thought about being a teacher, but I think I can influence more people through film."

"Influence them how?" Mary noticed the uncle listening while he processed her card and handed her the room registration.

"America has been very good to my family," the girl responded. "We have more things here, and more opportunities, than we ever would in India. The economy there is growing too, and more and more people are becoming quite wealthy. But most people remain very poor, and the competition for education, business, even just a loan, is deadly. In some ways it's a simple matter of numbers—a billion people there versus, what's our population here, 350 million?"

"That is a big difference, all right," Mary took her key from the uncle and signed the guest log he pushed toward her.

Eager to talk, the girl continued, as Mary pulled away from the counter. "So I want to make films about things you never see on TV or in the movies. About inequality, for example, and how that affects people's lives. Not just about silly stuff like having a huge house, but important things like who goes into the military and who doesn't, who loses their house when Wall Street screws up, and who doesn't. Who always gets by, doing well, and who never gets by, no matter what. Have you ever heard of Barbara Ehrenreich?"

"I have indeed," Mary smiled at the girl's eagerness. "I bet you're talking about her book *Nickel and Dimed*, right?"

"Yes," the young woman exclaimed with excitement. "A wonderfully horrible book, right? She was so good, taking those jobs so she could let the world know what life is like for those people, the ones who do the cleaning and work at Wal-Mart. This city is filled with those people, busy cleaning up after the millions of tourists and gamblers who come here. Even here at the motel, Mexican women do our laundry and make up the rooms. Anyway, that book should have been made into a movie."

"Wow, you've got some good ideas," Mary signed her credit card statement and entered the Lincoln's license numbers into the book.

Looking down at the log, the girl noted, "Mary Finnegan. Isn't that an Irish name? I'm Ajita, which in English means someone who wins, a winner. Great name to have in America right?"

"A lovely name," Mary agreed. "And I'd guess very appropriate. Finnegan is Irish, but it's my married name, my husband was Irish American. Me, I'm a Stein, my grandparents were German immigrants."

Coming around the desk and taking Mary's key, Ajita said, "Come. I'll show you your room. My auntie and uncle who own this place are immigrants. I came here as a baby to live with them because both of my parents wanted a better life for me. And now they are both dead."

Mary caught her breath. "I'm sorry. About your parents, I mean."

"Oh, it's OK, actually. I never knew them, you know. There are photos, of course. And stories from my uncle, my father's brother. But he and his wife are my real parents. They have no children of their own, so I'm their kid!"

Opening the motel room door and ushering Mary inside, Ajita asked, "Your grandparents were immigrants? Everyone but the Native Americans immigrated here, really. Don't you think it's strange that so many Americans today don't like immigrants? Las Vegas, Los Angeles, San Diego, San Francisco—all of those Spanish-speaking people? The whites are shouting about keeping the Mexicans out, but don't they ever look around and see who's doing most of the work? Isn't it that way in L.A.?"

"Oh, of course," Mary replied. "If even just the illegal Hispanics went on strike—not even those here legally—the city of Los Angeles would shut down. And it's not just there. I have a sister who lives in the country in Minnesota, and she told me that at least half of the cows in the Midwest are milked by Mexicans. Some legal, some not. She said that the university there even offers courses to white farmers so they can speak Spanish with their employees," Mary harrumphed.

"*Sí, lo hablo un poco de español,*" Ajita said. "And am learning more. You have to, or you should. You should see my uncle and auntie trying to talk with the Mexican women who work for us. It's very funny and also kind of sad. A good movie idea, I think! And even more sad is that there are plenty of Indians here, from India, who look down their very brown noses at the Mexicans, the blacks, and the Native Americans. Can you imagine? Acting superior because maybe they have a motel, or a restaurant, or their parents paid for them to go to school to become a dentist or something."

"Well," Mary sank gratefully into an ancient chair in the room. "That always happens. My grandparents were actually upset that I was marrying an Irishman, because the Germans tended to think of themselves, even without Hitler's propaganda, as a superior people. And my husband Mike, his parents were terrible racists. Nice people, but they couldn't find anything good to say about black people, Native Americans, or Asians. They were devout Catholics, but one time the priest in their parish in New York City, in Queens, had to be away for a month or so, and his substitute was an Asian man, maybe even from India. Anyway, he spoke perfectly good English, and he was ordained by the church, of course. They, and many others in the parish, simply stopped going to mass while he was there. 'No darkie priest for me, thank you,' my father-in-law said."

"I understand all that with my head. But my heart? My heart doesn't get it! I'll leave you now. You look like you need a rest, especially from a chatterbox like me. But please come and get your car first, and move it back here."

Out in the blazing heat of the motel courtyard, Mary noted the total absence of any plant life. Not even a scraggly cactus or mesquite bush, just a very sad-looking, mostly dead vine strung over the edge of the roof. Apt really, she thought as she got into her very hot car, for Lost Vegas. Cement, macadam, and lots of lights. After parking, she went around to the passenger side and unbuckled her mannequin companion. "Time for a long nap, Mike," she said as she tipped him over gently in the seat and covered him with a blanket.

Back in the very warm room, Mary remembered to turn on the air conditioning, a large and very dated window unit that emitted an unpleasant odor the minute it was turned on. Well, it was old like the room, like the motel, and like Mary herself, actually. Although she hoped she wasn't yet giving off strange odors.

Pausing to look around the rest of the room, Mary considered the requisite crooked painting of someplace with palm trees over the bed as she reached over to straighten it. There was a *Gideon Bible* in the bedside table drawer. The owners were Hindu, so why not a copy of the *Kama Sutra*, she thought with a laugh.

She and Mike owned a very interesting illustrated version, and yes, they'd once tried some of the 1970s classic *The Joy of Sex*, bought because Mike had heard the British author was an anarchist. This they put to use, usually with much laughter. God, she remembered a time when she and Mike were in their fifties—was that right? Mike's nose would begin to itch violently every time he climaxed, he'd have to reach up to scratch it vigorously, which caused them both to laugh until they darn near rolled out of bed. Who knew why it happened, but from then on, every time they saw some hapless man rub his nose . . . .

"Miss you, Mike. I really, terribly do," Mary sighed for the thousandth time.

A low-wattage ceiling light was buzzing in the room. The dim lamp on the bedside table had maybe a 40-watt bulb. Apparently they assumed that no one read in motel rooms. The TV was across from the bed, no flat screen here, just a big, old electronic invader. The tiny bathroom, not surprisingly, had water stains in the sink, shower, and toilet bowl, and the requisite ceiling sunlamp. Mary turned it on and it gave off a low buzz too. Who used those things anyway, and for what?

Still, the room was quite clean. Very much like herself, Mary thought—worn out, but clean. She'd be even cleaner after a shower, however. So she turned it on, but after waiting a very long time for the hot water to arrive, she began fiddling with the faucet to get the right mix of hot and cold. Why are shower faucets all different from each other? She ended up spending less time in the shower than it took to get it set up. As she dried herself, she thought about people she knew who said they stayed in the shower for fifteen or twenty minutes, sometimes longer. Never giving a thought to the waste of water and electricity—or gas or time, for gosh sakes!

"Hey, it's a free country," Mike used to say. "Americans are free to be as stupid as they can be, and many are!"

"Let it go," she told herself. Think about the good stuff, like that wonderful girl she'd just met. There was hope. Smiling to herself, Mary thought how great it would be if Andres could meet the Indian girl. What was her name? Ajita! Right, Grandma. The old granny as matchmaker, cruising the nation in her Dreadnaught looking for lovely, bright young women to date her grandson! And thinking, more and more vaguely, of her grandson, then some neighbor kids, she fell sound asleep in the chair she'd hoped to do a little reading in.

Chapter 9

Driving the short distance to Theresa's, Luther lit another cigarette, exceeding his usual two-a-day limit. He was nervous, depressed, no . . . really down about the letter on the seat next to him. Should he even mention it to Theresa? Of course! He had no one else to go to, and she was good counsel. Well, almost always. The exception being the time years ago when he was having serious PTSD symptoms, night sweats, crying right in the middle of the day for no apparent reason, not eating—and she insisted that he join a veteran's therapy group in Rochester. She even drove him there the first two times.

Big mistake. He'd always disliked the concept of "sharing," and in the couple of months he was in the group, he came to truly hate it. The idea of telling a bunch of strangers what was going on in his crazy head. Sharing is what you do when you have something good to give to someone. Share your ice cream, your sandwich, your dope, your firewood. It wasn't *sharing* when you had something bad, terrible even, to unload on someone.

Hey, man, let me share my broken leg with you. How about my broken head, my busted spirit? Like to carry that around with you for a while? Jesus, what a dumb notion. Take a bunch of guys crazy from their war shit, put them together in a room presided over by a male Nurse Ratchett, and have them unburden themselves. The result was that Luther ended up with not just his own whacked-out story, but was weighed down with the miseries of eight other guys too. By the time he fled the whole scene, he was dreaming their dreams too. And crying their tears.

He'd apologized to Theresa for leaving the program. Then she apologized to him for forcing him to go.

"I'm sorry for recommending something I didn't know enough about, Luther. I heard about it and it sounded good. But your point about it being compounded misery makes total sense. I did hope you'd find some vets to bond with, though."

"Bond, schmond. I hated the military. Hated what it did to me and everyone else around me. Hated watching my few friends get totally, pardon me, fucked up. Two of them finally dead. Why would I want to be with veterans ever again in my life? So we could relive that misery? The whole VFW/American Legion thing is exactly the opposite of what I need. Guys getting drunk every night talking about their time in the military. And the guys who never saw war, never got close to combat, sitting on their fat asses celebrating their glory days? No, thanks."

Otherwise, Theresa had always been a wonderful source of advice and comfort. Yes, there'd been other women in his life, most of them lasting only a summer, arriving as "interns" to learn about his organic gardening methods. Almost every one of them had ended up in his bed—until he started sleeping with Theresa—but all fled by the end of the season, if not earlier. Only one, Susan, had actually stayed for a whole year. He guessed he'd loved her, and she him, but as she tearfully told him, standing in the kitchen before he drove her to the Greyhound in Winona, she just couldn't take how morose he was. Morose and silent.

"It's not even the scary PTSD stuff," she'd said. "It's the daily grind of trying to get you to be a little cheerful, to see things in a good light, and to *talk to me*, for God's sake. And when you do talk, often as not it's a rant, hollering about something or somebody, some asshole you don't even know that you've heard on the radio or read about. I mean how many times have you looked up from your precious lefty mags and simply started in? Y'know, at first I thought it was cool—the hip, old Vietnam vet with a serious chip on his shoulder, trying to get the world right. But it's not just something you do, Luther, it's who you are! Deep in your soul! Who you fucking are!" her voice mixed with anger and anguish.

And so they'd driven silently into Winona, the only sound her quiet weeping. At the bus, she'd just leaned over and given him a quick kiss. "Good luck, Luther. I love you." And she was gone.

He'd vowed never to "get involved" again. Except for the rare one-nighter, he'd kept his word to himself. Not fair to them. Not smart for him. Once or twice he'd allowed himself, out of self-pity, the crazy idea of getting an Asian wife, or a Filipina. His neighbor La Dean Johnson, a huge man with a booming, glassware-rattling voice, had married a young, tiny Filipina with limited English. His first wife had fled with their daughter but left La Dean their son. The second wife was basically a mail-order bride, just like the nineteenth century.

The poor girl had stayed with him, in his dark, filthy, old farmhouse, for just two years, then fled to who knew where. Some local women, especially Theresa, had initially done their best to welcome her, include her, make her life bearable. But all of them had to admit they'd never stay one night in La Dean's house, let alone let him paw them. The poor man was basically a decent person and a good farmer, and he was good to his son. He'd come over to Luther's in the summer and stand there ogling the young interns working the gardens.

"Who's that creepy guy?" they'd invariably ask. And while La Dean ogled, in his booming voice that could reach all the way down to Winona, he'd lament about how badly he'd been treated by women.

"Just up and left. Not even a goddamn note, Luther. Two of them!" he'd bemoan. Luther knew La Dean actually didn't get it. He was clueless about how women reacted to him. The man had a kind heart, a little money, good land, and a nice truck. Sure, the house was a little shabby, but wasn't that supposed to be one of the things a woman did? Keep house? A man like La Dean would certainly think so. In a way Luther envied the man his innocence, because Luther knew exactly what his own problem with women was. Exactly! Just as he knew there was nothing he could do about it.

Pulling into Theresa's yard, Luther saw her dog Mose down by the barn. That meant she'd be there too. Hearing the truck, Mose came to greet him, looking for an absent-minded pat or three as Luther headed to the barn, a building he loved almost as much as its owner. Why, he wondered? Because, he supposed, it represents an entirely different, infinitely more hopeful way of life than the ugly, modern, steel pole sheds. The people who built Theresa's barn and all the buildings on this place, and his, had fully expected that they, and the life they represented, would last. Maybe forever. Whereas nobody today thinks of pole buildings—or farming—as lasting. It was as uncertain an occupation as any on the planet.

Opening a barn door, he almost knocked Theresa over as she emerged with a bale of hay.

"Here," he took the bale from her, "let me."

"Hi. Thanks," Theresa smiled as he hauled the bale to the edge of the goat yard, where he broke it into books of hay, distributing them at intervals along the inside of the fence.

"A 'book' is a great name for a section of a hay bale, isn't it?" she reflected. "I mean, if you're inclined, you can read each one. Here's some clover in this one, a big piece of thistle in that. Uh-oh, bits of a dead vole here, caught in the mower, or baler. Timothy, big bluestem, ragweed, and some box elder airplanes."

"Yeah," Luther agreed. "And the really loose books tell you that the Moe brothers were a little sloppy with their baler that day, the really tight ones just the opposite. And the twine? I think it's sisal, so it comes all the way from someplace like Bangladesh. Now there's a story!"

"Sloppy or not, I'm just grateful they still put it up in small bales. They're both older than me, so I worry they're going to have quit soon. Then where will I get hay?" She grimaced.

"The only way John Moe will quit baling hay is when he gets caught in the baler. You'll open a bale one day and find his cap or parts of a boot.

And if you're lucky, all the rest of him will be in bales somebody else bought. Hopefully that silly horsewoman down in the valley. The one that's always late paying the Moes because she knows that even though they grump around, they'll always sell her hay. John said some years she's been more than six months behind," Luther scowled.

"Wow, Lute, that's a dreadful thought—John's boot in a hay bale." Theresa shivered. "You must be in a great mood!"

"I'm OK. I cut wood today. You know how much I like that. I love my new tractor, so thanks for talking me into taking my old man's money. I'm thinking about spending a chunk of what's left on alternative stuff—solar panels, a wind machine maybe. What do you think?"

"Wonderful! That could actually be a selling feature for your produce. 'Organically produced with alternative energy' would be a good sign to have at the markets."

"Maybe. We'll see. How are the goats?"

"They're all good. Look at them. The only thing they need right now is to have their hooves trimmed. So I was wondering?" Catching the goats had always been very challenging, with the does weighing in at about one hundred fifty pounds apiece, and the buck at closer to two fifty. But now they were impossible for her to catch on her own. Then, after you caught them, you had to hold onto them while you trimmed their hooves. It simply couldn't be done by one person, no matter how agile they were.

"Of course. Let's put it on the calendar tonight. But where's Sebastian?" Luther referred to the breeding buck of the herd.

"Hear that hollering? He's penned up until November because if he starts in on the does now, I'll have kids early in January, in the miserable cold. I want them to come in April, in the spring, so the poor guy just has to endure awhile. He'll survive his horniness," Theresa shook her head in sympathy.

"He'll survive," Luther grinned. "But I bet he's started to stink. In fact, I think I can smell him way out here. He's probably curling his upper lip as we speak, turning his head back over his shoulders like he's sniffing the air for girls. Which I suppose he is, come to think of it."

"Yeah. I've never seen another animal as sex-driven as a buck goat. When we had cattle Tony always kept a bull, but they were positive gentlemen compared to goats. I suppose that's why we call some men old goats? Seems appropriate."

"Well, I feel sorry for that boy being stuck in there while his ladies are cavorting out here," Luther frowned. "But that's how it's got to be. The way our government is headed, they'll be following Hitler's lead soon, controlling which people get to breed and which ones don't. They'll turn it into a serious moneymaker. Controlled breeding for humans too!" He hit a wooden fence post for emphasis.

"Fascists in sheep's clothing—I mean goat's clothing," Theresa added and they both laughed.

"Goat's clothing? That's good," Luther chuckled. "I know I've asked before, but did you ever think about saving the hides after they're butchered? I mean some of these does are beautiful."

"Tony tanned a couple back when we first had them. It was a lot of work for some very small hides that we didn't know what to do with. It does seem a waste. I'll ask Jonas what he does with the hides next time I'm in there."

Jonas was the butcher Theresa used, Jonas Marks Meats. The local joke was that Jonas did indeed "mark meat," cutting out the best portions for himself and his large family. Theresa very much doubted it, as had Tony, who said that every butcher who ever lived had been accused of the same thing. "In fact," he'd say, "when our ancestors killed a mammoth, there were always some in the back of the cave who accused the hunters of having eaten or hidden the best parts for themselves. 'Where's the liver, Grog? I bet you and your brother ate it!'"

"Ask Jonas? Good luck with that," said Luther emphatically. "Any day when I'm feeling like the most grumpy, most antagonistic dude on the planet, I only have to remember Jonas—the ultimate grump. The guy never smiles. He's always, unfailingly, rude. He makes me look hail-fellow-well-met!"

"I know. But think about his job, Lute," Theresa said sympathetically as they started to the house. "The poor man has spent his life killing things, really big things like cows. Then he has to cut them up, quickly. They're always in a hurry in there, and they do the whole thing in the cold. I can't even go into their store without a sweater, let alone the locker. I don't know how he, or any of them, can do it."

"By drinking lots of beer obviously. Or booze in Jonas's case. Look at his nose, that man could guide the Christmas sleigh with that honker!"

"You're probably right," Theresa admitted. "But like the Moe brothers, I'm glad Jonas Marks Meats is here because what would I do without him? And are these for me?" she gestured to a basket of tomatoes on the fender of Luther's truck. "These are those great Russian ones, right?"

"They are," Luther was proud. "As ugly and tasty as ever. What did you make tonight?" Pausing on the tidy porch to leave their shoes and barn coats, they headed into Theresa's equally tidy kitchen, a great contrast to Lute's messy home.

"It's just stew—meat, carrots, potatoes, onions, garlic, and lots of gravy. I know I make it all the time, but it's easy and I know you love the dumplings. How about a cocktail first?"

"Yes, please, a large, stiff one. Plenty of gin and a tiny bit of tonic." Just as he sat down, Luther got back up. "Hey, is this the new chair Rusty made for you?"

"Isn't it wonderful?" Theresa beamed. "It's based on a design by a man named Nakashima. George Nakashima, I think, who was one of our premier woodworkers last century. I love how simple it appears, how elegant it looks, and that the walnut came from the farm here. A log you probably helped Rusty harvest. Sit in it, it's not gonna break, and it's really comfortable," she pushed the small chair toward Luther.

"It is nice. Typical Rusty work! But you said one of *our* premier woodworkers? How could that be with a name like Nakashima?" Luther ran a hand over the chair's outlines.

"Rusty told me he was actually born in the U.S. at the turn of the century, went to college and studied architecture, I think. Then at some point he began making furniture. But, and here you're partially right, he was interned along with most other Japanese Americans during the war. Still, he got on with his work afterward and became famous. Rusty took me to see a couple of his pieces at the Minnesota Landscape Arboretum up in Minneapolis."

"Man, if that had been me, interned because of that racist bullshit, I would've left and never looked back at this miserable country," Luther seated himself gingerly in the chair. "You're right, it's comfortable. But I'm going to sit in that sturdy armchair, OK?" The lovely chair was really too small to contain Luther's lanky body.

"Here's your drink," Theresa curled up in her new chair across from Luther. "So tell me what you want to talk about, Lute."

"Am I that obvious?" he grimaced.

"To other people? I don't know. But to me you are, especially when something's really bothering you. You brood and brood until you hatch giant lines of worry on your forehead. Actual brooding lines."

Luther's face twitched involuntarily, as if trying to erase the worry it showed. He looked around uncomfortably. Finally, he took a great draught of his gin, then set his glass on the floor and put his hands on his knees like some sort of supplicant.

"It's Azteca, isn't it? How bad is she?" Theresa worried.

With palpable relief Luther answered, "Not good. Bad, in fact. She's in a lot of pain, so a couple times a day I give her meds I got from the vet, which seems to help a bit. She can't walk though, and her hind legs are shot, so I have to haul her out to pee. She hasn't pooped in several days since she's not eating. She has this real low-pitched whine. You can hardly hear her. It breaks me up."

"What did the vet say?"

"The old guy, Gus, is still in there, but the other three are women, and they all look about fifteen years old. Anyway, the one I talked to told me there's nothing more to be done. Azteca has cancer in her hip joints, not uncommon for an old, large dog. And there's nothing to be done but put her down. I just haven't been able to bring myself to do it," Luther looked down at his boots.

"Why not let them do it, and save yourself the pain for once, Lute?" Theresa asked gently.

As he answered, Luther's hands moved back and forth in a kind of rocking motion over his knees. "Nope, I have to do it myself. They charge way too much money for everything they do there, and this is something a man should do himself. She's my dog. I'm gonna do it real soon. Put her out of her misery, then bury her with the others."

"She's only your third pup since you've been here, right?" Theresa noted. "Your dogs live a long time, so do mine."

"Yep, three dogs. You know they live so long because they're in the country, where they belong. Big dogs in town, where they don't get enough exercise and just eat store-bought food, have miserable, short lives. Azteca, Pepe, and the first one, the big Rottie Hans, were all free-range pups. They roamed the farm, and if they found a dead coon, ate all of it they could. Then they'd come back and lay in front of the stove, farting something awful. Man, the stink! And the occasional puking during the night. Wolves and dogs are basically scavengers. Fresh meat is nice, but rotten is good too! Like us and our cheeses, I guess." Luther smiled at the memory of his beloved dogs.

"I don't remember, did you have dogs growing up?"

"Not a chance," Luther snorted. "The old man didn't much like people, but he detested dogs. He grew up on a hardscrabble farm where dogs were only for work, never for pets. Too urban and effete. Christ, even poor people now get their dogs clipped and washed, spending big money at the vet's. My father had none of that. On the rare occasions we visited some relative's house and they had a dog or cat or even a bird in the house, he'd bitch about it all the way home. 'Disgusting! A filthy animal right in their home, full of fleas and who knows what diseases! Might as well live in a cave.' That was my old man's take on pets."

Theresa laughed, "My parents weren't crazy about pets either. Not as severe as your dad, though. And because my father had a tender heart, he actually bought me a cocker spaniel when I was about ten, much to my mother's dismay. But the deal was that I had to take care of it, walk it, feed it, comb it, and so on. Which I dutifully did, so there was a pet truce with my mother. Her name was Missy. I loved her."

"What happened to her?"

"She got run over out in the street one day. My brother was playing with her. He threw a ball and it went into the road. The dog chased it. Bam, dead Missy. I was heartbroken. Of course I wanted another puppy, but my mother stood firm. No more pets, not even a fish. I think for her it wasn't about a dog being dirty, it was about it being an extravagance. Spending money on something so unnecessary when she'd grown up so poor, and she and Dad never having much either."

Luther nodded, drained his gin, and asked, "Just another bump, please."

"Sure, but we're having wine with dinner, too, you know."

"Good. I'll drink that too," Luther was firm.

Reluctantly bringing him another drink, Theresa worried about his alcohol use, or abuse. She was fortunate to have him as a friend. A large, angry man. No doubt he'd be angry until he died, but never angry at her. And how many other women her age, or women of any age, had a genuine male friend? Someone they could talk with openly. Also, the man was competent, could fix about anything. An added bonus she didn't like to dwell on, since it raised the specter of her dependence. Was she good to him because she needed him? Of course, but it was so much more than that.

He came into the kitchen. "Can I help with anything?"

"Nope, thanks. While I'm putting dinner on, why don't you take a closer look at Rusty's chair," Theresa offered.

Which Luther dutifully did, taking it into his lap, putting on his broken reading specs, taped together at the nosepiece, to look at the elegant joinery, the clever design features. The chair didn't seem so special at first glance, but grew in significance the more you studied it. Like good people, Luther thought. Like Theresa.

"Theresa," he ruminated aloud, "do you think inanimate things, like chairs, have souls, some kind of life? That they can speak to us if we listen closely enough? I know it sounds crazy, but I think this chair has several voices. The walnut tree that Rusty and I took down, maybe some of the squirrels and owls and coons that lived there. It was a female, I remember, because of all the nut casings laying around, so the squirrels would remember it. Then there was the mill we took it to—Eli's, remember? John Moe worked there some, he was probably the youngest man there and he was in his seventies at the time. But the loudest voice is Rusty's, just booming out of here. Not that Rusty's any kind of a noisy dude. And the Japanese guy must be in here, too, I'd expect."

Theresa was setting the table. "Well, you know native people all over the world thought the entire universe of things had life, had souls. I've just been reading about it. Everything was animated until the big religions came along and started dividing things up—bodies here, souls there, hell there, heaven up there. Which happened about the same time that we got division of labor, dividing people up to do this little thing, that little thing. Very useful for those who sat at the top of the pyramids, to have the ordinary people believe that those divisions were ordained by the gods. Or God."

"Wow," Luther grinned. "You're getting radical on me. Speaking of churches, how do you reconcile this with yours? Tell some cardinal that this chair can speak and he'll have you committed, or not too long ago, burned at the stake."

"OK, OK, Lute," she raised her hands in protest. "Don't, please, get going on that again. I love the Mass. Did as a little girl, do as an old lady. Those pews? If you think that chair has things to say, imagine what the pews at St. Stan's can tell. But let's eat, my friend."

"OK, sorry. We're going to disagree about church until one of us packs it in, I guess. Hopefully me. Then you can come to where I'm buried on my farm, preferably in a raised bed, and continue the discussion. Just be sure to bring some gin to pour on my grave, OK?" he said as his face relaxed into a smile.

"Nice thought. Please open that wine."

Luther sat, took the bottle of red wine—something from Spain, he noted—and removed the cork with the handy little plastic device Theresa used. Small and cheap-looking, he was always amazed at how well it worked. He loved tools that worked well because they were designed well, but he was always suspect of plastic. "Tell me again. Where did you get this opener?"

"That came from that little French foreign exchange student we had. Dorothée. Remember her?"

"Yeah. Vaguely."

"Doesn't it work great? It is actually a piece of Tupperware. Or, as she said it, *Too-pair-where*. Her mother, who lived out in the middle of nowhere in rural France, raised her and a sister and brother by selling Tupperware. The dad was long gone. She made a good living at it, Dorothée said. I've got some good bowls too, that I've used for storage for years. Good-quality stuff."

"Hey, it makes plenty of sense that the French would need a good wine-bottle-opening tool." He held the device up for yet another inspection.

Lute then poured them each half a glass as Theresa lit two candles on the table, although it was still somewhat light out. Tony had been dubious about candles when she'd starting using them, but surely, she thought, if anything was animate, it was light. A candle was a whole conversation in itself, especially when an occasional breath of breeze entered the room, as it was now doing.

They ate in comfortable silence for a while. But the peace was broken when Mose, lying next to the table in hopes of a scrap, made wind. Considerable, stinking, dog wind.

They both laughed.

"Nice move, Mose. Couldn't you have waited? See now if I'll save you any meat. Which by the way, Theresa, is delicious as always, really wonderful. And your bread! How long have you had that starter?"

"Pride goeth before a fall. But I have to brag that I had that starter when Tony was still alive. About twenty years. I make the sponge the night before and then the first thing I do when I get up is look into the bowl to see how wonderfully much it's risen overnight, with all the little waves of bread life moving across its surface."

"Yeah. Hey, I'd probably join you at your Mass if the host was made out of your sourdough."

Ignoring his comment, Theresa raised her wine glass. "A toast to bread, my friend."

"To your bread, anyway." Luther touched her glass lightly and finished his wine in one gulp.

"Yeah, starter. Seeds." He took a drink of water. "When I start seeds, almost overnight, they start making waves too, in the soil. So of course they're alive, with plenty to say. I swear I can hear them talking about stuff in the greenhouse when I'm stone sober. Those great Georgia Flame peppers I've been growing, that actually come from the country of Georgia? Just imagine their story, Theresa! A pepper, that has its start probably in Peru, where your brother was, and ends up in a place most of us know nothing about and would never visit. Although at the rate we're going, our government is probably just about to bomb it. Think I'll pay more attention to those peppers this year."

"Good. Let me know what they have to say, will you?"

"Fine," Luther said absentmindedly. They resumed their silence, which by meal's end had reached the point of discomfort for Theresa. Something was still wrong, she knew, and it wasn't just Azteca.

"Let's sit in the living room. Bring your wine." And when they were seated, she asked "Mind if I say something?"

A look of alarm crossed her friend's features, but he swallowed and said, "Of course, what's up?"

"I don't know, Lute, you tell me," Theresa replied carefully. "I know you drink, but you're usually pretty careful around me, yet tonight you're pouring it down. You've just about finished the wine. Which is OK, but I'm not sure it's about you enjoying it so much as simply using it to squelch something. I thought it was Azteca—and it was, but there's something more, isn't there?"

Another long pause as Luther set his wine glass on the floor, his hands grasping and then kneading his knees. But he finally answered, "OK. OK. You know, you should have been a shrink."

"No. I'm not trying to analyze you. But you're working hard at avoiding something. Does that paper sticking out of your pocket mean something?"

Drawing the white envelope slowly out of his shirt pocket, Luther reluctantly answered. "Yes, it means one hell of a lot. Read it, will you?"

Taking the envelope, Theresa noted the return address was a law firm in Rochester, Manning, Fairbody and Dumermuth. "Aren't these the lawyers who handled your father's estate?"

Clearly agitated, Luther answered, "They are. Just read the letter, please."

Theresa read the letter quickly through to herself, then aloud, slowly.

MANNING, FAIRBODY AND DUMERMUTH LLP
Attorneys at Law
Wells Fargo Bank
223 South Seventh Street
Rochester, MN 55033
(507) 333-9999
dmuth@mfdlaw.com

September 25, 2012

Mr. Luther Rasmussen
Box 4504
Moeville, MN

Dear Mr. Rasmussen,

This is to inform you that our efforts to find and contact your sister, Eunice, have yielded the following results.

The agency we hired discovered that Eunice had lived in northern California, in the town of Garberville, for many years. Sadly, the agency also reports her passing. Eunice died several years ago, on August 7, 2007, in a

Garberville clinic. We have information regarding the circumstances of her death, which will best be discussed with you in person.

The agency informs us that your sister had a child, a son named Chester, born to her on April 15, 1971. Chester is, as Eunice's sole known offspring, Eunice's heir. This means that the monies coming to Eunice from the estate of your father, Dr. Lars Rasmussen, will now be conveyed to Chester. However, the agency has, as yet, been unable to locate Chester at several places he has inhabited in recent history. The agency has left word at those locations of the need for Chester to contact us. Again, more information is available, but we would like to discuss it with you in person.

Sincerely,
Quentin Dumermuth
Attorney at Law

Drawing her breath in sharply, Theresa sat quietly holding the letter for a few moments. Looking at Luther, she noticed that his hands were still on his knees, not moving now, but gripping them as he rocked in a very small motion back and forth.

"Luther," she broke the silence. "I'm so very, very sorry to hear this. When did you get the letter?"

Looking out the window, he sighed, "I don't know, couple days ago. I wasn't sure what to think about it, still not sure. Not surprised really. I thought she was probably dead years ago. In fact, it's a surprise to find out she lived as long as she did."

"You haven't really ever talked about her."

"Not a lot to tell, I guess. She was four years younger than me and my total opposite. No gloom and anger. Mostly upbeat, bright, and cheerful—despite our father. While I took offense at everything, and was locked head to head with the old man since I was born, she mostly just laughed stuff off. Which drove him crazy, or crazier, because me he could understand, poke me with a stick and just as he'd expect, I'd bite like hell. Poke her and she'd just let it go. Never seemed to hold a grudge, whereas I was full of grudges. Still am, as you well know. I've thought about it, about us and our so-called family for years, and concluded that the way she was wasn't just an act, a way of getting by in a shitty situation, but the real thing. Her chemistry was different than mine, than our father's, even than our mother's."

"Where was your mother in all this?"

"Silent mostly, a ghost. I've told you the way he punished us was by not talking. Do something he disapproved of, even a minor thing, and he'd give the three of us the silent treatment. Sometimes for over a month. He'd come home, not say a word, we'd eat supper together silently, then he'd head to his study, read or whatever, and sleep there on a hide-a-bed. The only reaction our mother had was to sometimes just sit there at the table and cry quietly, tears dropping onto her plate. At first we'd try to comfort her after the old man left the table, but she'd just wave us away. Tell us to go do our homework or something. Every once in a while I'd hear them arguing, her pleading with him, I think. But mostly . . . silence. We grew up in a tomb! A fucking, I'm sorry, tomb!"

"Did he ever shout at you? Hit you? Threaten you?" Theresa reached tentatively for Luther's knee.

"Never," Luther sat back in his chair and took a deep breath. "I had friends whose parents were yellers, even hitters, and I actually envied them—the kids. But who knows? They're probably right now bitching about how badly they were raised, blah, blah, blah. Man, when I heard about some of the things that happened as kids to those GIs I was in the therapy group with, I just shut up about my life. We were never beat. Always well fed, well dressed, in a fancy house. Nice cars. Paid for my college. Neither of them drank or smoked. I had piano lessons for years. So the old man didn't talk to us, maybe we were lucky. I don't know."

"Come on, Lute, of course you know. There are different kinds of abuse, and not talking to your own children was certainly, for sure, abuse. It plain was!" Theresa was emphatic.

"Well, anyway Eunice, we called her 'Euny,' fled the whole thing. No college for her. Just took off with some friends for Haight-Ashbury—they'd been reading about the scene there—right after graduation. Gave me a hug, hugged Mom, then climbed into a VW bus, and we never saw her again. Frankly, I think the old man was relieved, it saved him her college tuition. I knew even then that he was someone who should never have had kids. He just plain didn't like us, let alone love us. Didn't like anybody, I think—including my mother, his wife. When I was pretty young I'd ask her why Dad wouldn't talk to us, and she'd try to say something soothing like 'Luther, you know your father really loves you and Euny. He just can't come out and say it.' But by the time I was a teenager, I knew that wasn't true. And she knew I knew it." Luther grimaced.

"But why didn't you ever go looking for her?"

"I went into the Marines not too long after I left college in Decorah. Luther at Luther!" He looked out the window again, into the past. "They shipped my sorry ass to Vietnam. And when I came back, you know the story. When Mom died, not long after Tony, I tried to contact Eunice. Talked to some old friends of hers, including one who'd been on the trip out to sunny Cal. All she knew was that my sister had gotten heavily into the drug scene almost as soon as they got there. Suppose I could have gone looking for her, but where? I had my place, the gardens, to care for. Still do. Keeps me sane, but if I'd gone to California and started a search, I would have been a menace. Probably be in the pen right now, if I was even alive."

"I'm not criticizing you, Lute, you know that." She got up and hugged him, holding his shaggy head against her breast. "I'm so sorry about this, the letter, its news."

"Yeah, I am too, I guess. But I think I'm mourning, if that's what I'm doing, a little girl right out of high school. Actually, once I went to Decorah I was never home much. The old man paid my tuition, but for extra money I worked the whole four years. A few campus gigs, but the job I really liked was on a farm, a small dairy farm. I've told you. That's where I got my taste for this life, thank God!"

"Yes, you've talked about that before many times. That must have been a good time for you, I think."

"Real good," Luther replied. "If I'd been half smart, I would've hidden out on some hippie farm instead of enlisting. But so should millions of other guys too. I mean, that's why Uncle Sam likes kids, we're stupid and vulnerable. I still don't get the guys I see in Winona or Rochester who advertise that they were in Nam on their license plates. Just advertising how dumb they were!'

"Yes, you've mentioned that once or twice. Or many, many times. Can I talk you into two things, please?"

"Sure, anything for you, you know."

"One, I'm going to open another bottle of wine, and two, will you please sit down at the piano and play just a couple pieces?"

Hesitating, Luther took a breath and pushed himself up from his seat, gladly accepting the offer of another glass of wine. "What do you want me to play?"

"Did your sister take lessons too? How about something she liked?"

"Yes, she did. She loved to play, was actually much better than me, more tuneful, had a good ear. Where I struggled, going over and over a piece to get it, she'd jump right in and have it down, pronto. I envied her."

Taking his wine to the piano, he played some Chopin nocturnes his sister had loved—Op. 27 no. 2, then Op. 48 no. 1 and 2—followed by Beethoven, the lovely adagio from the Piano Concerto no. 2 in B-flat Major, and the rondo from the same piece. Finally, the heart-stopping Hungarian Rhapsody No. 2 in C-sharp Minor by Liszt, a piece so familiar that Theresa could play it in her head while she gardened.

Playing the music transported him, as Theresa had known it would. But at the end, he was quietly tearful . . . not weeping so much as just very, very sad.

"Hey," she put a hand on his shoulder. "Why don't you stay here tonight? Let me make you breakfast in the morning?"

Reaching over his shoulder to clasp her hand, Luther sighed. "Sorry. I'd love to, but there's Azteca. I've already been gone a long time, and recently the only way she stops whining—I know she's in wicked pain!—is when I lie down next to her, and pet her until I fall asleep."

"Next to her?"

"Yup! Couple blankets, a quilt, whatever," he explained. "Man, when she looks at me, I know she's asking for comfort. It's no big deal to do what I can. She doesn't have long, you know, I'm just putting it off."

"Luther, you're really quite a man, you know," Theresa gave him a quick hug and let him out the door. Only then did she realize that she hadn't told him about her sister Mary, en route to visit. It seemed unfair, in a way, that she and Mary were still very much alive while Luther's sister, much younger, was dead.

Chapter 10

MARY AWOKE SUDDENLY FROM HER NAP in the motel armchair. Confused, she thought she was at home and called for Mike to get the door. Then she remembered she was in a motel. In Vegas. But why was someone knocking at her door? Leaving the chain on, Mary opened the door just far enough to peer outside into the gathering dark, where she saw it was the young girl—what was her name?—knocking.

"Hello, hello," the girl gave an embarrassed smile. "It's me, Mrs. Mary. Ajita."

"Oh, hi," Mary opened the door.

"Hi, did I wake you? I'm sorry, I just came to invite you to supper with us, with my uncle and auntie and me. It's Indian food, but not too hot."

"Oh, thank you. I'm glad you woke me. I had the A/C on too high and was starting to freeze my old bones. I'd love to eat with you, how nice. Let me freshen up, then I'll be there in five minutes, OK?"

"Great, just so you know though." Ajita was hesitant. "The meat is goat. It's really good, one of our maids and her husband raise goats. We buy it from them and send it to a butcher here. I know some people don't eat goat—"

"Actually, I'd love to try it." Mary smiled.

The girl smiled with relief. "Good. Come over when you're ready, OK?"

"Sounds good, thank you," Mary closed the door.

She turned the air conditioning way down, washed her face and hands, brushed her unruly salt-and-pepper hair, and called Emma's house on her cell phone. Carlos answered since Emma was teaching at the college that night. He asked how and where she was.

"I'm in Lost Vegas, Carlos, decided to stop early."

"How's Mike? Your mannequin companion?"

"Fine. But guess what? The owner here thought I was trying to cheat him by asking for a single room. He saw the mannequin in my car and thought it was a real man. Very funny."

"Yeah. It is. What happened?"

"I took him out there and showed him the real Mike, so to speak."

"The real Mike. Yeah. I get it."

"You're such a clever man, Carlos. Especially for a math teacher. And the other thing is that they have a lovely girl who just invited me to eat dinner with them. Guess what we're eating?"

"Couldn't begin to."

"Goat! They're Indians. The kind from India. So probably curry!"

"Who'd of thought? Take care of yourself, Mary, and give Mike a pat on the head for me, will you?" Carlos hung up.

Putting on a sweater in case her dinner hosts' home was cold, Mary walked up to the office and entered, a bell ringing as she did so. Ajita greeted her, motioning Mary into the motel's inner sanctum. It wasn't too cold, a bit warm if anything. And quite lovely. Lots of beautiful cloth in vibrant greens, reds, and purples arrayed in marvelous patterns in the many curtains, in cushions of all shapes and sizes, and on a tablecloth so beautiful it would be a sacrilege to spill on it. And thick, beautiful carpets that were covered with many small rugs. And finally, wall hangings, a mix of cloth and ornaments that looked much like very large earrings.

"You have a lovely home, so many wonderful colors. Thank you for inviting me. And oh, it smells so good, the food I mean." Mary stood and admired the room, thinking it was like a lovely indoor garden.

"Please to sit here," the uncle offered, directing Mary to a seat on what looked like a very large ottoman. Were ottomans Indian, Mary wondered? No, Turkish, she thought, the fabled empire, with turbaned sultans, Ali Baba and magic carpets flying all over the place. Not that these carpets weren't magic.

As Mary sat, Ajita introduced her uncle and aunt, hovering in the background. "This is my auntie, Nikita, and my uncle is Raj."

"Nikita like the Russian leader, Kruschev?" Mary asked. "And Raj?"

"Yes, but our Nikita is very different than the Russian one, though it's spelled the same in English. Raj means rule, or ruler, but it's also a very common name for men in India, like Mike, or Bill in America. Right?"

"My husband's name was Mike," Mary settled on her ottoman. "He died a couple of years ago, but he would have loved this, you inviting me in."

"Oh, I'm sorry to hear that. That he's dead, I mean."

"Well, I'm sorry too. I miss him a lot. I've been very lonely, so I'm on a trip across the country to visit my sister. I haven't seen her in a long time."

"Where does your sister live?" Raj asked.

"In Minnesota. Do you know it? The Mississippi River?"

"Yes, we know that," Raj replied eagerly. "I have a cousin who has a restaurant in the city with the hospital. Mayo Clinic, do you know it?"

"Oh, that's in Rochester, in the southern part of the state," Mary explained. "My sister lives only an hour away from there."

"Oh yes?" Raj sat down. "And what is she doing? She has a family, yes?"

"Yes. Her husband is also no longer alive; he died many years ago. But she has a son who lives near her, and he has two children, grown by now. And she has a farm. A beautiful place in the hills above the Mississippi River near a small city called Winona. Lots of snow in the winter, and many farms."

"Please?" Aunt Nikita said, finally speaking up as she gestured to the table. "Can we sit to eat now?"

"Yes, yes," Raj agreed. "Please sit here, by the window," Raj invited as he pulled out a chair for Mary.

Mary and Raj sat while the two women of the house served. And when they were all seated, the Indian family bowed their heads while Raj said a brief prayer, followed by each of them crossing themselves.

Surprised, Mary asked, "I'm sorry, but I didn't quite hear your prayer. Was it Muslim, Hindi?" She knew, of course, the sign of the cross, so much a part of her childhood that she almost crossed herself when they did. But she couldn't quite believe that these wonderfully exotic people were . . . Catholics?

"No," Ajita responded. "Catholic. We are Christians."

"Catholic? I had no idea," Mary could not hide her surprise. "Are there many Christians in India?"

"We are from state of Kerala," Raj explained as Ajita passed the dishes. "And yes, almost twenty percent of people there are Christian, mostly Catholic."

"Oh," Mary spooned curry over her rice. "I know a little about Kerala because my husband Mike was very interested in socialism—really any alternative to American-style capitalism. Wasn't there a communist government there, and I thought he said Kerala had a very high standard of living because of it?"

Ajita, not waiting for her uncle to respond, took the conversational reins.

"Yes, Kerala, which was founded as a state in the 1950s, has always had a communist party. And it's mostly they, the communists, who have made Kerala a very important state in India. It has—maybe you know this—about a 99 percent literacy rate, men and women, a very good public health system, free and very good public education all the way through college or technical school, and so on. You know the Human Development Index?"

"No," Mary admitted.

"Well," Ajita smiled, "and now I suppose I'm sounding like some-one from the tourist bureau or something—"

"Not a bit, it's very interesting. Please go on." What a wonderful girl!

"The index is simply a new way to measure the standard of living, and includes things like health, education, and welfare, not just income. So by the index, Kerala measures up to most First World, wealthy nations, meaning that people there live as long as we do in the U.S., are just as healthy, and so on. This in India, a country where millions of people are still illiterate, especially women, and go to bed hungry each night. It's really rather amazing." Adding, as she grinned, "and now I'll climb down from my podium."

Raj, who hadn't started to eat, couldn't stay out of the discussion. "Yes, these things you say are true, but there is also much poverty in Kerala, as incomes are very low. Which is why we came here, to America, where we can live like rajas compared to what we would have in India."

His animation revealed that this was an oft-visited topic between him and Ajita, who in turn responded with, "But that, Uncle dear, is *exactly* what's so amazing. That there's a place where, despite not having much money, people are still well-off. I would even say that the poor of Kerala are better off than the poor of America, who probably have more money, but little care from anyone, especially the government."

Nikita, looking increasingly desperate at her end of the table, finally spoke up, urging Mary to take some of the many condiments—banana slices, shredded coconut, mango and papaya chutneys, and raisins—to add to her curry. Thanking her, while wishing also to enter the conversational fray, Mary thought better of it, took the food, and kept her silence. Meanwhile, Raj asked her to please excuse his niece, who he said often sounded like a communist when she talked this way.

Wanting to object, Mary refrained, the better part of being a guest. Good thing Mike wasn't here. So they ate in uncomfortable silence for a minute or two until Mary realized that the talking ball was now in her court. She had to move the conversation along, since the others were perhaps embarrassed by the hint of disagreement between niece and uncle.

Let's see, how about religion? And without further reflection asked, "Do you attend a church here in Las Vegas?"

Visibly pleased, Raj answered that yes, they did. It was nearby, and named Santa Teresa, a church largely attended by Latino people. He then asked Mary if she was familiar with the saint?

"I am actually, yes. My sister, the one I am driving to see? Her name is Theresa, after the saint. We were a Catholic family, and our brother became a priest."

Ajita, not able to stop herself, asked with a grin, "And is your sister very saintly?"

Mary laughed. "That depends on what we mean by a saint. She married and had a child, so she certainly wasn't celibate. But she's a good person. Always was."

"What did she do when she was younger?" Ajita hadn't even started to eat.

"She was a teacher. Because of her name, and because our parents were devout Catholics, she actually went to a women's college called St. Teresa's in the town of Winona that I told you about. After she graduated, she taught English for a time in a local Catholic elementary school, then went on to teach in a public high school in Winona. I don't know for sure, but I'd guess she was a very good teacher."

"And you?" asked Raj. "Do you also have a profession?"

"I did, but not with people, with plants," Mary explained. "I was a landscaper, designing and installing gardens in Pasadena, where I live. I'm OK with people, but I like plants more. They don't talk back, and more importantly for me, they don't tell you what to do."

"So." Ajita ignored her aunt, who clearly wished she'd be silent and eat. "You're what they call an 'independent.' Right?"

"Yes, I guess. The reason I didn't go to college like Theresa was that I couldn't bear the idea of four more years of being told what to do—or when or how to do it—after I got out of high school. My Catholic high school back then was quite strict, and taking orders wasn't my strong suit, as they say."

Silence ensued for most of the rest of the meal, with Mary commenting several times on how good the food was, and asking a desultory question or two about Las Vegas.

Finally, Ajita asked, "What does your sister do now that she is retired?"

"Her farm is up in the hills above Winona. She's lived there for almost sixty years. Her husband was a farmer. After he died, she had to rent out the land to neighbors, but she has always kept animals. Chickens and a small herd of goats. She loves those goats!"

"Really, so she doesn't eat them?" Ajita asked.

"No. I mean, yes, she eats them. They're her main source of meat. In fact, she often makes goat curry, like this. Probably not as good, of course." Mary declared as she smiled at Nikita.

"So," Raj asked, "does she kill the animals herself?"

"No, her husband used to do the butchering, but since he died she takes the goats to a butcher."

"She has to bring the animal there, all by herself?" Ajita wondered.

"No. She has friends, neighbors, who help load them into a truck and bring them to the butcher for her."

"But if she loves them, as you say, how can she eat them?" the girl wondered.

"I don't know. In fact, I've often wondered that myself. I'll have to ask when I get there. But you know if you eat meat, somebody had to raise it, and someone had to kill and cut it up," Mary justified as she felt herself getting defensive.

Sensing this, Ajita changed the topic, "How long will it take you to reach your sister, do you think?"

"I'm not exactly sure. About three more days, I hope. Maybe a little more. It depends on my car, which is old but in pretty good condition. Like me, I guess. And that reminds me that I want to get up quite early tomorrow and get on the road, so thank you very much for this lovely supper and the interesting conversation."

At this, Raj stood, then Nikita. Ajita helped Mary from her chair, offering, "Please let me walk you to your room."

Thanking her hosts once more, Mary shook their hands and let the girl escort her out a back door and to her room, where they talked briefly at the door. Ajita said she might visit her relatives in Minnesota so she could come and see Mary and her sister, and the goats! They both laughed, and Mary took some paper from the table and wrote her cell number on it.

"You're a lovely young woman," Mary said warmly. "Meeting you and your family has been a nice addition to my trip. Not to mention, of course, the meal. Please thank your aunt, and your uncle, again for me." At that Mary gave the girl a brief hug as she entered her room. A hug? When did she start doing that? Mary asked herself as she went to bed.

Chapter 11

Joni Adams began to have trouble with her ancient Civic shortly after she got to Sacramento, the City of Trees. Lots of trees, yes, and they looked pretty nice from the freeway, but Geeville had *more* trees—it was basically *in* the freakin' woods! Joni had worried because as soon as she got on the interstate, the Honda started to get funky. Nothing too alarming, just a little slow going through the gears as the automatic upshifted.

When she stopped for gas just out of the city, she checked both the engine oil and transmission fluid, pleased that she knew how to do these things thanks to her dad, who taught her basic car maintenance. Both dipsticks showed sufficient fluid. So there was nothing to do but touch her dashboard talisman for good luck and continue on to Tahoe, then Reno, then on to someplace where she'd find a quiet street and sleep for a couple of hours. No motels for her, too expensive. And she was so wired about leaving Geeville she wouldn't sleep for long anyway.

Joni had always driven just a little over the speed limit, and she'd been ticketed several times accordingly. On major highways and the interstates, she looked for anyone going real fast and immediately tailed them at a discreet distance. A former boyfriend, a biker, called the maneuver feeding the bear. The bear being the Smokies, the state troopers. The idea was that the cops would go for the speeding car ahead instead of the car following it, as long as you kept a weather eye in your rearview mirror.

Too often, though, the speeding car was a Beemer or a giant Mercedes, tough cars to keep up with. Sometimes it was a 'Vette, always driven by some guy with gray hair, the only ones who could probably afford that kind of iron. A few years ago, on the 101 down to L.A., she'd stayed with a guy driving some rad sports machine, a Ferrari maybe? Up to a hundred and ten, then chickened out when her front end starting getting squirrely. Yikes, slow down, girl.

What was that boyfriend's name? Something country, Clark or Trevor? Yeah, Trevor, a real asshole. Nice at first, lots of fun, great sex. The guy could even cook! But after he moved in with her, against her grandmother's warning—"that boy's a doper I tell you, I can smell the meth on him"—he became rapidly less nice, bringing his crazy speed-freak buddies over at all times of night, yelling at her. He even pushed her against the wall a couple of times. He'd apologize profusely the next day, begging forgiveness, offering the biker mantra, "I'm sorry, babe, but shit happens, you know."

"Yeah," Eunice had said. "With bikers shit does happen, 'cept it's mostly to women! Kick his sorry ass out, girl, before I tell your dad. Then shit really will happen. He'll probably set the guy's bike on fire before he busts his miserable chops!"

The prospect of her father gone wild again, with cops and jail and all the crazy bullshit, scared her more than the boyfriend. So one night she simply double-locked the door, ignoring his pleas and threats after she yelled: "Get the fuck out of here, you goddamn loser, or the cops will be here pronto!"

"You stinking bitch," he'd screamed. "What about my goddamn stuff?"

"Your shit will be on the doorstep tomorrow, loser," she'd hollered back.

And since she couldn't begin to sleep, she'd gathered up his few things—jeans, underwear and socks, boots, a jacket, five or six stupid country-jive CDs, and his precious stack of porn videos full of doped-up women with fake plastic tits. Next day, she put the box on the step and thankfully it was gone when she got home from work. As was he. He never bothered her again, probably because someone warned him about her father. Chet did have his uses now and then.

Would she ever see her dad again? Who knew? If she did, it would be because she made it happen. He'd never leave his hideout, running into the woods every time a chopper or a small plane went over the cabin. Jesus! But she smiled fondly anyway, crazy fucker! As violent as he was, he'd never raised a hand to her, and she knew he loved her in his loony, a-little-too-huggy, weird kind of way. Shit, like Eunice said, you didn't get to choose your parents, did you? But you *did* get to choose to have kids, or not. At least *she* was choosing, and for sure she was *not* going to get caught in the parent trap. No freakin' way!

Time to pop in a CD, Dianne Reeves, one of her grandma's favorites. Doing a cover of that Joni Mitchell song "River," which Eunice said Reeves did even better than the original. God, it was a wonderful song. Reeves with that great voice, the song so plaintive. "Oh, I wish I had a river I could skate away on. . . . Gonna quit this crazy scene."

Now that was true, Joni thought, she *was* leaving that crazy Geeville scene! Less crazy than boring, though. It had taken her a while to realize that was her main problem. She was bored. No one she cared particularly to see, tired of the worthless guys hitting on her and her reputation as a local "hotty," hating her job at Worst Western, same old crap on TV, same dumb stations on the radio. She'd been worried that she wasn't doing anything with her rapidly passing life. Chet's letter, whatever happened with it, made the difference, got her over the hump. Now she was eager to see what was on the other side.

Man, she was hungry. She reached over to grab some more raisins from the bag on the passenger seat. Maybe she'd treat herself to breakfast . . . Perkins potato pancakes with extra applesauce and bacon? Would there be a Perkins on I-80? Meanwhile, she had to admit she really was enjoying the beautiful scenery east of Sacramento. Mountains, steep ups and steeper downs, were probably hard on the Honda, but just look at it all.

She'd been this route before, just after high school with a much older boyfriend she'd eventually found out was married. He'd taken her sorry young ass to Lake Tahoe for the weekend, and the sex wasn't really all that bad, as she remembered. But at some point, she'd realized this wasn't his first visit to Tahoe with a lady friend. He was just a liar. Still, he'd wined and dined her, and they both agreed the lake and its surrounds were beautiful.

Hey, she thought, maybe I should jog over there just for old time's sake? Right, you couldn't buy a cup of coffee in Tahoe for less than ten bucks. The place was flush with rich people, the truly rich, all living in beautiful wood and stone homes butted up against one another, thick on the lake. She figured the last thing she'd do if she had that kind of bread is live right next door to anyone. She'd buy a chunk of land in the boonies somewhere—get away from nosy neighbors, cops, the whole thing. Whoops. Was that too much like Chet?

Joni skipped Tahoe and continued on to Reno. She knew it was a stretch for her and the Honda to keep up with all the new iron on the highway with giant SUVs and pickup trucks clocking an easy eighty to ninety miles an hour. How come everybody but her seemed to be driving new stuff? Wasn't any-fucking-body poor anymore? Soon enough there was Reno with its casinos right off the freeway, including the truly gigantic Nugget.

Yeah, I bet, Joni thought. Nuggets for the owners of that monster, busy mining the fools who showed up to lose their bread! She thanked the small gods she didn't gamble, had never been interested. Money was way too scarce to waste on stupid bets, at least that's one thing she could brag about. But who would listen?

"Hey, I don't gamble, y'know," she said out loud.

"Really? Wow! You must be some kind of special person," she answered.

Joni didn't steal either, never took even a lousy bar of soap from the Worst Western. And when she'd find shit like an earring in a room, she always took it right to the desk. She guessed Eunice had drilled that into her through scary stories of when she was a junkie in Oakland and would go from car to car looking for anything that could be sold or traded for dope. Eunice had also been frank about how she'd routinely sold herself for dope.

Joni had never been paid for sex and couldn't imagine she ever would want to. She was actually pretty careful—never even gotten an STD or anything. And she was more and more careful as she got older. She'd been practically celibate for most of the last year. Nothing against screwing, just nobody interesting or smart to do it with in Geeville.

What about the other possible sins, Joni wondered as she kept on truckin' down the road? There was lying, just the usual kid stuff when she lived with Eunice, who almost immediately found out that, for example, she really hadn't done her homework or she'd taken the car without permission.

And booze? Alcohol was OK to relax with, or to take the edge off at parties, but luckily she had a low capacity for drinking, ready to puke after three beers or a couple of shots. So no problem there.

Dope? Eunice's horror stories kept her far from anything serious like crank or smack. "You're real pretty, Joni girl. Got beautiful clear skin. Be a goddamn shame to mess up those arms and legs with needle tracks," her grandmother had told Joni more than once. Seeing Eunice's struggles up close didn't hurt any either.

She'd tried coke once or twice at parties. It just got her super wired, like way too much coffee. Not for her.

Weed? Her dad smoked bales of it, and when Eunice started getting real sick, she used it to ease her pain and anxiety. But Joni could take it or leave it. Nice to have a buzz when listening to good music, but she didn't need it daily, and it was too spendy anyway. Even with the new clinics.

Really the biggest danger with weed was how hungry you got. A person could OD on pizzas for sure. Thinking about that, she was now even hungrier—and getting just a little tired as she left Reno and headed into the barren Nevada desert. Finally, stopping for gas about an hour from Reno, she peed, bought a dark-chocolate Mounds bar, her favorite, then took out her map. Damn, she'd hoped to make it to Salt Lake, but it was just too far. So she'd drive until she had to quit, as long as it was in some decent-sized burg. Pulling off the road out in the empty desert was too scary. No way she wanted to wake up in the dark with some crazy person tapping on her window!

She drove until her vision started to seriously blur, and the lights from oncoming vehicles turned into fuzzy streaks. She pulled off in a place called Elko. Three exits, so it had to be of some size. Joni took the one where she saw a Wal-Mart just off the freeway. She pulled over to a far corner of the lot next to a couple of semis and an old RV, locked her doors, climbed into the back seat, and got into her sleeping bag. Hmm, she thought as she drifted into a deep sleep, I've never used this car for camping before.

The next morning she woke early, just a little cold. Her phone showed 6:25 and was in need of a charge. And hey, she didn't have to show up for work anywhere! But now she was really starving as she remembered the elaborate so-called free breakfast buffets she'd help serve at the motel, with guests heaping on enormous portions of eggs, sausage, biscuits, and gravy to tide them over until lunch. Yuck, obese America, way to go! But man she could sure use some of that chow now.

Getting out of the car to stretch, she popped the hood and checked the oil. Down half a quart, good thing she had more in the trunk.

She couldn't check the tranny fluid until the car warmed up and was running, so she vowed to take care of it after she'd had breakfast. She pulled out onto the main drag in front of Wal-Mart and started looking. On the other side of the interstate she found the Oasis Eatery. "Breakfast Served All Day." It was tiny, with just eight or nine tables and a counter with six stools. A harassed-looking middle-aged guy with a red, sweaty face manned the counter, and a teenage boy took her order. Probably the guy's son, Joni figured. Two eggs up, sausage links, whole-wheat toast, and coffee.

When the coffee came, it was surprisingly good, but something in the place was wrong. Just as her eggs arrived, Joni realized what it was.

At a corner table, by a window looking out to the parking lot, four or five old men were drinking coffee. And—Joni could scarcely believe it—smoking. Yes, smoking cigarettes right there in a restaurant, something she'd never witnessed in her life. Sure, you'd see it in the movies, and Eunice told her it used to be common, even on airplanes. Which was hard to believe. But here she was, trying to eat breakfast, and cigarette smoke was wafting right over her food. Nasty!

"Hey," Joni summoned the waiter kid. "Isn't that illegal?" she asked, pointing to the obvious.

"Yeah, guess so, but Dad feels sorry for those old guys. They like to come here, drink coffee and whatnot, so he lets 'em smoke," the kid shrugged his shoulders.

"But what about the cops, and food inspectors and stuff?" Joni was incredulous. "What do they say?"

"Not much. Cops stop in here for coffee regular, just joke about the smoking. Got better stuff to do, Dad says, than worry about it." The boy started to move back to the counter.

"Wow," Joni said aloud. Then she hurried to finish her meal, still not really believing she had to eat in a room filled with cigarette smoke.

"Oasis, my ass," she muttered as she picked up the bill, counted out the $4.50 and left a buck tip. Too much she thought, given the smoke. But it wasn't the kid's fault, and since she'd been a waiter too she was duty bound to leave at least 20 percent even if she could barely afford it.

Hastily exiting the restaurant, still amazed at the smoking, she started the Honda and let it run for a bit before opening the hood to check the transmission fluid. As she waited, a nice-looking young guy strolled over and asked if she needed help.

"Nope, thanks. Gotta check the tranny fluid when the motor's running," she said over her shoulder as she pulled out the dipstick and wiped it with the rag she kept under the hood.

"Hey, I'm impressed," the man said, as he lit a cigarette. "Most guys I know don't even know how to do that, let alone a chick. I mean woman."

Noting happily that the dipstick read showed it was full, Joni slammed shut the hood and turned to the man, "Well, this chick does know how to check fluids, and she also knows you could be smokin' that ciggie inside the restaurant. Weren't you at the counter?"

"Yeah," he acknowledged with a sheepish smile. "I saw those old guys in there smoking. But, man, I couldn't light up in a restaurant to save my ass."

"Yeah, totally weird if you ask me. Spoiled my breakfast. Adios." With that she jumped into the Honda and sped out of the lot. The guy just probably wanted to talk to a pretty girl, but she didn't have the time. Or the inclination.

"Some other time, man," she said aloud. He was cute, but she had places to go.

Chapter 12

Leaving Las Vegas, Mary thought. Like the title of that depressing movie. She pulled into a Starbucks drive-through and ordered a large coffee with cream and sugar, thinking, "Yes, Mike. I know you disapprove of Starbucks—can't exactly remember why—but I love this kind of coffee. Besides, who was it who bought this giant car?" Mary poked at the mannequin next to her as she settled the coffee carefully into a cupholder in the middle of the seat. "And I know," she added, "you're probably mad at me for leaving you under a blanket all night too. Sorry."

Despite a slight hunger pang, she felt the need to get on the road right away. So even though she usually ate a leisurely breakfast, she told herself the coffee would have to do. She might stop for an early lunch, however, depending on what was available. If she stuck to the freeway, there wouldn't be much. She'd just have to take her food chances, which so far, given last night's curry, had been excellent.

"Gosh, Mike," Mary said to her silent mate. "You would have loved the evening, especially when you heard that those folks were from Kerala. Remember, that Indian state you loved to cite in support of the possibilities of a communist government? And you know what else? They're Catholics! You'd have had trouble swallowing that, I tell you!" Mary chuckled as she glanced over her coffee cup at her companion.

Let's see. I didn't get through to Emma, but I did talk to Theresa. Mary smiled as she remembered telling her sister about her nutty mannequin, at which Theresa paused, then laughed, saying "You're crazy, Mary, and I can't wait to see you—mannequin, Lincoln, and all!"

"Likewise." Mary recalled how much she'd always enjoyed their time together—even when they were kids, as different in temperament as they were. She was headstrong and impetuous, while Theresa was careful and obedient. They'd gotten along well. Differences between them now? Let's see, both widows, both of us have children and grandchildren. Was Theresa close to Rusty's kids, Mary wondered? What are their names? One was an academic superstar, she'd been told, and the other had trouble figuring his life out.

Her sister still went to Mass, something Mary had stopped doing as soon as she left Chicago as a young woman.

"What would you think of that Mike, me going to Mass?" Mary asked the mannequin. Smiling as she recalled Mike's disgust with the Catholic Church, a feeling she largely shared, albeit less vocally. Their disenchantment was established long before the pedophile scandals. The Los Angeles archdiocese, the largest in the country, had infuriated Mike and many others with its cavalier treatment of Latinos, the cultural background of most parishioners.

The L.A. church, Mike said, was like a medieval fiefdom run by one Irish prelate after another, following the tradition that dated back to the early Spanish missions, which had virtually enslaved local native populations as part of the conquest. The church leaders in L.A. were wholly at odds with the bulk of their parishioners. Time after time the vast numbers of Latino parishioners were forced to submit to cardinals like McIntyre and Mahony who treated them with little respect. But then that was true of the whole country if you thought about it—millions of people putting up with inadequate, often venal, leaders, giving little thought to those they were actually leading.

"So, Mary, stop thinking about this stuff that will make you crazy."

Unlike Mike and Emma, who had fallen not at all far from her dad's tree, Mary didn't thrive on controversy. She wasn't afraid of it, she didn't back down when pressed, but it didn't make her gleeful like it did her husband and daughter.

"Mike," she'd say, "how can you read that gloomy stuff that makes you furious night after night? Try something easy on your soul so you can get a restful sleep for once!"

"And what would that be, sweet spouse o' mine?" he'd respond in a mock Irish brogue. "Maybe I should be readin' say, *The Lives of the Saints*? Lift me spirits to be tinkin' on the holy martyrs y'know. Like say, Catherine of the Wheel, queen of Christian fireworks?"

Mary reached for the playlist of the tapes Andres had made for her—there it was, keep your eyes on the road, girl. Let's see. *Winter Moon*, Art Pepper, perfect to pop in and take a listen.

Talk about soulful, she couldn't help shed a tear or two as she listened, remembering that she and Mike had been in the audience at a club Pepper played in not long before the man died.

"Where was it, Mike?" she asked her mute companion.

Echo Park? No, that's where he lived whenever he wasn't in jail. Venice? No, Malibu. That was it. Impossible to remember the name of the club though. Had to hand it to Pepper, he played marvelously through all his troubles. Probably one of the greatest alto players of all time despite being sick on junk, stealing, even armed robbery, and serving time in San Quentin. She thought how great it would be to listen to the recording with Theresa while sharing a little of the marijuana she had brought with her.

"Whoops, woman," she reminded herself out loud. "That probably won't happen with Theresa, even though it's 'medical' marijuana." She'd purchased it legitimately with her marijuana card at a clinic. What was this batch called? White Widow, how appropriate.

Still, probably not a good idea, sharing her stash with her sister. Unlikely that Theresa would approve. Emma certainly wouldn't, so she hadn't bothered to tell her. Carlos would just laugh. But eventually he would tell Emma; the man could *not* keep a secret from his wife. So it was Mary's own quite wonderful secret, even Janet didn't know. Did they have marijuana clinics in Minnesota? She doubted it. Too bad. Maybe the folks there wouldn't be so woebegone if they could get a little high.

And the medical part wasn't any joke, it had certainly helped Mike die a much less painful death. And when Mary's stomach acted up, the best thing to do, by far, was smoke a little medicine. But she'd read that the authorities all over the country were still busy locking people up, screwing up their lives, just because they used marijuana. And Art Pepper would've probably lived beyond his fifties if he hadn't been hounded into prison for his heroin habit. So many of those great bebop-era musicians were junkies, and so many went to jail uselessly.

Mary looked at the playlist again. Great, Andres had put Gene Ammons on there too. He was a great black saxophone player from Chicago, with that wonderful album *The Boss is Back!*, celebrating his return from prison, where he was sent for using. He served nine lousy years for possession. Ammons was very different than Pepper, but also wonderfully mellow when he needed to be.

Could she get into trouble for transporting her ostensibly legal drug across the country, she wondered suddenly? She didn't know, and God forbid she'd have to find out. At least the stuff was securely hidden in the Lincoln's vast trunk. Big enough to put a VW Beetle in there, Mike had joked.

Whoa, the coffee, so good earlier, was now was making her pay dues in the form of an urgent need to pee. Where was she? Just inside Utah—and hey, there was a rest stop right here! Pulling into the area marked for cars, she locked the Lincoln and almost ran to the bathroom, which was empty.

Once in the stall, she noticed the toilet had the autoflush system she always called the private eye, since the ominous little red light behind the stool did indeed watch your privates. Easing herself onto the seat and starting to enjoy a much-needed release of her bladder, the toilet all of a sudden flushed, scaring her into standing but not before icy water soaked her behind. Stupid thing!

More careful this time, she eased down again, but with her hands underneath her bottom, ready to launch off the seat if it happened again. Which it did, two more times before she finished. What a ridiculous device! And now she had to stand stooping in the stall and use about half a role of difficult-to-retrieve toilet paper to dry herself.

Out of the stall and at a sink, Mary realized her pants were still quite wet. They were a synthetic fabric so, unlike her cotton underwear, they wouldn't dry for a long time. A long time to sit in the Lincoln with a wet butt. She took them off and rotated them under the electric hand dryer. Push the button, turn the pants, push it again, turn them again.

And of course someone came in, looking startled at the sight of an elderly woman in her undies. A middle-aged white woman in a brown pantsuit, very Reagan era, she almost backed out of the room. But Mary spoke up and told her briefly what happened.

"All I can tell you is be careful in there," she warned to the uncomfortable stranger as she motioned to a stall.

"Y'know, I don't think I have to tinkle as badly as I thought. Guess I'll wait for a gas station," the woman hurriedly exited.

Pants now dry, and still upset but chuckling about her dousing, Mary walked hurriedly to her car, sticking the key into the door lock but getting no response. Oh hell, now what?

WhoopWHOOPwhoopWAILwailWAIL.

She'd set off the car's alarm system. A horribly loud, siren-like sound warned the whole world that someone might be trying to steal this car. In her haste she'd forgotten entirely that she had to punch the keyless entry code into the buttons on the edge of the door. The loud shrieking made it hard for Mary to think. She tried to focus on what she should do to stop the noise. She didn't have a clue, but she got into the car and started pressing buttons, almost weeping from the horrid noise and her growing anxiety.

Jumping out of the car like it was on fire, she looked around the lot but no one was visible. Suddenly a very large black man emerged from the cab of one of the semis in the adjacent lot. He came over quickly, asking her what was wrong. Mary explained, yelling over the noise, what she'd done and he laughed, not unpleasantly, and asked if he could maybe look at the car.

"Of course, please do," Mary shouted while holding her hands over her ears. "And hurry, it's driving me crazy!"

The man folded his great height into the driver's seat and reached under the dash where he pulled the lever that opened the car's hood. He then ran around to the engine, grabbing a large multi-tool from his belt. Opening the tool to its pliers, he quickly disconnected one of the battery cables. Bingo, silence, blessed silence.

"Shut the power, see, and it get still, y'know?" said the man as he turned to Mary with a lovely smile.

"Thanks! Phew!" Mary exclaimed. "But now what? Won't the noise start again when you reconnect the battery?"

"I don't think so. But let's see now." He tightened the clamp back on the battery post and lo . . . no noise. "Now please see if the car start, OK?"

Mary put the key in the ignition, held her breath, turned it—and bingo. Back in business with no alarm sounding. She smiled up at the man, turned the car off, and got out to shake his hand.

"I'm Mary, and I have to thank you a thousand times for helping me. I had no idea what to do. None!"

"That's OK, it's fixed now, ain't it? And my name is Lazarus. That's my truck over there," he pointed to a huge, white tractor-trailer rig.

"Lazarus? Like in the Bible, the man raised from the dead? Well, you sure raised me from the dead!"

"Yeah, that's me, so. Where I comin' from . . . I coulda been dead many time too, y'know?"

"Really? Where are you from?"

"From Liberia, you know that place?"

"Not well, but don't you have a female president right now, like the first one in Africa right?"

"You're right, how do you know that?" the trucker was surprised.

"Well, it was in the news," Mary explained. "But really the only other thing I know is that your country was founded by African American slaves, sent there by one of our presidents right?"

"Hey," Lazarus was appreciative. "You know one bunch more than most people here. I tell them I'm from Liberia, and from what they know it's a country by Poland, you know? But I tell you something, there were already a lot of peoples in that place when those Americans came, you know? Maybe thirty-some different African peoples, and that's why we got so much trouble, you know?"

"You mean conflict between all those different groups?"

"Mostly between them Americans and the rest. We got a terrible war there not so long ago. It's a small country, but we had maybe a couple hundred thousand dead. Ruin every damn thing. Me, I got shot twice. But I got my lucky name my mama give to me: Lazarus, you know? And then I get more luck . . . come here to America. Safe, got work, make a little money. Back there, everybody so damn poor you can't believe it."

"I'm sorry to hear that, but I'm glad you're safe here now. And extra glad you were here to help me."

"Where you goin' in that big car, and why you got that thing sitting in the seat, I wonder?" He pointed at Mike.

"I'm going to Minnesota actually. To a town called Winona. It's on the Mississippi River. My sister lives there, in the country. And the dummy? I've got him because I want people to think I have a man with me, for safety. Probably silly, isn't it?"

"Not so." The trucker smiled. "This is a pretty safe country, but still you got—how you say?—dangerous men on the road, cause trouble. Even me, a big guy, sometimes those people cause me some problems. But I just laugh, say 'you tryin' to give me some griefs, man? You got no idea what I seen. So just go away!' But Winona, I know that place. I truck down there sometimes, not far from my home. Minneapolis."

"Really, what a coincidence. How on earth did you end up there?"

"Lot of African peoples live there, and I got an uncle, he sponsored me. Crazy, huh? We from a tropical place, warm, very warm, all the time. Sweat all day, sweat at night too, and we come to a very cold place. Never see no snow before. But me, I rather see snow than a bullet, you know? So what does your sister do in the country?"

"Well, she's a retired schoolteacher. But she has a small farm, where she gardens and raises a few animals."

"What animals?" Lazarus was intrigued.

"Chickens. Goats. Cats and dogs. A dog, actually. Mostly for herself and her son, but she does sell a goat occasionally. To people from Rochester. Somali people, Mexicans, and Hmong."

"Say, maybe she can sell me some too," Lazarus asked eagerly. "I like to eat goat, but hard to find in the city, would she sell to me?"

"Of course. I can give you her phone number."

"No, I get you my card. Everybody got a card now, so I got one, in the cab," Lazarus trotted back to his truck to get it. "Maybe you call me when you get there, on the cellular, you know. Then I'll come down—bring my boys," Lazarus offered.

"You have boys?"

"I do, two of them," Lazarus smiled broadly. "They're still pretty small, you know, five and eight. But now, I am sorry, I gotta leave. I got a schedule, and I'm gonna be late. I am very glad to meet you, Mary. Keep safe on your journey."

"You too, Lazarus, and thanks again," Mary waved good-bye, started the Lincoln, hooked her seatbelt, and turned to her silent companion. "What a lovely man. Imagine . . . Lazarus! A very big, very black man from Liberia, and he's driving truck across country. A big *white* truck. Things in this country can't be all that bad then, can they, Mike?"

Uh-oh, it dawned on her that she'd actually expected him to answer!

Chapter 13

Getting home from his dinner with Theresa, Luther rushed into his house to get Azteca and carry her outside to pee. Which she promptly did, her rear legs shaking as he held her up. Back inside the house she whined loudly, then more softly, as he put her down. He got her pain meds, coated each of three pills with peanut butter, and tried to get her to take them. Not too long ago she would have gulped them down, but now they just lay slack in her mouth and soon spilled out on the floor. He tried again, but this time she actually growled at him.

"Sorry, girl. Guess the old rub-a-dub will have to do," he said as he stretched out on the wooden floor beside her pallet and began to stroke her back. She stopped whining, mostly, although occasionally still gave out the most pitiable moan. After a half hour or so, Luther knew he wasn't going to be able to sleep without some help, so he got up and rolled a joint. He sat down across from the large wood stove that Azteca had laid in front of winter and summer since she was a pup.

As he smoked, he considered starting a fire to see if that would help her, but nixed the idea because the night was unseasonably warm. Too warm. He let his mind ramble into a mini rant about the millions of idiot Americans, some of them his neighbors, who were denying climate change. The dog's whining and moans snapped him out of his preoccupation, and he saw that she was looking right at him, clearly asking for help in her pain. So he put out the weed, went into his bedroom and grabbed a blanket and a quilt, and returned to lie down next to Azteca. He fell slowly asleep with his left arm draped over his pet.

When Luther awoke, his dog's cries cut through the haze in his brain. Outside it threatened rain. He recoated Azteca's meds with peanut butter, but to no avail. They just dropped from her mouth again. And her rear leg, where the vet said the cancer had started, was almost three times as large as it was yesterday. As he started his morning coffee, Luther knew that today had to be the end for his dog. Keeping her alive was cruel, and he was doing it because he couldn't let go, didn't want to do the deed. God, he thought, could he really shoot her? As he carried her outside to try to pee, he found she couldn't go and even trying was clearly painful for her. Then, a good thought amidst all the gloom—why not ask his crusty old neighbor John Moe to put Azteca down for him? Leaving the dog lying in the grass, Luther ran to the phone in the kitchen and called John.

"Be home, old man. Please be home," he worried as the phone rang, and rang, and rang. But John wasn't home, and there was no answering machine. God forbid John would have such a silly thing. Luther had one because of his veggie and wood businesses, but he knew the Moes scorned such fripperies. Moes, plural—that was it! He called John's brother Donald, and his wife Gerda answered on the fourth ring. "No, he's not here. They're cutting wood over at John's place, behind the pasture. Won't be home till supper as I sent a lunch along."

Luther went out and gently picked up Azteca, bringing her into the house and onto her pallet. She moaned the whole time. He then ran to his pickup and drove, too fast, skidding badly on some gravel in a corner, over to John Moe's pasture, driving through it right to the back where the woods began. There the brothers were busily running their chainsaws until his frantic gesturing caught their attention. Pulling earplugs out of his ears and wiping the earwax off them on his shirt, John asked Luther what was wrong.

"Can't shoot my dog, John, just can't," Luther expressed painfully. "She's terribly sick—cancer—and in real pain, so I have to put her down today. But I just can't shoot her. So . . . ," he trailed off looking at his boots.

"You want me to put down that pup? I didn't know you cared so much about animals, Lute."

The Moes were old-school. For them, animals belonged outside in the barn, or a kennel, but never in the house. Sentiment for pets was not high on their list. Pets themselves weren't high on their list.

"Yeah, I do, John," Luther admitted. "Sooner the better. I just can't bring myself to shoot her, and I'm not hauling her in to the vet and paying a huge bill to have a stranger kill my dog. Just do it for me, will you? I'll pay," he added, to put on the pressure.

"No, no," John said waving his gloved hand at Luther. "No, you're not gonna pay me a goddamn nickel. I'll do it, of course I will. You got her in the truck?" John spit a mouthful of snoose on the ground.

"No, I couldn't get her in. Just jump in and I'll have you back here in half an hour. You're not gonna miss him, are you, Donald?"

"Guess not, if you say so," Donald spit a stream of snoose, black as coal, onto a log. "Go on, John. Help the boy out."

"Got a gun?" John asked as they got into Luther's truck.

"I do." Luther sped out of the field, onto the road, and back to his own yard. He went into the house and found and loaded his old single-shot .22, bringing extra bullets he prayed wouldn't be needed. After handing the gun over to John, he went inside and got his dog, talking to her as he carried her into the yard. He gently placed her under his favorite tree, a Kentucky coffee he'd planted years ago. Appropriate, he thought, that Native Americans called them the dead tree.

"I remember this pup," John said as he strolled over with the gun. "God, she's a big animal. You had her a long time, right?"

"Yeah, she's fourteen, which is real old for big dogs like this. But all my dogs live a long time, they love it out here." Lute fought against tears.

"OK, then let's get it over with. You gonna watch?"

Luther took a breath, "Got to. Go ahead and do it, John."

Placing the long gun gently behind the dog's left ear, John pulled the trigger and stepped back. Azteca convulsed briefly, and a puddle of urine formed beneath her while blood leaked lightly out of the bullet's entry point. All of it seemed to happen at once for Luther, the rush to get John, the rush back, getting and loading the gun, getting Azteca, and then John shooting her. He'd worried about weeping in front of the old man, but instead he felt strangely numb, like watching a movie he was in but somehow not part of. Like it was sometimes in Nam, and sometimes in his nightmares.

Handing the gun back to Luther, John spoke, "Well, that's about it, Lute. Sorry about your pup." The old man looked back at the pickup, signaling his desire to leave the scene and get back to what made sense, which was work. Luther drove him back, saying as he dropped him off that he owed him one.

"All right," the old man laughed, "maybe I'll have to ask you to put me down one of these days. No way I'm going to the g-d nursing home!"

Neither am I, Luther thought as he drove back home to start digging a grave for Azteca, finally allowing himself to cry a few low-key tears. She had been a splendid dog, easy to train and basically obedient but not timid. Playful up to a point where it was best to back off, so not a good children's animal, but he didn't have kids. Some came with their parents to get produce, though, so he always left her in the house then, since he knew children could be mean to animals. And while some dogs would put up with it, not Azteca.

One of her greatest contributions to the farm was just her presence, made known morning and night when she went out and patrolled the farmyard and gardens, barking in her deep basso. Hence no deer, rabbits, squirrels, or raccoons spoiled his gardens. They must have gotten the message, staying away even long after her ability to chase anything had ended.

She was part Rottie, so this was a breed trait, a peaceful one really, wherein these large, potentially dangerous animals much preferred to bark rather than bite. It reminded him of one of the toughest guys in his outfit in Vietnam, a little Puerto Rican man from the Bronx—short, not especially piped, his only tat a small cross on the back of his left hand. He'd been very quiet but, as he'd proved, very dangerous if provoked. When somebody, usually drunk, would mess with him, he'd say in a low tone, "Don't fuck with me, man. Just don't do it. Leave it be." Very authoritatively matter-of-fact, with a slight Hispanic accent. He'd only been in a couple of scrapes before everyone got the word: Don't mess with the little guy, he'll eat you alive!

Placing his dog gently into the hole, Luther said with tears, "I'll miss you, babe, one hell of a lot. Adios, girl, best friend, and all that. Yes, you were. Hope I was!"

Going back to the kitchen, he retrieved a sack of big bones he'd been saving in the freezer in case she recovered. He brought them to the grave and tossed them in with her. "Don't know about heaven for people, girl, most of us don't deserve it. But sure hope there's one for dogs full of bones and stinky dead deer." With that he began to cover the dog, filling the hole, tamping it down to keep critters from digging in it and getting at her. Promising that he would soon make a memorial for her out of an oak board and attach her dog tags to it.

Dog tags, same things you wore around your neck as a GI. Government Issue—same as a jeep or a gun, a goddamn *thing*, not a person, a human being. In Nam, he'd taped his together so they wouldn't rattle and give away his position. Other guys wore one around their neck, another tied to a bootlace. Either way, when they found your body lying in a rice paddy, they put those tags between your teeth, so they knew your ID and could tell your folks you'd bought it! Nowadays he'd see fucking college kids at the farmers' market sporting tags, the idiots! Course they were all tatted up too, like sailors or jailbirds or stupid bikers! Fucking punks.

But hey, he had to get ready for Saturday's farmers' market in Winona. Get to work.

Chapter 14

ALMOST EVERYONE WHO KNEW ANTHONY KOZLOWKSI JR., known as Rusty for his red hair, liked him. Always friendly, he was genuinely curious about everyone he met. Funny and smart, but never sharp, he'd probably never hurt anyone's feelings his entire life. So the mystery was why and how he stayed married to Carmen, who most agreed was a shrew. A very pretty, highly animated shrew. She was a marvelous seamstress—"that woman could make a wedding dress for a pigeon I tell you!"—but trouble brewed in every pot of coffee she made.

Was it her Polish background? She was a Syzmanski, but then Rusty was a Kozlowski. Couldn't blame the Poles. Firstborn? No, she was the third of five daughters, none of the rest of them a bit like her. Her father? No, the poor man was so overwhelmed by living with and supporting six women that he simply faded into the woodwork, usually aided by several brandy and Cokes. He loved his wife and daughters, sure, but what a burden.

Then it had to be her mother, Wanda. Was she a scold? Not a bit. Many said she was a saint. Saint Wanda. But saintliness is always a double-edged kitchen knife. How could you explain a woman who routinely rose high above the general hurly-burly of Winona's working-class life, seemingly never bothered by chaos or strife. Always serene, appearing to glide from room to room of her large, old, and dilapidated house, cleaning, arranging, making wonderful meals, and sewing elegant clothing for her daughters on a tight budget. How did the woman do it? She never got angry, never hectored her husband Bill about fixing stuff around the house, the sagging gutter over the porch, the steady drip, drip in the basement laundry sink, the windows that didn't close properly.

Was she on drugs? No. Did she drink? Not that anyone could see. Was she a Holy Mary type who made a show of piety at Mass? No. In fact, she always sat somewhat to the rear of the church and dressed modestly. She held her head high as she went up for Holy Communion, hands folded in front of her, but with none of that "just about to scourge myself, Dear Lord" look that some of the parishioners displayed prominently.

Did she, like many others, gossip about everything and everyone, getting her digs in, making fun of those who weren't as able as she? Not a bit of it. So what could anyone say about her? Wanda was just . . . a saint. Always had been, and still was in her late eighties. Bill had long since passed. But Wanda was very much alive and now greatly involved, in her low-key but emphatic way, in the lives of her grandchildren and great-grandchildren. She made them huge batches of her wonderful kolacky pastries, filled with sesame paste or apricot jam. She sewed all kinds of garments for them. Even shirts for some of the boys. Not that they ever wore them except at family gatherings where Grandma was sure to be. Wanda even babysat the newborns and infants so the young parents could go to a movie.

So where did Carmen come from? Some said maybe she was just the jagged edge of the kitchen knife. Wanda's saintly serenity on one side, Carmen's sharp and ready tongue on the other. Some people, especially women, were bothered by Wanda's manner. Not aloofness exactly, but something that kept her slightly apart, slightly above everyone else. Carmen was, they surmised, a penance of sorts. "'See, even Saint Wanda managed to have one difficult child," they said.

Even as a girl, Carmen was moody and quick to anger, taunting her sisters like some wicked child in a grim fairy tale. You certainly couldn't call her the ugly duckling, as she was beautiful even in the midst of her worst behavior. Yet her father adored her. He probably admired her spunk, which he lacked in spades. But she sure could ruffle his feathers easily with some snide remark, or as a teen, by dating the biggest loser in high school. Whereas Wanda couldn't be ruffled. She didn't respond to Carmen's tantrums, extreme willfulness, or deliberate anarchies in an otherwise orderly household.

So there they were, Rusty and Carmen, married now close to thirty years. They had two boys. Patrick, an academic superstar with a full boat to a private college back East was now in grad school, planning to be a world-class meteorologist and take on the challenges of global climate change. The other, Duane, lived at home again after several unsuccessful tries at being on his own. He was a good kid, but apparently, some thought, was stunned into apathy by his younger brother's overwhelming success.

For now Duane helped his dad install cabinets, but he really wasn't interested in learning the trade, maybe not even capable. Not because he had any inherent lack of ability, but he lacked spirit. Nothing really seemed to turn him on. He did smoke some weed, but not enough to hamper him, Rusty hoped. He drank beer with his loser buddies, all stuck in Winona. "Nobody *wins* in Winona, man!" they said.

Today Rusty had to drive to the Amish community in Harmony, about an hour away, to pick up some lumber. Quarter-sawn white oak, hard-to-find wood he needed to make a couch for a local doctor's wife. A copy of a Stickley couch first made about a hundred years ago in the then-popular Craftsman style. He knew that if anyone locally had the wood, it would be Jacob Hostetler, who in addition to the usual Amish farming chores, operated a sawmill and kiln and would also do the preliminary planing of your boards.

But it wasn't easy to make arrangements with Jacob. He had no phone. So Rusty had called the hardware store Jacob dealt with and asked them to relay his request. Several days later, he called them again, and learned that, yes, Jacob had been in and said he would have the one-hundred-some board feet of lumber ready in a week or so. That meant two weeks, and it had been two and a half weeks. So Rusty felt mostly confident his lumber would be ready.

He enjoyed the drive to Harmony with fall just starting to change the color of everything. Even the soybeans were now a beautiful rust brown. It wasn't Rusty's favorite crop because of what it symbolized about the decline of small-scale agriculture in the region. Did the Amish plant soybeans? He doubted it. Corn, hay, oats, all in rotation according to a system that Midwestern farmers had used for generations, striving to keep their land productive while also paying their bills. Now only the Amish still farmed that way, along with a few young farmers who called it "sustainable agriculture."

The Amish farming methods were only one of the many things Rusty admired about these people who had mostly managed to avoid joining the mad rush of consumer capitalism that was sweeping the planet. Maybe the Amish, or people like them, would be the survivors? At least they'd be able to teach the helpless app-dependent urbanites how to survive. A rather rigid form of living, admittedly, but probably that sort of discipline, which could be especially harsh for women, was what you needed to keep Wal-Mart and reality TV at bay.

Rusty slowed down considerably when he sighted his first horse and buggy. They no longer displayed the bright-orange slow-moving vehicle sign required on farm equipment used on public roadways. The Harmony Amish community had won a legal victory allowing them the religious freedom not to desecrate their carriages. Who really could object, he thought? If you couldn't see a horse and buggy in front of you and notice it was moving a lot more slowly than cars, you shouldn't be driving. Still, the State of Minnesota had spent a lot of time and money fighting the matter.

Typical government bullshit, Luther had said to Rusty. "'You let some get away with it, and soon everybody's going to do it.' Same stuff the bureaucrats always say, worrying about their silly jobs!"

Aside from the buggies, Rusty knew right away he was in Amish country. It was as if he'd entered a different zone of being—and he had.

No electric lines running to the farmsteads. Horses clustered together on every place. Grains, oats, and barley shocked in bundles to dry, making him think of the hard, hot work they required. Houses all white with tiny windows. Vast amounts of laundry filling the lines in untidy yards.

Years ago Carmen had come here with him, and had immediately seized on how "messy" the Amish yards and farmsteads were. Lawns? Hah, not really! And the kids, mostly barefoot, looked dirty too. And there were so many of them! Bringing her had been a mistake.

Jacob's place was as disorderly as always, piles of logs seemingly stacked at random everywhere. Large stacks of lumber. A couple of horses tied in the yard, and several scroungy dogs. Fortunately, Jacob was home. Rusty didn't like going up to the house to talk with Jacob's wife. She was very shy, and he always felt like an intruder. Jacob wasn't shy, just reserved. Not rude, but far from garrulous.

"Yes, crops look good now that harvest is on," Jacob said when Rusty inquired how he was. "And the children are healthy with the older ones becoming good help." He shifted on his feet, probably impatient to get back to whatever job he was doing.

He and Rusty spoke a little about trees, oak tree blight was indeed an ongoing problem. Red elm at anything but a small size was impossible to find, but there was still quite a bit of walnut around. These observations occurred as they loaded Rusty's trailer.

When they were finished, Rusty paid Jacob in cash. They shook hands, and Rusty drove away. He kept his speed down until he was well out of the community, feeling the whole time he was like some kind of alien intruder among the peaceful lives of these horse farmers.

"Well," he thought, "I am an intruder. What was the Amish word for everyone else? The English? Sure, I'm the English!"

Heading back, Rusty decided to stop and see Luther. After that he'd visit his mother. Now that he had the lumber for the fancy couch, Rusty knew exactly what he had to do, and more or less how long it would take him. Barring any unforeseens, the lady would have her furniture well before the promised date—reflecting his long-standing practice of scheduling much more time for each job than it needed.

Carmen, he pondered, usually did exactly the opposite, so work she promised almost always came in just a little late, resulting in much anxiety. "Is my dress really going to be ready for the prom?" a client would be left wondering. Or worse yet, the same for someone's wedding gown. Carmen rarely, if ever, apologized for the stress she caused her clients, and almost seemed to take a little delight in their anguish. Still, most people came back to her even after harsh words had been said on both sides. He had, once or three times, gently suggested to his lovely wife that she adopt his approach, but she scorned his advice. Go figure.

Pulling into Lute's yard, as unkempt as Jacob's, Rusty thought his somber friend might have made a good Amish man. Physically strong and a working fool, he would've entered willingly into the intense labor required to work a farm without modern gas-powered, electricity-aided machinery.

And like the Amish, he disapproved mightily of the "English" world outside his farm. And he was very moralistic, many thought excessively so, ready at the drop of any tiny suggestion to cite data—he was well informed—about most anything going on in the larger world. American foreign policy, probably of little concern to the Amish, made him apoplectic. But then so did almost all domestic policy, especially agricultural. "Washington policies," Lute would thunder, "ensuring the continuing ruination of the land and water and farm families and rural communities throughout the nation." Rusty saw Luther working in one of his greenhouses in nothing but a pair of shorts. That wasn't a bit Amish and neither was the beer he had next to him.

"Hey, Rusty, good to see you, man," Luther said when he spotted his friend. Not the most intimate of men, he shook Rusty's hand. Rusty was a hugger, but he took Luther's hand and avoided the awkwardness of an embrace, something he'd tried several times over the years and embarrassed both of them.

"Get you a beer?" Luther offered.

"A little early, but I guess I will. Don't bother, I'll get it. Give me a chance to see if you have any company I don't know about," Rusty smiled.

"Yeah. Let me know, will you. There hasn't been anyone in that bed but me for a hell of a long time. And prospects aren't good either."

"Aw, Lute," Rusty protested, "come on, half the women at the farmers' market would love an invite up here—and not just to gawk at the cauliflower either."

Rusty barely registered Luther's muttered denial as he turned toward the house to get a beer from the fridge in the old pantry. Two, actually. He'd noted that Luther's bottle was almost empty. It really was too early to be drinking, but it was only beer. If Lute had had a large glass of gin out there this time of day—that would be cause to worry.

Looking at the label on a bottle as he went back to the greenhouse, Rusty noted that it came from La Crosse, just across the river. It wasn't one of the more popular mediocre beers that had long been made there, though, not with the name Catfish Flats. It was a porter, one of those heavy, dark beers that was almost like drinking cereal.

"You know with this craze for everything local lately, people start to think that just because it's from around here, it must be good," Lute remarked. "Which is a foolish notion, Jesus, some of the produce I see for sale at the market I wouldn't feed to your mother's goats! And I've had a few beers from nearby that weren't worth the money. Don't get me wrong, Rusty, I'm as happy as anybody that there's at least some effort to take back what we eat and drink from the agribiz greed heads, but still—"

"Greed heads? That's a new one," Rusty smiled as he opened their beers with his favorite tool, a Leatherman, and prepared himself for the inevitable Luther lecture.

"You know what I mean," Luther took a large draught from his beer. "The people who smell money every time they step outside, their dollar radar beeping like a cop's on the freeway. They're already trolling in this locavore thing, buying up successful small breweries and bakeries then churning out their own cheap replicas. It's just more bullshit. But then, Americans crave it."

"What?" Rusty took a slug of his beer and encouraged Luther to continue.

"Bullshit. Remember, we live in a state that elected a pro wrestler as governor, and in a country that elected a minor-brain B actor president. Twice!" Luther banged his bottle on a work table for emphasis.

Rusty drew a breath. Reluctantly, he had to disagree with his friend. "Yeah, I know, but my customers aren't into bullshit. They want quality stuff. Not to brag up my work, but you know what I mean. And your customers, the ones at the farmers' market? You've got people who've been buying your veggies for years, paying a lot more than at the supermarket, right?"

"OK." Luther agreed reluctantly. "But they're a minority, our customers. Hey, *skol*." The two friends clinked their bottles together and continued drinking in silence. A silence broken finally by Rusty asking Luther what he was working on. Luther explained that he needed to get the greenhouses tidied up after the frantic summer, and today was a nice, not-too-hot day to get a start on it. Rusty helped him for a bit while they talked, piling up the plastic trays Luther had been rinsing out, trays he would start his seedlings in next winter.

"Hey, I just noticed, Lute, where's Azteca?" Rusty asked as he looked around for the animal who was always with Luther anyplace on the farm.

"Jesus, Rusty. I had to put her down a couple of days ago. Terrible. It really busted me up." Luther drained his beer, jamming the bottle into a tray of dirt.

Rusty wanted to hug his friend, but refrained. "Hey, Lute, I didn't know. I know she was sick when I was here before, but not that she was that bad."

"Yeah, she had cancer, or that's what the vet said. They actually talked about taking off the leg where it started in hopes of stopping it and keeping her alive, but her back legs were already weak and I knew she wouldn't make it as a tripod. She was real old you know, much older than most big dogs like her. I miss her like sin, man." Luther sighed.

"I can imagine," Rusty sympathized. "You've always been tight with your dogs."

"Yeah, they're a whole lot easier to deal with than people—you and your mom excepted. Dogs don't lie, don't mess with your head, they're faithful, loyal. Remember that old poem? It ends with "get a good dog, boys, he'll be your best friend!" You know, Azteca never kissed my mortal white ass, like some dogs do, she had real dignity. Integrity. Remember she bit me once, scared the hell out of me?"

"Really? I didn't remember that."

Luther smiled. "Yeah, I'd been drinking and was messing with her, teasing her by pushing her, tapping her on the mouth. She liked that kind of stuff, up to a point, but I passed the point. Got too rough, I guess. So she just turned and came at me. Bam! Knocked me down on my dumb ass and grabbed my arm. I gave up right away, of course, and she backed off. Still, that was a lesson."

"Man, I've seen her devour a goat's leg bone in minutes, so I know how strong her mouth was. Shit, Lute! I'm really sorry." Rusty drained his beer. "So . . . another pup soon?"

"Not too soon. Have to show some respect, some restraint, you know. Wouldn't be right to run out and replace her when she's not even cold in the ground yet." He sighed once more.

"Suppose you're right. But let me know when you're ready and I'll ask around. Whoops, shit," Rusty exclaimed looking at his watch. "Hey, I told my mom I'd stop for lunch, and I'm late. Good to see you, Lute, and I'm real sorry about your dog. Stop by the shop, or the house, next time you're in town, OK?"

"Sure, Rusty. Thanks for stopping, man. And say hello to Theresa," Luther said, thinking that the likelihood of him stopping at Rusty's house, where the formidably cranky Carmen held forth, was very low. How could such a nice guy, enviably easygoing, stay married to such a harridan, he wondered for the five hundredth time?

On the short drive to Theresa's house, Rusty wondered if he'd handled the death of Luther's dog right. He was quite comfortable with dogs, if not cats, but then he'd grown up on a farm. Carmen hadn't, and her mother Wanda had wanted no pets in her home. She passed her prejudice along to all of her daughters but one, the youngest, Ava, who was a confirmed cat nut with maybe a dozen of them in her house at any one time. All of them overweight, noisy, and smelly. Rusty smiled, remembering a conversation with one of Ava's ex-beaus, who told him that he couldn't have sex with her. It was just impossible.

"Why?" Rusty wondered.

"Cattus interruptus, man," the guy had grinned as he punched Rusty's arm.

Because of the cats, Carmen wouldn't even visit her sister anymore, her disapproval and disgust was so great.

"She can come here anytime," Carmen said. "She's my sister, always welcome. But I'm never going back into that house again. It's like a zoo . . . no, zoos are much cleaner than that!"

No one but Rusty could understand how the Ava apple had fallen so far from the Wanda tree. It was a simple matter of the daughter reacting extremely to Wanda's rigid beliefs. A no-pets rule as a child resulted in too many pets as an adult. Like farm kids who decided to become vegetarians in the midst of their meat-eating households, insulting their parents' livelihood, driving their mothers to distraction trying to feed them. Rusty smiled as he pulled into Theresa's yard. Look at him after all, his mother was a teacher, and he didn't go to college. Well, he went, he just hadn't stayed long.

Going into the house and giving his mother a long, deep hug, Rusty stepped away from her and asked, "Mom, do you think I'm shallow?"

"Why would you ask that?" she replied in wonder.

"I don't know," he mused. "I stopped at Lute's and he told me about Azteca. You know he had to put her down?"

"No," Theresa said sadly. "But I knew it was coming. He was over here for supper the other night and told me how bad she was. How's he doing?"

"Not great, I think. I mean, he's so morose anyway, he sure didn't need that. But what I was getting at was how I responded to how sad he was, about the dog. I wasn't sure exactly what to say, or do, you know? I wanted to hug him, but that wouldn't be cool with Lute, so I just mumbled something about what a great dog she'd been, blah, blah. Just a shallow response, I'm sure." He sat down heavily on a kitchen chair.

"Don't worry," Theresa also sat. "I probably won't do any better. Most of us do badly with death of any kind. Say what you will about religion, at least we have a means for dealing with it."

"With the death of a dog? Come on, Mom, Christianity has always put animals at the bottom of the heap. Go ask your priest what prayers he has for dogs!" Rusty grinned.

"OK, OK, but what about St. Francis?" Theresa objected.

"The exception to the rule. Many non-Christian peoples, as you know, Ms. Teacher, worshipped animals. Lionized them, pardon the pun. But the good padres soon put an end to that wicked heathen idolatry, didn't they?"

"Well, they did and they didn't," Theresa pointed out. "I've just been reading about the Mayans that built the great jungle cities. They've been Christians, more or less, for about 500 years, but many of them still have strong connections to their old beliefs, including that people have an animal as well as a human soul. So a person can have a goat soul, or a monkey soul, even the soul of a jaguar."

"Thanks for the lesson, Mom, always learn something here. But what about lunch, and what about my problem? You know . . . sometimes I wonder if I'm a lightweight." Rusty got up and walked to the window over the kitchen sink.

Theresa also stood and began to heat squash soup on her stove, going to the fridge to get out her refrigerator pickles, which Rusty loved, a big chunk of Amish blue cheese, and the sourdough bread she made weekly.

"Compared to Luther, we're all lightweights. He's carrying the whole world on his shoulders. But you," Theresa sighed, "look at these wonderful cabinets, look at the great chair you made. Inconsequential people don't do that kind of stuff. Where on earth did you get such an idea? Having a problem responding with Lute's dog's death doesn't mean you don't care, that you're not thoughtful." Theresa served the soup and Rusty sat down, bowing his head as Theresa said a brief, familiar grace.

"Butternut, right?" he asked. "The squash I mean. You know it's hard to believe something this good can also be OK for you, not make you fat. Oh, fridge pickles! Just make 'em?"

"I did," Theresa said, pleased her son was appreciative. "And I'm sending a jar home with you." Theresa passed the cheese to Rusty.

"OK, maybe I'm worrying unnecessarily. Jeez, wonder where I got that from, Mom?" He made a face at his mother. "Still, when I get around people like Lute, so serious, I always feel a little uneasy. Even Carmen thinks I'm just too nice, too easygoing." Rusty slurped his soup noisily, and his mother refrained from admonishing him. She tried that years ago, and failed, so why keep at it?

She moved uncomfortably in her chair in her effort to address the Carmen question. Yes, the Carmen question, requiring great delicacy on her part.

"Well, Anthony," she began formally. "There's not necessarily a connection between being easygoing and friendly, like you, and being shallow. There are plenty of people who are very serious, not a funny bone in their bodies, and also very shallow. A scowl, and I don't mean Carmen, of course, does not denote depth, son." Theresa felt herself scowling.

"Hey, Mom. You do mean Carmen when you say 'scowl,' come on. She's plenty deep, as you know, a veritable Polish American well, several hundred feet down. And I'm the guy with a flashlight peering down in there trying to figure out what's going on." Rusty smiled ruefully.

"I know she's not a shallow person, Rusty. I know that, dear. But neither are you, so please continue being who you are, a lovely man, and stop fretting." Theresa reached across the table and put her hand on her son's. Just holding it there for a moment, not patting. She couldn't stand patters, people who felt compelled to pat you awkwardly on the back when they hugged you.

Mother and son spent the rest of the meal discussing her garden, his trip to Amish-land, the couch he was going to make, and again, Luther's dog. Theresa also told Rusty she thought Luther was sad not only about his dog, but also because he'd had bad news about his long-lost sister. She explained that because of the will Lute's father had left, the attorneys were compelled to find the sister, which is how they had discovered she'd died in California. She told Rusty how Luther found out he also had a nephew who was probably about Rusty's age, a ne'er-do-well, apparently, so who knew if Lute would ever see him? It probably didn't make much difference that Luther hadn't seen Eunice in many years, she was his sister, and now she was dead.

"No wonder he was drinking beer in the morning," Rusty reflected. "I would too. His sister, then his dog. Will he be OK, you think?"

"I think so. This is a very busy time of year for him. Wrapping up his gardens, the fall farmers' markets, cutting wood, one of his favorite chores. He'll drink too much, but not do anything foolish. Smoke too much marijuana probably. And I'll keep close in touch, so he has someone to talk with." Theresa smiled reassuringly.

"Right, well I'll make more of an effort too," Rusty promised. "Maybe I'll get back up here soon and spend a day cutting wood with him. Beer, marijuana, cigarettes—a woods party! And speaking of sisters, have you heard from Mary?"

"Yes, she called this morning just before she left Las Vegas, where she spent the night. We had a nice chat. She actually ate dinner with an Indian family who owned the motel. And listen to this—she got a male mannequin, dressed it up in Mike's clothes, and has him strapped into the front seat next to her!"

"Very weird. Why?"

"To make it look like she has a male companion and isn't traveling alone—for safety. She said the motel owner was trying to charge her for a double room until she brought him outside and showed him the dummy. Can you believe it?" Theresa smiled at her sister's audacity.

"Wow. What a notion, what a woman. I can't wait to see her again."

Rusty laughed, but also made a mental note to be sure *not* to tell Carmen about his aunt's gambit.

They laughed a bit more about Mary and her mannequin, and then Rusty left, a large jar of pickles in hand that he safely stashed on the floor next to him in the Blazer. His would tell his son Duane about crazy Aunt Mary, but swear him to silence.

Chapter 15

AFTER RUSTY LEFT, THERESA FOUND HERSELF WORRYING about Luther. Drinking beer in the morning, smoking too much marijuana. Cutting wood all by himself he could get into a lot of trouble if he were just a little bit drunk, or stoned. So she got into her very old, very durable Subaru wagon with 273,000 miles on the clock and took a quick drive to Luther's house.

Getting out of her car, Theresa was relieved to see that Luther's tractor and the old manure spreader he used to haul wood were sitting in the yard. She went to the house, knocked, hesitated just a polite moment, and went in. Luther wasn't the tidiest of men, but the large stack of unwashed dishes on the sink and stove top was unusual. He did generally wash up after each meal. Passing the stove, she noted that several pans still had some food in them. Not good, an open invitation to mice, which began to come indoors in the fall to find shelter and food.

In the combined living and dining room, every available surface was covered with books, magazines, and the local *Shopper* sales newspaper. This was actually not so unusual. Next Theresa tiptoed quietly into Luther's downstairs bedroom. He wasn't there. The bed was unmade, but that wasn't rare either. So then up the creaky old stairs she went to Lute's so-called study, where he kept his computer and business paperwork.

Very messy, but always was. And there was that big Frank Zappa quote in bold print on the wall: "It would be easier to pay off the national debt overnight than to neutralize the long-range effects of OUR NATIONAL STUPIDITY."

Theresa looked next in the spare bedroom. Since it faced south, it was brilliantly illuminated by the afternoon sun. More books and mags on the tiny bed, but no Luther. So back outside, where she actually called out loud for him to no response. She went into the little barn where he kept his laying hens. Chickens, yes. Luther, no. She tried the machine lean-to on the side of the barn. Cats, yes. No Luther. Then on to the greenhouses where she finally found him, sound asleep in the fetal position with his coat wrapped around him, lying on a potting table and snoring to beat the band.

"Let him sleep?" she wondered aloud. No, it was well into the afternoon and time to wake the man up.

"Lute? Luther?" she shook him gently, remembering that he often awoke violently. Suddenly he leapt from the table with a loud, frightened shout, "What? What? Jesus Jumping Christ!"

Backing away a little, but not a bit afraid of the big, crazed-looking man, Theresa said firmly, "No, Lute. It's not Jesus, just Theresa. Your friend, remember?"

Holding what was probably his aching head in his hands, Luther rocked back and forth for a moment, then looked up. "Hey, Miss Tee. I'm sorry. I scared the crap out of myself. Did I scare you? Sorry . . . ."

"Not a bit," Theresa replied with a sympathetic smile. "I know what a wicked waker-upper you are. But at two in the afternoon? What's going on?" Theresa reached over and touched his arm.

"One hell of a hangover. That's what! I got way into the booze last night, then to take the edge off the gin, smoked a pipeful of that quality dope I've been growing. Over on that shithead doc's place?" Exercising his jaw up and down, Luther tried, but failed, to take the awfully doleful look off his face. "Had a lousy sleep, even with the weed. So I got up real early . . . still dark . . . and came down here to work. Which I did until

Rusty came. He was here, you know . . . then I guess I just fell asleep. What a jerk, right?"

"Listen, Luther, it's fine. You're going through a lot. You're just sad about stuff you should be sad about—your dog, your sister. It's OK to be sad. You know I'm still sad about Tony, and it was more than twenty years ago." Theresa smiled ruefully.

"Yeah, but you lived with him, slept with him, did it all. But my sister? Hell, I hadn't seen her in years. Hadn't a clue about her or her life. So why am I sad?" he asked, shaking his shaggy head.

"Well . . . ," Theresa pondered as she hoisted her short self up on the dirt-strewn table, wincing from the pain in her arthritic hands. "Not being able to climb inside your very large brain, I can't say for sure. But I'd guess you're mourning the girl you knew. And you're also probably very sad about not having her in your life all this time. But nothing can be done about that now."

"Yeah, I guess," Luther admitted as he leaned forward to brace himself on the work table. "You know better than me that I'm like the least introspective guy on the planet. I've got this little man in my head—probably Vietnamese—who's my gatekeeper. Every time I'm inclined to peer into my funky head, he jumps up, slams the gate on me, and says 'Don't go there. Stay out. Go back to work and forget about it!' In English, of course."

"Well, I have some good news at least," Theresa said. "My sister Mary is coming for a visit."

"Hey. That is good. Wasn't too long ago her husband died, right?"

"Yes, sadly. Mike."

"Sure. I remember when they visited years ago, particularly because he and I got right into it about the politics in this miserable country of ours. We had a lot of the same ideas. Wasn't he some kind of organizer?" Luther stood upright and stretched his arms over his head, trying to wake up fully.

"He was. For grocery-store workers. Before that he worked for years as what the English call a greengrocer. Kind of like you, in a way." Theresa smiled.

"Produce man, right? I grow it, he sells it. Or sold it."

"Yes. Although I doubt he sold anything as fresh as your veggies."

"Whatever."

Lute didn't take the opportunity to rant about the poor-quality produce sold, much of it from Mexico, in American supermarkets. For which Theresa was grateful.

"So—she's flying here, I'd guess?" he asked.

"Not a bit of it," Theresa smiled. "She's driving this monster of an old Lincoln that Mike bought just before he got sick. Her daughter Emma was *not* thrilled about the trip. But, hey, we all deserve a bit of adventure while we still can. And she's tough, and smart, and most of all determined. So there it is." She shrugged and hopped off her perch. "Meanwhile, I'm going in to clean up your kitchen."

"Hey," Luther protested, "you don't have to."

"Yes, I do. You've got the farmers' market soon right? You'd better get out there and start picking, Luther." Not waiting for his reply, Theresa went up to the house and began to stack the dishes she was about to wash. As she'd expected, she found little mouse turds on several plates and tiny footprints in a very greasy frying pan. I knew it, she thought, the little so-and-sos! She went straight to the telephone and picked up a pad of paper, writing on it in large letters: Dear Luther, Thank you for feeding me and my large and growing family. Please don't set any traps for us. Especially with peanut butter. Love, Mickey!

Tearing the note from the pad, she taped it to the refrigerator and began to wash dishes.

Chapter 16

Back on the slab, the bikers' name for the interstate, Joni noted that she was stuck in some totally boring countryside. No trees, just desert, with the occasional herd of cattle on some distant hillside. Now she had nothing to do but worry about the increasingly slow shifting of the Civic's tranny.

She patted her little bobblehead talisman and asked for some grace. "Just get me to Minnesota, Mr. Red Wing. Please and thanks."

Random thoughts bounced around in her head as she drove. Had she slept well? Yes, but she always did. A real blessing, as they said. Good to be short when you had to curl up in the back seat of a very small car. Let's see, at last measure she'd been a scant five two.

"Musta been your mom," Eunice had offered from her daybed just before she died, referring to Joni's height. Eunice had been tall for a woman of her generation, nearly five ten.

"Yeah, we Rasmussens were all Vikings. Shit, my dad was well over six foot, and my brother too," Joni's grandma had noted.

What was that brother's name, Joni wondered as she drove on through the monotony? Some kind of religious connection . . . a saint maybe? John? James? Paul? No. Pope? No, that was a last name. Pope Rasmussen—that would be weird! But really, what was it?

Luther! That was it, like the Lutherans! That was pretty weird too. She couldn't picture anyone named Luther. Bet he was straight as a string. Blonde wife, blonde kids, driving a Chevy. Probably played golf and sold insurance. Or maybe he was a pharmacist, a pill doctor. Well, she'd likely find out if and when she got there.

Some ways west of Salt Lake City, she started to encounter the lake, or something like it. Great stretches of white, was it salt? With small ponds right along the freeway. Really uninviting. Who in the hell would want to live here, Joni thought? Then she remembered, the Mormons. There were actually a couple of Mormon families in Geeville who had some kids in school. Always alarmingly polite, bugging you about whether or not you'd like to come to their church. Ugh.

"A goddamn cult," Eunice had said. "Some guy says he finds some golden tablets in his backyard and *bingo!* a bunch of loonies believe him. Now they own a whole freakin' state for God's sake!"

And now one of them was running for president. Eunice would have puked, Joni thought as she chuckled to herself.

Thinking of Eunice, Joni picked another of her granny's precious jazz CDs *Art Pepper Meets the Rhythm Section* to listen to as she cruised into Salt Lake. Just the right antidote to the Mormons, she thought. Great sounds, totally cool.

Joni remembered that Pepper, according to Eunice, was a junkie too. "Listen to that man play, Joni," she'd say. "He breaks your heart! And a goddamn junkie just like me. Well, not exactly like me since I can't play a lick except to bang a spoon on a pot! Jesus, he's something else. Something else!"

Now that would be something, wouldn't it, Joni thought now as she listened. Learn to play an instrument. Not to be famous or anything like that, just play for herself. Get real good at it. She'd envied the kids in school who were in the bands and orchestra. Mostly the rich kids who could afford private lessons.

While she hadn't liked most of her teachers, she'd always admired the music teacher, Mrs. Standish. From a distance, of course, since Joni never even tried to get into band. She liked the woman because it seemed amazing that she could take a bunch of basically dumb Geeville kids and make them musicians. Not exactly Art Pepper, but good enough that they didn't embarrass themselves, or their teacher, at their concerts. Joni went to most of the concerts, and there were even a couple of kids from her side of the tracks in the jazz band. When Eunice was well, she'd sometimes go to the concerts with Joni too.

"You oughta play something, Joni," Eunice would say. "God, it would make me happy if you were in that jazz band."

Why hadn't she at least tried? Had she been too shy? Totally scared of not being up to the grade? Well, there'd been no money for lessons or an instrument so there really hadn't been any point. Maybe, Joni thought, if this Minnesota gig actually turned out to be true—if there really *was* a pot of gold at the end of this road-trip rainbow—she could afford to buy an instrument and pay for lessons. It wasn't like she was too old to learn or anything.

But she shouldn't count on it—the money. Probably just a wild-goose chase. Got her out of Geeville though, didn't it! But even as she cautioned herself not to expect anything, she felt a surge of exhilaration. Whatever happened, it was going to beat the hell out of changing stained sheets at the Worst Western!

Leaving Salt Lake and Utah and its Mormons behind, Joni threaded her way into Wyoming, The Cowboy State. Well, from the interstate, she wasn't seeing anything cowboyish at all. Not that she was disappointed, horses and big hats weren't exactly her thing. Getting to Minnesota was her thing, and she was more and more worried about making it. Her car was shifting ever more slowly, and was sloppier each time she slowed down. She finally was so worried that she even gave up the comfort of listening to her CDs so she could focus all her energy on the car.

Some people her age went around glued to their iPods, and she'd often been told she should get one. No more hassle with little discs that got dirty or cracked or lost, they said, and jillions of songs you could download for free. A whole 'nother musical world, they said. She never got one though. Too much money, and even more, too steep a learning curve for a girl who didn't even own a computer. Maybe in Minnesota she'd get a laptop, take a lesson or two, and join the digital party. Meanwhile, little Honda, please don't let me down. Just get me to the Midwest!

On and boringly on, Joni drove. God this ride was bleak, she thought, just goddamn nothing. Whoa! There was a sign for Rasmussen Road. That was Eunice's family's name. An omen maybe? Hope it's a good one! She needed to stop for gas and a Coke in the next town, which turned out to be the bleakest of places. Just bunches of trailer homes on both sides of the highway and yards filled with all kinds of equipment.

Wamsutter. Strange name for the place, she thought as she pulled into a small station and gassed up. When she went in to pay and get a soda, she noticed the very large sign warning: No Bathroom Use for Non-Customers. Then, in the bathroom itself, another warning: Please Leave This Toilet as Clean as You Found It!!! Whoa, careful when you pee, girl. It *was* really clean for a gas-station crapper, but heck. At the counter, a nice-looking woman, maybe in her fifties, with lots of cowgirl-style hair, smiled at Joni as she deposited her Coke on the counter.

"Going far?" the woman asked as she rang Joni up.

"Yeah, I am. To Minnesota, actually. If my car holds out," Joni nodded to the Honda outside.

"Never been there, but it's gotta be better than this godforsaken place. Where you from?" the attendant handed Joni her change.

"California. Place called Garberville, up north in redwood country. Not exactly L.A. or the fancy Bay Area," Joni grimaced as she pocketed her change.

"Yeah, we went to see the redwoods years ago. Pretty, but too dark and wet for us. Course, as you can see, we could sure use a few trees here in Wamsutter. Think there's probably a half dozen of them in the whole town," the woman said, grimacing in turn.

"So what's going on here?" Joni pointed to the heavy equipment visible through the window.

"Believe it or not, it's actually a boom town, y'know, like the Old West? But the boom isn't for gold, it's gas. Natural gas. You know BP, British Petroleum, the gas stations? They're here, and the rest of those big gas companies. This is BP's largest gas field in the whole freakin' world, can you imagine! We call 'em Big and Plenty," the woman smiled. "Don't know how long the boom will last, so nobody builds an actual house. Everyone lives in trailers, got our own big double-wide out back. Many guys just pull up with an RV and live in it while they're here."

"Gets pretty hot here I bet?" Joni wondered.

"Hellish so. And cold as a witch's tit in the winter, let me tell you."

"So is this your place?" Joni opened her Coke.

"Me and my husband," the woman explained. "He has his own rig, hauls gas in a tanker. Tractor's his—ours—and the tankers are some other outfit that rents to BP, Amoco, whatever."

"Hauling gas? That's gotta be dangerous huh?" Joni queried.

"Not really. Those rigs are pretty safe. Biggest risk is in the winter, running off the road 'cause of snow, ice, wind, fog. Gets real hairy then. I'd rather he did something else and we lived somewhere else, but while we're here, we at least got this station. Something for me to do, and make some money too." The woman smiled and patted the register.

"I get it," Joni said as she turned to leave. Clearly the woman could use some company, and it was nice to talk to somebody, but she had to hit the road.

But that didn't exactly happen.

Joni couldn't get the Honda out of the station. The engine started fine, but it wouldn't shift into drive. The engine just raced. The car moved a little in reverse, but not much, and she couldn't reverse her way to Minnesota.

Panicking, she turned off the motor and got out of the Civic, slamming the driver's door shut as hard as she could. Just then, a young man came out from the garage attached to the station.

"What's the matter?" he asked as he wiped his hands on a rag.

"I think my tranny's shot. Just won't go, 'cept in reverse, and not much there either," Joni said.

"Can I take a look?" the man asked. He was a boy really, short and greasy, sporting a baseball cap with St. Louis printed on it.

"Sure. Man, it'd be great if it was just something simple, you know," she replied anxiously.

The kid got in and started the car. Raced the engine, shifted the gears, and got a slight response in reverse but that was all.

"Hate to tell ya, but I think you're right. No tranny. Prob'ly didn't keep fluid in it!" he pronounced with youthful male authority.

"Wrong," Joni insisted loudly. "Check for yourself. I kept it full of tranny juice." God, she hated men being snotty about simple car stuff, or anything actually.

"Well, we can't leave it here," he said. "Help me push it over there by the dumpster, maybe we should just toss it in there, huh?" He laughed an annoying kid's laugh.

"You're a funny dude, y'know?" Joni said sarcastically. "Is there anybody else can take a look at it, a grown-up maybe?"

"Oh. So my opinion don't count, huh?" When she didn't answer, he added. "My dad'll be here soon. He's over-the-road and prob'ly late as usual, but he's like an ace mechanic. Just have to wait. What's your name?"

"Joni," she offered. "Guess I'll just sit in the car and drink my Coke till your dad comes. What's your name?" she asked reluctantly.

"George."

"George? Like the president?" No one she had ever known personally was called George.

"Yeah," he replied defensively. "Not like that dipshit prez from Texas, y'know, but like the old-time rocker George Thorogood. You ever heard of him?"

"Nope, never," Joni shook her head.

"Yeah, pretty much no one ever has, but my parents liked him. 'Bad to the Bone,' 'Move It on Over,' 'The House of Blue Lights'—that was his stuff, I guess." He waited for Joni's recognition.

"Nope, sorry, never heard of him or those tunes." Nor was she interested, Joni thought as she got into her car and began to shut the door on him. Just leave me alone so I can sulk in my broken car, goddamnit!

"My folks saw him live once, best concert they ever saw, I guess. Wish some good bands would come play somewhere around here. I've never been to a live concert," he added ruefully as Joni closed her door.

Just then a pickup pulled into the gas pumps, giving Joni a chance to escape from George when he went to provide the service. She drank her now-warm Coke and sat, disconsolate, in the Honda.

"Bobblehead," she accused as she pointed at her good luck charm, "looks like you let me down, dude. Bad!"

Then she put the seat back and promptly fell asleep. It had been maybe half an hour when somebody knocked on the car window. Groggy, she half-stumbled out of the Honda and leaned on a fender.

"You OK?" A larger, older, and much cleaner version of George asked.

"I'm fine. Just catching up on my zee's. Car's not so good though. Mind taking a look?" she asked.

"Sure, pop the hood. I'm Sam, the owner, by the way. My kid told me you got tranny blues. Start it up, will you?"

She did and saw him checking the tranny fluid. Of course they didn't trust her.

"OK, fluid's good. Let me in there, please."

She got out and he got in to do the whole race-the-engine, try-the-gears thing. Nothing, this time even reverse failed to move the car.

"Linkage might be loose, but it doesn't feel like it. 'Fraid it's a blown tranny," Sam got out of the car and looked at her not unkindly.

"Can you do something?" Joni asked without much hope.

"Not really." He shook his head as he wiped his hands on a rag. "These old Civics are great cars, but even they don't run forever. Could probably find you a used tranny, but it would take a week to get here. Tranny plus shipping would be about eight bills. George and I'd have to charge you at least five to swap trannies. My opinion, car's not worth it.

Put a new tranny in and the motor could go, or not. All depends." He smiled a nice, kind smile.

"Doesn't make any difference," Joni shrugged. "I don't have that kind of bread anyway. Got just about enough for gas money and some cheap eats to get to Minnesota. Is the car worth anything at all?"

"Nah, it's starting to rust bad. You got California plates, but this ain't no L.A. car," Sam pointed out.

"No, I'm from redwood country," Joni explained. "Lots of trees and lots of rain, so plenty of rust."

"Well . . . ," he paused. "I can scrap it out. Salvage this and that and send the body to the boneyard. Another dead automobile, courtesy of our lousy twenty-first-century transportation system," he intoned in a solemn voice.

She looked at him with some disbelief, "Wow, you make your living driving truck and owning a garage, but you're down on transportation? How does that work?"

"Who better than someone in the thick of it to smell the shit? Pardon my French. What's your name?" he asked.

"Joni, and pardon *my* French, but I'm fucking screwed! Shit. Does the Greyhound stop here?"

"In Wamsutter? Not a chance," Sam laughed. "Probably catch it in Rawlins. But the bus has gotten really spendy—gas prices, insurance, you know."

"Jesus, I *am* screwed!" Joni grimaced.

"Listen, why don't you stay here tonight? I mean with us? My wife's makin' chicken and dumplings, great grub! We got a spare room. Then you can take off with me in the morning. I'm heading for Omaha. Big truck stop there, I bet you can catch a ride to Minnesota, no problem!"

"Seriously? Are you sure I won't be too much trouble?" Joni was doubtful.

"Let's see," he said as he gave her an appraising look. "You're about—what? Maybe a hundred pounds or so, five three at the tallest. How much trouble can you be?"

Feeling a little uncomfortable, Joni nonetheless liked his easy manner, and the offer could not be turned down unless his wife objected. But Patty was just as friendly as she'd been in the station. Still pretty in her fifties in a country-western kind of way, with that big hair and lipstick—she couldn't believe some women still wore it—Patty found an old Joni Mitchell album and played it for Joni while putting supper together, the station having been shut down for the night.

"Nothin' to this meal, honey. The pressure cooker does it all. Course I take a little care with the dumplings, 'cause they can turn to lead if you use too much egg. Now, tell me again where you're from?" Patty smiled at her.

"From a place where people are afraid to use pressure cookers, that's for sure," Joni said raising her eyebrows. "I was raised by my grandma and she was terrified of those things. My dad brought one home from a garage sale one time, brand new, and she made him throw it out. Right into the dumpster. Couldn't give it to the Goodwill. She said that was just like giving them an explosive device. You're not afraid of it?"

"Yeah, I know some people feel that way," Patty rinsed flour off her hands in the sink. "I was raised with them. Canned and cooked with these things my whole life, never even close to an accident. You're much more likely to get hurt with a sharp knife in the kitchen than a cooker."

Patty had lots of questions about Joni's past and her plans for the future. Yes, she'd graduated high school. No, she hadn't gone to college. No, she didn't have a boyfriend. Yes, she had kin to visit in Minnesota. But Joni said nothing about the potential inheritance.

Uncomfortable with the questions, Joni knew the woman meant well, just wanted to talk. And she had to admire Patty's easy confidence in the kitchen. Joni could barely boil water. How lucky this woman was, Joni thought, to be so comfortable in her own place, even if it was in a horror like Wamsutter. Patty drank a beer while she worked, but her radiant face showed no trace of boozy excess, or any other kind, for that matter. She offered Joni one, but she declined.

"See all those veggies in the stew, and the chicken?" Patty pointed out. "In our last place, in Colorado, I would have raised all that myself. Had a big garden and chicken coop. But here, not hardly the best place for growing stuff. Boom ends and we're outta here like shot from a cannon, lemme tell you, dear!" Patty said, taking a swig from her beer. "Want to grab a shower while I'm finishing up here? Down the hall, grab a towel from the cabinet."

After a wonderful shower and quick exam of the tiny room she would sleep in, noting a picture of a pretty young woman on the wall behind the bed, Joni helped Patty put the supper on. She asked casually about the girl as she set the table.

"Oh, you noticed that," Patty said, with a flat voice. "Yeah, she's George's sister. Been gone for a while now, don't see much of her."

"Your daughter?" Joni asked the obvious.

"Yup, Jean Anne. Graduated from high school back in Colorado and left that town like it was on fire!" Patty shook her head.

"Oh, is she married? Kids? Where is she?" Joni wondered, taking her turn to ask questions.

"Tell the truth, I don't know. We had a kind of a family feud, and she split. A couple of years ago. We haven't heard diddly since we moved here," Patty's kindly face was somber.

"Wow! That's harsh." Joni proclaimed.

"Well, nothin' to be done about it, I guess," Patty stated. Then she added in a defiant voice, "Just show me a family without trouble and I'll show you a pack of liars!"

"Can't disagree with you there," Joni nodded. "My people are totally wasted, but you know when I was a kid I used to think that lots of the other kids probably had great families—their moms picking them up at school, dads taking them fishing and showing up for sports stuff, you know. But by the time I got to high school, and Geeville is a pretty small place, I found out that even the rich kids with big houses, new cars, and cool clothes had trouble at home. Booze, sex, money—just stir the town pot a little and the crap soon floated to the top. Man, even with this car trouble, I'm so glad to be out of there!"

"Well, I'm glad you're here. Try to talk you into staying here a bit, no trouble finding a job with the gas boom on, but I'm guessing you're determined to move on?" Patty said, ending with a question. "Hey, go call the men in, will you?"

When they were all at the table, Sam, Patty, George, and Joni, they joined hands as Sam mumbled a brief prayer. Mercifully brief, Joni thought.

Smiling at her, Sam explained, "We're believers, have to believe in somethin'—but we're not church folk. Too many rules and too many bastard pastors, if you know what I mean? Just don't like people telling us what to do. Which is why we got our own business here, and I'm over the road in my own rig. What about your people?"

"Church?" Joni asked. "No, never. Neighbors tried to take me to Sunday school a few times when I was a tyke, but my grandma just chased them off. As for my *people*, there's just my dad, and he's an odd-jobs kind of guy, logging mostly. Some carpenter work, like that. I haven't lived with him since high school. We get along, but better when we're in separate spaces. God, this chicken is good, Patty!" Joni was eager to change the subject.

"It is, isn't it?" George chimed in. "Mom's the best cook in Wamsutter, by far. I keep telling her we should open a restaurant here at the station, but she won't do it."

"Wow, 'best cook in Wamsutter!' Which is like saying some weight-lifter is the strongest man in a bunch of kindergartners! Thanks, Georgie." Patty glared at her son. "'Sides, because someone can cook at home in no way means they can run a restaurant. Look at those folks back in Fort Collins. That's where we lived before," she explained to Joni. "They opened up a restaurant because both of them were such great cooks. Restaurant flopped within a year. Too risky, and certainly no way I'd do it here, in the middle of nowhere!"

"Yeah, and in this horseshit economy, too big a risk," Sam added. "Everybody keeps talking about a turnaround, but I ain't seeing it, even with the gas boom here. My guess is it won't happen—the turnaround. Whole country's on a downhill slide, far as I can tell. How are things back there in California?"

"In Garberville there's just lumber and tourists," Joni responded. "And dope, which is by miles the biggest moneymaker, especially now with the medical marijuana thing. So the dope's kinda legal, although the feds are always sneaking around trying to bust people."

"There you go," Sam slammed his hand on the table. "Goddamn government always messing in people's business! I don't smoke myself, gotta piss in a bottle to keep my license up. Hate to do it, but it's my living."

"Yeah," Joni agreed. "I don't care if people smoke some weed and make some money growing it. But for me, dope work's too dangerous. Man, one dude up there had tigers patrolling his stash!" Joni savored her last bite of dumpling.

George jumped in, "Tigers? No shit? You mean like Bengals, the really big ones?"

"Far as I know," Joni said. "I never saw 'em, never wanted to. Not exactly a cat lover, y'know? So I was in the tourist end of things, a maid at the big motel in town. Just got tired of cleaning other people's crap up. No future in it. So, off to Minnesota." Saying this, Joni remembered her plight. "Somehow, hopefully."

"Don't worry," Sam assured her. "We'll get you there."

"Where exactly *is* there?" Patty asked.

"Rochester, you know, where the fancy Mayo Clinic is? That's where my uncle lives," Joni lied.

"Never hauled there," Sam noted. "And hope I never have to go, to the clinic, I mean. Good if you get cancer, I guess."

"Yeah, I heard that too," Joni said. "I don't care about that though, just needed a change from Geeville, you know?" She looked around the table.

The conversation continued with this and that, those and these. Joni was actually enjoying herself with these friendly people, although George made her a little uncomfortable by just plain staring at her.

Finally even Patty noticed, "Say, George boy, are you just totally fixated on Joni, or are you in a daze from drinking too much brew out in the garage?"

Red faced, he snapped to, saying he'd only had two beers all afternoon. After that, he didn't look at Joni for the rest of the evening, which ended quickly because Sam pointed out he and Joni would be up and out at five a.m.

Chapter 17

Bidding adieu to her Liberian savior, Mary determined to make some mileage, especially in light of the short distance she'd traveled on her first day. Ten hours of driving was a bit of a stretch . . . but she felt fine, albeit a bit guilty for not yet responding to the message on her cell from Emma.

"Mom, hey, how are you? *Where* are you? Call please. OK?"

Next stop, she'd call. Her daughter probably wouldn't answer. She'd be in class. But Mary would've done her duty, telling Emma to call her tonight after she stopped. Which would be, if all worked out, somewhere in Wyoming.

So settle in for a long haul. Starting with Tierney Sutton singing her great version of "Route 66." Something she'd considered, for about five minutes. Taking the fabled road. But she decided it would be far too complicated and uncertain. She and Mike had talked about doing it in the Dreadnaught once, but he got sick . . . and died. God, she missed that crazy little man. She reached over and gave the mannequin a poke.

"Hey, buddy. I miss you awfully. You'd have loved this trip. But maybe you're here for all I know." Grinning a tight little smile, she sighed heavily.

Mike was often angry, but rarely at her. Almost every day he found something or someone in the papers or on the radio to illustrate his firmly held belief that America could be a crappy, vicious country. She didn't miss his rants. While she did agree with most of them, they were tiresome. Not that there weren't some humorous moments out of Mike's political bent, she thought, remembering a guy she used to work with at a nursery, a wonderful plants man but otherwise ignorant about many things. He attributed almost anything going wrong in L.A., the nation, or the world to "just 'nother comnist plot!" At first she didn't get what he was saying, but eventually she realized he meant a *communist* plot. And he believed it, along with millions of Americans stuck in the 1950s. What had been LBJ's response to the black riots in Watts in the '60s? Hadn't the president himself called the riots a communist conspiracy?

Over the several years she worked with the guy, Mary realized that he apparently did believe the *comnists* were actually trying to undermine America. He was intent on placing blame on a distant enemy for everything that was wrong right here. Once, the guy actually had the gall to denounce Mary's husband when he learned Mike was not only a union member, but an organizer. She'd been so angry at that—she smiled at the memory—that she yelled at him, right out there among the shrubbery and cactuses, calling him an ignorant old fool. Not long after, the nursery's owner fired her.

"Regrettably," her boss had said.

It was actually fine. She was highly employable, and ended up at a much better place. And for the rest of their lives together, she and Mike had chuckled as one or the other of them attributed almost all bad news to being a comnist plot! God, even when they got the bad news about Mike's "failure to thrive," as the doctors called it, he'd managed a grin and croaked out, "Comnist plot. Goddamn comnist plot!"

Now she couldn't stop thinking about Mike. Stop, already, Mary!

"OK, one more reminisce? Or is it reminiscence?" She looked over at the mannequin. "The Zinn book?"

Howard Zinn's *A People's History of the United States* was a book Emma now used in her course at City College, and often cribbed from for her high-school classes. Jeez, Mary remembered the time Janet and

James invited them over for dinner along with a colleague of James's, a historian. Mike, never abashed by someone else's title or claims to status, immediately began to question the guy's knowledge of American labor history. Defensive, the man challenged Mike's sources, and when he heard Zinn was one of them, began to deride the book that Mike held as sacred. What a disaster of an evening, with Mike yelling at the guy that maybe if he'd ever done anything besides sit in an office, he'd have a better grasp of reality—and insulting their friend James in the process. The guy, red-faced and angry, had left shortly after dinner and Mary, embarrassed again, hauled Mike home soon after.

"Come on, Mike," Mary demanded. "You know history isn't a big stone laying there with the truth on it for all to read. He's got his version, you and Zinn have yours, and I don't need to be embarrassed at dinner with our friends!"

"Yeah, you're right. One big difference, though, is that me and Zinn got it right!" Mike wasn't quite chastened.

The man had been impossible, she loved him, but impossible. Whoops, was that a tear? And appropriately, Tierney Sutton was now singing "Crazy," that great Willie Nelson song. They had always liked Willie: almost as old as them, smoking weed everywhere he went, a successful outlaw, if that was possible.

Mary's favorite female artist was Nina Simone and, yes, Andres had included one of her albums in the tape mix. That wonderful throaty voice, so authoritative. Don't mess with her. She popped out the Sutton tape and inserted Nina into the player, punching ahead to Mike's favorite Nina song, "Mississippi Goddam," where she denounces the South for its treatment of her people, Mississippi being the worst of all. On this version, Nina was in front of a live audience, and the applause and cheering when she finished were grand. What a woman! Now this was the way to take a road trip! Great music, and the miles flying by quickly because the desert scenery, here anyway, was pretty scant.

Mississippi. Mary had never been in the South and really had no desire to go. Mike had been in Biloxi during his stint in the Air Force right after World War II. The black guys from up north never left the base, she remembered him saying. They were scared of going into the dinky beachfront town, all bars and cheap hotels and chock full of racists.

Mike had told her Biloxi was the first place he'd ever gotten drunk. Puking his guts out in front of some sleazy bar, drinking some sweet cocktail like a Tom Collins or a Manhattan. He'd laughed, "I got sick of course."

Gin and tonic, she'd brought a bottle of each and some limes in the small cooler Emma had loaned her. And she was certainly going to have a drink tonight when she got to her motel to celebrate a successful day on the road. Meanwhile, she was plenty hungry so she pulled off at the next exit with signs indicating gas and food available, with a good portion of Utah remaining. Pulling into the larger of two stations, she glanced over at her companion, deciding to pick the most remote of several pumps so no one could scrutinize his plasticity.

She pulled up to the pump, got out, and opened the gas hatch. Then she plugged in her credit card and punched "yes" for a receipt. She was going to keep track of how much it cost to get to the woebegone north. Eighty-seven octane, whatever the dickens that meant, she thought as she filled up. Carlos had explained it to her once, but who cares? Octane, octogenarian, whatever. Well, neither she nor Theresa was eighty-seven yet. She'd call her tonight, and Emma, she thought as she returned the nozzle to the pump.

Gas-up done, receipt in hand, Mary got back in the car to search for a drive-through. A short distance from the gas station she pulled into Dairy De-Lite and ordered a burger and coffee with cream and sugar. No fries for her—too much heartburn!

"Sorry, ma'am," the pimpled kid at the window said. "We're having a small problem. Will you please pull over there in front of the building? We'll bring your order in just a minute, OK?"

She'd gone to a drive-through to avoid problems with people gawking at her companion. Now she had to sit there in full view and wait for her meal. Talk about a full meal deal! Darn! But moments later a cute little blonde girl skipped out with the burger and coffee, pausing just a minute as she handed the bag in to Mary.

"Excuse me, ma'am, but is your husband OK?" she asked inquisitively. "None of my business, but?" The girl stared at the mannequin.

Right, none of her business. "That's OK, dear. He's fine, just a little under the weather from car sickness. Thanks for asking." Mary forced herself to smile at her as she set down the bag and secured the coffee, eager to pull away.

"OK, bye." The girl ran back into the building.

Mary turned to Mike. "Well, Miguelito, I've crossed the line. Pretending you're real, I mean." She fixed her coffee, tasted it—awful! But she needed the caffeine, so she'd drink it anyway. A bite from her burger—not bad, but not good either. Road food, or roadkill? She pulled the Lincoln back onto the highway, and headed off toward Salt Lake.

On the road, Mary turned off the tape player, taking a break from the music. Glancing over at Mike she wondered, what if by continuing to talk to him she would eventually animate him, bring him back to life? There's a notion.

Maybe she should have brought more of Mike's clothing so she could have changed his outfit every other day or so. Heck, the living Mike would wear the same thing for days. Years, actually, since he wasn't hard on clothes or shoes. Why not keep them forever instead of wasting money on something as foolish as new clothing?

"Mike," she'd say, "I can see right through that shirt. You give *threadbare* new meaning."

"So what? It still fits, doesn't it?" he'd retort.

"Here's what, honey. *I* have to look at it, much more than you do. Remember when I cut my hair and you didn't like it, and you argued the same thing? You said *you* looked at my hair much more than I did, so you had a right to weigh in. So now I'm weighing in—please throw that shirt out. Goodwill doesn't want it, but Carlos might for cleaning his motorcycle. And I'll go with you to buy a couple of new ones. Some pants too, maybe?"

"Pants?" Mike raised his eyebrows. "This is getting out of hand!"

"Yup, pants! Those things you use to cover your little Irish butt. That pair you have on now you wore at work for years. They still have lettuce stains on them," Mary noted.

"These are, dear wife, honorable trousers. Working man's pants, I *did* stuff in these."

"I know, the evidence is all over them. Tell you what, we won't throw them out. We'll stash 'em in a trunk for the grandkids to find and put into Mike's Museum."

And so it went about his clothes. Not that Mike was cheap, anything but. He just didn't get the idea of caring about clothes for men beyond the minimum necessities. Growing up, he just figured that any male who had an interest in clothing was homosexual. But then one of his best allies in the grocery union battles turned out to be gay, and he dressed as carelessly as Mike. That guy drank beer, sported a notable paunch over his belt, and swore worse than Mike too, dispelling all preconceived notions. Go figure.

Mary drove onward through the high midday sun, thinking about her own clothing habits. She wasn't exactly a clotheshorse, also wore things for years. She thought she still looked pretty good in them since she'd kept her figure as she aged. Far more than how her favorite clothes looked, she loved how they felt, soft and comfortable, but sturdy. Mary also cared about her clothes' history, even now remembering that great little black cotton dress, simple but sexy, she wore when she and Mike went dancing. There had been many requests from other men to dance with her. One idiot had actually said . . . what was it? "You know for a short woman, you have a great body!" Thanks, Quasimodo, she'd thought. Is that a hump on your back or are you just happy to see me?

She had understood Mike's allegiance to his old work pants, but there was a limit. If she spilled wine on a dress she liked and couldn't get the stain out—she threw it out. Right now she was wearing a great pair of pants Janet had made for her. The pants that had gotten wet from that automated-flush toilet this morning. Mary laughed out loud at the memory of standing in the bathroom in her underwear trying to dry her pants when that woman had walked in.

Moving back and forth in the seat, she tried to get comfortable. This was a pretty big car for a short woman to drive such a long distance. She'd always wanted to be a little taller. Not much, but something slightly above her now-fading five one. Five three, maybe, or ooh, five five—a giantess! One of the many great things about so many of the immigrants pouring into L.A.—the Latinos and Asians—was that most of them were short too. Helping drive the average height down nearer her level. Some of the women, say from Vietnam or Thailand, were even really much smaller than Mary.

She gripped the wheel after a large semi sped by, rocking the Dreadnaught in its windy wake. This was her least favorite part of road tripping, being on a multilane freeway sandwiched between lots of cars rocketing well over the speed limit and frantically changing lanes to break out of the pack. She was old enough to know that her best bet was to slow down and let the pack split around her, leaving her behind to quietly tool along at a more comfortable speed.

Passing a minivan packed with what appeared to be a large family with kids of all ages, Mary remembered the story Mike would tell about his tiny beginnings. He had been about eight pounds at birth, the joke being that he scarcely grew after that. Topping out at five seven as an adult, he was taller than Mary, but among Anglos he was a small guy. Unlike Mary however, he never wished for more height. What did he need it for, he'd ask? He'd say that when he was a kid back in Queens, and then in the Air Force, it was mostly the big guys people picked on. What glory was there in beating up a little guy like Mike?

Not that he didn't get into scrapes with his big mouth, his never-ending bulldogging about justice and fairness. But still . . . God, was that a Lincoln? Mary wondered as a very large four-door pickup truck passed and pulled in front of her. It was, but a Lincoln truck, what for? Her own car was small in comparison. Andres may call the

Dreadnaught a VLA, very large auto, but it was nothing compared to that beast in front of her.

"Hey, Mike," she said aloud. "Check it out, that thing makes our Dreadnaught look like a VW!"

He would have been livid at that thing, but also secretly pleased because it was so much more outrageous than his own big car.

She was getting tired, being on the road with nothing but a mannequin to talk to was wearing her out. She needed to find a way to stay awake so she could log a few more miles.

"Livid, livid, livid. Livid, lily, liver," she chanted a nonsense sequence aloud. "Hey, Mike, speaking of livers. Remember liver and onions? Now that was a delicious treat until they told us it was bad for us. And I guess our livers survived all those gin and tonics too, huh?"

They also drank wine, and the occasional beer, but mostly in moderation. They used to laugh that they were too small to hold too much liquor. Or, more probably, just genetically lucky. Otherwise, who knew, they might have been in downtown L.A. with all the other homeless folk. But that drink was going to taste good tonight. *After* she'd called Emma and Theresa, of course!

Well, there'd been nothing much to see in Nevada. She didn't even remember crossing into Utah, heading for Salt Lake City. Just as boring, maybe more so, than Nevada. Talk about bleak and godforsaken. What in the devil did the Mormons end up here for, she wondered? Was this landscape some kind of penance? Penance. Penitentiary? Penile? Penis?

"Stop it!" Mary scolded herself aloud.

Tiresome scenery, tired old lady who needed to stop and take a nap at the next rest stop. And here it was, thankfully. Mary locked the car and headed in to pee. This time she used the coded numbers on the car door to get back in. No more alarms, please and thank you.

Back in, she locked the door, moved the seat and fell asleep immediately, her last conscious moment was noticing a fellow traveler passing by as she walked her dog. Her restless dreams included a neighbor's vicious dog when she was little, or was it that dog on her block in Pasadena? Kids running in a yard. Greeting customers at some unidentifiable nursery.

Mary finally woke when she got chilly. How long had she slept? Almost an hour, no harm in that. The nap would let her drive all the longer today. Starting the car, now fully awake, she tried futilely to remember her dreams. She never could, whereas Mike would recount many of his in great detail. So much detail that both she and Emma regularly accused him of making stuff up.

"Why would I do that?" he'd scoff.

Janet had several books on interpreting dreams and had offered to loan them to Mary. "No thanks, dear," Mary told her. "I can't remember them, just can't. And, truth told, I don't care about them. Even if I could remember."

Back on the highway, the view was just as boring as before. But wait—huzzah—signs for Salt Lake signaled progress. Skirting the city by hooking up with I-80 on the southern edge, Mary was careful not to pick the wrong lane and miss her route. As she climbed out of the city, it was at least more scenic. There was Park City, famous for what? Oh yes, the movie festival. Robert Redford's Sundance.

She stayed on the movie track to occupy herself. What was that great movie with him and Paul Newman? There was the cowboy one, what was it called? Where they jumped off the cliff at the end? Then the funny one . . . *The Sting* . . . where the two guys pulled some flimflam to cheat some mobster out of his stash. That was a good movie.

"Wait a minute, *Sundance*, that was it!" Mary said aloud. "*Butch Cassidy and the Sundance Kid*, that was the great cowboy movie, Mike. Remember? Where the two of them jumped off a cliff into a river?"

"And what was that other one you loved and watched so many times?" she asked her silent seatmate. "Remember, the one from the book about the Latinos in New Mexico foiling the developers? Miracle? No . . . *Milagro*! *The Milagro Beanfield War*! Who did Redford play in that? Or was it Newman? Memory, ahh, memory. Hey, it was neither one!"

"Do you remember, Mike? Redford *directed* it. Now those were good-looking men, both of them. But of course, they were movie stars."

Mary remembered the neighbor they'd had years ago who worked in The Biz, as they used to call Hollywood. He'd told them about working on the set of an early Newman movie where everyone had just assumed the young actor was gay just because he was so handsome.

No one could ever say Mike was beautiful, Mary thought. Not even ruggedly handsome, as was said about some men. The love of her life had a round face, a small, upturned nose, and regular kind of eyes—green, and always sparkling, even just before he died. They'd been his best feature, those eyes. Oh, and his unruly, thick black hair and truly huge eyebrows were memorable as well. Those brows got more and more bushy as Mike aged, and he wouldn't trim them. Or let Mary near them either!

She laughed just thinking about those crazy brows! "Makes me look like some kind of Mick Mongol, you know," He'd joke to her. "I need them to help scare the bad guys off."

"But, Mike, birds can perch on those things!"

"As long as they don't crap on my face," he'd say with a grin.

And the other features of the real man were also distinctly different than the plastic model next to Mary. Mike had a small mouth. Physically small, that is, but running most of his waking hours. Really, his mouth was even more bristly than his eyebrows.

And, as if the man's wild dreams weren't enough, he also talked in his sleep! He'd sit bolt upright in bed and say stuff out loud—crazy stuff. But it was always clear, no mumbling. Wherever you are now, Mary thought, I'm sure you're jabbering. Entrancing some people, pissing off a bunch of others. But who would you be talking to? People, ghosts, spirits?

Turning to the mannequin, she asked, "Where are you, Mike? And who are you with?"

More than once he'd said, "Lucky Emma took after you, Mary, y'know. She looked like me, she'd have been an old maid for sure."

And, yes, their daughter was pretty, and she had her namesake's, Emma Goldman's, anarchist spunk, which was what really counted.

Now, still climbing out of Salt Lake on 80, Mary began to think about stopping for the night. There were signs ahead for gas, restaurants and motels in a place called Coalville. Still part of the nicest landscape she'd seen since her trip began, lots of mountains and trees. Mary exited and began looking for a motel, pleased that she'd successfully navigated the bypass around Salt Lake. She was also pretty proud of her amazing bladder for holding out this long.

Whoa. She was suddenly really tired. Her stay in Vegas seemed days ago rather than just last night. But here was a funky little motel, the somewhat less than grand Grand Vista, right next door to a Los Caballeros Mexican restaurant. She'd check in, have a gin and tonic from her cooler, maybe even a cocktail at the restaurant, then fall into bed.

Pulling into the dusty motel parking lot, she almost drove up to the entrance portico before she remembered to pull out of view of the office and put Mike to rest under his blankie. Whoops!

"Good night, Mike. I love you. Or loved you! But sorry, no dummies allowed in this fine place." She tucked him in carefully.

Then backing up slowly, carefully, how long was this car anyway? Mary pulled up next to the office and went in to ring the bell for service. It was hard to hear over the noise of a TV in an adjoining room, and when no one came, she rang again. And then once more, taking a deep breath as she tried to be patient.

Finally, a man came in, smoking—was that even legal? In his sixties, and balding with a comb-over, which looked ridiculous. He was skinny too, with chicken arms hanging out of his wifebeater. A wifebeater, Mary thought, was this some kind of 1940s noir movie? Who still looks like this?

"Yes, ma'am? Need a room?" the man asked with the cigarette still in his mouth.

"Yes, I do, please. A single, just for the night."

"We're not busy, I can give you a double, much bigger bed, for just ten bucks more," he offered hopefully.

"No, thanks. A single will be fine. How much?"

"Let's see . . . with tax . . . fifty-seven eighty-two. Seasons starting to slow down, so that's a fall rate," he explained as he pulled out the paperwork.

"Fine, I'll take it. Visa OK?"

"Rather have cash," he suggested. "Damn card companies take a big bite out of my living."

"I know, I'm no fan either, but I don't carry that much cash," Mary handed over her card in a hurry to get away from the smoke.

"Don't suppose, traveling all alone and such. That's a fine car you got there, ma'am. Town Car?" he asked as he slowly ran her card.

"It is. It's old—an '89. But still runs well. Comfortable ride for my old bones."

Ignoring Mary's obvious desire to get a move on, the man went over to the window, still smoking, and looked out at the Lincoln. "Hey—white leather interior? I love those older Lincolns. Had a '79 Town Car myself, monster motor. Got about twelve miles per, but gas was a lot cheaper then. God that was a car, probably about nineteen feet long, I kid you not! Sure miss that ride."

"What happened to it?" Mary asked politely, wanting to leave, but he was still holding her card.

"Sign here, please," he said, finally handing her the slip and returning her card. "Yeah . . . loved that car, but one of my goddamn, pardon my French, kids ran it right into the ass end of one of them Winnebago motorhomes. Drunk. The kid, I mean."

"Oh, was he OK?" Mary handed the signed paper back to him.

"Yeah, just fine. Y'know how they say if you're drunk enough, your body stays loose and you don't get hurt? Well . . . that was him. Stupid kid! Car got totaled."

"I'm sorry to hear that. But say, which room am I in?" She held out her hand for a key.

"Seventeen. Here, a real key, not like them stupid cards they got in the motels nowadays. It's on the far side over there. Just park right in front of the room. And if you're hungry, you can try the Mexican joint next door. Not my kind of chow, but plenty people go there."

"Thanks," Mary headed eagerly for the door. As she was leaving, the man asked "Wouldn't want to sell that car, would you?" But she ignored him, got into the Lincoln and drove slowly to room seventeen. She let out a big sigh and reached over to pat Mike good night.

It was late afternoon really, with a fading fall sun. Mary put the key in the room's lock, opened the door, and turned on the light. A 'No Smoking' sign hung on the door, but the years of smoking in the room had left its stench, which brought another sigh. "Always ask to see the room first, Mary," she muttered as she dropped her bag on the bed. Well, she and Mike had both smoked, eons ago, so she could stand the smell for one night. Time to shower!

Chapter 18

Joni awoke with the sudden realization that someone was, or just had been, in her room. Right away she knew it had been that creepy little George.

"What in the fuck did he want?" she wondered under her breath.

Getting up, she placed the room's only chair with its back up against the bottom of the doorknob. That's what the kid was, a goddamn knob! And what did he want? The usual guy bullshit? To touch her, or failing that, handle her goddamn underwear? Something creepy, for sure. And now, of course, she couldn't go back to sleep and just lay there for the next hour or so until Patty knocked at her door.

Joni got up and got dressed. And, yes, her bra, panties, and socks were still there. Then she washed her face and brushed her teeth in the bathroom. Downstairs, she grabbed a travel mug of hot coffee and a fried egg sandwich from Patty and gave her a hug. Joni really liked her, she thought, as she thanked the woman for her hospitality and headed out to climb into Sam's monster semi, all warmed and ready. They rumbled out onto the highway, another freakin' adventure.

Sipping their coffees, eating the sandwiches, neither Joni nor Sam said a word for probably the first half hour. He had some radio station on with country music. Not Joni's favorite, but hey, it was his truck.

Sipping the last of his coffee, Sam looked over at Joni and asked, "Your dad? He still around?"

"Yeah. Sort of. Lives in the woods, real paranoid about cops, kind of hiding out."

"Oh. What's he done?" Sam wondered.

"Nothing, really. Used to booze it a lot, and got into trouble—fights mostly. But he's sober now. Just paranoid. That's it, the long and the short." Joni really didn't want to talk about Chet. She grimaced at a small flood of memories about her dad and his loony endeavors.

"Yeah," Sam noted. "My old man wasn't exactly a winner either. Got shot up in Korea and never got over it. They called it shell shock back then, now it's what they call PTSD. Same thing, where a soldier never really gets over being in combat, I guess."

"Guess so. My dad was never in the military, but he had a couple of drinking buddies who were in Vietnam. One, I think, was a chopper pilot. The other a gunner—y'know, the guys you see in movies shooting from the door of a helicopter? Chet, my dad? He could get crazy, but those guys? Totally out there. Nothing they wouldn't do when they got loaded," Joni elaborated. "I remember one time, both of them got some women's stuff, dresses and aprons from the Goodwill, put them on and went into the most badass bar in town. So, of course, the local dudes couldn't help saying stupid stuff. And then those Nam guys just started smashing the place up, beating the shit out of people, wrecking stuff . . . ."

"Jesus. Dresses? Why'd they do that?"

"I'm not sure. I think they just wanted to see what would happen. But they knew what would happen. Go figure." Joni made a wry smile.

"Well, my old man wasn't that far out. Mostly just a drunk. Had a hell of a time holding a job. Miner for a while, uranium in Utah. We lived in some Podunk place out in the desert. Working there probably shortened his life by a chunk. He died in his early fifties. Course the booze didn't help either. He drove truck for a while, some logging, and then at the end he worked bagging people's groceries in the town where I went to high school. Man, that was embarrassing." Sam winced at the memory.

"And your mom?" Joni asked.

"She tried. Did her best, I guess. But she liked the booze too, so the worse the old man got, the more time she spent at the bars. Hung in there a lot longer than he did though, died in her early seventies."

"Any sisters or brothers?" Joni continued.

"A brother, but he's dead. He didn't want to go to Vietnam, so he starved himself down to nothing. Looked like those people in the Nazi camps by the time he went before his draft board. They knew what he was up to, but couldn't do squat about it. Couldn't force-feed him; fatten him up for the Cong to kill. Trouble was, he got sick from being so thin, so wasted. So every goddamn thing that came along after that, he got. Stuck it out till he was forty, got the flu bad, then pneumonia, and it took him."

"Were you in the service?"

"Nope, lucky me, my feet are flatter 'n a board. Never knew it till I went in for my physical—and, stupid me, I was disappointed. All gung ho to go over there and kick some gook ass. Guess you could say my feet saved my bacon!" Sam looked over at her and grinned. "There's a guy in Wamsutter who works the rigs, he was in Nam. He's got all kinds of stories. Said he worked with some guy who talked all the time about his time over there, blah, blah, blah. Had a couple of Purple Hearts he bragged about, but then he got killed in a motorcycle accident. His pals in Wamsutter contacted the military and told them he should get a real soldier's funeral, twenty-one guns and all that. Funeral home kept him in the cooler waiting for the government to get off its fat ass. Then a letter, all official, finally came. Guess what?"

"Can't guess," Joni shook her head.

"The guy was never in the Marines, or anything else. Can you beat that?" Sam turned to her for emphasis. "When the draft was on? Nobody wanted to go, did shit like my brother to stay the hell out. But once the war was over, and there were all those hero movies about it, all of a sudden all kinds of people were braggin' about being there. Shit, you can buy all the medals you want in any truck stop. I'll show you when we stop later."

"One of Dad's buddies, one of the guys in a dress, said that most guys over there never saw combat other than a bar fight. And those are usually the guys who got the license plates bragging about being a Vietnam veteran."

"Yeah," Sam agreed. "Those are probably the guys that changed the sheets on the colonel's bed, loaded shit off and on planes, and cooked crappy food in the mess hall. Who knows? I'm just glad I missed out, believe me!" Sam downshifted as they approached a slight rise in the highway, the huge diesel engine rumbling in response.

Joni agreed, "I never really thought about it, I guess, but a couple of girls in my high-school class went in the military. Navy or Air Force. I don't know. I think one of them might still be in, but the other one came back pretty messed up. Main combat she had, she told me, was fighting off all the asshole guys she worked with. Officers were the worst of all, she said, basically expected her to put out. Why else had she enlisted, they asked her. I mean, come on, obviously they were just looking for a way to get out of town, maybe get some money for school, right?"

"Bastards. What? There aren't any hookers over there in the desert, women all veiled and shit, so female troops are fair game? Can't stand guys trying to take advantage." Sam said as he hit the dash for emphasis.

"Yeah," Joni agreed less emphatically, thinking of Sam's son George and his midnight foray into her room. The little creep!

Changing the subject, Sam asked her if she'd ever ridden in a big rig before.

"No, never," Joni replied. "Pickup truck, sure, but no—wait a minute. I caught a ride out to my dad's place once in a logging truck. The kind with the big boom on the back?"

"I never drove one of those. This isn't a bad gig. Pays well. Pretty safe except when there's ice on the road. Then, whoops, there you go into the median, or off in a field or something. Scary shit, but it's never happened to me, knock wood," he said, tapping his forehead with a fist.

Sam had turned the radio way down while they were talking, but now turned it up again. More country-western stuff. Yuck.

Feeling sleepy, and feeling even more like she wanted to tune out the station, Joni said, “Hey, Sam, I’m wasted. Still recovering from that long drive, I guess. Mind if I catch forty while you drive?”

“No, go ahead,” he said. “But don’t try it there, just climb into the sleeper in the back. That’s what it’s for. Get some serious zee’s in there, kid.” He motioned to the large, dark space behind him.

“Thanks, don’t mind if I do. Wake me whenever, OK?” Joni climbed into the sleeper and dropped off within moments, a song about a pickup truck echoing in the background.

Chapter 19

Mary woke with a serious headache. Where'd that come from? As she brushed her teeth and stared at herself in the bathroom mirror, she began to put last night's events together. She'd showered, changed her slacks, and put on a top she had from Mexico to wear to the restaurant next to the motel. The place turned out to be very noisy, and totally full, so she had to wait at the bar for a table.

"Table for one, señora?" asked the very non-Hispanic girl seating folks. "I'm sorry, but you'll have to wait a little."

God, Mary thought. She hated "table for one," which was why she never went out by herself back in L.A. At the bar, where she took a stool, she told the young, good-looking bartender how to make her a Mexican martini. A couple ounces reposado tequila, an ounce or so of Cointreau, fresh lime juice, and fresh orange juice. He didn't have fresh juice, so it came out of a jug in the fridge. "Oh, and a little bit of olive juice and two olives, please," Mary added. He did it as she asked, more or less, as busy as he was. Good kid, she thought. Bet the drink even intrigued him a little. Mary downed it quickly and had ordered another just when the girl arrived to seat her.

Mary got a tiny booth in a corner, which was perfect. The waitress, also not remotely Latina, brought her the new martini. And Mary ordered a chile relleno and a side of beans. "Not refried, just plain beans in a bowl with onions and green chile, please."

Now, the next morning, looking at herself in the bathroom mirror and feeling her aching head, Mary realized she'd sat in that restaurant and gotten thoroughly potted. Potted because she'd actually had one more martini with her dinner. Heck, she'd told herself, I can handle my booze, and I sure don't want to go back to that motel room and try to watch some crappy TV. She'd thought she was simply enjoying the noisy crowd, all white people, not a Mexican in the bunch.

But truthfully, she was just drinking and feeling sorry about being alone. Drunk, but fully upright, she had luckily gotten back to her room. She remembered she wanted badly to hear some music and to dance, so got her screechy little portable tape player out of the Lincoln and brought it into the room. Then she went and got Mike out of the car, hauling her silent companion in as well. She put in that Nina Simone tape, and began swaying around the room, with the mannequin in her arms, to some of her and Mike's favorites. "I Put a Spell on You" and "Don't Smoke in Bed," and another of her favorites, Billie Holiday's "Don't Explain," a real weeper. Halfway through that wonderful song, she dropped Mike on the floor and fell into bed, crying herself to sleep. Yes, it was all, painfully, coming back to her.

Silly old woman, she thought, as she took some aspirin. Was this trip such a good idea after all? Well, she was committed at this point. Time to pack it up and head out for the day. But she'd better call home first. She knew she'd be in trouble there, having promised Emma she would call every evening.

And sure enough, there was a message, "Hey, Mom. Where are you? You said you'd call, and you've missed at least twice now. Am I worried about you? Of course I am! Mom, call me, will you?"

Feeling not nearly as guilty as Emma probably would have wanted her to, Mary called her daughter's cell, knowing she'd be in class and unable to answer. "Hi, honey, sorry I didn't call. It was late when I got in to the motel. Then after I showered, with good intentions of calling, I just fell asleep without even getting under the covers. Sorry, honey. Promise I'll call tonight. And I'm fine, by the way."

Not exactly true, but she wasn't sick, just a little heartsick. And the Dreadnaught was running fine. The guy in the motel even wanted to buy it. All right, time to move on, old lady. Move on out of this little burg. She needed to get back on the highway, she and her mannequin.

Mary eased the big car back out onto 80. Hey, she was eighty too! All systems a bit fuzzy this morning, so no music for a while. Not after last night. She had to remember to call Theresa when she stopped next for gas. Uh-oh, she probably should have filled up back in Coalville before she left this morning. She would have to watch the gauge; she could probably go at least a hundred miles and check the oil when she stopped.

It was nice countryside as she left Coalville, a wide valley on both sides of the highway with lots of cattle and horses on ranches or farms. What was the difference between a ranch and a farm anyway? Well, Theresa certainly had a farm, not a ranch. But out here, maybe it would be a ranch?

As Mary drove, things leveled out again into more desert, desolate and bleak. This was no place to have a breakdown. No place to travel at night either. It probably wasn't really so bleak if you knew what to look for, she thought as she remembered all the desert plants she'd used in her landscape designs, and in her own gardens. Walk out there, away from the highway and the stupid billboards, and you'd probably find some good things to look at.

Plants. So much easier to deal with than people. So much more likely to survive climate change than most of humanity. What was that figure she'd seen recently, about what a tiny percentage of Earth's mass all forms of life occupy? Less than one percent, if she remembered right. Which means people, even in the billions, are a miniscule percentage.

"Hey, Mike," Mary said turning to her companion. "Remember how mad you'd get at the climate-change deniers?"

God, even some of her fellow landscapers argued that the drought in the West was just a normal occurrence. Don't worry, they'd say, things will turn around again soon. But Emma told her, time and again, that the only "normal" thing was for civilized human beings to go on about their daily business while the vast systems they depended on collapsed around them. Mesopotamians digging out canals in the desert that had silted in hundreds, if not thousands, of times due to bad ag practices. Easter Islanders carving yet more massive statues as their resources dwindled to rats and a few bird eggs. Americans plowing up the fragile grasslands of the Great Plains, only to watch them vanish into dust in less than a generation. Mayans farming fragile hillsides until all the soil was gone and the whole thing collapsed!

And now, here Mary was in Wyoming, site of the world's largest open-pit mine—coal, of course. Digging out vast tons of the black stuff to be shipped on trains to the East, where it was burned to create electricity for people to microwave junk food and watch TV, creating massive carbon emissions.

"You would really hate to see this carbon catastrophe, my dear," Mary said aloud to Mike.

But, after all, there was nothing she could do about it right now. She needed to focus her energy on this trip, miles zipping by. She planned to stop for gas at that next town, Wamsutter. That was a strange name. And what a very bleak place, she thought as she exited the interstate. She found a gas station just off the freeway and pulled up.

A kid came over and asked if he could "fill 'er up?" Mary rolled down her window and replied, "Sure, and check the oil, 5W-30, will you, please?" Going in to the station, Mary noticed the very large sign warning that only paying customers could use the bathroom. And then, the sign inside the restroom asking help in keeping it clean. "Well, somebody has time on their hands," she thought. Stopping at the counter to pay, the pleasant woman with big hair asked Mary where she was headed.

"Minnesota," Mary answered.

"Hey," the attendant replied. "There must be a run on for that state. Young girl came in yesterday going there too. Her old car crapped out so she spent the night, heading for Nebraska this morning with my old man in his rig. Don't remember exactly where she was going, or I'd give you a couple small boxes of her stuff to haul for her," the woman smiled. "Someplace to do with cancer, I think."

"Could be the Mayo Clinic, in Rochester, but who knows?" Mary gave the woman her Visa card. She had no intention of taking anyone's crap with her.

"Yeah, that was it, Rochester. But she didn't leave an address, so probably not a good idea for you to haul it. How would you find her anyway?" The woman ran Mary's card.

"Right." Mary responded absentmindedly.

"That's OK," the woman said. "Told her I'd send the stuff when she got settled and sent me an address. Speaking of cars, that's a nice old Lincoln you got there."

"Old is right," Mary nodded in agreement. "It's an '89, solid though, and real comfortable. Perfect old-lady car," Mary smiled as she signed the credit card slip.

"Don't mind my asking," the woman said, "how old are you?"

Mary grimaced, "Eighty, actually, and counting."

"Really, you got to be kidding! Don't look a bit of it!" The woman smiled. Nice smile, Mary thought. Nice person, but too chatty. Probably bored silly in this godforsaken place.

"Thanks, but I *am* eighty, and nothing to do about it either. Bye now." Mary picked up her receipt and started out, followed by the woman yelling after her in jest, "Don't get lost in Wamsutter. Big place, you know!"

At the car, Mary was pleased to note the boy had washed her windows . . . all of them. He came out of the garage and said the oil was fine.

"Not much on big iron, ma'am, but that's a beauty!" he said, touching a fender.

"Thanks, it is." she agreed, climbing in and hoping that the young man had not seen Mike. But so what if he had.

She drove away from the station, not back to the highway, but toward the south of town until she found a spot next to a huge compound filled with all kinds of machinery. Nobody around, so she got out and went to the passenger side to set Mike up properly, as she'd just more or less dumped the dummy into its seat when she left the motel. She seatbelted him in and put his cap on at a rakish angle. What irony, Mike had rarely worn hats, even in the blazing sun. Said they made his head itch, and reminded him of his time in the Army Air Corps when hats were mandatory. "Too bad, buddy," she said as she got behind the wheel, "got to have a lid on now, my man!"

And then she *did* get lost, kind of, as she tried to get back to the freeway, which she could see easily just a few blocks to the north. She saw several other enormous machinery yards en route, and several trailer courts—just empty spaces filled with an odd assortment of trailer houses and RVs of all ages, including an old Airstream. Then there was a trailer sitting by itself, dubiously labeled the Wamsutter Library. Just further on, was a space with a sign declaring it the site of a "Future Supermarket." Another space proclaimed "Pecos Bar and Grill: Coming Soon." And just before the highway, she saw the Coastal Supply Company.

"Coastal?" Mary wondered. The sign said the store carried oil-field supplies, including Carhartts and Red Wing Shoes, which Mary remembered came from Minnesota.

Finally back on 80, Mary encountered many more bleak and boring miles. About the only visible distraction being trains, incredibly long and astonishingly slow. Did they ever reach their destination? Or were they ghost trains, forever moving to nowhere, visible only to people in the last stages of life? Now there was a gloomy notion to be discarded before it took hold.

"Start thinking like that, Mary," she said out loud, "and you might just as well take the nearest road out into the desert and give it up."

Both Mary and Theresa had been frightened of ghosts as little kids in their creaky old house in Chicago. Once their father had told them how it had been an old farmhouse out in the country, moved to its location on the South Side just before the Steins bought it. And since it had maybe been built when there were still Indians in Illinois, the girls had started to conjure up all sorts of ghostly beings when they went to bed at night.

Konrad didn't help when he made occasional raids into their room, whooping like a movie native. That fright didn't last long, maybe just one summer, Mary remembered. Maybe it was just a way to beat the boredom, with both parents at work and the house empty. This was before the television when there were just board games, Monopoly especially, and endless bike rides to the nearby park, circling round and round, believe it or not, a statue of an Indian.

And once in a great while their Mother would let them come to work with her, which was a great change of summer pace. They would get up early, hurry breakfast, and take the bus to Halstead to the tiny storefront that housed the electric business where Mom was the secretary, bookkeeper, and Gal Friday.

It had a big, dirty window in front with small lettering . . . surprising how much she could remember, Mary thought. Anast Electrical. If you peered through the window, you'd vaguely see an astonishing clutter of wire, radios, lamps, and toasters, not to mention boxes filled with tubes, light bulbs, junction boxes, and any number of other things unknown. Tools—pliers, small hammers, wire-pullers—were strewn about. And the small counter was likewise covered with stuff, including a thick coating of dust. Then behind that, what had to be Chicago's tiniest office, a small, very dark place with a single buzzing fluorescent light overhead, and a gooseneck desk lamp from the early days of electricity working about as well as the dim overhead.

That was Mom's office, where the girls would sit on the floor and color, or be given some old gadget to take apart and try to put back together. Just across from the office, a tiny toilet with its permanently stained bowl beside a dripping faucet. It was often short on T.P. so the girls more than once had to use napkins from their mom's desk instead. They always brought lunch in a brown paper bag, usually a PB & J sandwich, apple, and cookie, times three. After she left home, Mary refused anything peanut-butter based—sandwiches, cookies, ice cream—saying she'd had more than her fair share as a child.

Beyond the office was an open area packed with still more parts and tools of the electrician's trade. This led to a large double-door that opened on an alley, where the boss, Mr. Alexis Anast, parked the company car. The car too was filled to overflowing with tools and supplies. Mary knew that car was also the only transportation for Mr. Anast's family of five, so she'd asked her Mom once how they could, for example, get to church in such a dirty car?

"I don't know, dear. That's their business."

Their mother, Gertrude, had gotten her job because both Ernst Stein and Mr. Anast were members of the KCs, the Knights of Columbus.

Let's see, Mary thought as she drove, family history? Might as well occupy my mind with that during this boring drive, then see if Theresa will have any of the same memories. The story was, more or less, that Dad's work as a housepainter was insufficient to pay all the bills, so just after Mary was born her mother went to work. Her first job was at a local funeral parlor they were connected to via church. What was the name of that place? Mary couldn't remember. Mom didn't like working there, though, too spooky and the owner too demanding for the scant pay she got.

Somehow Anast had found out about her plight, and offered her the job at his place. His shop had never had a real secretary. Though she'd tried to help, Mrs. Anast's native language was Greek, so she couldn't type English, and her math skills were subpar. So Gertrude took the job she'd hold for more than forty years. There was nothing much else available to a woman with only a high-school education back then. Besides, their mother wasn't a risk-taker by any means. She was just grateful she had a job at all and that she got along well with the Anasts.

One time of great anxiety for Mary's family had been when Old Man Anast began to slowly turn the business over to his son Gregory, who Gertrude thought was not remotely up to the responsibility of the shop. She had cherished the elder Mr. Anast, and she worried Gregory couldn't handle the work itself, and more importantly, the customers. For months, it was the topic of many conversations at the Stein supper table.

"And I don't want you to say a word about this to anyone, you girls understand?" Gertrude would admonish them, Ernst busily nodding agreement from the head of the table, and adding an unnecessary, "Not a word!"

Mary smiled as she remembered, who did they think we were going to tell?

Who at school or church or in the park cared about Anast Electrical? But they were always being told as children, mostly by their anxious mother, to not repeat anything they heard at the family dinner table. A rule they mostly followed, because none of it was a bit interesting. Unlike the Victory Garden some neighbors planted in the empty lot across the street during the war, which was *really* interesting. Their parents didn't participate, too busy and not at all interested in growing stuff. But Konrad and the girls did, helping whenever they could with whatever they could. Maybe that's where Mary caught the bug for growing things, and her lifelong love of plants?

Six or more local families had gardened there, one of them being some terribly exotic Italians! Mary couldn't remember their name, something with a D . . . D'Amato, Di Tomasso, who knew? Maybe DiTomato since the family's mother grew great tomatoes. Ernst didn't really approve of Italians, but he'd admit they had gardening prowess when he snuck across the street to peer at the garden, or enjoy the paper bag Mary and Theresa would bring home filled with the largest tomatoes anyone in their family had ever seen.

The girls also played hide-and-seek in the gardens, racing around in the squash and cucumbers, peering out from behind trellises bursting with peas or beans, and routinely being yelled at by the adults working there. Not exactly a trip to the circus, but at least it wasn't as boring as so much of the rest of their lives. Boring Catholic school with boring old nuns, boring piano lessons with a cranky old nun, and boring morning Mass with the priest spouting Latin in his high-pitched, tremulous old voice.

Mary remembered her mother eventually admitted that Gregory Anast, the young whippersnapper did amazingly well taking over the electric shop, despite her dire predictions. Mary's mother always talked about him being so young, but now that she thought about it, he was probably middle-aged at the time, which meant he was likely closer to her mother's age than his father had been. She must have just been so unsettled since he was younger than the boss she was used to.

Mary thought Gregory had even given her mother a salary bump, probably a small gesture to gain her confidence, since he needed her to keep things running. He had also brought his own three girls into the place on a number of summer weekends to actually clean it up, bringing some order and light to the previous jumble. Her mother had described the girls as spoiled before that, which maybe was just a bit of jealousy that they had more than her own girls.

She remembered how odd it seemed that although her mother had always complained about the mess, when Gregory and his daughters cleaned it up, she didn't like that either. Likely just her reaction to so much change all at once. Then she'd come home worrying that one of those too-cute girls was going to end up taking her place in the office too.

But her mother's anxiety must have clouded her judgment, because the Anast girls went from high school straight on to college. It didn't take too long before Mary's mother settled in again and really began to be happy in the cleaner, more-organized version of her job. She worked there until she retired, so all of her initial fears must have been unfounded, Mary thought.

Thinking now as she drove about the odd significance a parent's job can play in their children's memories of childhood, Mary wondered if the Anast daughters had also grown up with much of the adult dinner conversation focused on that tiny business? Then she remembered a time two of the Anast crew, a couple of older men, had come to the Stein house on a weekend to do some long-overdue wiring for Mary's family. They must have come on the weekend so the regular rates wouldn't apply. And, of course, young Gregory gave the Steins a big break on the wire and switches too. Mary's father Ernst, quite pleased with the arrangement, had gone out and bought some beer for the workers. This story was committed to memory since it had become family legend!

Not a drinker himself, Mary's dad had followed a friend's advice and bought two six-packs. But because he didn't drink, Ernst gave the beer to the crew as soon as they arrived at the house. Welcome, welcome, have some beer! Long story short, the men started drinking and wiring at the same time. With the long-lasting result being that the switch at the bottom of the stairs did not turn the stair light on, but instead turned on the light in the bathroom. You could turn the stair light on with the switch at the top though, and so it went for about eight different lights.

Gertrude was furious at her hapless husband, but never in a million would she even think of telling Gregory about what happened, or asking for it to be fixed. So the Stein switches and lights stayed that way until their father's death. The incident went down in family lore as a means of describing pretty much any giant mess with poor decision-making and a side of drinking. Mary laughed out loud even now by herself in the car just thinking about how ridiculous it was.

War in Vietnam? "Stein wiring job!" Mary and Mike would say.

Unnecessary freeway construction project that fixes nothing? "Stein wiring!" And so on.

Mary suddenly noticed signs for Cheyenne, her last big stop in Wyoming, thank the Lord. Slowing near the city, she decided to wait to pull off for gas outside of what looked like a busy downtown area. Passing a truly enormous—blocks long—and very dirty-looking structure on the north side. Probably a refinery, she thought, and right in the middle of a big city. What was that about?

Then she saw another very large building, the Sierra Trading Post, what was that? But, ah finally, a sign for a Campstool Road exit with a very big Pilot truck stop in view on the other side of the highway. Mary exited, pulled next to a pump, and got out to fill up. When she was done, she hung up the nozzle, grabbed the receipt, and went inside to pee. It was a huge place, but she found the women's bathroom right away.

Coming out, she paused to grab a small bag of Fritos, paid and headed back to the car, opening the bag on the way.

Closing the Lincoln's driver's door, Mary had a slight shiver of apprehension immediately verified by the frightening feel of a sharp object on the back of her neck. A snarky male voice, high-pitched and nasty, behind her said, "Hey, old lady, nice move with your dead guy in the seat there. Too bad it didn't scare me off. Did it?" He then pressed the knife, or whatever it was, tighter into her neck.

"N-no, I guess it didn't," Mary replied shakily. "What do you want? And please, get that thing off my neck." This was really bad!

"What do I want? Just about every goddamn thing I don't have, how about a house, car, wedding ring—nah, forget the ring. But a car would be good, and looks like I got me one here, don't it, granny? I'm in charge now so," his voice dropped to a whiny kind of hum, "you, grans, are just gonna put your key in that ignition and move us on out of here. Slow and careful, got it?"

"I do. But where are we going?" Mary asked with more than just a slight quaver in her voice. She thought suddenly about how someone, who was it, had wanted her to take a pistol with her, just to scare people off?

Pulling out onto the highway, Mary felt the object on her neck removed and she relaxed just a little. Who was this person? What did he want? Stupid thoughts raced, like glad I peed or I'd be doing it now!

"So, gran," the nasty voice resumed. Mary didn't dare look at the mirror to see his face. "We're gonna stay on this freakin' road. Fucking Campstool, what a stupid name. Then head north right under 80. You got it? Then we get down the road just a bit, and you're gonna turn when I tell you, so don't crank it, OK? Just nice and slow. Once we're down that road, we're gonna stop at like some really remote spot, you got it? And then I take this great old ride and whatever you got—money, food, dope. Bet you ain't got any kind of dope, right? No Vicodin or oxy for you, old lady. Right?"

"No, sorry," Mary said, wondering why she was apologizing. "Just aspirin, but what happens to me with my car gone?"

"Well, that's for you to worry about, gran, since I'm just now making up my mind what to do with you. Kill you? Dispose of your old body someplace they won't find it for like ten years. Or just leave and let you do whatever you got to do to get some help, but then of course you tell the fuzz what I look like, blah, blah. That's not cool, now is it? Guess we're just going to have to take it as it comes," he said, giggling now in his strange, strangled voice.

Now Mary was, if possible, even more scared. What would Mike do, she asked herself? Something crazy and desperate she figured, that's what. Probably getting himself, or them, badly hurt or killed. So . . . what should *she* do?

"Hey, gran, slow down and turn on whatever is the next right. And nothing fancy to attract no cops, got it?" he snarled, pushing the sharp object back into her neck.

Crazy, she thought, or maybe high? Which was bad, or could be good if he was really out of it. Who knew though?

"You don't have to kill me, you know? What glory is there in hurting an old lady like me?" Mary asked. "Who are you going to brag to about that? You must have a mom or a granny like me yourself. You wouldn't want anyone to hurt them, would you?"

"Wrong, bitch!" He came back at her with venom in his voice. "If I ever saw either one of those stinkin' women again, they'd be fuckin' dead. Slow like, as in roasting over a goddamn barbecue pit. Instead, my guess is they're both roastin' in hell, no fucking doubt!"

Well that was a mistake, Mary realized. Now what? Best shut up, she thought, listening to the man's odd wheezing breath, and some slight sound of . . . what? . . . was he mumbling to himself?

Driving on the deserted road for what seemed forever, but what was probably only fifteen minutes, Mary finally passed a right turn onto a gravel road.

"Hey! Whoa, old lady. Stop and back up!" her captor demanded.

Mary stopped and turned around in the middle of the road since there was still no traffic either way. Not good!

"OK, turn there," he barked. "Into that gravel pit! And hurry the fuck up and stop the car!"

This also wasn't good, he was getting nastier. Now what, Mary wondered?

"All right, sweetheart. Here's where we part ways," he announced from behind her. "And me still not sure what to do with your old bones. Don't worry, I'm not into fucking old ladies, just taking their shit! Gimme those goddamn keys. I gotta piss like a racehorse. Then we'll just see what I'm going to do with you." He grabbed the keys from her and got out. Then waved what turned out to be a very small knife at her window threateningly.

A Swiss Army blade, Mary thought, could that thing really hurt her?

Beginning to get hold of her panic, Mary got a good look at the skinny little white man with his butt crack showing above some ragged jeans as he shuffled away from the car. Nasty man. But what could she do? Certainly not just sit there waiting to be killed, or whatever.

Gently pounding the steering wheel in her fear and frustration, Mary suddenly remembered the extra set of keys she kept in the cup-holder in the middle of the front seat. Carefully . . . very carefully . . . shaking as she opened the lid of the device, Mary reached inside for them without turning her face away from the window. She kept her eyes on the man as he stood there urinating and ranting something unintelligible.

Glory be! The keys! She had them in her hand, but he was coming back toward her. Without looking down she put the key into the ignition. Whoops, dammit! The wrong one. OK, the other must be the ignition key. Yes. In, turn, start the car, and put it in gear!

Oh god, he heard the motor and started running toward her, screaming as he stumbled-ran.

Not hesitating, Mary aimed the Dreadnaught right at him.

"Go ahead, Mary," she told herself, "he might kill you!"

And then suddenly he was right there grabbing the door handle, screaming at her. "Fucking bitch, I'll kill you!"

She knew it was time to hit the accelerator and spin the big machine around. God, the door was starting to open. Mary hit the gas again, speeding right through a pile of brush. Then there was a thump as she careened over a big lump of dirt or something, and the car lurched through the bushes.

Jesus, Mary, and Joseph—now the driver's door was swinging wide open, him still hanging on and screaming as Mary gave it more gas. This was crazy. She had to knock him off, get him off the car!

With the Lincoln lurching crazily, the door suddenly slammed closed again and the man hit the ground. Mary swung the car around in the direction she'd come from, gave it the gas and zoomed across the pit toward the road. Glancing briefly in the mirror, she saw the skinny thug standing there throwing something, rocks or dirt, toward the car. In vain. His screams, however, stayed with her for several miles down the road.

It was just noise she told herself, just silly noise from a nightmare. Go back to sleep, Mary, because this couldn't be real, not a bit of it. But, oh God, this was not a bad dream, she thought as panic rose in her throat, this was the real thing! A rushing sound filled her ears as she tried to focus on getting back to the freeway. Drive as fast as you dare for as long as you can, she told herself. Drive, drive, drive.

And that's just what Mary did. Shaking for a very, very long time, she kept her hands gripped on the wheel and her eyes focused straight ahead. In some part of her very frightened mind she realized that the sensible thing to do would be to stop and calm down. But she couldn't, because another, more urgent, voice kept telling her to drive as fast and as far as she could to get away from everything that had just happened.

So she drove until her bladder hurt so bad it was giving her a stomachache, meaning either a toilet or wet underwear was in her near future. Happily, it was the former. It was the most welcome rest stop she'd ever encountered, just across the border in Nebraska. She slowed down, pulled into a parking spot, and shut the car off. Then she started to shake uncontrollably. Started to weep uncontrollably too, wrapping her arms around herself and rocking a bit to calm down before she could even open the car door.

"OK, Mary," she said. "You're not a weeper, so let's just calm down so you can go into the restroom and pee." Still shaking, she opened the car door and shut it carefully as she looked around her. Then she stood very still and locked the car, repeatedly pushing the button to make sure the doors were actually locked.

Inside, she peed. Torrents, it seemed. Then at a sink, she ran warm water on her face again and again. Of course, there were no towels, just those lousy blowers, so Mary grabbed a big handful of toilet paper to wipe her face. Once dry, she stood and held onto the sink, closing her eyes until she felt steady. Then she walked slowly back to the car to unlock the door. She still couldn't stop shaking.

Once in, she locked the doors again and sat still for a moment. Then she remembered the second set of keys. The blessed set of keys. Emma and everyone else had told her it was silly to have an extra set of keys *in* the car. "Mom," Emma had insisted, "they have to be *outside the car* in case you lock the main ones *in* the car. Just get one of those magnets so you can hide them under the fender." But those keys in the car had probably saved her life. A small point, but just enough evidence of her competence to remind her that she could still make this trip.

Feeling like her head was finally beginning to clear, Mary wondered what the prudent next step should be. Should she contact the police? Probably not since she'd lose a day or more filling out forms, getting checked at a clinic, and raise the alarm that she couldn't finish the trip alone. That crazy guy was certainly a predator, but she never even got a good look at him. Couldn't identify him at all, really, just as a nasty, skinny little asshole. She could certainly remember that horrid voice of his, but she intended to block that memory out entirely. Turning to the useless plastic man beside her, she said, "I need to get out of here. I am too old for this shit. Somebody else is going to have to deal with that miserable man!"

Mary got back on the road determined to leave all that had happened in her rearview mirror. She needed to put a few more exits between her and that man, and then she'd pull off and get some coffee to steel her for the rest of the drive. Black, forget the sugar and fake milk. It was time to start paying attention!

Chapter 20

When Theresa got the call from Mary that night, she wasn't sure why, but she knew something was wrong.

"Are you OK?" she asked her sister.

"I'm fine. Why are you asking?" Mary said firmly.

"I'm not sure. I guess you sounded a little shaky. Long day?"

"Well . . . I'm eighty, shaky goes with the territory, and this *is* a long drive. I'm fine. I should be there in a couple of days."

"OK." Theresa still felt anxious. "Mary? Be careful, please. There are all kinds of bad people out there. On TV last night there was a report about a woman up in Minneapolis who was abducted right outside a grocery store. So please, dear, no hitchhikers or anything like that. Oh, and call your daughter! She's worried about you."

"I know, I know," Mary sounded tired, but less defensive. "I'm calling her right after this. I'll see you soon, Ms. Tee."

Something was wrong with Mary, Theresa knew it. All these years apart from her sister and yet there was still something fundamental between them. Some sort of deep understanding going back to their childhood. They had both known more or less at the same time, she remembered with a pang, when their brother was dying. Mary, by far the less sentimental sister, generally pooh-poohed such things. But Theresa did not.

Right after Tony died, she'd seen him very clearly, down in the barn. He was facing away from her, feeding a calf, but she knew him right away. It frightened her, but she stayed, watching him do something he'd loved. Finished with the calf, he turned and smiled at her, and was gone. She'd seen him four or five times over the years, by the woodpile, in the garden, leaning on a fence watching the goats, but never in the house. Was that because she and Lute had slept together, she wondered?

After Konrad died, she did see him in her house, smoking on the porch one wintry morning. He turned slowly to look at her, then disappeared, cigarette and all. Was there a faint trace of tobacco smoke in the air?

When Mary got here, Theresa would ask her about Mike. Had she seen him since his death? Mary would probably scoff. Something was definitely amiss with her sister, but there was really no way to find out until she got there. And Theresa would never worry Emma by asking her. Like her aunt, Emma was a born worrier: There's a cloud in that bright-blue horizon somewhere, and if not now, there would be one soon.

Well, Theresa thought, I sure need some company. That was another difference between the sisters. Mary had few friends as a child. It hadn't been that she wasn't liked, she just didn't seek people out. She was always a little aloof, and as an adult she said quite plainly that she mostly preferred plants to people. But not Theresa, she needed to talk. In fact, she should find someone to distract her from worrying about Mary. Luther! She'd go over there and help him gather produce for the Winona Farmer's Market. Maybe even go there with him on Saturday?

Lute's house might be literally over the hill, she thought as she headed down the road, but she herself was still holding on pretty well. Some arthritis in her hands, and she moved a little slower than before, but she was basically of sound mind and body.

She'd worn glasses since she was ten and had moved on to bifocals about fifteen years ago. But that wasn't unusual for someone her age. And her hearing had been twenty-twenty, or whatever was considered good, at her last checkup.

She weighed a bit more than she had when she was young, but nothing notable. She figured she'd probably stay a small woman until she passed on, unless something drastic happened. The list of opportunities for something "drastic" was pretty long and she tried to turn her brain away from the golden opportunity to worry. What if people not only gained weight as they aged, she wondered as she caught sight of Luther in his yard, but grew taller? Now there's someone who's taller than average. A *lot* taller, she thought, smiling!

Luther greeted her warmly, "Hey, Theresa, and Mose! Thanks for bringing the pup, reminds me to get on the ball about getting another dog before winter. You know what a pain it is to house-train one, and it's a hell of a lot worse with snow on the ground."

"Have you started looking?" Theresa asked as they watched her dog sniff around the yard.

"Yeah. Got on the Internet last night, but felt guilty as hell about it with Azteca not cold yet, you know?" He looked forlorn.

"She'd forgive you." Theresa touched Luther's arm. "*Is* forgiving you, depending on what you think about a dog's afterlife."

"I've often thought that if there is a heaven, it should be for animals since they almost always behave better than humans!" Luther smiled at the notion. "Y'know, I was wondering after Azteca died, do you think dogs dream?"

"Of course," Theresa replied immediately. "Mose chases stuff in his sleep, legs moving like crazy, little noises he makes." She rubbed her dog's head.

"Yeah, all my dogs did that. But what do they dream about?" Luther wondered, reaching over to pat Mose also.

Theresa chuckled, "I don't know for sure, but I imagine it's like us, stuff from our waking life all jumbly when we're sleeping. Rabbits, squirrels, deer, other dogs, and cats. Maybe we show up in there once in a while. But I'll ask Father Terence about dog heaven."

"Right," Luther snorted. "I dare you! He'll shit a Catholic brick right there in the vestry!"

"So." Theresa changed the subject. "I actually came over to help you with the market if you could use me, not to argue theology—as pleasant as that can be with a skeptic like yourself. Can I pitch in? I really need something to do. Mary called a while ago and sounded a little spooky, but of course told me she's just fine. Since there's nothing I can do about it until she gets here, I need a distraction." She grimaced.

"Should you call her daughter?" Luther asked.

"Not a bit of it!" Theresa was emphatic. "Emma is a worse worrier than me, or so Mary has always said. She didn't want her mom to take this trip in the first place. No, I just have to wait until she shows up to get the details."

"Hey, relax, lady," Luther put his arm around her. "She'll be fine. But until then, you can help me. Hey! Cut that out!" he hollered at Mose, who was facing off with one of his ancient barn cats.

"Mose, c'mere!" Theresa demanded of her errant dog. "Come on, leave the cat alone!" The dog slowly, reluctantly, turned and trotted dutifully back to them, his head down.

"Hell, I wasn't worried about that cat," Luther reassured Theresa. "I was worried Mose would get his nose torn off. That cat's a serious fighter, got into it many times with Azteca until the dog finally left her alone. Thinks she's a tiger!"

"Maybe in a former life she was!" Theresa grinned.

"Happy to have your help. We can talk while we work," Luther turned and strode—he really never walked anywhere—to one of his gardens.

Theresa hurried after him, Mose beside her.

Once they reached the garden, Luther laid out the plan. "OK, here's the deal for today. For the last of the tomatoes, or almost the last, pick a lot of the green ones so I can let them ripen upstairs in the house. Then we pick squash, some pumpkins, although it's a little early to sell them, cabbage and other brassicas like broccoli and cauliflower. Then bunches of kale and chard, and some early beets. Oh, and potatoes, always potatoes. Then eggplant . . . the list goes on."

"Eggplant—how about I start with those? You always have such interesting kinds. I like to check them all out."

"OK, they're down there, by the woods. Pick—I don't know—about a dozen of each kind. More of the little ones. There are the bushel baskets." He pointed to a pile.

Calling Mose, Theresa went to the eggplant patch, going down on her old knees in the straw Lute used for mulch, and began picking. She was grateful for the row markers he'd made naming the varieties, which included the small pink-and-white Asian ones, appropriately named Fairy Tale. She picked two dozen of them. Next were some quite narrow, violently purple ones about a foot long, Pingtung. Then some very small white ones called, who'd have guessed—Casper, like the ghost.

Next she focused on a long, slender, green variety called Thai Green. Followed by a pile of small, round, orange Goyo Kumbas. Where were they from? Theresa wondered, but Lute was too far away to ask. Finally she gathered some that looked more like traditional eggplants, somewhat round and very dark purple, almost black, with a great name: Barbarella. Like that silly Jane Fonda movie from the '70s, although that couldn't be the connection! She would definitely have to remember to ask Luther about that one! Where do eggplants originate, she wondered as she stood up to see if she had picked all the varieties. Luther would know, and he loved talking about his veggies. One of the reasons he had so many loyal customers at the market.

Finding a cart, Theresa loaded her two bushel baskets of eggplant into it and headed for the big greenhouse, where she unloaded them. Then she and Mose looked for Lute, with the dog making a half-hearted run at another cat before returning to Theresa's side.

"Lute! Luther?" she called several times while standing outside the greenhouse and scanning the gardens. She finally saw him wave as he was coming up a small rise with a wheelbarrow filled with cabbages, huge ones.

"Wow," Theresa hefted one. "These are huge. How much does one weigh? What kind are they?"

"The customers love the names for all this great stuff, and I actually need it for keeping track of so many different varieties. You don't always see the variety names of veggies in the grocery store, just 'broccoli' and 'celery.' They could be from fucking Mars for all you know. Pardon my French."

"Mexico, more likely," she noted as she followed him to unload.

"Well, these beauties are called, believe it or not, Premium Late Flat Dutch. Sounds like a can of paint, I know, but they're great, weighing up to fifteen pounds apiece! People mostly buy 'em to make kraut. They're great for that. But they'll keep in cold storage a heck of a long time too."

"Hmm," Theresa pondered. "I think you've given me some before for kraut. Save me three or four, will you, and I'll have my sister help me make some when she gets here. It should be fun. Mike, her husband, would have loved this, all you've done here and how much you know."

"Who knows? Maybe he'll get another shot at it, come back as a veggie hippie," Luther said, referring to his name for himself. *Just an old veggie hippie*, he'd say, *wandering around the gardens growing shit!*

"That's a nice thought. So now what? I put the eggplants—they're wonderful by the way—in the greenhouse. I was wondering where they came from, you know, their origins?" Theresa looked up at her tall friend.

"From India, they come from a wild plant in India. They're actually part of the nightshade family—potatoes, tomatoes, and believe it or not, tobacco. Same family as our local poison plant, deadly nightshade, that we need to watch out for. You know, with the small purple berries? Anyway, eggplants have a great name in French, *aubergine*. The Brits call it that too!"

"Great name," Theresa agreed. "And what about those little orange ones with the odd name, Goya something, like the painter. Are they Spanish?"

"Nope, it's *Goyo* with an O, and they're African. I don't like 'em much, not enough flesh under that tough skin. But there are African students at the U who love them, so they buy 'em. You ready for more picking? How about some squash?" he asked.

"Lead on, MacLuther!"

Theresa and Mose followed the veggie hippie into what seemed the most distant garden, huge and pretty wild in appearance.

"I know, I know," Luther harrumphed as they got closer. "It looks pretty messy. It's what happens with squash, spreads out all over, overflows the gardens, gets all tangled. Sure you want to work in here?"

"Got to be done. Let's get going. I even have a knife," Theresa said resolutely, pulling a utility blade out of the pocket of her garden trousers.

"Great, start in that corner. You're gonna find some mix-ups, overlaps. Just put the same kind with each other up there on that grassy knoll. Like Kennedy, remember? I have to get the tractor and a wagon—there's so many of them, and they're too heavy to haul in baskets," Luther headed back for the tractor.

With Mose napping in the grass near her, Theresa began to pick and haul the squash, one at a time. Some she was long familiar with, of course. Acorn, and butternut, her favorite for most squash dishes. The odd and variously colorful streaks of white and green in the Turk's Cap. And sure enough, they were mixed up, long vines intertwining, hundreds of them. There must be a thousand squash altogether, she thought. And some were really different, like the blue ones, funny-shaped and elegant. She would have to ask Lute about those later.

As the day wore on, Lute and Theresa worked separately, but stopped often enough to chat about the afterlife, former lives, squash names, dogs, cats.

"Y'know, my friend," Theresa said as she and Mose got wearily into her car to go home, "for a hippie hermit-type guy, you're pretty chatty."

He laughed and waved as she drove away.

Chapter 21

Tired and shaken, Mary still couldn't stop driving, not yet. She had to stay on the interminable I-80 just a while longer.

"A lot of help you were, Mike. You were supposed to protect me."

She couldn't play music just yet—and couldn't keep her thoughts from returning time and again to what had happened in Cheyenne.

So many white places with Indian names like Cheyenne. We took their land and then their names. How different this country might have looked if we'd taken a lesson or two from the Indians, with their anarchist systems of governance, their absence of land ownership, their respect for all life.

Mary helped Emma with a paper about the Cheyenne back in high school, and thought she remembered they originally came from Minnesota maybe. But they were pushed westward as Europeans started to take over North America. The Cheyenne then changed from a farming culture to a horse-riding nomadic group who hunted buffalo. They were routinely attacked by U.S. Army forces, including the notorious Sand Creek massacre in Colorado, where women and children were slaughtered. Not exactly history to be proud of.

"OK," Mary said, "these depressing thoughts are not helping a bit with how awful I feel."

There was just enough daylight left to read the Nebraska road signs, and the next one was strange. "Drug Dog in Use Ahead," it proclaimed.

Meaning what? Had she really read that right? "Well, plunge on, old lady, and hope no drug dog starts sniffing in the Dreadnaught's trunk!"

The traffic, trucks especially, had increased tenfold it seemed since leaving Wyoming. Lots of giant RVs too, which made Mary nervous with their swaying. She remembered the occasional Sunday drive with her father and, like Mike, how he'd always wonder at all the traffic.

"Look at all these cars! It's Sunday—where are they going?" he would demand. "Why aren't they at church, or at home?"

And from the time she was about eight she would reply, "But what about us, Daddy? Why aren't we at home?" Which would be met by silence. Then they'd all start laughing.

Mary did need to pee . . . again. Maybe it was a reaction to being so frightened. She would stop again and hopefully get some more coffee, but no nap today, it was just too cold and too late for that. She would have to find a motel sooner or later.

Pulling into the next rest stop, near Kimball, on the north side of the highway, she parked, got out and carefully locked the doors before she headed to the bathroom. Next was hot coffee from the machine. God, how did truckers and other people who had to be on the road all the time do it, she wondered? Bad coffee, boring highways, smelly toilets. Was she really going to drive all the way back home to Pasadena after visiting her sister? Who knew, right now she just had to get there.

Drive on, she told herself, drive on.

Chapter 22

Standing at the wood splitter with hearing protectors jammed in his ears, Luther didn't hear John Moe approach, noticing him only when the old man was standing right in front of him. He throttled the engine down and pulled out the earplugs.

"Hey, John, what's going on?" Luther asked even though he couldn't hear the reply as he worked to shut the engine off entirely. "What? Didn't get that," he said once he silenced the machine.

"Don't s'pose you heard about Elmer Tofte?"

"No, I didn't. What is it?" Luther reached into his shirt pocket for cigarettes.

"Well, the old bugger finally did it. Killed himself!" John spat a greenish-black stream of snoose onto the ground.

"Really? How? What happened?" Luther lit his smoke and inhaled deeply.

"Rolled his goddamn tractor into the ditch," John was matter of fact. "Over on the coulee road. 'Bout midway between here and my place. Broke his neck, sure did!" Another stream of snoose spat out for emphasis.

"Jesus, hell of a way to go." Luther shook his head.

"I don't know," John scratched his armpit. "Bet he was half in the bag, so no pain. It's probably why it happened. Quick death, I expect. No laying there half-alive till somebody found him."

"Who did find him?"

"Lydia. Lydia Berglund. She's older than me you know, and don't get around good. So imagine she didn't actually get down in the ditch. Just saw the tractor and him laying there, and called me when she got home." John explained as he scratched himself again.

"Not the sheriff? Not 911?" Luther wondered.

"Lydia don't know no 911 from a monkey's butt," John snorted. "So I called 'em, the cops. Then I went right up there myself. And sure enough, that old Case was tipped on its side, Elmer lying there like a broken stick. Don't see a lotta dead outside the funeral parlor, kind of spooky. I did check for a heartbeat, y'know, but of course he was stone cold. Skin all gray like a January sky, eyes rolled back, shoot!"

"Deputies get there?" Luther asked.

"Yeah, took their time, ambulance too. Put him on a stretcher and took off. Sheriff took a bunch of pictures, then asked if I could get the tractor out of there. County's pinched for money these days, they claim, so save a lot if they don't have to call a wrecker. 'S why I'm here, ask you to help me with it," John explained.

"Sure, of course. We'll use my rig. It's little, but has plenty of torque and the four-wheel will let us get a grab on it. That Case was just a little tractor, wasn't it?" Lute took a long drag on his cigarette.

"Yep, was just a row cropper, kind of a glorified garden tractor," John mused. "Couldn't have been more than fifteen horse or so. Heck, got lawnmowers now with more than that!"

"Yeah, well, we both know about the horsepower bullshit. Or should I say *horseshit!* I love my new machine, but it will never have the torque my old H had, and it's rated at about ten more horsepower. I don't get it—the horsepower thing is bogus." Luther shook his head in perplexity. "That Case had a narrow front, didn't it?"

"Yep. Dangerous as hell on the highway. Put it in third and prob'ly goin' only 'bout fifteen miles per, but she wandered all over the road like crazy. That's what killed him sure." John nodded solemnly.

"No," Luther disagreed. "The booze killed him. Just like it killed his brother. What was his name?" The two men had begun to walk up the hill to the shed where Luther kept his tractor.

"Lloyd," John offered. "Froze his goddamn feet off, the fool."

"Oh yeah, I remember." Luther stood outside the shed to finish his cigarette. "A few years after I got here. Was that what killed him?"

"More or less. Colder than a well-digger's butt and he got stuck outside." John leaned against the tractor shed. "Couldn't get back in the house. His brother was all boozed up, so he never heard him holler. Just couldn't open the goddamn door, laid out there all night. Feet froze, had to cut 'em off, never was right after that."

"Hell yes, I remember that old son of a bitch. Somebody told me those old boys had a manure spreader for sale, so I stopped by there that spring," Luther remembered. "Knocked on the door several times. Finally somebody yells, 'Come the hell in.' So I go in. And just about shit myself 'cause as I get just inside, it's dark as hell, and I barely see this guy, must have been Lloyd, laying in a bed right there by the door. He has a goddamn shotgun pointed at me, says something like 'How about a taste of lead, you hippie son of a bitch?' I had this crazy thought, like—shit I made it through the Nam, and now I'm gonna get wasted by this old farmer loon. Jesus!" He took one last heavy draw on his smoke, then stomped it out.

"Don't know that I heard that before," John mused. "But those boys were sure as hell mean when they'd been hitting the cider! Get that spreader?"

"You're kidding," Luther said as he climbed up onto his tractor seat. "I just backed out of there and bolted. Get shot over a spreader? No thanks!"

"Well, you heard about what happened with that spreader, didn't you?" John smiled, relishing the tale he was about to tell.

"Nope."

"Story was," John paused, "that the Toftes—they were twins, y'know—got to fighting in the barn, and Lloyd takes a pitchfork to his brother's leg. You know, the old three-tine fork? Goddamn sharp! Sticks 'em good, so he's bleeding like a pig. So what's Lloyd do while Elmer is hollering and jumping around, blood everywhere?"

"No idea." Luther answered from his tractor seat. "Stick him some more?"

"Nope, he knocks him down and ties up the leg above the wound with baling twine, a whole shitload of it. A tourniquet, y'know. Then he hooks up the tractor, same one we're aimin' to get, to the manure spreader, heaves Elmer into the spreader right over the side into some cow crap, and heads for town, for Doc Detlefsen's," John says, shooting another wad of snoose on the ground for emphasis.

"Christ, did he make it?" Luther was incredulous. "Shoot, s'pose he did, didn't he, since he lived long enough to scare the hell out of me!" Luther shook his head at the cruel story, and reached for another cigarette but thought better of it. What was happening to his one-a-day pledge to himself?

"Yep, Doc patched him up and prob'ly lectured them boys about the booze. Didn't do no good, of course," John offered.

"Didn't they have a car, or a truck?"

"Nope, that's why they drove that tractor everywhere," John explained. "Sheriff took their licenses away, 'cause they'd been in the ditch so many times. Afraid they'd kill somebody with their boozed-up driving. And musta been bad, because back then nobody ever heard of a DWI, whatever they call it. Shit, people drove around with a six-pack right on the seat next to 'em, get stopped weaving all over the place on a Friday night. Deputies would just tell you to be more careful, that's all. So them Toftes musta really screwed the pooch to lose their licenses like that!"

"But it was OK to drive the tractor?" Luther didn't get it.

"Sure, don't need no license to do that," John said. "That's why you see eight-year-old kids hauling wagons up and down the road!"

Shaking his head, Luther started his tractor, the noisy little diesel roaring to life like a machine twice its size. He backed out and began to follow John's pickup, rusty sides flapping even at that slow speed, out of the yard and onto the back coulee road.

They were at the accident site in minutes. They found no one there. Surveying the tipped tractor, they tried at first to right it by simply pushing from one side, but it didn't budge.

"Didn't think that would do it," John noted. "So we'll put a chain on 'er and hook it up to your machine. You'll pull it upright, then we'll see where we're at."

Up in the road, Luther backed his tractor as close to the edge of the steep ditch as he dared while John hooked a heavy log chain to the base of the Case's seat and gave Luther the go-ahead. Putting his New Holland into the lowest gear possible, and making sure the tractor was in four-wheel, Luther eased on the throttle. Nothing happened at first, so he gave it more gas and got a fright as the front end of his machine lifted for a moment. Whoa. But before he could back off the gas his little blue tractor's front end dropped back down, and he started to ease the old Case upright. Once he got it to a tipping point where the ratty-looking, off-white machine suddenly came fully onto its feet, John motioned Luther to ease off.

Looking the Case over, the men concluded that it was unlikely to start, as most of its fuel had probably drained out of the fill cap. John showed Luther the near-empty dipstick of the oil too and pointed to a large stain in the ditch where the tractor had lain.

"Shouldn't even try to start her, then, or we'll ruin the engine, if it ain't ruined already," John unhooked the log chain from the tractor's seat.

"So," Luther asked. "What do we do?"

"Well, that little machine of yours ain't gonna do it by itself. But I reckon with both of us, we can haul it out of here and onto the road," John suggested. "We'll hook you up to the Case's front end, then I'll hook my truck up to your front end, which will make sure you don't come up in the air again and break your goddamn neck. Bet that will do it!" The old man looked down at the chain in his hand.

"Sounds fine," Luther said as he looked around, spotting a broken bottle of Jim Beam on the ground. "You see that, John? What the hell . . . ?"

"Sure do. He was on a booze run," John said. "See that wood box behind the seat? No tools in there, that's what them boys used to go get groceries and booze. Usually *after* they'd spent as many hours as they had money for at the bar. See?" John opened the broken lid on the box in question, and sure enough there was a loaf of white bread, a jar of strawberry jam, some cans of sardines, an onion, and a jar of peanut butter jumbled in there, along with a half pint of rye whiskey and a six-pack of Old Milwaukee.

"Jesus, what a sorry-ass life they had," Luther grimaced as he stooped to hook the chain around the tractor's front end. Looking up, he asked John, "What the hell do we do about the steering? Gonna go all over the place."

"Right, I'll get that rope I've got along and tie it down." He anchored the steering wheel tightly to the lower part of the tractor's seat as Luther watched, admiring how easily such problems were solved by his old, and usually grumpy, neighbor. I'd never have figured out about hooking our two vehicles together to get the Case out, Luther thought.

John's plan worked well. With their two machines pulling at once, they hauled Elmer's machine out of the ditch with scarcely any trouble and Luther's front end staying firmly where it belonged, on the road. Then, leaving John's pickup parked on the roadside, they shortened the distance between the Case and the New Holland. John took off the rope he'd tied to the steering wheel, and got in the Case's seat to steer the machine back to Elmer's place. They encountered no one as they made their way down the three miles of gravel road.

At the Tofte homestead, a place Luther had passed plenty of times but only visited once—the shotgun incident—the two men towed the tractor next to a shed and unhooked it.

"Should we try to put it inside somewhere?" Luther asked.

"Where?" John demanded. "The barn and every goddamn shed is chock full of shit. Couldn't squeeze a garden spade in any of 'em. Just leave it sit here. Prob'ly never been in a shed its whole life." John took out his snoose can and took a pinch of snuff.

"Yeah, bet it's got stories!" Luther lit another cigarette, feeling the occasion allowed for it.

"Whaddya mean, stories?" John cast him a suspicious glance.

"Well, if the Case could talk, or these buildings . . . all the shit they've seen?" Luther suggested.

"Well, I don't know what you're smoking there, neighbor, but last time I heard, tractors don't talk!" John pushed the wad of snuff into a corner of his mouth.

"Tobacco's what I'm smoking, John, and don't get your panties in a twist. It's just a figure of speech, a way of saying there's probably a lot to tell about this place and the Toftes. Is this where they were born?" Luther looked dubiously around at the place, which seemed to be one big junk pile.

"Well, Lute, the day's half shot. And you're all curious and whatnot. Let's pop one of those Old Mils, take a couple sips of Elmer's rye—and take a seat," John suggested.

Amazed that John, a working fool if there ever was one, was willing to take a break, drink some beer and talk, Luther readily agreed. When he thought about it a day or so later, he reasoned that his elderly neighbor, tough as he was, must have been a bit shaken by what happened to Elmer Tofte that day.

Hauling the six-pack and the small bottle of rye to a fallen tree, one of many scattered over the property, the men each popped open a can of beer, took a couple of slugs, then shared a heavy sip of the rye.

Smacking his lips, John wiped them with the back of his hand, and spit out some snoose. "How in the hell," Luther wondered, not for the first time, "could these old farts drink beer and chew snoose at the same time?" Then John started to tell about the Toftes.

"Yep, them boys was born here," he started. "Not in no hospital, right here in that house. Their father—same name as you, actually—Luther was, if anyone was, a goddamn working fool. Like everybody back then, he had a little bit of everything on this place. Milk cows for making butter they sold to the creamery. One of the only ways, back then, to get cash. A few steers for beef, not for sale but to eat on the farm. Hogs, called them mortgage lifters 'cause if the price was good down at the auction in the fall, you'd come away with some serious money. Serious for then, anyways. And maybe you'd give some to the banker to cut some slack on what you owed. Chickens, they were for the women to take care of, maybe sell a few eggs. A few turkeys and ducks and geese. Horses, of course, I think they had Percherons, if I remember right. Not like today, where all these wannabe cowboys move up here and get some useless horses right away."

John stopped to take another swig of his beer. "Glad they do 'cause that's mostly who buys my hay, but those horses back then weren't goddamn pets! Hell no! They were what made the farm go 'round, plowing and planting and hauling. And in the winter, when money was extra scarce? That old man went logging. No chainsaws and such, of course. Axe, crosscut saws, bow saws for the small stuff. Ropes and chains, and the most important part, a team that he'd trained up himself for working in the woods in the winter. Swear he and them horses could haul logs out of hell."

"Got the wood around here?" Luther asked.

"Yep," John replied. "Gotta remember there was a lot more timber here back then. Farmers was anxious to get more land to plant in and they needed the money from the timber, so the old boy kept busy. Kept them twins busy too. Shoot, both of 'em could drive a team by the time they was six years old, I swear." John took another hit from the rye bottle.

"Jesus, six?" Luther shook his head, thinking of how he was barely able to wipe his butt when he was six.

"Sure, course they was big for their age," John explained. "And back then kids were supposed to work, not like today. Donald and I were both heavy at it round the home place by that same age too. Milked cows—by hand, of course—morning and night. Ran the separator, sawed firewood with the Swede saw, slopped hogs. Whole different life back then and, hell, it wasn't that long ago, y'know?" John again spat snoose for emphasis.

"So what happened? I mean look at this place, crap everywhere, can barely walk around. It's a shithole!" Luther gestured at the yard strewn with broken machinery, dead cars, bicycles, batteries, windows, and doors. An endless and depressing mess.

"Real shame," John agreed. "Old Luther would cry out loud if he saw it now. Not only was he a working fool, he kept the place neater than most women do their kitchens! Everything in its place, all the machinery oiled and greased and shedded. Horses groomed day and night, shoot, even the pigpens were cleaner than anybody else's! Go in the barn, all the shovels and pitchforks, the ropes and chains, hung tidy. Like going into a goddamn store, neater even. Never was in the house that I remember, but everybody said that was just as clean as the outside. Man you'd look down one of his fence lines and there wasn't a quiver, straight as a goddamn arrow. Straighter!"

"So . . . ?" Luther prompted.

"Better have me 'nother of those beers, I guess. Help the memory." John popped the lid on a can, took a serious draught, then continued. Luther, amazed to see his elderly neighbor drinking more than a single can of beer, opened another for himself, backing it up with another slug of the rye.

"So what happened nobody coulda guessed, not a soul! Terrible thing you won't hardly believe!" John took another drink. Pausing in reflection, he let his thoughts gel. "See it was a Sunday, and they, Luther and his wife and the boys, was in their car—they had one back then, you see—pulling out to go to church. Went to that Lutheran church in Moeville, one that's still there on the corner?"

"Never been in it, but they keep it nice. I'm no church man, but I do like those old churches with the high spires—if they're kept up, that is."

"Well, so they were all got up for church, motor running, and the old man says he's just got to check something in the barn. Be only a minute. Jumps out of the car and runs to the barn, that one right there," John pointing to an enormous building with its gambrel roof sagging, broken-backed.

"So . . . ," John paused, "they wait awhile until the wife gets anxious. Can't be late for church, not their style! So she sends one of the boys, not sure which, to see what's going on and Christ Jesus! You can't guess what he saw, that boy!"

"What? Old man fell down in the cow yard? Sunday best all covered in shit?" Luther half-laughed at the notion.

"Nope, not fallen down, but *hung up!* Right there in the haymow," John proclaimed. "Old Luther put a rope around his neck and jumped off a pile of hay. Still swinging, eyes bulging, when the boy found him. Damnedest thing!"

Hearing this, Luther was staggered. He actually rose up off his seat on the log they were sitting on, then sat down again with a thud. Later he would wonder why this ancient news had affected him so.

"God, really?" Luther clasped his hands on his knees. "Man, that is hard to figure. Why in the hell?"

"That's just it. Didn't have a clue why he did it. No note, nothing. Just that body hanging there, mute as a bale of hay." John hit his knee in emphasis.

"But shit, there must have been something," Lute protested. "Farmers kill themselves all the time, not as bad as vets, but damn near. Usually it's money trouble, right? In debt, discouraged, leave some insurance money for the family, that kind of stuff."

Shaking his head, John replied. "Nope, nothing like that. They actually owned that farm, free and clear. Probably only place around here then that wasn't mortgaged to the hilt. Had just bought that car, a Ford four-door, and rumor had it he'd paid cash for the goddamn thing. Shoot, nobody around here could do that."

"Booze? Dope? Women?" Lute offered the usual short list.

"Not a one!" John insisted. "Man had no time for any of that, would get in the way of his work. Maybe he rubbed a little snoose, but maybe not. Probably saw it as a waste of money!"

"Hard to believe. All these years and nobody came up with anything about why he did it, the hanging?" Luther took another drink and scratched his head.

"Yep, real mystery."

Intrigued, Luther wanted to find out more. "What happened then, to the place? The boys, how old were they?"

"Not for sure, but I'd say around nine or ten. Find their father hangin' in the barn like that?" John put his hands around his neck to make the point, leading Luther to conclude that his usually undemonstrative neighbor was starting to feel his liquor. "Can't imagine what it did to them."

"Shit, no wonder they took to booze!" Luther emphasized this with a slug of rye, emptying the bottle.

"Well, jeez, Lute, them kids didn't just up and start drinking, y'know. C'mon, man! They was only kids."

"What did happen then?" Luther asked.

"Just toughed it out, their mother hung in there . . . shit. Shouldn't have said that!" John pulled his greasy cap down over his brow.

"What?" Luther wondered.

"'Hung in there!'" John repeated. "But she and them twins did what they could to keep the place up. Folks around here tried to help, you know. Few old Norskie bachelors came sniffing around, she wasn't that old, and not bad looking. But she drove 'em off, wanted to be sure her boys got the place—this place! But things kept slipping, boys was just too young to fill the old man's shoes. And shoot, think what it must have been like each morning and evening, milking cows, pitching hay, right there where their father had done the deed. Hard for anybody, but young kids like that?" John followed Luther's suit with another beer.

"Can't imagine, just can't," Luther said. Now on his third can of beer and having finished the rye, he was feeling just a little lit. Be great to smoke a J right now, but he couldn't do that around John. No way.

Popping the top on his beer, John continued. "Not sure what happened, there was lots of gossip, of course. But I think the old lady, the mother, started to come a little unhinged. All the work, the responsibility. They stopped the milking, really didn't have enough cows to make it worthwhile and woulda had to spend a lot of money to upgrade the barn to meet the new state specs for a dairy. So they just upped the size of the beef herd, more hogs, this and that. But the buildings stayed unpainted, always a sign. Machinery began to get crappy. Maybe their heart wasn't in it, y'know?" He sipped his beer contemplatively.

As Lute lit another cigarette, John took notice. "You really puffin' today, ain't you?"

"I am indeed. This story has really got me kind of wigged out, feeling strange, y'know. And of course when I'm having a beer or two, nothing's better than a smoke to go with it."

"Tried it when I was kid, near choked to death. Snoose is my sin," John offered, spitting a gob of it on the ground.

"Know you're still wanting to hear the end of it," John continued his story at length. "Well, them boys, teenagers, had enough cattle to haul to the sales barn that they talked their ma into buying a cattle truck. Not a semi like them cattle jockeys got now, just a three-four ton rig, wooden sides, tarp roof, load 'em with a ramp. But soon's they got it, everybody wanted those boys to haul their stock to the sales barn, so they hired out. Made a business out of it. Got busy enough they stopped putting in crops. Rented the land to neighbors on shares, y'know."

The old man took just a sip of beer, nearing the end of the can. "Well, don't know for sure, but story had it that one of the big buyers at the auction, Winona man, started taking the boys out for drinks. Liquored 'em up to take advantage. Maybe happened, maybe didn't, don't really know. But did know they started hitting the booze pretty hard. By the time they was in their twenties, still young, they lost the business. So, they started working as hired men around here. Good men if they were sober, but that was less and less. Mother died or went into the home, not sure which, and they started selling off the land to pay the taxes, buy groceries, booze. Bought that tractor, lost their licenses, and you know the rest."

"God, that is one sad son of a bitch of a story, John." After a moment, Luther stood and walked to the edge of an old plow to take a piss. Despite the rust, he noted right away it was a John Deere, two-fourteens, a pull type. That little Case would never have pulled that plow, he guessed.

"Must have had some bigger machinery around here at one time, don't you think?" Luther asked as he pointed to the plow and walked back to the log.

"Nah," John responded. "When they wasn't buying booze, they bought every loose piece of junk in the county. Got so that at the end of any auction, the auctioneer would point to the crap that was left over and yell, always gettin' a big laugh: 'Hey, Tofte twins, want the rest of it? Gimme a bid. Ten bucks? Five?' And so they'd buy it, whatever it was. Broken machinery, doubt that plow works, boxes of canning jars too old to use. Piles of moldy magazines, pianos and pipe organs couldn't make a sound, full of mice. Look at this place!"

"I *am* looking, neighbor, and it makes me damn ready to get the hell out of here. Hop on the tractor, and let's get your truck and go home," Luther climbed onto his tractor while John grabbed the roll bar and anchored his shaky self onto a fender.

At home, Luther made himself a late afternoon pot of coffee to kick the alcohol so he could get some more work done. Work was the best he could do to beat back the depression that had grabbed hold of him like the flu after John's sad tale.

Chapter 23

JONI, ASLEEP IN THE CAB OF SAM'S SEMI, awoke with a start to find Sam in the back of the cab with her. Sitting up and rubbing her eyes, she realized he'd been touching her. Drawing sharply away from him, she said, "Hey! What are you doing?"

Smiling, he responded, "Nothing much, just givin' you a little back rub."

"A back rub?" Joni was indignant. "I didn't ask for any back rub, man!"

"Take it easy, little girl," Sam protested. "It was just a back rub, I didn't mean anything by it. Don't get your back up." He gave her a leering smile.

Definitely a leer, Joni thought, goddamn men! What in hell was she going to do now?

"Hey, listen, Joni," he continued. "I just saw you sleeping there so nice, I thought a little back rub would be good. Me? I love a nice rubdown." Said with that same shit-eating smile.

Joni began to clamber out of the sleeper toward the passenger door. Not looking Sam in the face she said, "Yeah, well, I gotta pee."

Out of the truck, Joni headed right into the large Pilot truck stop where they were parked. In the bathroom, she leaned against the side of the stall, realizing she had to get out of Sam's truck and away from that shifty smile.

"A fucking back rub!" she murmured to herself. "No thanks, buddy." Men were just fucking untrustworthy. And dangerous goddamn knuckle-walkers, right out of the stinking cave. And now there was no trusting Sam. If they stopped somewhere quiet up the road, he'd like as not try to jump her bones. But he had her backpack with her money and clothes. She could do without the clothes probably, but not the bread. How in the hell was she going to get her stuff and get away?

Coming out of the can, she scouted the store for Sam but didn't see him anywhere. He could be in the crapper, she thought, or maybe still in his truck. Then she spotted him over near another rig, about four trucks away from his own, jawboning with some dude. "OK, girl," Joni told herself. "Let's get into stealth mode!"

Heading out the door, Joni slipped over to the far side of the first semi, going carefully from truck to truck. Then suddenly—*fuck!*—loud and frantic barking scared the hell out of her. Looking up, she saw a huge dog slamming at the window in a cab above her. Joni froze for just a moment, and then tiptoed away from the dog, who was still barking frantically. She stopped to kneel down and look under the trucks toward where she thought Sam was, or had been. But she saw nothing, nobody. "Hey," she thought, "I still have to try."

Joni continued across the lot, very quietly, very carefully, until she reached the rear of Sam's semi. And then, shit, there he was, heading right for the truck. Just outside his door he stopped, looking up at the cab. Apparently not seeing her there, he turned back to the station and went inside. Joni seized the moment to jump up into the cab—thank God he'd actually left it open—grabbed her large, heavy backpack, and threw it out onto the ground.

Flinging herself off the truck and grabbing her pack, Joni started hoofing it. But where could she go to get away from him? There were a couple of nearby motels, but she might not make it to them before he came out. And it would take too long to register if he came looking for her. There were also a couple of restaurants, but too many people might notice her, and tell him if he asked. And she was pretty sure he would.

Joni noticed a store with a great, big stone-and-timber entrance. Some kind of farmland Taj Mahal? The sign read Cabela's, and the place was huge. Probably her best bet, she figured as she ran across the lot and through the giant doors where she came face to face with an enormous display of dead animals. "This can't be a museum," she thought as she scoped out her best route for disappearing in the place, "there are too many racks of clothes in here."

"Ma'am," a woman at a counter said, looking at Joni. "Sorry, but no packs allowed in the store. Please check it here, and you can collect it on your way out."

Joni gladly handed over her backpack and took the receipt as she looked over her shoulder to see if Sam was headed her way. With no sign of him, she headed into the bowels of the freakishly huge two-level store. Starting in, she suddenly went back to the entrance.

"'Scuse me, ma'am? Can I ask a favor?" Joni asked the lady at the counter.

The woman smiled back at her, "Sure, honey, as long as it's not for money!"

"No, it's just," said Joni as she hesitated and looked toward the door. "I just had a fight with my asshole trucker boyfriend, and he's probably gonna come in here looking for me. Just don't tell him you saw me, OK? Please?"

"Asshole trucker boyfriend?" the cashier smiled, lowering her voice. "You mean there's more than one of those? Been there, done that, little sister. I ain't sayin' Shinola to nobody. Get your butt into the store. Hide in the ladies, if you like." She pointed to the back of the store. "If he's on the road, he won't spend too much time looking for you."

Joni thanked her and almost ran to the back of the store, where she spotted the restroom and practically dove into it. Sitting down on a bench, shaking, it dawned on Joni, that the very helpful woman at the counter had the exact same big, poofy hairdo as Sam's wife, Patty. What are the chances of that?

Probably never get my shit mailed to me now, she lamented. But then again, Sam couldn't exactly, wouldn't exactly, tell Patty why Joni had split. Or maybe even that she split at all!

Let's see, she calculated: creepy little son George sneaking into her room plus creepy dad Sam cozying up to her. Maybe there was a reason George's sister left that family and never looked back. Too many back rubs!

After fifteen or twenty minutes Joni decided it was safe to leave the bathroom and check the place out, keeping a wary eye out for Sam, of course. The store was cavernous. All wood and stone inside, just like the entrance. It must have cost serious dollars to build someplace like this, Joni surmised. And out here in bum-fuck nowhere. Where was she anyway? Joni had lost track of where they were when she went to sleep in the truck and now realized she didn't even know where she was stranded.

Pretending to be an interested shopper, Joni wandered around the place responding, "No thanks, just looking," for almost an hour in hopes of evading Sam. There were lots and lots of outdoor clothes in this place, with enough camo to outfit the Mexican Army, she thought. And against one wall, more guns than she'd ever seen.

The guy behind the gun counter couldn't help but notice her wandering aimlessly. "Pretty young lady like you's gotta be careful. Looking for something nice to conceal and carry?" he asked hopefully.

The guy looked like a freakin' walrus with that giant handlebar mustache, Joni thought. Oh, that's right, this store was probably out in the middle of nowhere so the cowboys could ride right in off the range to get their guns and shit. She wondered if after they stocked up they ate at the Chinese place across the street?

Smile at him, Joni told herself, say something.

"Nah, just looking. But what's that?" she asked, pointing to something that looked like a cross between a rifle and a bow and arrow. Reaching for it, he laid the thing on the counter. Jesus, it was scary!

"This, ma'am, is a crossbow," he said proudly. "Shoots a bolt, kind of like an arrow. More accurate than a shotgun, and with a greater range. Real deadly weapon, I tell you."

"Never heard of one. What's it for?"

"Killing things," he said with a nasty grin. "Deer, elk, antelope, coyotes . . . even buffalo. Wolves too, now that they took the goddamn critters off the protected list."

Joni had no idea what he was talking about, and no interest either, but she did know he was staring at her tits like he'd never seen any before. Another idiot.

Smiling weakly, she moved away.

"Hey, what's your hurry?" mustache man called after her. "Let's talk guns!"

Yeah, she thought, that's real high on my list, you pop-eying my tits while telling me about killing stuff. Like the enormous stuffed bear in the corner, and hundreds of horned heads on the walls. Upstairs, safely away from the gun department, Joni wandered into the boot and shoe department aimlessly, until she ran into a stuffed leopard. A leopard—were they here in the United States? This creepy place had kept her safe from Sam, but it was time to go for sure. So she finally gathered the courage to head downstairs and collect her backpack.

"Didn't nobody come in lookin' for you sweetheart," the nice big-haired lady offered. "If that boy was on a schedule, bet he's drove off by now. Find himself another woman down the line. We girls don't use the brains the Good Lord supposedly gave us when it comes to men!" Taking a slug from a can of Coke, she smiled kindly at Joni.

Taking her pack, Joni thanked the woman and exited cautiously into the store's parking lot with an eye out for Sam. Halfway through the doors she turned back suddenly and approached the cashier again. "Say, I know this sounds dumb, but I was in the sleeper when we got here. So . . . where *is* here?"

"Sidney, sweetheart," she answered. "Sidney, Nebraska. Basically a truck stop on 80 famous for one thing only—this store. This was the first Cabela's in the country, I'm proud to say."

"Sidney, huh? Thanks," Joni said as she went back outside toward the truck stop very carefully. Where was Sam's truck, she wondered as she scanned the lot? So many damn machines, most of them running. A few truckers hanging around, smoking and kicking tires. After a pretty thorough look around, Joni concluded he was probably gone. Unless he'd moved it to fool her, but he wasn't that crazy was he? It was getting late, on toward dark. She wondered how long she'd actually been in the hunting store. No telling now. She was hungry as hell, so she might as well get something to eat and figure shit out, like how she was going to get out of here.

There were plenty of restaurants to choose from, China One Buffet, something called Runza, Arby's, and hey, a Perkins! She could get potato pancakes, applesauce, and bacon there. She headed down the road toward the familiar green roof and giant flag, and was pleased to find that inside it was just like all the other Perkins in the world.

"Can I have a booth please?" Joni asked at the counter.

"Sure, honey, right back here," the hostess said. Joni followed the very large woman from the counter to a booth in the back of the restaurant, where she unloaded the pack into one side and sat on the other.

"You want anything to drink?" the woman asked after she handed Joni the menu.

"Yes, some coffee, please, with cream," Joni said, smiling up at the waitress as she remembered her many mornings serving people at the motel. That experience had left her very sympathetic, probably forever, for wait staff.

Joni was pleased to see that her favorite, potato pancakes, were still on the menu. The waitress took a long time coming over to the table, which was just fine with Joni since she needed to make her time here last while she figured out what to do next.

When the coffee finally came, it wasn't bad. Perkins must have caught the coffee craze and upgraded from the light-brown liquid they used to serve. Joni looked around, still worried about Sam turning up, but then figured if he was here, he'd have seen her and been over to her table by now. There were lots of single men sitting alone, probably truckers. And a table of four older women, one with what Joni now thought of as Patty hair.

Too bad about Patty, she'd really liked her, and Sam too until he'd groped her. Why had he done that? Was he just another horny dude under that smile and small talk, or was he seriously creepy? Either way, lucky she'd scooted when she did.

Joni truly regretted that men, especially older ones, found her so attractive. She had given up dressing provocatively years ago, in her late teens, when it really wasn't fun anymore because she attracted the wrong kind of attention. She didn't walk around looking like some kind of hooker. Her auburn hair was cut short and very simply, no fancy, high-maintenance cut for her. And sure, she figured she had a good face, with her little nose, big green eyes, straight teeth, and a nice smile, people said. Heck, what was she supposed to do, mess up her face or gain a hundred pounds so men stopped staring at her? Shit!

The waitress came back and Joni noticed that she was a big woman—like wow, really big. Not fat, just really tall with broad shoulders. Her name tag said Loretta, but it was barely noticeable in the sea of her serious knockers. And she was chewing gum like there was no tomorrow.

"I'll have the potato pancakes. And can I get two extra sides of applesauce? I love that stuff," Joni asked.

"Sure, honey. Want a refill on that coffee?" The woman wrote down Joni's order.

As she moved away, Joni thought more about waitresses. This lady was right out of some movie, big cowgirl named Loretta calling all her customers *honey*. It's weird how waitresses and truck drivers so often seemed to fit some mold, there was probably one for hotel housekeepers just like her too. When you work in a place with the same people long enough, maybe everybody starts to look alike.

Joni wondered if she sounded and acted like a housekeeper? Whatever. As bad as things were, like being stranded here, at least she didn't have to clean any more hotel bathrooms! Don't look back. It was time to figure out how to get to Minnesota and see those lawyers about that inheritance. If there was one . . . .

Chapter 24

Theresa got up late, at eight o'clock. She'd actually been more or less awake for probably a half hour, but the house was a little chilly and she loved the feeling of turning over, stretching, wiggling her toes, then curling up again in the flannel sheets she'd made the bed with yesterday. Used to be she'd wait until serious cold, around Thanksgiving, to put on the flannels, but the last several years she put them on sooner and sooner. Just like her silk long underwear, putting it on earlier and earlier each fall as she aged. Remembering how as children she and Mary had always giggled at their Grandpa Meyer when he pulled up his trouser legs on a sweltering Chicago July afternoon to reveal a glimpse of white long underwear.

Guess he was old and cold, just like you, Theresa told herself. Getting out of bed, she let Mose out the kitchen door and went to pee, sitting there briefly thinking about how good it was that she was still able to enjoy such simple things as her flannel sheets. Not even an indulgence really, since she'd had them for years. It was probably time for a new set. She'd order them from right across the river, The Company Store in La Crosse, when they sent their catalog around Christmas. Treat herself, maybe.

As she put on her Carhartt workpants, which were just as old and comfortable as her sheets since she hardly ever wore stuff out, she couldn't recall a time when her mother Gertrude ever wore pants. What a shame, since wearing them was one of the truly liberating things about being a modern woman, Theresa figured.

For years Mary had been saying that women getting the vote was humbug, but wearing pants, now that was freedom.

Women, it was said, might "wear the pants in the family," but that phrase never gets turned around. No one ever says a man "wears the dress in the family," do they? How about the shoes, hat, belt, stockings, or purse? She laughed as she continued to put on her outdoor gear. How about "that man certainly wears the stockings in that house"?

Purse. Theresa hardly used a purse anymore, whereas her mother had never gone out of the house without one. More liberation she figured. What used to be carried in a big, old purse anyway? A wallet for money and family pics, a comb or hairbrush maybe, depending on your hair. Hers was always unruly.

"Brush your hair, Theresa," her mother said almost every day, "you look like a ragamuffin." Her mother wouldn't be a fan of the barn look Theresa was sporting this morning!

Now there was a word, Theresa thought as she put on her rubber barn boots, puffing just a bit at the exertion of pulling them over her thick socks. *Ragamuffin*. She'd have to look up the etymology of that when she came back inside.

Meanwhile, she opened the kitchen drawer where she kept two stainless steel, lidded trays. The one on the left was for compost scraps, mostly coffee grounds and egg shells, and the other was for food scraps she gave to her chickens: old bread, vegetable peels, meat scraps, and anything from her frig that had 'gone over to the dark side,' as Tony used to call spoilage. When people asked why she didn't give eggshells to the chickens, she told them of how initially, ignorantly, she had, only to find that the birds soon developed a taste for their own eggs. Nothing more disappointing than to collect eggs and find several of them broken into! She dumped the chicken scraps into a plastic ice cream pail as she ticked off a list of other things that used to fill a woman's purse.

Keys, a handkerchief, or for the more modern woman, Kleenex. And candy maybe, or some sort of mint or gum to freshen your breath.

What else, Theresa wondered as she walked to the barn? Some of those old ladies she remembered from her childhood had enormous purses. What *was* in them, groceries?

She tried to recall what had been in her purse when she was still in high school. Makeup, of course—lipstick, sometimes two shades, a compact with a mirror and some blush or powder, and some girls even carried eye shadow or mascara. Both verboten in the Stein household.

And then of course maxi pads or tampons, ugh, that was something she didn't miss in old age!

Imagine, she thought while following Mose down to the chicken coop, calling those things feminine *napkins*. Let's see, napkins at the table, and napkins between your legs. Please! That was a comparison she'd never had her students make while they explored the English language in her classes. She smiled to herself as she opened the door to the coop, throwing the kitchen scraps onto the straw-covered floor amid the cacophony of chickens.

"Hey, Mose," she commanded to the dog who had snuck in behind her. "Out!"

He'd eat all those table scraps in just a gulp or two, whereas the chickens would peck away at them for hours. And they needed a treat to divert them from their otherwise boring lives in the coop and the outside run connected to it. She couldn't let them have the run of the farm, however, at least not until mid-October, when most of the garden was done, because that was always the first place they headed. They went right into the garden to eat everything they could, and leave a big mess. Then they'd come up to the nice stone patio Rusty and Lute had laid for her by the south porch and poop all over that! She remembered how much fun it had been to put in that patio—she even did some of the smaller stones, finding one with a lovely fossil on it, while drinking a little too much gin. The two men in her life had been wonderfully at ease with her and with each other. A fond time.

Theresa gathered the eggs, there were four, one of them slightly brown. She'd started the flock last spring and they were poor layers, ornament being their specialty, but they produced enough each week for her and an extra dozen for Rusty and Carmen.

Theresa got them from a man in Iowa who saved, raised, and sold heirloom chickens, small flocks in danger of disappearing. She thought she'd do her part by buying and raising some, but couldn't really make up her mind about a particular breed since there were so many to choose from. So she ended up ordering a mixed flock and let the breeder decide what to send her.

And what a mix! From tiny little red chicks the size of large quail, to several monster gray birds, probably eight pounders, with feathered legs. Her favorite was a rather smallish rooster, mostly white but with a mane and tail of large, brilliant black feathers topped with an outsized comb. And all of them, like most poultry, were very, very noisy.

Almost every morning she felt just a little bit guilty that she couldn't identify the various breeds on sight. When the chicks had arrived back in March, a sheet naming them had been with them, but it was just names, nothing about size, color, egg-laying, and so on. The expectation apparently was that you would do your homework about them on the Internet. But Theresa didn't have a computer, and she wasn't about to get one to identify her chicks.

Not that she was a Luddite, decrying these new technologies. Just that she really liked her current life and its various habits, one of which was extensive reading, and really didn't need any more busyness. Lute and Rusty both, of course, had offered to look online to help her figure out the chicken breeds, but she declined. They each had plenty to do, and if the chickens added a little anarchy to her life, so be it.

Back in the house, Mose gobbled his doggy breakfast so fast that great gobs of saliva ended up on the rubber mat under his bowl.

Thinking of Mary, Theresa said, "Anarchy."

Her sister had actually named her daughter after the famed anarchist Emma Goldman, once proclaimed "the most dangerous woman in America." Theresa hadn't a clue who called her that, nor did she much care. Unlike Mary and Mike, or Lute, Theresa wasn't particularly interested in politics. She voted, which if she remembered right, both Mike and Mary did not.

Neither did Lute, at each major election he'd say, "Don't vote. It only encourages the bastards!"

Not that she had any illusions about her vote making much of a difference. One reason she did it, she knew, was out of deference to and affection for her parents, who voted with the same fervor and loyalty with which they attended Mass, believing those things to be an essential feature of both their humanity and being American.

And what irony, she chuckled as she poured her coffee, that Emma Goldman should be, like Theresa's very conventional parents, buried in Chicago. Their brother Konrad, despite being a priest, had really shared much of Mike and Mary's ideas about the false gods of consumerism and the state as simply instruments of the capitalist elite—having witnessed the effects of same on the wretchedly poor folk he lived among in South America. And in later years, he even came to fully admit the complicity of much of Holy Mother Church in keeping the poor poor and in their desperate place.

"Church, like state," Mary's Mike had said more than once (he said everything more than once, Theresa remembered), "just another capitalist tool!" Well, Konrad hadn't been a capitalist tool, she thought sadly as she cracked a couple of eggs into a pan already filled with peppers and onions. Not exactly a revolutionary, but certainly, as they said of Jesus, Konrad had been "a man for others."

"A wry man, your brother," someone or other had said of Konrad, referring to his highly developed sense of irony. A quality he'd had even as a child, always a bit askance from the noise and hurry of family life, school, and the neighborhood. He was a loner at school, and apparently in the seminary as well. He even stood apart in their family, making fun of her and Mary and even their parents. Then he was ordained and was sent right away to an isolated rural parish of mostly Polish people in northwestern Wisconsin.

He'd told his family that normally he'd have been paired with a senior priest somewhere until he got comfortable, then on to his own parish. But there was a sudden opening when the pastor in the church had died, so Konrad went there on his own—and hated it. He wasn't familiar with how a parish ran, and in this case, a handful of women, including his devout elderly housekeeper, considered the church, rectory, and tiny elementary school their bailiwick. They resented Konrad from the day he showed up for being young, not Polish, and too good-looking. The young girls and even some younger wives in the parish actually giggled when he was around!

Not familiar with the ways of women, Konrad's enormous and everlasting first blunder was to tell the council that he didn't need a housekeeper and could care for himself, which would save money that should properly be spent on the school. That had been a bad move, and Theresa smiled remembering how she and Mary had both told him that he should have asked them first. Any woman could have told him that you don't mess with an entrenched housekeeper.

Konrad had continued to step on toes there, including trying to correct the misinformation the old nuns were teaching the children. He had told Theresa in desperation over the phone that they didn't seem to have any information about modern teaching methods or curriculum.

"I swear, Tee," he'd said, "the nuns here think, no kidding, that even Jesus was Polish."

After a miserable year there, when Konrad was told by the bishop that he was being transferred, he was thrilled to leave.

As Theresa finished breakfast and began to clean the kitchen, she tried to remember where Konrad had gone next. Yes, he taught somewhere, she thought. What was it, that Catholic high school maybe, in Eau Claire, La Crosse, Stevens Point? Yes, that was it, Theresa remembered, Stevens Point, another Polish enclave.

Konrad had really teased her too, Theresa remembered fondly, when she had married Tony and become a Kozlowski. Tony had left the church as a young man and was much amused by his brother-in-law's encounters with Polish Catholics. He never missed an opportunity to razz his brother-in-law about the old Polish ladies when they saw each other.

That high school had also not been a stunning success for Konrad. Still, the young priest stoutly maintained that he had a vocation—just hadn't yet found where to vocate. So when an opportunity arose to go to South America, to Peru, he seized it. And he came back on his first leave, or whatever the church called it, a changed man. A real priest, as he'd called it.

Sitting on their patio during a visit, lighting yet another cigarette, Konrad had inhaled deeply—the man loved to smoke—and asked Tony and Theresa if they remembered the warning he'd gotten in seminary about his irony, about using it to distance himself from others.

Long familiar with it, Theresa had nodded.

"Well, they were right. It was why I screwed up so much my first few years. Well, apparently, what my cold German soul needed was some heat. Not just from the sun, though there's plenty of that down there, but people heat, human warmth to get my blood moving in the right direction. You know, when I got there I bet the locals thought they'd gotten some kind of zombie padre. The people there, mostly Indians, are touchers. When they talk to you, they get right up close—in your face, we'd say—and start to touch you, just part of their conversation. I practically jumped out of my skin. Touching? Me? And my Spanish was terrible. But they persisted, God bless them—warmed the ice in my veins, fed me lots of rice and beans and hot peppers. Oh, those peppers! Sent a few senoritas my way to test my vows. I passed, I guess. We got a little school started, hooked up with a wealthy parish in Chicago to get regular shipments of used clothes, books, food, and canned goods, mostly. You just can't guess the poverty there."

He'd continued to tell them how he undermined the local elites, who were worried he might be some kind of commie padre, by hooking up with his resident bishop, who yearned for educated company and for someone who could keep up with his considerable fondness for expensive brandy, a taste Konrad soon acquired. If Theresa remembered right, her brother had eventually convinced the man he was no threat, no red priest, and he got the go-ahead, and modest support, for his efforts to help his charges.

Remembering all this, sad about both Tony and Konrad being gone, Theresa scraped the last glint of butter from her plate into Mose's dish before washing it.

That good butter she got from Quint Schumacher, her neighbor with two Jersey cows he milked by hand. Lute called the man an honorary Amish man since he wasn't really Amish, but he farmed like them, with horses and old machinery, and did as much as he could by hand. Quint also sported an enormous beard, wore shirts without collars and black wool pants, even in summer. And he treated his little wife like a servant, nothing violent or anything, just an obvious assumption that men were meant to run things and be obeyed, and women were to do their husband's bidding.

The man failed the Amish test however, by driving a pickup truck and using electricity, not to mention chewing tobacco. None of that mattered to Theresa though. The butter he churned by hand and sold illegally was wonderful. You just went into Quint's garage, opened a large freezer and took as many pounds as you wanted. He charged three dollars per plastic container, and you just left the money in a gallon jar on a nearby table. Butter. Ah. Cholesterol. At eighty-two she couldn't care less about monitoring it, so maybe she should take up cigarettes and whiskey too! The dishes done, she picked the sunniest spot at her dining room table and opened the novel she was currently reading, a new Benjamin Black mystery set in 1950s Dublin. She sipped her second cup of coffee while she read. Pausing for a moment, she thought how wonderful it was going to be to have Mary there, to have someone share her meals if only for a week or two. Maybe the worst part of living alone was eating alone. A thought she'd had far too many times.

Chapter 25

ABSORBED IN HER POTATO PANCAKES and increasingly anxious thoughts about how in the hell she was going to get out of Sidney, Nebraska, Joni listened to the loud waitress speak to whoever it was that had taken a seat in the booth behind Joni.

"Saw you pull in in that car. Late' 80s Town Car, right?" the waitress asked.

The customer behind Joni answering, "Yes, it's an '89."

"Thought so," the waitress answered. "I used to have one, an '87, loved that car. Truth told, I prob'ly married my ex as much for that car as for him. And ended up liking the car a lot more than that sorry man too! Where you headed?"

Joni could have sworn the woman said Minnesota.

"I'm going to visit my sister," Joni heard the woman say. "She has a farm there, in Minnesota."

Minnesota! She'd heard it right. Now what to do, Joni wondered, as she listened to the rest of the conversation.

"Long ways, but plenty doable in that rig," the waitress was saying. "Like a living room on wheels, I remember. What can I get ya?"

"Well, it's supper time," the woman was saying, "but I'm going to have breakfast. Just two eggs, over, sausage links, whole wheat toast, and coffee, please."

"Got it," the waitress replied as she left.

Twice Joni lifted herself almost out of her seat before she finally got up enough nerve to stand and turn toward the woman behind her. What was the worst that could happen, after all?

"Hi, excuse me. Did I hear that you're headed for Minnesota, ma'am?" Joni addressed the tiny elderly woman huddled in an outdoor jacket.

"I am, yes," Mary replied quietly to the pretty girl who stood at the edge of her table. "Why?"

"Well," Joni hesitated, "I'm headed there too. Do you mind if I sit for a minute?"

"No, sit down," Mary gestured across the booth, curiosity evident on her face.

"Well . . . ," Joni hesitated, "I'm just going to blurt this out. I need a ride. My trucker boyfriend and I had a fight, he's gone now and I'm stuck here, clueless about how to get to Minnesota. There," she sighed, "that's it!"

Now it was Mary's turn to hesitate, Emma's warnings about hitchhikers echoing in her mind as she appraised this young woman sitting across from her, looking desperate. Normally she wouldn't have given the kid a ride, as she wasn't keen about company, especially from a probably gabby youngster. But something about this girl struck her.

"Well," Mary sighed. "I'm going to blurt a little too. I'm eighty years old and driving halfway across country, much against the advice of my family, especially my daughter. And she of course, among her many warnings, issued a fierce one about hitchhikers, which you aren't in the strictest sense, but still . . . ."

Joni nodded in agreement and looked down at the table. "When I learned how to drive, my grandma, who raised me, gave me the big beware-all-hitchhikers speech. You know, highway murderers, the whole thing. So, of course, I never picked anybody up, not that many people hitchhiked in the boony town I'm from."

"Where's that," Mary asked?

"Garberville. Garberville, California. Little nowhere place up in the redwoods."

"Oh, California. I'm from Pasadena," Mary offered.

"Really, Rose Bowl, Parade of Roses, and all that?"

"Yes, all that," Mary gave a nod. "So why are you going to Minnesota?"

Joni was flummoxed, she hadn't really thought about an easy answer to that one. She'd already told one lie to this apparently nice old woman, and she shouldn't compound it with another. But the waitress intervened, bringing Mary's meal and giving Joni time to think.

"Hope you're not trying to buy this lady's car," she said to Joni. "'Cause if it's for sale, I'm first in line!"

Mary smiled. "Well, easy for both of you, it's not for sale. Not a bit of it!"

"Can I grab my plate and join you?" Joni asked. And not waiting for Mary's assent, she moved over, hauling her backpack into the booth with her.

"So." Mary nodded as she sipped her coffee. "Minnesota?"

"OK, it's a bit weird, kind of a *Tales from the Crypt* sort of thing," Joni said with a nervous laugh. "The dead guy in this case is my great grandfather, a guy I never met, but I guess his hand kinda reached out of the grave and into my life in Geeville a couple weeks ago. My dad got a letter from some lawyers in Minnesota, in Rochester. You know, where that fancy Mayo Clinic is? Turns out my great grandpa was a doc." The remaining potato pancake getting cold on her plate, Joni sketched out the rest of the story for Mary. "Guess it's kind of hard to believe, huh?"

Mary smiled, feeling far better than she'd felt since the afternoon assault, which seemed now like it had happened on another planet, eons ago. And she knew, gut instinct, that this girl wasn't lying. And that she would actually be glad for her company.

"No, it's actually farfetched enough to be believable. Either that, or you're a novelist trying your story out on me—in which case, I'll buy the book, my dear!"

My dear, Joni heard. That was a good sign; this old lady had class, and seemed to like her. Saying nothing, Joni dumped the rest of her applesauce onto her cold pancake, and finished eating.

Mary ate quietly for a bit too. Then after a long sip of coffee, she cleared her throat and said, "Yes, I'll give you a ride. And you're in luck, my sister doesn't live far from Rochester. She can probably help you find the lawyers you're looking for. So why don't we go together to her place—she has a little farm—and then get you to those lawyers from there."

Giving Mary a long look, Joni finally asked, "Are you sure? And, by the way, I'm Joni," she said, extending her hand across the table.

"I'm Mary. And I have a notion . . . listen. I suppose you have a driver's license?"

Joni nodded.

"Well, I'm already behind in getting to Minnesota. I'm really tired and can't drive anymore tonight, would you mind taking the wheel for a couple of hours to get us that much closer?"

Chapter 26

Mary explained Mike the Mannequin to Joni without telling her about being attacked earlier in the day. Was it just this past afternoon? Mary wondered. Joni understood the mannequin's purpose right away, so Mary suggested they leave him where he was, strapped in the passenger seat. That way the person who wasn't driving, in this case Mary, would stay in the back seat and rest. They agreed to at least try it out.

As Joni took the wheel of the Lincoln, Mary stretched out on the back seat, too tired to worry whether or not she was making the right decision. She fell asleep within minutes of getting on the highway.

God, Joni thought as she moved the seat back and down to find a comfortable spot, electric seat controls and cruise control! She set the speed at seventy-three miles per hour, a safe three miles over the limit. No use attracting the fuzz.

You lucky girl, Joni thought, somehow you got out of the fat, but for once, *not* into the fire.

She wasn't sure what she did actually get into in this case, though. Hey, girl, forget about it, she told herself. You have simply, for once, gotten lucky because you were smart enough to ask this old lady for a ride. Maybe your luck is changing.

The car sure was comfortable, Joni realized. She'd always been scornful of these big old cars, gas hogs, road hogs, tanks—but, man, it was comfortable, and unlike her old Civic, the heater worked great. The seat was luxurious . . . it was freaking white leather! Who knew?

Relaxing into the ride, she did feel a little guilty about dissing the Honda, it had really been a great car for so many years, despite its age. Feeling in her jacket pocket, she made sure she still had the dashboard bobblehead she saved before she ditched the Honda. He'd failed to keep the Civic running, but she figured he got her as far as he could, so she stuck the figure on the Lincoln's dash, hoping Mary wouldn't mind. Doubting she would.

What a great old lady she had stumbled into! Of course the dead hubby in the passenger seat was a bit weird, but Joni reminded herself it was just a mannequin, for safety, and she relaxed. And it did make sense for an old lady traveling alone, to keep the creepos at bay, she figured. Joni glanced over at "Mike," his hat pulled low on his forehead, the mustache, the painted lips. OK, again, weird. But unlike the late unlamented Sam the trucker, at least Mike the Mannequin wasn't about to put the moves on her. At least she hoped not!

As she drove she saw signs for Ogallala, North Platte, Kearney, Lincoln, and Omaha ahead. She should look at a map. Did Mary even have a map? She'd have to look at the next stop. What was the name of that last place—Sidney? What a shithole! Still, she got her lucky break there, and that break was now gently snoring in the back seat . . . on white leather! She still couldn't get over it. Jesus, she wondered how many hides it would take to make these seats. And how did they make them white? Albino cows? It was dark out there on the road around her except for the more or less constant stream of semis. Maybe one of them was Sam, the fucker, Joni thought indignantly.

On nights like this Joni's dad used to make some racist remark—a nigger's asshole?—to describe the darkness. She wasn't even sure if that meant her dad was a racist, he just said shit like that, not even thinking it was right or wrong. There had been two, maybe three, black kids all the way through school in Geeville, so it wasn't exactly a color-friendly kind of redneck town. There had been only one black kid in her graduating class. And he was adopted, his father was a white doctor. The kid took shit but he was pretty tough too, Joni remembered, he could give it back. And given the town's not-so-subtle hierarchies, a rich doctor's kid, black or not, had some power.

Grandma Eunice always said she liked black people, loved their music—soul, R and B, bebop, jazz. But her favorite jazzman was Chet Baker, or was it that other one, Art Pepper? Both white guys, if Joni remembered right. She and Eunice had watched a movie about Chet Baker once when her grandma was starting to go downhill. The guy was a total asshole, Joni remembered. Pretty much everybody hated him, but loved his music. Go figure.

Eunice blamed it on the junk. "Show me a junkie—white, black, man, woman—who's not an asshole when they're using, and I'll eat a pound of dog shit." And Eunice ought to know.

At least Joni's own interest in drugs was scant and she wasn't crazy about booze either. She just wasn't into losing control, letting herself get so vulnerable. Not to mention getting sick, thinking of all the cleaning up she'd done in the rooms and hallways at the motel. Why in the hell would you want to do something that made you sick? She figured she was lucky she apparently didn't inherit her dad and grandma's addictive tendencies. She'd always been able to choose whether or not to get wasted.

This old lady, Mary, said she was eighty? With a totally wrinkled, heavily tanned, face from what Joni could see. But she must have led a clean life, to live that long. And she seemed pretty loose. No St. Christopher medal on the dash, no fish bumper sticker. Both good signs the woman wasn't some kind of devoted Jesus jumper who'd try to convert her.

Her thoughts spinning randomly, Joni passed the exit for Ogallala, feeling good enough that she was sure she could drive through the night. Why not? As long as Mary slept, why waste money on a motel? Joni hated the thought of actually walking on the nasty carpet in one. People just didn't know what happened on those carpets, how much puke and sex and beer and piss got on them. Sure, the surface got cleaned up by the Jonis of the world, but underneath, where they couldn't easily clean? Yuck.

She thought it would be nice to listen to some music. Mary had told her the Lincoln only had a tape player and a radio, so CDs were out. And really, she couldn't play anything anyway if she didn't want to wake Mary. It would be great to surprise her by getting as far as, say, Lincoln or even Omaha, before Mary woke. Shit, Joni thought, what in the hell do the long-distance truckers and salesmen do over the many thousands of miles they drive?

Maybe they listen to music or talk on their CB radios. She hadn't even noticed if Sam had a CB. Maybe you had to be just a little bit crazy to spend all that time behind a wheel, get lost in your head while you were driving from A to B, stopping to piss and grab coffee and a shitty sandwich at a truck stop. Didn't seem like much of a life.

Joni was interested to get to Mary's sister's place. She'd never been on a farm and wondered what it would be like. Her mind wandered, imagining what the farm might include. Tractors, cows, chickens, hay bales, and all that? She didn't think she'd ever even seen a real farm on TV. Then she wondered why there weren't any farm shows, a farm sitcom or maybe even a farm reality show?

Well, if this all worked out, she'd soon know something about a farm. Joni realized Mary hadn't mentioned that her sister was married or anything. She'd have to ask Mary about that tomorrow. Could an old lady run a farm by herself? But then what did "running a farm" even mean! Joni smiled to herself as she floated along the highway, picturing an old woman sitting on a stool milking a cow, must have been something she'd seen in a book when she was a little kid. Joni pretended to read a children's book out loud to her mannequin seatmate, "Look. Here is Mary. She is milking a cow. And here is Joni. She is milking one too."

Joni suddenly froze. The rearview mirror. Shit, fucking cops! She slowed and edged right, expecting the flashing red lights to pass her. But they just stayed right behind the Lincoln. Joni talked out loud to calm herself, "OK, slow down, pull over. Here he comes, big hat, big flashlight. Push the button for the window, Joni. Whoops, wrong one. OK, got it. Be fucking polite, Joni, whatever you do."

"Yes, officer?" Joni said, giving him a wan smile.

"Did you know you have a taillight out, ma'am?" he said, leaning in toward her a little.

"No, sir, I didn't," Joni told the truth.

"Well, I'm not going to give you a ticket, just a warning, but I'll need your license and registration, and proof of insurance, please," he said as he waited expectantly.

Oh shit, here we go, Joni thought. Keep smiling while you look for the shit, girl! Handing him her license, she then opened the very large glove box and pulled various papers out of it, making a show of looking through them, when the truth was she hadn't a clue where the registration and insurance paperwork was.

"Ma'am?" the cop said pointedly.

It was time for Joni to fess up. "Well, officer, this isn't my car," Joni explained. "It belongs to the lady asleep back there, she needed some zee's so I'm driving. I don't like to, but guess I need to wake her . . . do I?"

"Yes, you do, miss," he instructed, shining the light inquisitively into the back seat. Mary was just starting to wake up as the officer's beam lit on Mike. "What's that?" he demanded with a note of surprise.

"Just a mannequin, officer," Joni explained. "He's there to keep the bad guys away." What else *could* she say?

"Bad guys, what do you mean?" the officer asked.

"Oh, you know, two women traveling cross-country pull into a truck stop. Having this guy makes it look like we have a man on board," Joni explained, giving him a girly smile and letting him know how necessary men were.

"It looks pretty strange if you ask me," the officer stated flatly. "I'm gonna run the car and your license, then come back for the rest. So please wake your friend." And with that, he turned and walked back to his bright flashing lights.

Joni sighed and turned on the interior light as Mary sat up, rubbing her eyes and asking, "What's going on?"

"We got stopped for a bad taillight," Joni explained. "He needs the registration and insurance stuff, I pulled all this out of the glove box but . . . ." She handed the pile of papers back to Mary, who stretched, yawned, and got her glasses out of her purse to look for the stuff in the pile.

"OK, it's here in this folder." Mary pulled out the documents. "Mike was good about keeping it handy. Don't give the officer any grief, just hand it over." Mary passed the documents up to Joni, asking "How are you doing, driving I mean?"

"Fine," Joni said. "No sweat until the dude with the big hat showed up. By the way, he's not too crazy about our friend here." She gestured to Mike.

"Oh, why not?"

"Hey, he's a cop. They're suspicious about everything." Joni grimaced in the mirror at Mary.

The deputy returned a long time later, but instead of giving Joni back her license, he asked her to get out of the car.

"What's the matter, officer?" Mary called from the back seat.

"This young woman's license has been expired for over two months, so I need to be sure it's actually her license. Come with me to the car please, miss," the officer explained. Taking her arm a little forcefully, he led her back to his rig and placed her in the back seat. "What is your full name?" the officer began.

"Joni Eunice Adams," Joni replied.

"Your age?" he continued.

"Twenty-four," Joni answered.

"Height, weight, eye, and hair color?" he asked her.

"Five three, one fifteen, green, and brown," Joni offered, trying to keep her cool.

"Place of residence?" was the officer's next question.

"Sixteen zero eight Commack, Garberville, California."

"How long have you been driving with an expired license?" he questioned her.

"I don't know," Joni answered. "If I knew it had expired I would have—"

But he interrupted her, "OK, OK, I've got a call in checking you and your license and the car. Now, who owns the Lincoln?"

"Mary, I suppose," Joni said. "The woman in the back seat."

"Mary what, what's her last name?" he sounded incredulous.

"I don't know, we only just met," Joni explained, knowing the situation was getting worse and worse.

"You don't know? You're driving her car and you don't know her name?" the officer demanded.

"Well," Joni sighed, "I got a ride from her back in a town near the border, the one with the big outdoor store? She was tired, so asked me to drive. We never had enough time to get really acquainted."

"You were hitchhiking? That's illegal here on the interstate, you know." The officer was now turned around in his seat, literally glaring at Joni.

"I wasn't hitchhiking," Joni explained. "I met her in the Perkins, heard she was going to Minnesota, and asked her for a ride."

"Why are you going to Minnesota, and how did you get to Sidney?" he asked.

Oh shit, here we go, Joni thought. "I'm going to visit some relatives in Rochester, the city with the Mayo Clinic? I got a ride to Nebraska from a trucker."

"Why is the old lady going to Minnesota?" the officer wanted to know. "And you rode in a semi all the way from California? Who was driving, and what was he hauling?"

"Far as I know, Mary is going to visit her sister," Joni answered. "And no, not in a semi from California, but in my old Honda, which gave out along the way, so I caught a ride with the trucker."

"What was his name? Who was he driving for?"

"Sam. He had his own rig, and he was hauling propane."

"Last name?" he asked.

"I don't know. But wait a minute, officer." Joni was getting very edgy. "Why all these questions? I know I screwed up on the license thing, but why the third degree?"

"Miss, I ask the questions. I-80 is a major drug corridor coast to coast, and you and the old lady are from California. So for starters, we're going to have to search you, your luggage, and the car," he stated coolly.

"You're kidding!" Joni blurted, her eyes big. "I'm no doper, and I'd be an idiot to be hauling that stuff across country. And the old lady, Mary, you gotta be kidding!" She was indignant.

"My partner will be here with a dog shortly."

"A dog for what?" Joni asked, near tears.

With that, he got out of the car, instructing her to "Just sit tight!"

Christ, Joni thought, fucking Deputy Dawg *and* a real dog. Let the nightmare begin!

"Ma'am," the officer said, leaning in the Dreadnaught to speak with Mary, who was now seated behind the wheel. "I'll take those," he said, retrieving the registration and insurance papers, "and I'll have to ask you to step out of the car, please."

"Out of the car, what on earth for?" Mary asked, beginning to be angry. "It's cold, and I'm old. Eighty years old, in fact."

"OK, just sit there," the man relented. "May I have your license? And where are you going?"

"To Minnesota, to see my sister," Mary answered tersely.

Looking at her license with his flashlight, he verified that it was current, and also that the old woman really was eighty.

"Ma'am," the man sounded exasperated. "Can I ask? Why's an eighty-year-old woman driving all the way across the country with a dummy in the front seat? And with a girl who doesn't even know your name?" he asked, sounding skeptical.

"Is there a law against any of that deputy?" Mary's voice now had a real edge to it.

"As I explained to your passenger back there, we're going to examine your car and your luggage. The taillight was out on the vehicle and your friend was driving with an expired license."

Oh hell, Mary thought. What about my medical marijuana? Well, she did have her clinic card, which should exempt her. Her thoughts were suddenly broken by the wail of a siren from another car pulling up in front of the Lincoln. Turning to Mike as the officer went to greet his partner, Mary said quietly, "Nice going, buddy. Thought you were going to protect me!"

Waiting tensely in separate vehicles, Mary and Joni both heard the dog bark—loud, sharp, and insistent. It was pitch dark, late at night, on this lonely stretch of highway in the middle of nowhere. They each worried silently about the horror show unfolding at the trunk of the Lincoln.

"OK, ma'am," the first officer said to Mary as he held her door open. "This time I do have to ask you to step out of your car, please." Mary, having put on a jacket while she waited, reluctantly eased out of her seat.

"What we got here, Pete, a travelin' sideshow?" the second officer asked, holding his straining dog as he peered in the car on Mike's side.

"Leave it, Harris," the first guy said. "Just haul that backpack out and put it on the ground. Let Steel check it out." Then turning to Mary and handing her the keys to the Lincoln, he said, "Ma'am, please open the trunk for us?"

Mary fumbled a little in the cold and dark, tired and nervous. The dog climbed into the car, still leashed, and began a frantic sniffing. At which point Mary suddenly remembered the odd sign she'd seen when she drove across the Nebraska state line, something about a drug dog ahead.

Well, she thought as she lifted the trunk lid, they warned me!

The next few minutes, or was it merely seconds, went by for both Mary and Joni in a crazed and frightening blur.

First, Joni started to get out of the cop car, causing the first deputy to turn and yell at her, "Hey! Get back in that car."

Next, the dog barked frantically from inside the trunk of the car, clearly signaling something to Harris, its handler, who said loudly, "Hey, Steel got something here. Might have caught him a drug bunny! Good pup, Steel." He pulled the small German shepherd from the trunk, patted its head, and he gave it a treat from his pocket.

The deputy called Pete grabbed Mary's arm as she attempted to approach her car, saying, "Hey, lady, stand still. Don't get near that car!"

Mary pulled angrily away from him, agitated and yelling now, "Why not? It's my damn car! Get your hands off me!"

"Whoa," Harris remarked, holding the barking dog. "Watch it, lady. It will be very bad if you're hauling illegal contraband into our fair state! Let's see what's in that luggage." Even in the dark, Mary could tell he was hoping to find something.

Mary tried to approach the Lincoln again, and was close enough to see Pete's name tag now. Monson. He stood in front of her now, firmly blocking her path. Then he took her—gently, she remembered later—by an arm and brought her to the rear seat of his partner's car.

"Sorry, ma'am, but you'll have to stay here while we finish our search." Mary heard the car doors lock as he left.

Seeing this, something in Joni snapped, a "Chet moment" she called it when she thought about it afterward. She leapt out of the first cop's car, yelling, she wasn't sure what, but something like "leave the old lady alone, you bastards!"

Whereupon the second deputy, the one with the dog, which was busy with Mary's luggage, simply grabbed her, roughly, and pushed her back into the vehicle, yelling at her to "Stay the fuck in there, you little—," and locked the doors.

After what seemed a long time, but was probably only moments, the two cops conferred briefly. Then each got in his squad car, Mary in one, Joni in the other, and took off in a blaze of lights and sirens. Suppressing an angry sob, Joni asked Munson, "What about the car? Mary's car? The Lincoln? You just leave it there?" But she got no answer.

Mary, in the other car, feeling herself shaking, wrapped her arms around herself, just like she'd done when she'd realized one morning that Mike was finally dead. God, she thought, first the crazy man in Cheyenne, and now, these cops. Except for the day Mike died, this was simply the very worst day in her long life.

Chapter 27

Early Saturday morning, with the weak sun just breaking through the clouds, Lute loaded his pickup with the tables, canopy, signs, and produce for his farmers' market stand in Winona. En route, he breathed some relief that Theresa had called the night before and canceled coming with him. She was worried her sister would show up sometime on Saturday, and she wanted to be there when Mary came.

He loved Theresa, and almost always enjoyed—and was grateful for—her company. But when she helped in his booth at the market, he was usually uncomfortable. For one very clear reason—women! Lots of them. Yes, weird as it was, he had groupies, farmers'-market groupies. They showed up to buy some stuff, of course, but also to talk to him, and to flirt. Young women, girls really, from the U who wanted to be invited to his farm to check out the cool, hippie place. They at least moved on after they grew tired of him or graduated and moved away. But the older women from thirty on up to his own age . . . Jesus. There was a group of them, not together but in aggregate. Divorcees, widows, somebody's ex-girlfriend, they came like flies to sugar to his booth.

Theresa kidded him about it, in her gentle way, laughing about his Winona Harem. Couldn't blame them, they were all lonely, crazy, or crazy lonely! He certainly didn't encourage them, he thought, as he pulled out onto the main highway into town. But shit, he didn't mind a little attention from so many lovely ladies. They'd be standing there with their hips cocked, yakking about this or that. Jesus!

And he knew well enough that one of the reasons he liked seeing them all at the farmers' market was that it was a level of interaction that worked for him. No commitment, no requirement, no demands. They could flirt all they wanted, but at the end of the day, he could go home alone without the entanglement of a deeper connection with any of them. And then next week he could go back for a little more—totally self-serving, and he was fine with that.

Pulling into his space at the market, the Hmong family next to him was already there. Shit, did they sleep here?

"Hello, Ger," Luther greeted his very short neighbor, who waved back at him. And, of course, she'd brought her daughters with her. Also very short, with thick bodies and totally round faces. He didn't find any of the women in that family attractive, but they could sure grow the hell out of some veggies. Their stuff was often much larger than his. They said they didn't spray or use artificial fertilizer, but he doubted it. But, it was none of his business. Caveat emptor!

Luther put down the cement corner supports for his canopy, then set up the aluminum frame, always an awkward process. Pinching his fucking finger, well that was the norm. He snapped it together, stretched it some more and then his black canopy was in place. He then unloaded and put up two eight-foot folding tables, positioning two old kitchen chairs behind them. Now it was time to load all the veggies on the tables. This was the part Theresa was good at. She was much more orderly.

When he was done, he added the signs with quantities and price on each pile. Butternut squash 3@$5, red noodle beans $2.50/lb., purple ground cherries $2/basket. And so on, making a note to check his competitors' prices later. Finally, he stepped back to take a look, realizing—whoops—he'd forgotten to post his other signs.

On the left hand corner of the canopy, appropriately, he hung the quote from Ursula K. Le Guin, tattered and dirty after so many years: "You cannot buy the Revolution. You cannot make the Revolution. You can only be the Revolution. It is in your spirit, or it is nowhere!" Then on the other corner, in very large black letters: "One day the poor will have nothing left to eat but the rich!" Rousseau. Quote went well with the one from Le Guin. And it almost always got a rise out of some asshole. Wonder who'll bite today? He smiled to himself.

Then, finally, the big sign on a sandwich board standing by his booth: Raging Moon Farm, L. Rasmussen, prop., organic grower. It included a great 1970s painting, done by Liza, a former love who'd stayed one summer then split. The picture was of a crazed moon, all jangly angles, huge dark eyes, octopus rays, a little bit like her, actually. It got people's attention, back then, anyway. Now, it was only tourists who even noticed. Still, most other signs at the market were boring. Ger Xiong Family Farm, Trusty's Trusty Acres, Happy Daisy Gardens, and Sonshine Farms. The latter was the moniker of the Jesus-people family down the way. He couldn't stand them—the guy reminded him of Dickens's Uriah Heep, as unctuous as the day was long.

Whoa. Luther noticed a new outfit just backing in next to him on the north side. Shit, this dude had *semper fi*, NRA, and Harley stickers in the window. Triple threat. This was going to be interesting. The man drove a brand-new, giant, bright-red Ford F-350 dually, certainly not a farm truck. A woman got out first, smiling at him. Older, but fit and pretty in a careful kind of way.

The guy with her was tall, also fit, and bald with a trim goatee. He wore a wool vest, new jeans, big belt buckle, shiny cowboy boots, and he came right over to Lute with his hand outstretched. "Hi, I'm Hal, Hal Brekke. My wife, Georgia," he said gesturing toward the woman. "We're new here."

Yeah, I knew that, Lute thought, shaking the guy's big hand. He had one of those manly handshakes bordering on aggression. "Hi, I'm Lute, Luther Rasmussen. Not new here, been here forever, actually," he said as he turned and backed just a little away.

"Well, good then," the big man replied decisively. "You can show us the ropes." He turned to help his wife unload a couple of tables that she then spread cloths over. Wanting badly to split for coffee, Luther forced himself to sit in his booth to see what the new people's gig was. They pulled stuff out of cardboard boxes. Oh shit. Lamps, rolling pins, spoons—all wood, all real shiny. It was turned stuff done on a lathe. Weren't there already two or three others with the same shit in the market?

"Hey, Ger," Luther finally said. "Can one of your girls watch my stand while I get coffee, please and thanks?" he asked his other neighbor.

"Sure, Lute," Ger answered, then directed one of her daughters, in Hmong. Giggling, the girl came and stood behind Lute's tables.

Luther walked quickly to the south, rapidly passing many familiar booths, where almost all greeted him. When he reached the Amish lady's space, with her great old-fashioned baked goods, he bought two raised donuts. He nodded at her daughter in the white cap and long dress.

Then, down two more booths, he was greeted again, "Hey, it's Lute the Luther. Mister Rasmussen. Or is it Ras*muu*sen? Not here for coffee, are you?" The stand's small, dark, and very large-breasted proprietor, Lucy something or other, greeted Luther with obvious affection.

"No jive, Lucy," Luther replied, smiling at her. "Just java. Large dark roast, please?" Lucy was one of his groupies, a still-cute woman somewhere over fifty, who he figured wouldn't be bad to spend the night with. But nookie isn't free, man, he had to routinely remind himself. Nor should it be. You have to have a relationship, remember—romance, commitment, shared breakfasts, commitment, commitment.

"Jive? Me? Right here in bony old Winona? Not happening, mister," she said with a laugh. "Just a poor working girl trying to make her way in a harsh world, don't you know?" And she pressed Luther's change deep into his palm, winking at him.

"Donuts, huh?" Lucy pointed to the papered pastry. "No good for you, y'know, all that sugar. Know what it does, Luther?" She stepped back and shook a finger at him.

"Puts on weight, I suppose," he responded.

"Right, weight in the wrong places. Makes men grow tits. Keep eatin' them and you'll be wearing a goddamn B cup!" She wagged her finger again.

Never quick, and flustered as always being near this woman, Lute responded lamely over his shoulder as he headed back to his booth, "B cup, huh? Sounds more like a B movie to me, Luce!"

Well that was dumb, he thought, safely back in his space, where he thanked Ger's daughter. What was her name? Taub? It meant something like squash, he remembered. Why not call your kid a veggie name? Maybe it brought good gardening luck.

Several people were already milling around in front of his stand. A fat guy, big beard, suspenders, silly Aussie outback hat, was asking, "What do you do with these eggplants?"

"The long green are Thai, not as bitter as the standard Italian ones. I use them in stir-fry."

"I'll take three," the man handed Luther a five. "Try anything once."

Right behind him, a nice-looking couple—he knew she taught at the U—bought an acorn squash and a small sack of potatoes, German butterballs.

"How are you, Luther?" the late-middle-aged man, wearing a beret, asked.

"I'm fine. That sun breaks through, I'll be even better," Luther replied. The woman, always a little aloof, only smiled at him. Liberals, he thought. Nice people, but why shouldn't they be? Good jobs, nice house, car, wedding ring. He figured they were smart enough to know that the world was in a state of rapid decline, but why would they do anything when they had it so good? And to be fair, he pondered, what could they do?

Several other folks were just strolling, lolling around the booth next door, then his. The new guy now had all his stuff displayed. Shiny wood and bright brass on the lamp fixtures. Shiny like that big new truck, a freakin' dually to hold a few boxes of wood ornaments, Luther thought incredulously! Jesus-jumpin' land of wretched excess, Luther thought, and the guy had a shiny head too! Did the dude grease that dome of his? Luther looked over to see the guy's wife bending over to pick something up, and noted she had a real nice ass. What the hell was she doing with that dork?

"Excuse me, ma'am," Luther said to the customer standing in front of him, realizing he hadn't heard a word she'd said. She was a large lady, regular Valkyrie in wool armor.

"I asked about your beets," she repeated. "Do they keep well?"

"Sure do," Luther said, standing up to respond to her. "You can can 'em, of course, straight up or pickled. Or, if you've got a cold space, about forty degrees all winter? Just put a bunch of sand in a large container, stick in the beets. Last all winter and well into spring. Course they'll last in just your fridge for a real long spell too."

"Well." Did she actually huff a little? "I don't can, and I don't have a cold space. I'll take this bunch though, and just keep them in the fridge."

Handing her the change, he then turned to the woman opposite, a very small, quite elderly person who said with a smile, "I do can. So I'll take four bunches. These are lovely."

Bagging the beets, and thanking her, Luther wondered if he'd seen her before. He didn't think so. Now the mall in front of the market was really beginning to fill with the Saturday-morning crowd. Regulars, tourists, strollers, kibitzers, a steady stream of folks making it their mission to look in at every booth, buy something or maybe not. Lute told himself, for the thousandth time, that the market wasn't merely a place to sell food, it was a mini adventure for these house and condo dwellers. Kind of a Saturday fair.

And to remind him of this, there was today's musical entertainment, Lonesome Bill the Whippoorwill. The cat didn't have a bad voice, but he couldn't play the guitar worth a darn. And he sang all that sappy, country crap. Luther grimaced, figuring the guy was clueless about how bad it sounded. Ger's daughters both had their earbuds in—no fools they!

Some of the vendors had complained about Bill last winter at the annual market meeting where they elected officers. The treasurer had responded, "Hey, he's free so the music doesn't cost us a dime. And with the state of our treasury, I'd say we keep him." So "free" meant they were stuck listening to Bill, like it or not.

Uh-oh, groupie alert! Luther saw a familiar woman coming in strong at four o'clock, what was her name? Elvira, Elmyra, it was El-something. She was a midsized matron with dyed red hair to match her red cowboy—or cowgirl—boots. She was wearing plenty of eyeliner to emphasize her best quality, large, green luminous eyes. She had a pert little nose, a bit too upturned, Luther thought, and a small gash of a mouth. Her giant earrings were dangling almost to her shoulders, which were wrapped in a colorful poncho, and gold-chained glasses hung across her chest. It was a lot to take in.

"Hi, Luther," she said in her Hollywood-breathless voice. "I didn't see you last week."

"Nope," he replied. "In the fall I start to cut wood, so I'm here only every other Saturday."

"Well, too bad for you, last week I brought you that book I was telling you about," she continued.

"What book?"

"The one about astrology? I didn't bring it today, since I wasn't sure you'd be here. How are things up at Magic Moon Ranch?" she asked, smiling as she fingered the broccoli.

"Raging Moon," he corrected her. "Things are fine, thanks." She'd pulled that Magic Moon bit before, trying to get a rise out of him. It wouldn't work today. Just smile, dude, he told himself, keep on smiling. "Need some broccoli?"

"Yes, I'll take this bunch. I never remember, Luther, are you certified or not?" another poke.

"Nope, never was, never will be," he answered bluntly. "I farm organically, the whole nine yards, but I can't afford to pay for certification and I'm not crazy to have strangers poking around my place. People either take my word or . . . ," he trailed off, smiling at her.

"No, no, I believe you. But couldn't you sell at a lot more places if you were certified?" she asked, smiling back.

"S'pose so, but I like what I'm doing just fine. Do a few more local markets during the high season," he responded, giving her the change and putting the broccoli in a small bag.

"Well, stay safe. You'll be here week after next?" she asked in that husky voice. "'Cause if you are, I'll bring that book, maybe a couple of others you might like."

"Fine, and thanks," he replied, watching her stroll off, her behind twitching.

And so the day went. He took another break to get a buffalo burger with lots of onions from another booth, the Bullfrog Ranch Bison Farm. One or two more groupies showed up to kid him and sway their hips. The market officially closed at noon, but he lingered until about one, enjoying a sashaying group of college girls, still wearing shorts despite the late season, to show off their great legs. One—God, she was lovely—read his battered sign and asked who Ursula Le Guin was. Luther told her to read *The Left Hand of Darkness* first, his favorite.

Traffic slowed and it was finally time to wrap it up. The new guy came over, looked over Luther's signs, and paused in front of the poor-eating-the-rich one, asking, "So where's your place?"

"Up in the hills from here, near Moeville," Luther answered.

"Don't know it. We just moved here from St. Paul. It's a good place to retire, we heard." Pausing just a moment, he continued, "Sooo . . . what have you got against rich people?"

Oh shit, here it comes, Luther figured. Give him the judicious answer, not the rant. "Depends on who they are, how rich they are, and where they got their money. Especially that." Luther started to load stuff into his pickup, and the guy followed him.

"Well, I'm rich, or some people might think so," the man stated boldly. "We just bought a nice condo here in town. Got the retirement toys too, a new truck, new Harley. You ride?" the man asked.

"Motorcycles? No, just a tractor," Luther said as he kept working.

"Just a tractor, that's a good one," the dude smiled a tight little grin.

Should I give him the whole rap, Luther asked himself? About the wholly unjust distribution of wealth in this "free" country? He decided against it. No point, just get out of here.

"Know how I made my money?" the man asked, not giving up. "Airline pilot. Learned to fly in the Corps, then became a commercial pilot for Northwest and then Delta."

"No argument with that," Luther paused with a basket of potatoes. "Always thought you guys should be paid as much as you need, maybe more, keeping all those people alive up there."

The guy started to say something else, but happily was interrupted by a call from his wife. "Hal, we've got to go. Susan's coming, you know!" A slight chiding note in her voice.

"Well, nice to meet you. Plenty of time to hash these things out over the next weeks."

"Hash things out," Luther fumed under his breath. Fuck you, amigo, he thought, remembering those Mose Allison song lyrics: "Just another middle-class white boy, out trying to have some fun."

Luther reviewed the day as he drove out of Winona. Not bad bread-wise, two hundred-some bucks. Thinking again of the silly guy next door with his turned lamps—a fucking hobby! That was a word Luther hated, especially when someone would hear he had "only" a forty-acre farm and exclaim in all foolish innocence, "Oh, so you have a hobby farm!"

Hobby farm. Fuck you, he thought, come and work a day and see how much of a hobby it is! Glancing over at the seat next to him, he realized how empty it was now that Azteca was gone. Feeling a bit lonely, he thought of the lovely college girl, the one asking about Le Guin, and the pleasant view of her as she walked away.

Forget that, he told himself. It was time to get home, have a beer, and smoke a joint! The afternoon sun was nice. Fall gave the best sunshine, mellow, shining off the leaves that were starting to turn. He would make a veggie stir-fry for supper.

He remembered out of nowhere the enormous wok he'd seen when he went to take a piss in the back of some tiny restaurant in Saigon.

"Know what they fry in there?" One of his drunken buddies had asked back at their table. "Kids, little gook kids, prob'ly eatin' some now."

And then they'd all laughed drunkenly.

Stupid, he thought. Stupid war, stupid soldiers . . . stupid Luther for going there.

Chapter 28

Saturday, another day alone for Theresa, or hopefully not, since she really expected Mary to arrive. Who knew exactly when though?

Theresa stood in her yard after doing morning chores, surveying the place from a newcomer's perspective. Let's see, she thought, the large sugar maple probably close to two hundred years old was magnificent right next to the house, on the southeast side. Just starting to turn, its colors would be spectacular in a week or so.

On the south side of the house was a much newer tree, a three-clump river birch, one she'd planted as a memorial to Tony just after he died. Rapid in its growth, it now rivaled the maple in height, but was much more slender, and offered no color of note in its falling leaves, its gnarly white-black bark and graceful branching being its chief qualities. The birch had become infected with a boring insect two years previous, when a prolonged summer drought had weakened it, and Theresa had neglected to water it enough, considering it was a species that thrived naturally along riverbanks. This past spring, she'd given the tree a serious dose of a granular insecticide, which she was pleased to note had slowed the borer's top-down attack on the birch. Now, she knew, she was committed to using that chemical each year until either she or the tree died. Hopefully she would go first.

Recalling that drought, Theresa remembered how horrible it was, and just a few miles from the Mississippi, one of the world's largest rivers.

Theresa pondered what this wonderful area she lived in would look like as the planet heated up—palm trees, crocodiles in the Big River? The hardwood forests reduced to some sort of savannahs? She shuddered.

Just ten or so miles inland from Winona, Theresa's farm was located in the steep hills and valleys formed by the Mississippi over many millennia. Having lived in Chicago, flat, then in college in Winona, also flat, she was awestruck when Tony first brought her to his farm. The hills were all heavily covered with mostly oak woodlands. And the striking valleys, large ravines actually, were where people farmed, ran cattle, and operated small businesses.

Despite living on the farm for most of her life, she'd still never gotten over her delight at the wonderful place she was lucky enough to live in. The house itself was situated on a knoll near the base of a large hill covered with a mixture of red cedars, box elders, and poplars, trees of little consequence that soon gave way to a hardwood, mostly oak forest that ran to the hilltop, probably a third of a mile up from the house. Next to the house, on the south, was the wonderful limestone patio that Rusty and Lute had built some years ago.

It was too chilly now, but during the summer, she often had her breakfast there, seated at a table made from an old iron register mounted on legs from a treadle sewing machine. Rusty had made it for her. Leaning on the table, she hoped that she and Mary could at least eat lunch there if the weather warmed a bit, as it often did at the start of fall.

At a slight drop from the patio was a small section of lawn, pretty scruffy and hardly golf-course quality, that led to a very long alpine currant hedge which defined the gardens it enclosed. A wooden pergola marked the garden entrance, into the beds of flowers and vegetables. The pergola was covered with a vigorous wild grapevine, and a small bench rested on the structure's brick floor.

Rusty had built the pergola too, of course, out of his favorite red elm timber. Red elm was highly water-resistant, and he'd built it in a semblance of an arts-and-crafts style, which she liked. The bench was made from the same wood, just a simple seat and supports on each end cut from sections of a log. And the bricks had actually been pavers on a city street in Winona, torn up and thrown away to allow a modern road to be installed.

Sometimes, sitting on the bench, Theresa could imagine the bricks giving off the sounds and vibrations of horses and wagons and carts. Some of which certainly belonged to Tony's Polish relatives, who had once traversed them going to St. Stan's for Mass, or downtown for groceries, or to the river to see what a paddleboat had brought to the city. She had never shared those musings with Rusty or Luther. Only her dog Mose knew, since he'd join her there for a late summer afternoon cocktail. Mose could still smell the horses traversing the bricks, the dog urine long past, dead wagon-squished squirrels, and one or two pieces of kielbasa some child had dropped from her sandwich a hundred years ago.

Walking through the pergola, Theresa thought of how much she was going to enjoy telling her sister the landscaper about these little treasures. Like the large glass ball that hung in one corner of the pergola, partially encased in a rope net, still giving off the smell of tar left from its days, she'd been told, as a fishing float in some very remote ocean. Lute had been the one to tell her what it was, having seen many similar ones used as decorations in bars in Saigon. Tony had bought the beautiful blue-green globe at some farm auction eons ago, and who would ever know how it had gotten into the hills above the Mississippi? A good mystery.

Theresa headed into the gardens, a nice sunny day to be there. Her thumb was decidedly brown for the first garden she'd planted upon moving here. Tony had plowed up the space with his tractor, leaving her to break up the huge furrows with a rototiller he'd proudly given her as a birthday gift. God, that thing was a beast. She still had it, but could no longer run it. The monster had six tines mounted in front of the motor where it could do serious damage to large clumps of dirt—and even more damage to the arms, shoulders, and legs of whoever was operating it. Theresa smiled fondly at the memory of her first attempts to master that machine and Tony's astonishment at his new bride's willingness to tackle it.

After the awful tilling, she'd moved on to using a spade, fork, and rake to make her gardens. Also work she'd never done before, but soon learned to enjoy and, in the winter, even crave. She especially enjoyed the raking, when she leveled a bed, the soil fine and crumbly, was transformed into planting readiness.

"You'd never know she grew up in Chicago, where they think mowing a patch of grass in front of their house is a backbreaker," Tony would brag about her to neighbors and relatives.

Her first garden had simply been a series of beds measured out in the dirt. Peas here, pole beans there, lettuce there, and so on, with paths in the dirt between them. How crude, she smiled at the memory.

Then she'd started getting gardening magazines, talking to older neighbors and even to some of Tony's uncles who gardened in town. She realized her space could be much more productive and look infinitely better if she created a series of raised beds to grow in. And while Tony had very little to do with her gardening, he'd been helpful with the beds, hauling some trees to the sawmill in Moeville to make timbers and boards for her out of the farm's oak, red elm, and locust trees. These he and Theresa sunk into the garden and spiked together at the corners.

At first, they'd made only half a dozen beds, filling them with a mixture of black dirt, manure and sand. But over the years she'd added more. Now there were fourteen, filled and refilled over the years with sand and the wonderful compost she'd learned how to make. It had to be one hundred sixty degrees in the pile for the whole miraculous composting thing to happen. She measured it using the three-foot-long soil thermometer Lute had given her years ago for no particular occasion. The man didn't observe the holidays or traditional niceties—Christmas, birthdays, and so on—just gave you stuff when he wanted to.

Going over the virtues of raised beds in preparation for telling Mary, Theresa reprimanded herself. Hey, Tee, she's a professional gardener, remember? She smiled as she took in the garden's paths, no longer just dirt either, but filled with sawdust and wood chips Rusty brought from his shop. No muddy garden walks for her!

Now, let's see, she thought, taking an assessment of the state of the garden. The tomatoes were done, she'd have to pull the plants and discard them. The lettuce had bolted, so she'd feed the rest to the goats. A late planting of radishes was doing well, and there was a nice head of cauliflower there. And still some peppers, although frost would get them if she forgot to put a sheet over the beds at night. There were some cabbages left that she should make into kraut along with the ones she'd asked Luther to save for her. Theresa loved making sauerkraut. So simple, and so vital, at least in the old days, when the soured cabbage was the main source of vitamin C for local farmers.

Maybe when Mary got here they'd do it together, which would be fun. Worrying as she moved to garden two, she wondered, would making kraut be fun for Mary? Who knew?

Another currant hedge separated the gardens, and yet another one set garden number two apart from three, which was looking pretty scraggly. She would have to maybe get rid of some of it and replant next spring, she decided.

Then she remembered, she was eighty-two! Would there even *be* a next spring for her? God she hoped so, not because she was particularly afraid of dying, but because she so much enjoyed being alive. Yes, she was lonely, but there wasn't much to do about that. And where was her dear sister?

"Mary, you better get here soon," Theresa said aloud, a note of worry in her voice.

And then, "Hey! Out of here, you!" she said to a black squirrel scampering in her flower garden, certainly up to no good. Lute had offered to shoot it, or trap it, but she'd declined. If it had been a gray, she would've opted for the trap, catch it alive and haul it off somewhere far from the farm. But the black one, so unusual, had caught her fancy. So she just yelled at it when it was in her bird feeders or the gardens. By now, over a season, it had grown so used to her that it only went a short distance up a tree to wait until she went away, then returned to its task of eating and storing food. No black squirrel offspring last May. So was he a loner, she wondered, and why did she think it was a he?

Theresa did a quick inventory of the flowers, then picked a bouquet for the church tonight. She never knew if the flowers got used, that was up to the very officious Altar Society women at St. Stan's, but she brought them anyway. It was a cutting garden after all. She'd bring a bouquet to Carmen too.

Let's see, what's left? Cosmos, of course, all feathery and floppy pinks and oranges. It wasn't suitable for church, and neither were her garden phlox, abundant and thriving in their whites and pinks. Several large bunches of Shasta daisies remained, they'd be good in a bouquet, as would some of those Black-Eyed Susans, an old-fashioned favorite. She couldn't use the Osteopermum, as brilliant as they were. A new favorite of hers, they worked in some arrangements, but not in a large bouquet. There was some yarrow, very dusty yellow, and asters, still thriving in their purples and pinks. And, oh right, Heliopsis, bright-yellow flowers kind of like large daisies. The Gaillardia, or blanket flower, was still blooming in oranges and some lovely burgundies. And anemones—very, very white and also quite lovely. All of them would work. An autumn bouquet, wonderful!

That's why you planted them, Theresa, she told herself. The hydrangea tree situated right in the middle of the currant hedge, filled with very large and showy green-turning-to-dusty-rose blooms, would be perfect for the bouquets too. Did Mary have any of these out in Pasadena, she wondered? Or would she be scornful of such a limited palette, given what she could grow, like roses, out there in the perpetual sunshine?

Let's see, for church how about a couple of mums, a brilliant orange and a nice fallish red. Good, she thought as she went to get a shovel out of her garden shed. The shed was a lovely little building, quite ornate, but then Rusty had built it, so of course it was unique. And useful, saving her having to traipse up into the barn's hayloft where she used to store tools. In the shed, she grabbed a couple of plastic pots, then dug and potted the mums, leaving them there until she would put together the bouquets just before she left for church.

Theresa's last garden, garden three, was largest of them all, about fifty by fifty square. It was the "wild" garden, where Theresa grew her melons, squash, and potatoes. No raised beds, just plain ground. For the first month or so in the spring, after planting and when things were just getting started, this garden looked nice and orderly. The squash and melon mounds well defined from one another, the potatoes coming up neatly in their rows.

But by about midsummer, the garden was in riot, an anarchy of plants growing in and over and around each other, with the squash invading the potato patch, despite her best efforts to keep the vines away. She'd already harvested most of the squash—acorns and butternuts were her favorites—but she saw she'd missed some now that the first light frost had decimated the leaves on the plants.

There had been no leaves on the potatoes, hadn't been for a month or more thanks to the blight that always finally killed them. Still, once she'd pulled away the great tangle of squash plants from the potato rows, she knew that there'd be an abundant crop of Kennebecs, Yukon Golds, and those wonderful German Butterballs under the soil. She'd have to get to them soon too, thinking with pleasure about the wonderful storage her old farm cellar offered, with its limestone walls and gravel floor.

Rusty had even built her a squash room down there a few years back, insulating it from the normal thirty-five to forty-degree cold in the rest of the cellar, as squash needed it about fifty degrees to keep well into the winter, even until late February in some years. Whereas the potatoes would last until she was able to replant some of them in May, and likewise the carrots and beets. Stored in plastic pails filled with sand, they would stay edible until a new crop arrived. Not to mention her many shelves of canned goods: tomatoes in several variations from salsa to sauce to whole, pickled beans, lots of kraut, and several kinds of pickles, the best being the mixed ones with not only cukes, but also carrots, cauliflower, onions, and garlic.

She always made too much of her salsa, some of it had probably been down there more than ten years. Time to get rid of them, Tee, she told herself. The stairs down to the cellar, hidden under a trapdoor in her pantry, were steep and cramped, and harder and harder to negotiate, which meant one day she might just have to stay down there until they found her lying there staring up with a frozen smile at her lovely jars of raspberry jam! Not a terrible death, she thought, smiling again.

Theresa told herself not to think of things like that, especially not after her fall last winter. Standing in her lovely cutting garden, she remembered the incident. It was in late March, fresh snow had fallen over previously melted snow that had frozen, turning the farmyard into a sheet of ice. She owned a pair of boots with ice crampons fastened to them, but since they were hard to put on, she'd used her other winter barn boots with their simple rubber soles. Big mistake. About halfway down to the barn, her feet went out from under her and she fell violently backwards right on her head.

As good fortune would have it, she had on a thick woolen cap, but she still lay there dazed for a few minutes, with Mose sticking his cold, wet nose into her face. She had gotten up slowly and checked for anything broken. Her limbs were all functioning, so she went carefully back to the house and changed boots, by which time she had a seriously painful headache. She nursed herself with ibuprofen throughout the day, but foolishly told Rusty about the fall in a late-afternoon phone call. Foolishly, because Carmen had been pushing Rusty to get his mother to move into some sort of assisted-living place. Which Theresa was absolutely not going to do. So the poor boy was caught between a rock, his mother, and a very hard place, his wife.

"What would have happened if you hadn't been able to get up, Mom, just lying there until you froze to death?" Rusty had asked, worried.

"Well, it *didn't* happen. How about you, Rusty?" she had challenged him, defensively. "Driving around on these dangerous winter roads, picking up lumber, delivering cabinets? You could easily go off the road into a ditch, hit your head, and freeze to death too!" She'd immediately regretted she'd said such a thing.

"But, Mom, you're eighty-two. I mean how long can you live up there alone, it's dangerous!" Rusty had demanded, his usually calm voice rising a little.

"If I'm fortunate, until you carry me out of here on a board," was her quick retort, which she had also immediately regretted. "I love this place, I love my life here, and I can't imagine another. I've told you, if I lose my mind, you can put me anywhere because I won't know or care. Otherwise, it's the farm." Why had she told him about her fall? Silly old woman, she'd thought at the time.

She knew Mary had issues with her daughter too. Emma was worried about Mary staying in her own home too, not to mention taking this cross-country car trip. The same conversation was probably being repeated across the entire country a million times a day.

"Let it go," Theresa thought, turning to look over the valley where the bulk of the farm lay. The sixty-four open, unwooded acres divided into thirteen fields Tony had used for rotationally grazing his cattle. To prevent erosion, each field was its own separate erosion-resistant enclave, put in years ago with government help from the county soil service.

All the fields were now rotationally grazed by a young couple who rented from Theresa, great kids in their early thirties who actually had college degrees in something or other and had decided to become farmers. Peg and Adam Thorsness had bought the beat-up old Robideaux place between her and Lute. They were fixing up the house and outbuildings while raising two little kids—not to mention chickens, pigs, gardens, and their small Jersey herd. Wincing a little when she thought of them, she remembered their disconcerting tendency to wander around her place when they stopped by and simply asking for something they saw and needed.

"You're not still using that old side rake, are you Theresa?" Adam had inquired over coffee one morning.

"Why no." Theresa had answered.

"Can we have it then? We'll put it to good use. I'd offer to buy it, but we're cash shy, you know," he'd said, giving her his winning grin.

Of course, she'd given him the rake. She wasn't using it and it couldn't have been worth much at auction. Other requests had followed, however, including a small gas lawnmower, several pitchforks, and barn shovels, a coil of barn rope, until finally she'd mentioned it to Lute, who she knew wasn't particularly fond of the couple.

"Hey, Tee," he'd advised. "Better stop it now before they convince you to give them your farm."

"But I like them. They're smart and attractive and very charming. And I love what they're trying to do with that old place."

"I agree with you on that, and I appreciate the grazing thing. Have they been paying you what you asked for using those pastures?" Luther asked, looking at her with skepticism.

"Not exactly. They're a little late."

"How late?"

"About a year, I guess, more or less," Theresa said, wishing she'd never brought the subject up.

"Jesus!" Luther exclaimed and stood up, then just as suddenly sat down at Theresa's kitchen table, where she was serving him breakfast. "You know I helped them out at first too. A lot. Not just advice, but stuff, mostly gardening tools, a wheelbarrow, and so on. And soon as I did, they just started asking for more stuff they needed. Couple times of that and I just said no. Told 'em to go to an auction, pay for it themselves."

"But I know they're struggling over there," Theresa sipped her coffee nervously.

"But, Tee, we all struggled. You and Tony, me, the Moes. Hell, I'm still struggling, and so are they. Can you imagine John Moe coming over here and asking you for a cup of coffee, let alone a piece of farm machinery?" Lute challenged.

"No, I can't," she admitted. "And of course Tony found it hard even to ask you for help when he needed it. I used to tell him that you were his friend, and friends help each other, but he was always reluctant. You, in fact, are very much the same, my dear friend." It was her turn to challenge Luther.

“Well, better get your cash rent from them this season, Tee, or tell ’em it’s off for next year. You know you can always find other renters. In fact,” he looked hard at her, “I’d even be happy to go over and collect it for you. Those people, college educated, middle class, whatever, are takers. So sure they’re doing the right thing, and they take it for granted that we should all support them. And do they ever thank you?”

“Not really, and I do find that strange. But I certainly don’t want you traipsing over there and raising a ruckus about my rent. I’ll get it myself, don’t worry.”

Whatever, Theresa thought now with a sigh as she spied some of those lovely Jersey cows, in her field next to the road. The road was still gravel, thank goodness, ensuring that people had to slow down when they drove it. Not that everyone did slow down, but who cared about the dust when the house was more than a quarter mile from the road? A nice distance to walk to her mailbox in good weather, not so nice if there was heavy snow or ice. Banish that thought, Tee.

True. Not everything was perfect. Even here, there was some ugliness in the valley. To the east of her fields, a neighbor—she wasn’t even sure who owned that land now—had put up an enormous, shining complex of five steel grain-storage bins that, with all their interconnecting hardware, looked like nothing so much as a Buck Rogers space station from some 1930s comic book. Ugly, truly ugly, but tiny in comparison to similar setups that now dominated all the small towns in the area, including Moeville, Eyota, and Dover.

And dominate was the right word, the enormous structures literally looming over the towns like alien invaders. And alien was the right word too, Theresa thought. Lute explained that the bins, most of them brand new, were in response to the federal subsidy for corn-based ethanol. Lute wasn’t a fan of ethanol. He considered it a stupid idea economically, environmentally, politically, and every other way.

“Ruining the soil,” he said. “All those row crops, can’t hold the ground. Rain comes and the soil gets washed right down to the river, all full of fertilizer and chemicals so it ruins the rivers too. And are the farmers getting rich? Hell, some think they are, but those buildings cost a fortune to put up and maintain. Full of complicated computer-driven systems for moving the grain around. Means they have to borrow money, at high interest, and pay it back, even when prices go way the hell down, which they will and always do, leaving the farmers and this community holding the goddamn bag. Remember Harvestore silos?" Lute asked.

Harvestores were the big blue silos people put up all over the Midwest during the last agricultural boom back in the late 1970s, something having to do with selling wheat to Russia if Theresa remembered right. The boom busted, and many people lost their farms because they had bet heavily by borrowing the money to build the silos. But then they'd been unable to pay it back. And now all those silos, the blues and the cement ones too, with some farms in the area sporting eight or even ten of them, stood empty. Silent and empty but for pigeons and rats housed in them. And why? Because yet another technology, storing silage in huge plastic rolls on the ground, had supplanted them. Personally, Theresa thought those great white rolls of plastic were very ugly.

"And what do you think those bags are made from?" Lute had almost shouted when discussing it with her. "Oil, of course, the stuff we're running out of! And what happens when they're done with them? They either let them litter up the place," (and, yes, it was true that several local farms had a terrible mess of white plastic wrappers strewn around) or send them to the landfill. More stinking garbage!"

There was nothing Theresa could do about it except be happy Tony had never added a silo to their place beyond the small 1930s-era brown ceramic one that was there when he bought it. Despite several cracks, it was actually quite ornamental, and thank the Lord it never needed paint. Whereas the chicken coop and the barn did, and each could use painting now. But, Theresa thought, I'm not going to do it. Let Rusty take care of that when she was gone. And there was the granary, now a storage building full of stuff Rusty would have to sort through, and the attached woodshed, which could probably use a coat of paint too. Not doing them either, she smiled grimly to herself.

It was a good thing, a very good thing, that Tony had had the foresight to put steel roofs on both the barn and chicken coop. A little rusty by now in a few spots, but no real worries there at least.

Oh that one corner of the barn needed some stonework fixed, but she could get an Amish crew to tackle that next spring. In general, she thought with satisfaction as she surveyed the place, things were in pretty good shape. Not bad for an old lady, and nothing to be ashamed of when Mary showed up. And when, Theresa worried, was that going to be?

Strolling back to the house, she had an impulse. Hopping into her car she drove down to the road, making a slight left before pulling onto the grass margin. There, she turned off the motor and rolled down her window, trying to see her farm from her sister's eyes. Yes, nestled against the hillside, the gardens so neat, the buildings laid out in a line, house to granary to chicken coop to barn. The trees and shrubs and flowers, little bit of lawn, pergola there, trellis over there, and benches.

"Pretty as a picture," their mother, Gertrude, would have said. Remembering the one time her parents had visited the farm, taking the train from Chicago to St. Paul, then down to Winona. Dressed like they were going to a public event like a wedding or a funeral, certainly nothing that would be comfortable for rambling around the farm. They'd been politely and dutifully interested, but their discomfort was palpable. How had their smart, college-educated daughter married a farmer?

They liked Tony well enough—and thank goodness he was Catholic—but to them the country, actually the outdoors, was an alien place. To them, Theresa was living out in the middle of nowhere in an ancient, uncomfortable house and doing arcane things. Things their parents had fled from, like burning wood to keep warm, butchering chickens to eat, driving a godforsaken ten miles to her job in Winona.

Well, at least she'd had a respectable job teaching at a Catholic school. Funny thing, she now reflected, born and raised in a huge city and now she couldn't even tolerate the notion of living even in comparatively tiny Winona!

Rolling up her window and driving back to the house, Theresa remembered the saving highlight of her parents' visit, Mass at St. Stanislaus. St. Stan's. True, it was Polish, with that very odd dome, or basilica, and even offered Mass in Polish at the eleven o'clock on Sundays. Back in Chicago the Poles had their own neighborhoods, with their own churches and priests, with all the Masses in Polish. But despite the very Eastern European look of the church, the interior was spectacular, far beyond her parents' expectations of a rural church. She and Tony had taken them to the nine o'clock English Mass. Her father, Ernst, had commented after Mass, in a slightly disapproving tone, that he'd never been in a round church before, but Gertrude spoke right up and said she thought it was beautiful.

And the choir! "They probably thought Poles couldn't sing," Tony had laughed later.

"And with you, dear, they would have been right!" she'd retorted. The man couldn't hold a note to save himself, she recalled fondly, but that didn't stop him. She had often found him in the barn, or doing chores around the place, singing, The Beatles' "Can't Buy Me Love," his all-time favorite!

Now she went to church less often, especially in winter. But she'd go this evening to bring her flowers. In her mind she could see clearly the magnificent red brick structure with its enormous white dome. Tony had called it the Polish White House, with its formidable triple-tiered entrance, outlined in white and overseen by two towers topped with large white cupolas.

And inside, the marble and massive painted ceiling on the underside of the dome. The ornate Stations of the Cross, beautiful windows, and cut and colored glass made right there by Polish craftsmen, including Tony's grandfather. She knew that certainly when the church was built in 1894 such things gave great pride to the Polish people who had settled in Winona. Poor as they were, they could say they had the most magnificent edifice in the city.

They could leave the relative poverty of their own homes at any time to go sit in that beautiful building. Not to mention attend the daily

Masses, participate in all the many ceremonies and festivals. Now, she smiled to herself, she even had good thoughts about the corner bar Tony had complained about, with its roster of local alcoholics, not that she'd ever go in there. What was it called? There was always a cluster of men smoking outside, even in deep winter. Dan's Dugout, that was it. And right across from it, that very strange little ice cream place, Penguin Zesto.

The Polish Dairy Queen, Tony had called it. She had understood the Penguin part of the name, she'd told Tony. "But what's with the *Zesto*?"

"That's easy," he'd said with a grin. "It used to be Zestowski, they just dropped the *ski*!"

The day was so lovely that when Theresa arrived back into her yard, she returned to her cutting garden to sit on the bench and admire the light. Mose, who'd been distressed when she didn't take him on her five-minute car jaunt, came over and plunked his large head on her knee. Absently petting him, she thought about how she loved each season for its special qualities, but the light in fall was her favorite. The sun lost its summer sharpness and turned to a softer, more golden color, almost like the maple leaves as they began to turn, or the mixture of butter and honey she liked on her pancakes.

And what was that racket? Crows, of course. What was it called, a cluster of crows—a murder? That was the right word this time. They were harassing a red-tailed hawk who couldn't fly as deftly as his tormentors. Suddenly, the hawk made a spectacular dive toward the ground, confusing the crows, then just before hitting the field, straightened out and headed for a nearby copse of oaks, leaving the black birds in disarray. Hooray for the hawk, Theresa thought. Then she remembered the countless times she'd seen a crow harassed by smaller birds, and the times she'd been in the woods and come upon a noisy, very noisy, mass of crows harassing an owl.

Years ago, she'd actually sat quietly and watched such a scene for a long time, the owl simply sitting there blinking, with the crows, more and more of them by the minute, making an awful racket and feinting dives at the owl, but never actually hitting it. What a strange ritual, she'd thought, like a bunch of little kids harassing some street person. They'd pick on him, but only at a safe distance, fearful of what might happen if he grabbed them. Could a hawk, or an owl, actually seize a crow she wondered? She remembered going with Rusty to the National Eagle Center upriver in Wabasha and watching one of the large birds eat most of a rabbit—a dead one, of course—in several gulps, bones and all. Have to take Mary there when she gets here. Still worrying, Theresa went into the house to make lunch, determined not to call Emma. It would only upset the poor girl.

Chapter 29

Gary Wedemeyer, attorney-at-law in the small city of North Platte, Nebraska, sipped his morning coffee on Monday, October 3, 2011. Although he had the morning paper in front of him, he wasn't reading it. Instead he was thinking about the lovely evening he'd spent with his wife Alejandra. They had really gotten closer again and rekindled their sex life now that their kids had left home. Oh crap, he realized his cell phone was ringing. Where in the hell was it? Shit! Probably upstairs in the bedroom. Running up there, he grabbed it off the nightstand and answered it out of breath.

"Wedemeyer?" a gruff male voice asked.

"Yeah, sheriff. What you got for me?"

"Not the usual, tell you that," the sheriff answered. "Couple women, an old one and a kid, Munson brought them in Friday night—"

"What's the charge, DWI?"

"No. Listen, just get down here ASAP, OK? We gotta sort this out pronto!"

"OK," the lawyer answered. Closing his phone and pocketing it, he wondered what was going on. As one of two public defenders in Lincoln County, he ordinarily dealt with one of three things: a domestic, almost always a male beating on a female; alcohol, DWIs or some booze-related bust-up in a local bar; or drugs, marijuana mostly, kids getting arrested for possession or for paraphernalia the cops found in their car. Meth was a close second these days, with harder stuff like coke or heroin a rarity. So, two women, he pondered as he slipped on his ancient tweed sport coat, changed slippers for loafers in need of a serious polishing, and ran down and out to his car. A mother and daughter, he wondered? With what, booze, dope, or maybe a squabble serious enough to cause an arrest? Whatever it was it had Sheriff Summers's knickers in a twist.

Driving the couple of miles from the old neighborhood he lived in near the giant rail yard in town to the courthouse, Gary actually hoped the sheriff's distress signaled something interesting, something different from the run-of-the-mill cases that were starting to seriously bore him.

"What did you tell the officer?" Gary had asked a client a thousand times.

And the reply was usually something along the lines of: "Just that we was at a party and some dude gave me the weed to hold for him, you know? He asked really friendly like." Gary couldn't believe these guys, the details they would offer up to cops and then be surprised to find themselves arrested, time and time again.

Although there was that great case a couple of years ago with the guy who'd shot two or three sandhill cranes. He'd said they were in his garden ruining his bean patch or something, so he just opened a window and blitzed them with a 12 gauge. Crazy fucker couldn't get over the monster fine the judge stuck him with. He couldn't begin to pay it, so he had to do, what was it, thirty days?

"Listen," he'd told the middle-aged redneck, who lived alone so there was nobody to stay his stupid hand, "I did what I could, but you have to realize what those birds mean around here?"

"They're just goddamn birds," the moron had protested. "And there is one hell of a lot of them. Fucking thirty days I gotta spend for some birds?!"

Gary had explained to him that Sandhill Cranes weren't "just birds" but actually meant money for the whole goddamn state. He'd asked him what came to mind when he thought of, say, New York? "I don't know,

Twin Towers, 9/11, or—oh yeah, the Empire State Building and Statue of Liberty and that kind of shit," the guy had answered, confused.

"Right," Gary had said. "Now how about L.A.?"

"The movies, of course!" the guy continued. "Hollywood."

"Right again. I could go on—Paris and the Eiffel Tower, London and Big Ben. So when people think of Nebraska, what do they think of?"

"Big Red football and corn, I'd say," the criminal had offered.

"That's right—and they think of those birds! The same ones you shot, those sandhills are a claim to fame for this state. The judge, the cops, the prosecutor, they don't give a diddly-fuck about the birds per se. What they care about is that those cranes bring thousands of people and millions of big bucks to the state, even here to Lincoln County where we don't have that many. You shoot a sandhill, you're shooting the goddamn goose, or crane, that lays the golden egg, my friend. So count yourself lucky that you only got thirty days and not the death sentence!"

"Death sentence, now you're shitting me!" Gary's client said warily.

"Right. But, hey, in England years back, the big white swans swimming around in lakes and such? They were called the King's Bird, meaning they were protected by the king, so if you killed one guess what happened?"

"Shoot, I don't know."

"They hung you, no questions asked, no public defender to cover your ass. Just bang goes the gavel, and next thing you know you're climbing up on a scaffold and getting your neck stretched."

"That's wrong man, totally fucking wrong!" the guy said, starting to look worried.

"Here's some advice, amigo," Gary offered. "Next time you're itching to shoot one of those big birds, think about those swans and the hangman coming at you with a black mask over his head to put that rope over your head!"

Well, Gary thought as he pulled into the parking lot behind the courthouse, I haven't seen that guy back again. Maybe I did scare some sense into him.

He headed into the building and up to the duty desk to let the deputy know he needed to see the sheriff. A nice, fat, friendly cop greeted him and sent him right into the sheriff's office. When he opened the door he was just a little surprised to see the county attorney there also.

The sheriff, Clay Summers, had been in office longer than Job, or was it Methuselah? Summers was a large man, fit for his sixty-some years, very gray, and wearing the typical too-tight uniform. He was also quite dark-skinned, even in winter, leading to long-standing rumors that he had some Indian blood, or maybe Latino. As he himself was short, Gary always felt Summers's height of well over six feet was imposing. Perfect size for a sheriff, people said, and reelected him time and again. And Gary had to admit that over the many years of their acquaintance, Summers had been mostly fair, to him and to the many people he and his deputies had arrested, jailed, and released.

"Hey, Gary." County Attorney Dale Conroy shook Wedemeyer's hand. "Got a little something we need your input on."

Although Dale was also tall, unlike the sheriff, he wasn't fit. More like sixty to eighty pounds overweight, the mass of it protruding over his belt and out of his sport coat. Always hail-fellow-well-met, Conroy's bulk didn't impede his ambition, which was aimed at the statehouse in Lincoln. He hoped someday to be well ensconced in the capitol building.

As another local attorney had once put it, "Dale Conroy does not take a piss without considering its effect on his career." Once you knew this, and Gary did, it became relatively easy to deal with the prosecutor. You just had to think like he did. That strategy had made for very few surprises in the several years the two had been working together.

The sheriff turned to Gary. "Those women I told you about are in lockup. We'll move them into an interview room, and I want you to go down and get their story. Munson and Harris were the arresting officers—charged the women with obstruction and the young one with assault, and we found dope on the older one."

"Sounds serious," Gary said.

"Well," the prosecutor paused, "maybe, maybe not. Just go talk to them then come and give us a heads-up." He exchanged meaningful glances with the sheriff.

Not liking the somewhat peremptory tone in Conroy's voice, Gary turned and gave a half-assed military salute, leaving the room with a "sure thing, boss." Then he strolled through the cop shop and almost bumped into—was it deliberate?—one of the arresting officers, Harris. The man wasn't much liked by anyone, and behind his back people called him Deputy Dawg, saying his drug dog, Steel, was a lot smarter than its master. The consensus was that Steel should be the one with the badge, and Harris should be kept safely behind the wire divider in the back seat of his squad.

Down in the basement of the courthouse, which housed the small county lockup, Gary entered the nearest interview room. The rooms down here were all covered in the same ancient coat of hospital green, which strongly reminded him of his stint in the Air Force, where everything seemed to be painted that color: barracks, chow hall, clinic, workshops. Wishing he had another cup of coffee, he was just getting up to get some when the door opened and the two women in question were ushered in by the desk deputy.

"Here they are, Gary, all yours."

"Please sit," he said, and motioned to chairs behind the interview desk. He then busied himself with getting out a notepad and tiny tape recorder from his small briefcase, curious immediately about the unlikely pair sitting before him. He was intrigued.

He introduced himself as the public defender and asked them to describe what happened to them on Friday night, telling them that nothing they said would leave the room without their approval.

"But first, my mistake," Gary said. "Please give me your names, ages, addresses, so on. OK?"

Clearing her throat, the much older one, a tiny graying woman with short, frizzy hair and a deep tan complementing the many wrinkles in her still-striking features, gave her name as Mary, eighty years of age, from Pasadena, California.

Shocked by her stated age, Gary asked, "I'm sorry, did you say you're eighty years old?"

Mary nodded.

What in the hell were Munson and his dumb pal Harris doing putting someone this old in the can? "And you're traveling where?" he asked.

Mary briefly gave him the details of her journey, in a very cool and slightly hostile tone.

Looking for a moment at the police report, Gary then asked, "And what's the story with this life-size puppet, or whatever, that you were traveling with?"

Again, Mary gave a brief explanation, which struck him as a bit strange, but actually made some sense.

Thanking the older woman, or the *old* woman, he turned to the young woman scowling at him, asking her name and particulars. Joni gave them with outright hostility. Nothing cool there, just plain anger as the woman, very pretty despite her glare, told her story about leaving Garberville, her Honda breaking down, riding with a trucker until he hit on her, then meeting Mary and taking over the wheel of the Lincoln. Joni left out other details she had only shared with Mary over the weekend while they sat in jail, especially the part about a possible inheritance. The two women had talked through the bars between their cells, despite the noise coming from what seemed to be a drunken man across from them. The poor man retched periodically to confirm his infirmity.

Thanking Joni, Gary then asked Mary to describe what had happened once they'd been stopped by the deputies.

Mary related what had happened from being awakened by Joni, providing the car's paperwork to the deputy, the arrival of the other policeman and his dog, and her, their, subsequent arrest.

"Apparently," she said, "the officer's dog found some marijuana in my luggage. Which I don't understand—being arrested, that is—as my possession is perfectly legal. I have a medical marijuana card from the state of California that entitles me to purchase and use the drug. Grow it, even, if I choose to."

Well, ma'am," Gary sighed. "I'm sorry, but that card isn't legal here in Lincoln County, or anywhere in Nebraska. The possession and use of marijuana here is still very much illegal. Hence, your arrest."

Mary puffed her small self up, clearly angry. "Do you mean to say that something that's legal in one state can be illegal in another? What on earth is going on in this country?"

Gary sighed again. "Well, as to what's going on—that's a whole other discussion for a very different time. I'm not at all saying I agree with this . . . situation, but it's the law. For example, we have a rather famous and very large flock of very large birds that spend a lot of time here. They're called sandhill—like the Sandhills in our state—cranes. Maybe you've heard of them?

"Yes, I have. Lovely creatures that I've seen on television," Mary agreed.

"OK. Needless to say, those birds are fiercely protected in Nebraska. You look at one cross-eyed and you're in big trouble. But other states? Did I see that your destination is Minnesota? Well I've read, or heard, that there they're actually considering, maybe it's already passed, a law allowing a hunting season for sandhills. Different states, different rules."

"All right. I get it. No need for a further lecture," Mary folded her hands in front of her and sighed again.

"And you, miss?" He turned to Joni. "What's your account of Friday's arrest? Please go over it carefully. I see you've been charged with assault."

"Why? I didn't hit anybody, nothing like it." Clearly angry, but also plainly frightened, Joni told more or less the same story as Mary, adding the bit about her jumping out of the car and yelling at the deputies.

"That's it? You're absolutely sure. You didn't say anything threatening, or grab one of the deputies?" Gary quizzed.

"Grabbed? You must be kidding. I'm not a genius, but I don't grab cops, for God's sake. I was mad at them for messing with Mary, shoving her into that squad, so I jumped out and yelled at them. Told them to cut it out, or something like that."

"Then what happened?"

"The guy with the dog jumped me, grabbed my arm, hard, then shoved me back into the car and locked the doors."

"Anything else?" Gary knew that with Harris, there well could have been something else.

Joni grimaced. "Well, I don't know if I should say . . . ."

"Please," Gary urged her. "It stays here with me if it's something you don't want anyone else to know."

"Well, I asked him about the car, Mary's car, but he didn't answer. Then, a minute or so later—the dog was just quiet up there in front with him—he starts needling me, asking me about my old-lady doper friend, did I want to do serious time, I was kinda pretty and did I know what happened to pretty girls in jail, that sort of stuff." Joni looked at Gary defiantly.

"You're sure about this?" the lawyer felt compelled to ask once again.

This time a visibly angry Mary answered. "Why do you keep asking her that? 'Is she sure about it?' Why would she lie? What's your point?"

"OK, OK. I'm sorry, but it's just standard procedure. No two accounts are ever the same, and over time, the same person can have several different accounts. Just part of my job." He sighed. "But I can tell you this, it's certainly not part of a deputy's job to harass young women, or anybody, for that matter."

To herself, Mary could almost hear Mike, or Emma, chuckling in the background. *Not part of a cop's job to harass people? Hell, that's a good one!*

"OK, just one more thing, please." Gary looked at both of them. "What about the dog?"

"What about it? Joni responded, laying her hands flat on the table, then wrapping them over her knees. "That dog was fine. Sniffed at me a little bit, that's all. Much better behaved than the cop."

Heard that before, thought Gary.

But now he had to give his spiel. "OK, I can't help noticing that you both sound pretty hostile, so here it is. I'm not a cop, not a bit of it. My job is to help you out of this situation, legally, of course. So now we've gone over the arrest period. So let's move on with how you were treated once they brought you in."

Joni answered first. "They took our prints and took our stuff, all of it. Really no rough stuff once we got here, crappy food but who was eating? But there's Mary's pills!"

"Pills?" Gary's ears practically leapt off his head. "What pills, what for?"

"I'm eighty, so I take a few pills to keep me alive, like most old people do," Mary looked at him witheringly. "Let's see, there's Synthroid for my thyroid, a baby aspirin to keep my old blood thinned out, simvastatin for high cholesterol, and a tiny little guy, lisinopril, for my high blood pressure."

"You have high cholesterol and high blood pressure? Heart problems?" Gary repeated, thinking this was really alarming.

"Nothing in particular, but just trying not to have 'em," Mary answered. "Heart problems go back a ways in my family."

His strategy already mostly clear, Gary outlined it to the two now-attentive women. "OK, here's the bottom line, and I use that phrase on purpose. One, we arrest a lot of people here every month for drug-related offenses. Mostly teens and college kids smoking weed, I mean marijuana, but some meth cases too. So why bother, you say, when half the nation and probably half or more of the adult population in this town either smoked the stuff or still do? Well, ladies, the answer is simple—money!"

"They don't confiscate the stuff and turn around and sell it like bad cops on TV or anything. They do actually burn it out in a special dump we have. But for almost every arrest there's a fine attached, anywhere from $250 to $500, depending on circumstances and whether or not the judge is in a good mood! So whatever happens, the two of you are going to have to spend some money to get out of here."

Joni and Mary blurted out at the same time, "How much?"

"Well for you, Joni, driving with an expired license, the fine is not adjustable. It is what it is: three hundred dollars. As for the assault charge, the things you've told me about the arrest, the so-called assault, I think the prosecutor will be inclined to drop that," Gary continued. "Frankly, the deputy in question—"

"You mean the deputy with the dog?" Joni asked.

"Right," Gary went on. "Just between us, he has a bad reputation and is skating on thin ice around here. In a small town like this, police can get away with abusing poor people, the few blacks and Latinos, folks in the trailer courts. But you basically don't mess with middle- and upper-class folks—give them a ticket, maybe a small lecture—but Harris, that's his name, has gotten heavy-handed with some kids whose parents count in this town."

"Same as where I grew up!" Joni added.

"Well, be that as it may, our real ace in the hole is you, Mary," Gary suggested. "Your age, of course, but most importantly your medical status. Did you ask for your medications this weekend?"

"I did, several times. Nobody brought them, and on Sunday, when I asked a deputy, jailer, or whatever, he said he'd go get them, but never returned."

"OK, then, our real trump card here is those meds," Gary made a couple of notes.

"How come?" Mary asked.

"You know what the one thing a small jurisdiction like this fears more than anything? Housing a mass murderer?" He paused for effect. "Nope, that's nothing compared to having a prisoner with a serious medical condition. Because . . . if you get sick on our premises, you get sick on our dime."

"I don't get it," Mary wondered.

"OK," Gary said, warming to his topic. "Imagine you have a stroke, we rush you to the hospital. My wife's a nurse there, by the way. And you stay x or y number of days, get a load of meds, have several CAT scans. The county is liable for all of that. Big money we really don't have. The sheriff has to go to the commissioners to justify his budgets, even if they love him, and some always don't. He'll get a hell of an unwelcome grilling about why the county owes the medical folks large sums. Frankly, he and the prosecutor fear that more than anything because it can easily become a reelection issue too."

"Really," Mary said, "I had no idea."

"Yes, ma'am. I can't tell how you many warm bodies they've booted out of here because someone thought the prisoner might be sick enough to be hospitalized." Gary put both of his hands on the table. "Sooo, now you get it. I'm going upstairs to tell the sheriff and the county attorney that they have an eighty-year-old female prisoner with a history, never mind it's just your family history, of heart disease, and that the staff in this fine institution failed to provide you with your meds when requested. My best guess? I'll have both of you out of here by this afternoon."

"With my marijuana," Mary demanded.

"Sorry, that's not going to happen," Gary said. "They might want to lay a fine on you for that too, but I'll try to talk them out of it. I'll be back soon."

Opening the door, he called for a deputy and left the room.

Chapter 30

On Monday as Mary and Joni were hoping to leave North Platte, Theresa, by now quite worried about her sister, knew she'd told Luther she was just going to stay and wait for Mary, but she really needed to divert her anxiety. So she decided on a little grocery shopping and lunch with a friend in Moeville. The friend, Carla Schuman, was a former colleague of hers at the high school, where Theresa had taught English and Carla taught speech.

Never what her mother would have called a clotheshorse, Theresa had nonetheless always taken some care in her dress. Let's see, she thought as she decided what to wear to the village, was her wardrobe stylishly sensible or sensibly stylish? Who knew?

She had, in recent years, actually started buying a few things from the many catalogs that came in the mail, her favorite being Lands' End in nearby Wisconsin. She justified the catalog purchases by her age, figuring it was simply too much work to get out and go shopping like she used to, which was true in the winter but hardly so in the other seasons. There really weren't any good clothing stores in Winona anymore, though, and even Rochester didn't offer much these days.

Maybe catalogs were the reason the shops had closed, not to mention of course Wal-Mart, where she tried not to shop since she'd heard many negative things about its effect on small-town businesses.

Target probably wasn't much better, but she went there for underwear, socks, and such.

She did miss Davidson's, the three-generation clothing store in Winona that had finally folded last year. What a shame, she thought, remembering the pretty young girl who was the last Davidson to run the store. She told Theresa tearfully that the bank refused to renew the annual loan her family had depended on for generations. Small, family-owned businesses, just like small farms, really had become a thing of the past. Theresa remembered that almost everything her parents purchased back in prewar Chicago had come from small stores, with only an occasional foray downtown, usually to Marshall Field's at Christmastime, more of an outing than a shopping trip.

Looking through her closet now, she saw some stuff to give to the Goodwill so she set it aside. For today though, she contemplated the gray-green trousers with a slightly silky sheen, an off-white blouse, and a sweater—probably the dark-green cardigan with those lovely wooden buttons. For earrings, she opened the wall-hung cherry jewelry case with the full-length mirror Rusty had made for her and selected a tiny pair of turquoise hummingbirds, remembering fondly how horrified her father had been when she came home from college one Christmas with her ears newly pierced.

He'd been truly upset in his own mild way. "That's for savages," he'd told her.

Mary had been delighted, and promptly went out and had her ears done too. Their father had refused to speak to either of them for what, about half a day? All he was capable of, unlike what she recalled Luther saying about his father, punishing his family by not speaking to them for months on end. Well, Luther, had many reasons for being so somber, that not the least of them.

What shoes, she wondered? The brown suede lace-ups, her favorite go-to-town footwear, she decided, reflecting on how lucky she was to have small feet. Heck, she could wear her barn boots and still have them look OK because they were so small. Something Carla, whose feet were very large, would almost certainly mention at lunch, as she had done many times during the more than thirty years of their friendship!

For the final step, she considered her hair. Maybe her untidy mop, as she referred to it, was payback for her small and still-slender body and her tiny feet. Going into the bathroom, she put her head under the faucet and let lukewarm water run over her head. Then, looking in the mirror, she ran her hands through the tangle of curls and spikes, now mostly gray, and left it at that. So be it. What was the name of that salon in Rochester, Hair Police? What if they went around giving tickets for unruly hair? She'd pay a heavy fine for sure!

Leaving the house, she gave Mose a bone, telling him to stay on his rug, but knowing he'd end up on the couch. As she went out the kitchen door and toward the Subaru, she thought with a grin about the various people who came to her place now and always locked their cars with some kind of gadget on their keys. Lock your car out here? In the middle of the day in the middle of the country, your vehicle just yards away from the house? Silly. No one had ever stolen a thing from her place, not a tomato, for gosh sake!

The trip to Moeville was one of her all-time favorites. Even if it was a gray day, offering no color off the autumn leaves because there was no sun to augment it? Yes. Sure that lowering sky might bring rain, but thank heaven it was far too soon for snow!

Driving, Theresa thought again of trying to see this route from her sister's eyes. There were the lovely rolling hills, all of them covered with trees. And while many of the small farms were no longer operating, most of the farmsteads were still here, each of them surrounded by coveys of buildings large and small. Every single one of them with trees in the yard, windbreaks of cottonwoods, oaks, maples, and a few poplar or basswood. These places looked like they were right out of some rural calendar.

There were also plenty of cows to see, of course, with just one small herd of sheep on this route. And then some not-so-calendar-ready scenes with mobile homes and prefab houses. Notable not just for being new, but usually stuck right in the middle of a field on the very edge of the highway without a single bush or tree in the yard. Often just cars, trucks, swing sets, and monster propane tanks. Soon, once the snow came, there would be snowmobiles too. Machines she was not shy about saying that she just plain hated, especially after hearing that some people actually used them to run down and shoot foxes or other wildlife. Lute had once said he might get a snowmobile to run those guys down!

Theresa reached the bar, the Last Round, just before the turn into town from the west. There she got her first sight of the enormous, and truly ugly, set of grain-storage and -transfer buildings they'd just put up a couple of years ago in response to the boom in corn prices. Moeville had never been a quaint place, nothing special about most of its buildings or its tiny main street, but these huge bins dominating the skyline as shiny as new quarters were simply hideous. The village, Lute had remarked angrily, looked like a bunch of hobbit homes clustered around the terrifying castle of some grain-gulping giant keeping them in thrall. Not a bad analogy, she thought, given the power of the farm business giants in the countryside. Lute had also suggested Moeville's houses could be slave quarters in the antebellum South, sequestered around the master's plantation house. An ugly and enormous steel plantation house, in this case.

Easy, Tee, she told herself. You're starting to think like Lute. She was now driving slowly past possibly the strangest non-ag building in the village, the Holy Bible Church, led by Reverend Clark Oakes. A simple name, for a not-so-simple place, built on three descending levels, with three different types of siding and competing rooflines. The sign outside offered daily admonitions, today's being "Pray for sun, Pray for snow, but Pray most of all that you may GO . . . TO HEAVEN!" The pastor, it seemed, was a poet.

Next on the main street, Weston, a nondescript former home was now The Hair Shack, Moeville's latest salon. There were now three, if she remembered right, none of which could do her mop any good! Who owned this new place? She didn't know, but did vaguely remember a picture in the county weekly of a somewhat heavy young woman with a very large head of frosted hair standing in front of her new business, accompanied by six or so local business types, as she cut a pink ribbon. Next was an empty lot with two or three blue dumpsters, then the old Edmonds Bank of 1894, constructed the same year as St. Stanislaus. The bank building was a very narrow stone structure that now housed an antique store, open on summer weekends and supposedly by appointment. The sign said Antiques and Collectibles, the latter a word that always bothered her, the former English teacher.

Was "collectible" really a word? And why was it either *-ible* or *-able*? The latter made some sense, one was "able" to collect something. But *-ible*? Either way, the place was rarely open even in summer. It was launched about three years ago by a woman who had retired to the condo life in Winona and thought she needed something to keep her occupied. Nice enough person, Theresa had visited with her once or twice, but really it wasn't truly a store, just a bored woman's hobby.

Whatever had been on the next block had been taken down to make room for the gas station, a QuikTrip, which reminded Theresa that she had better get gas. She pulled in behind a dually pickup truck the size of an army tank, the tailgate, well-rusted, sported the bumper sticker "Fish Fear Me . . . Women Love Me." The apparently much-loved and feared fisherman turned out to be a very large older man, suitably sized for his vehicle, wearing a Green Bay jacket. He emerged from the station with a microwave sandwich in one hand and coffee in another, nodding to Theresa as he got in and started his loud, smelly diesel engine and drove off.

While she filled her tank, Theresa read the sign on the pump for snuff, or snoose, which included the prominent line "Warning: This product can cause mouth cancer." Yikes, she thought, mouth cancer had to be nasty! She recalled her doctor years ago telling her he'd stopped smoking not out of fear of lung cancer, but cancer of the throat. He volunteered monthly at the federal prison in Rochester, where many of the old mafia dons living out their days there had lost their vocal cords from years of smoking and were forced to speak with those weird voice boxes. Lung, mouth, or throat cancer, Theresa thought they all sounded bad.

She was thankful she'd never smoked a single cigarette and had certainly never remotely considered putting a pinch of snuff in her mouth. Ugh!

In the station, paying with cash, Theresa greeted the young and very overweight female cashier she didn't know. Then got her change handed back to her over a heaping tray of enormous multihued donuts. Not very appealing by any means. Lucky again, Tee, she thought as she left the station.

She started the Subaru and headed for the grocery store down the street, Hal's Valu-Wize Market. Never mind the missing E in "valu," what she really hated was that Z! "OK, Theresa, calm down, because who really cares?" Parking in front, Theresa recalled at least two of the building's previous incarnations—a combination lumberyard and hardware store that had lasted about ten or so years. And prior to that? Yes, a small feed mill that had also been, more or less, a ten-year operation. The yard had been locally owned by the Amundsens, who were now long gone from the village. But the mill had been part of one or another of the many farm co-ops that were routinely, and bravely, established in American agriculture's long-standing efforts to fight off the industrialization of farming by the monster firms like Cargill, Monsanto, and such.

Sighing, Theresa entered the dimly lit store and was promptly greeted by the owner, Hal Baumgartner, a small, round man in his late fifties with an ingratiating manner.

"Missus Kozlowski, how are you? Haven't seen you in a while," he wiped his hands on his apron in a gesture he repeated hundreds of times each day.

"Hi, Hal. Sorry, I was disloyal and bought groceries when I went to Mass in Winona last week at the big Cub store." Where, in reality, the fruits and vegetables were much fresher, the meats more appealing, the variety huge, and the lighting excellent.

"Ha, ha," Hal forced a chuckle. "Cub! More like a grizzly! Can't compete with those big boys, no siree!"

"I know, and I very much appreciate your being here, Hal, which is why I do most of my shopping here. I think everybody in the village is grateful to have your store," Theresa offered kindly as she picked up a shopping basket from the stack near the entrance.

Theresa was then greeted by a cashier at one of the two checkout aisles—Lydia Cook, who was almost as old as Theresa, certainly well into her seventies.

"Hi, Lydia, how are you?" Theresa asked as she paused to talk with her. Lydia was a woman she'd always liked but knew very little about, other than that she was a widow. Her husband, long-passed like Tony, had been killed in a tractor rollover. Or was it a bull that gored him? Theresa tried to recall as they spoke.

"Fine," Lydia responded. "I'm just fine, enjoying this great fall weather with the leaves turning, although today's not so good with the rain."

"Yes. There are things I love about every season, even the deep of winter, but as I age, I'm coming to think fall is my favorite." Noting that Hal had gone back into the store, Theresa edged closer to Lydia and asked in a lowered voice "How are things here at the store? Is he hanging in there?"

Lowering her voice in turn, Lydia responded with a rueful look. "Can't say for sure. I'm down to three days now, but that's OK, I've got so much to do at the farm. On Wednesdays and Thursdays, he's here by himself running the store and the checkout. Don't know how he does it!"

"And the other days?" Theresa asked.

"Well, let's see. I'm here Monday, Tuesday, and Friday. Greta is here on Saturday. And Billy does some stocking and carryout for them that wants it."

Greta, Theresa remembered, was in her sixties, and Billy was in his fifties. He was intellectually disabled, known by everyone in town and treated unkindly by no one. When he wasn't working, Billy walked around and around the village, smoking endless cigarettes, going into the stores and churches, and stopping to chat with folks he knew, and the few he didn't know. He talked nonstop about whatever was on his mind, usually something TV-derived and always a little hard to understand as his speech was slurred and getting worse as he aged. Billy lived in a battered trailer home placed smack up against the formerly grand Victorian-era house his ancient mother lived in but rarely left.

"I think Hal should be open on Sundays. People would come, don't you think?" Theresa continued in a whisper to Lydia.

"I agree. I told him that, but you know he won't. Both of the preachers in town would raise a ruckus. That new pastor we've got at Bethany?" Referencing the small Lutheran church she attended way out in the countryside. "Pastor Linda? Said she wouldn't care. She knows how tough it is to keep anything going out here in this economy."

"It's a shame," Theresa agreed, "but I better get shopping or Hal's going to think I just came in here to talk!" Moving off down the first aisle, Theresa got several cans of soup and two cans of fruit cocktail—light, of course. Then she realized her basket was already too heavy, so she went back to the front of the store to exchange it for a cart. She was happy to see that several more people, no one she knew, had come into the store.

With her cart, she gathered a large box of oatmeal and a package of that great local Sturdiwheat buckwheat pancake mix. That was really amazing fast food. She had only to add water to the mix to make really excellent pancakes or waffles. She then selected a couple cans of black beans for her variation on Mexican food, thinking she'd have to get some advice from Mary, with her Latino son-in-law, on that. Spaghetti noodles or "pasta," as everyone called it these days, came next, then over two aisles to canned meats for sardines and a tin of tuna. She also picked up some saltine crackers and peanut butter. Like the sardines, they were leftovers from her childhood menus. The most common thing her mother packed in their school lunches was white-bread sandwiches with peanut butter and grape jam. Ugh, she couldn't imagine eating that now!

Theresa also picked up some doggy treats for Mose, a silly purchase because they were *so* expensive and he gobbled them in seconds. Package of English muffins. Bag of chips for her home-canned salsa—hope Mary would like it—and an eight-pack of those small Diet Cokes.

"Find everything OK, Missus K.?" Hal asked, hovering at the end of the aisle, wiping his hands again. "There's also a sale on bread this week, two loaves of Bountiful for two and quarter. You can't beat that!"

"I'm sure you're right, Hal, but I make my own bread," Theresa replied, "I can't make my own English muffins, of course." And she held up the package for him to see.

"Right, right," Hal acknowledged. "I forgot that you bake, it must be a chore though, all that kneading?"

"You mean a chore for an old woman like me, Hal?" Theresa teased him.

"No, no, I didn't mean that at all!" the grocer insisted. "Sometimes I just say stuff that comes out wrong. I don't mean that, you know."

"I know, Hal," Theresa assured him. "And I'm not a bit offended. I've done that my whole life."

"Kneaded bread?" Hal inquired.

"Well, yes, that too, but I meant saying one thing and meaning another."

"And you, a teacher!" Hal shook his small, round, and very bald head in mock reproach as he turned away. "Anyways, nice to see you, Missus K., and thanks for shopping."

"My pleasure, Hal," Theresa said to his disappearing back. Heading to the checkout counter, she looked up just in time to see that she wouldn't be able to escape talking with the priest from Immaculate who was shopping today in full priestly collar and black suit, of course.

"Ah, Missus . . . ," the priest began, struggling to remember her name.

"Theresa, Father. Theresa Kozlowski," she smiled at him. Someone she felt a great deal of sympathy for, thousands of miles away from his home in India, stuck in tiny, out-of-the-way Moeville and the other parish he served, she couldn't remember which one.

"Oh yes, Missus Theresa. We have not seen you at Mass recently? Have you been ill?" This asked in his sing-songy English, which so annoyed some locals, but she found charming, although the man himself wasn't particularly so. Maybe it was a cultural thing, maybe a language problem, but Theresa found him abrasive, and it was too clear that he was uncomfortable with women, or American women, at least. Or rural Midwestern women. Or . . . .

Placing her groceries on the counter, she turned to face Father Thomas.

"No, Father, I haven't been ill. I've been attending Mass in Winona. At St. Stan's?"

"Stan's?" he asked.

"Oh, I'm sorry. St. Stanislaus, the big church in the east end of town? Local people call it 'Stan's,' which comes from a nickname."

"Nickname?"

"Yes. Like Joe for Joseph. Liz for Elizabeth. Harry for Harold. A pet name, if you will."

"OK. I understand. But . . . a pet name for a holy place?" The man shook his head in disapproval.

"Well, Father. I really don't think any disrespect was, or is, intended by the name. Some families, mostly Polish Americans, have been worshipping there for three generations." Theresa felt her discomfort growing as she shifted from foot to foot and realized how eagerly Lydia, at the cash register, was listening to the conversation, to be repeated word for word to many others in the following week.

"So, you are Polish?" The priest was apparently not going to let go.

"No, Father, I'm not. But my husband, Anthony Kozlowski—that's a Polish name—was, and his family worshipped at St. Stan's, I mean Stanislaus. Anthony, Tony was his nickname, has been gone for many years, but some of his cousins and their children and grandchildren go to Mass there, and I like to see them." Gosh, she thought, do I really have to excuse myself to this man?

"But, you are still a member here, are you not?"

"Yes, Father. I am. I send in my contributions, and I attend here about half the time I go to church, which in the wintertime, with the weather, I do less often." Theresa sighed and turned to her purchases, pushing them toward Lydia, hoping to signal that the conversation—or was it a confrontation?—was over.

Not quite, as Father Thomas said, very loudly and in an admonishing tone, "OK, but we hope to see you more often, here in your home church, Missus Theresa," turning to walk back into the store.

"Wow," Lydia shook her head. "He don't let go, does he?"

"Guess not." Theresa shook her head too. "I feel sorry for him, posted out here, so far from his home. Must be awkward."

"Well," Lydia snorted. "He's certainly awkward. Glad I'm not Catholic."

Theresa let that one go, knowing it had multiple meanings, whether intended or not.

Theresa put her groceries in her car and walked across the street to Molly's All-American Café to meet Carla, who was already seated in a booth by the large window facing the street.

"Theresa, there you are," Carla greeted her, resplendent in one of her many seasonal outfits. Today she was dressed for fall, in beige knit slacks and matching jacket over a light-orange blouse draped with a very large turquoise necklace. She got up and hugged her friend tightly.

Too hard for my old bones, Theresa thought, but her friend had always been an ardent hugger and was unlikely to change now. "Hi, Carla, how are you?" Theresa sat down in the booth.

"Fine, fine. All right, I guess. For someone my age, you know." Carla grimaced.

"I do know, I'm the same age, remember, my dear." Theresa smiled at her friend.

"I know, I know, but you always look so fit. Those tiny feet, a person could think you were a lot younger."

There, she'd said it, at least it was out of the way, Theresa thought. "What the size of my feet has to do with it, I'm not sure. But you look great, and true to form, you're easily the best-dressed woman of a certain age this side of Chicago," Theresa smiled again.

Pleased, Carla beamed, turning her head in profile for Theresa's benefit. "Like my new cut?"

"I was getting to that too," Theresa insisted, "but first I had to admire your outfit. Both are lovely!"

"Well, we have to try don't we, Tee? I never understand women who give up, stop taking care of themselves and wear the same old thing day in and day out. I mean, there's a woman in my condo, can't be a day over seventy-five and plenty of money, I'm sure, or she wouldn't be there. She wears, I swear, the same pair of slacks every day. Every blessed day, I tell you!" Carla shook her head, mortified.

"Really? Maybe she just has many pairs of the same pants." Theresa suggested with a grin.

"Well, that would be even worse wouldn't it?" Carla exclaimed. "But about my hair, Sue at my old salon did it. I don't trust anyone else. There's a new young man she's got in there now. I'm sure he's gay, and everyone seems to want to go to him, but not me with my old head of hair. Sue's the only one I trust!"

"It looks wonderful, very chic." Theresa actually reached over and gently touched a lock of Carla's hair.

"Thank you. I love it. Let vanity have its day, I say. You know you really should try Sue, she's a miracle worker, Tee!"

"Not Sue," Theresa shook her head, "not the young gay man, not the leader of the free world, no one can do anything notable with my hair. There are these old pics of me when I was little, all dressed up for church? Cute little outfits my parents probably couldn't afford, and Mary in her new Easter clothes. But my hair? It was sticking out all over my head."

A small woman of uncertain, age, wearing an apron over a pair of jeans and a Western-style blouse with steel buttons came to take their order. Molly was the owner and the waitress.

"I'll have the beef-barley soup and a small salad with vinegar and oil," Theresa said.

"Coffee?" Molly asked.

"Yes, please, with sugar and cream."

"Cream's right there on the table. And what'll you have?" Molly demanded, moving her eyes to Carla.

"I'd like a grilled cheese, and can I have it on sourdough? And can you put a couple of slices of onion on it before it's grilled? And coffee for me too, please." Carla smiled at the woman.

"Sourdough? You mean bread? Sorry, this ain't the Cities," Molly tossed at Carla. "We got white or whole wheat!"

"Whole wheat then, please," Carla replied, taken aback by the lack of hospitality.

"Sourdough?" Theresa laughed with Carla as Molly went into the kitchen.

"I know, I know," Carla said throwing up her hands. "Here I am bringing my highfalutin' Winona, capital of the foodie universe, tastes to lowfalutin' Moeville. Excuse me! But," Carla said, looking around the restaurant, "I must say, I love Molly's décor."

"Just be happy if she actually puts that onion on your sandwich," Theresa offered, laughing. "I agree about the décor she has going on. Elvis, Marilyn, James Dean, and all the cars." The women glanced around at the numerous photos and posters depicting Molly's idea of an all-American style.

"But what's with those Welcome, Bikers signs she's got up?" Carla wondered aloud. "I see them everywhere these days."

"Oh, you know, the river road is a hot spot for all those men riding those giant motorcycles up and down during the summer. I hear those machines cost lots of money, and it's not like the businesses in these small towns couldn't use the money. So, 'Welcome, Bikers.'"

"God. Harris, my second?" Carla said, referring to one of her three former spouses, "he thought motorcyclists were the scum of the earth. I had to restrain him more than once from running one over."

"Well, good thing he's out of the picture then, right? He wasn't exactly the most tolerant of fellows."

"Boy, that's true! I don't miss him one bit. But what I will miss is that once again you refuse to even consider going with me this winter to Costa Rica? Getting out of here when it's twenty below and your old bones are aching? Why don't you want to go someplace nice and warm and welcoming?" Carla demanded as she took a bite from her sandwich, which Molly had put on the table while they talked.

"Let's see," Theresa pretended to ponder as she spooned up some soup. "How many times have we been over this in the eons we've been pals?"

"Plenty. But I've got to try, don't I? Not to embarrass you, but if it's money, I'll happily pay your airfare!"

"Thank you, you're a very generous woman. But you know very well my interest in traveling is about the same as my interest in those motorcycles," Theresa paused and looked at her friend. "But there is something else I want to talk to you about, although I realize I risk offending you by bringing it up."

"At our age? My dear Tee, my most excellent friend, I can't imagine you saying the remotest thing to upset me. Unless of course it was about my clothes, or my hair, or—" she grinned.

"OK, it's no secret that Albert left you, shall we say, well-off? You don't have children, and from what you say about your sisters' offspring, leaving them much would only make matters worse. So—and this is of course just a suggestion . . . ."

"Go on, Tee, spit it out," Clara encouraged as she sipped her coffee, looking up with a bemused expression at her struggling friend.

"You know those two kids I told you about? The ones renting my land? The young couple with two little children?"

"Vaguely."

"Well, they're farming, and I think doing a decent job of it, because they got help from a local nonprofit group, the Land Stewardship Project. They actually recruit young people to get back on the land. Help them out in lots of ways, including, if I remember right, some kind of beginning farmer course. Anyway, I think it'd be wonderful if you took the money you were going to spend on my plane ticket and donated it to this organization. It's tax-deductible, I think." Theresa noticed that she had folded her hands, as if in supplication.

"That's a good suggestion. I'll consider it. Where can I find out more about them, and maybe send a check? If I like what I see, of course."

"They're headquartered over in Lewiston. Actually, you could stop there on the way home if you have time. Pick up some of their literature. It's just a tiny little office front. You'll see it. And, Carla?"

"Yes?"

"Thank you for considering it. I'm sorry I won't go with you to Costa Rica, or to New York, Paris, or London."

"You bet. But in the meantime, guess what?" Carla harrumphed. "She didn't put any onion in this sandwich!"

"Not surprised," Theresa laughed. "She was probably offended at the suggestion."

"OK," Carla wiped her mouth with a tiny paper napkin. "Now's my chance to potentially offend you! I have a question about your little community. What on earth is a *meat raffle*?"

Theresa, her soup finished, motioned for Molly to abandon the magazine she was reading at her lunch counter, and deliver them some more coffee. Smiling, she answered her friend's question about this bit of rural trivia. "Easiest thing to do is describe one to you. You know that bar you pass as you drive into Moeville from the east, the Stumble Inn?"

"Stumble out, more likely," Carla replied. "But yes, that's where I saw the sign today. Actually I've seen them all over the place around here. Even, I think, at the Legion in Winona."

"Well, so here's how it works here in Moeville. Immaculate Conception has a tiny, I mean tiny, parochial school attached to it. Literally, it's a little brick one-story that's connected to the church hall. They've got two or three teachers and a principal. No nuns, since there aren't any more left, but older local women with teaching degrees. Well, paying those teachers their scant, and I mean *scant*, wages is an annual nightmare for the parish. The parents pay something, but it's not much, and money is always scarce. So they have the meat raffle once a month, raising maybe a thousand or so dollars a year."

"A raffle for the church school, held at a bar, for people to win meat?" Carla was dubious.

"Yup," Theresa laughed. "The two institutions are sort of joined at the hip. And, as I said, they raise about a thousand dollars a year, I'd guess. And it brings plenty of people into the bar too."

"It's not much though, is it, a thousand dollars?"

"No," Theresa, sipping her coffee, agreed. "But every bit counts, and they have other fundraisers too. So on the third Thursday of each month, people come to the bar and buy a paddle, a piece of cardboard attached to a tongue depressor, with a number on it. Somebody, maybe one of the teachers, spins a wheel and if your paddle number, for which you paid maybe two dollars, comes up, you win a thirty-pound package of meat. Almost always beef."

"Steak, ground meat? What?" Carla wondered. "And is it fresh or frozen?"

"Frozen, and all of the above, some burger meat in one pound packages, some steak, stew meat, you name it."

"Liver? I hope not!" Carla said, wrinkling her nose.

"In the past, I'm sure. But not now, nobody eats liver anymore."

Carla, still making a face, agreed. "Ugh, I certainly don't. So where does all the meat come from?"

"It's all local, of course. When the farmers in the parish send an animal to the meat locker, they'll tell the butcher to set aside a certain number of pounds for the raffle. But that never adds up to enough for the whole year, so the school ends up buying, say, one or three steers, usually. Which, of course, they get from a parishioner to be butchered and raffled too."

"And what does the bar get out of it?"

"Oh, they make the real money. They sell the beer and the liquor and the sandwiches while the raffle is going on. Raffle night has, over the years, become something of an event. Kind of a party, so that even people who don't like Catholics and the school come, bid on the meat, and have a good time."

"Well . . . a meat raffle! Who knew about the quaint goings-on out here!"

"In the sticks, you mean?"

"OK, if you will, *the sticks*!" Carla laughed.

"Hey—quainter still is what they used to raffle!"

"What? Children, dogs?" Carla guessed, as she raised her considerable eyebrows?

"Not quite," Theresa's eyes twinkled. "It was liquor! Not beer, mind you, but real booze like Jim Beam and Johnny Walker!"

"Wow, I guess there's more than one way to fund a parochial school!"

"Yes, it was a time-honored tradition that I think was ended when we got a new priest. The Indian man I told you about? I guess he pointed out how inappropriate it was to run a school with alcohol-fueled funds. It took an outsider to do that, and I heard there was some grumbling. So the meat is actually a step up." Theresa raised her hand in a flourish.

"Did you? Do you—?"

Theresa laughed. "Me? No, never. I've always had plenty of meat in my locker, besides, I'm simply not comfortable in a bar. Never was."

"I know, me either," Carla agreed, "although I will certainly partake of drinks on the beach in Costa Rica!" She gave a broad grin.

"I suppose that's different, with the beach and all." Theresa actually couldn't imagine it. Was there an actual bar right on the beach or what?

Molly finally came over and filled their coffee cups, asking pointedly if they wanted pie, which both declined.

"So, your sister is coming? Mary, right? When?"

"Well, actually, she was supposed to be here this weekend. But I got a call from her son-in-law in Los Angeles saying she'd had car trouble somewhere in Nebraska, so I'm hoping to hear from her soon about where she is and what's going on. Of course, part of me is worried sick." Theresa folded and unfolded her hands in one of her nervous gestures.

"You, worried?" Carla said, not surprised. "My advice? You've heard it before: Don't worry until you have reason to. Pardon my trite saying, but no news is good news!"

"Right, I'm trying to believe that."

"Isn't she almost your age?" Carla asked. "Why on earth is the woman driving across the country?"

Pausing, Theresa thought for a moment. "I'm not entirely sure, but part of it is that she's simply stubborn, very stubborn. 'Mary, Mary, quite contrary!' we used to say. She always was, so when the whole family, including her daughter and I, objected to her driving here, she dug in her heels and got behind the wheel. Also, she has this great big old car—a Lincoln, I think—that her husband loved. They never really got to take a trip in it before he died, so the trip is sort of an homage to him, to their marriage. That part I fully understand. That's very much a part of why I intend to stay on the farm until they carry me out in the proverbial pine box. I owe it to Tony, and to our life together."

"Well, Tee, as I've said many times before, I can respect that. But it's a good thing I don't have the same feeling about my men. Let's see, Harris only ever wanted to play golf once he retired, and hoped to die on a golf course. So, of course—did I say 'course'?—we had to live on a golf course. Remember my place up in Lake City, where the golf course went broke? I cared for the man, mind you, but living there? It was a nightmare that only ended when he passed. Didn't die playing golf, if you remember, but eating a bowl of his favorite ice cream while he was watching TV. Some show he loved on public TV about investing. He went out with stocks, bonds, and ice cream—three of his favorite things!"

"Yes, I remember. Poor man!" Theresa replied sympathetically.

"Poor? Not a bit of it, dear," Carla shook her head. "I hope I can have as easy a death, believe me. Maybe I'll be sipping a mai tai on the beach in Costa Rica and simply keel over from sheer delight!"

"Yes, I guess you're right," Theresa looked wistfully out the window onto the street, not a bit of traffic in sight. "I remember asking the coroner and my doctor about Tony's death. They both assured me he probably felt no pain other than a brief burst of something in his chest. I kid Rusty, and I know it's cruel of me, about finding me dead in the barn some morning, my hands folded saint-like over my chest."

"Well, you *are* named after a saint, aren't you? Whereas there's no Saint Carla, believe you me!" her friend offered.

And so the friends, lingering over Molly's thin coffee, continued their wonderfully animated conversation into the afternoon.

Chapter 31

As Mary and Joni boarded the Dreadnaught, having stowed their luggage and safely strapped Mike into the back seat, Joni looked over the courthouse parking lot and noticed the cop Harris watching them from where he was smoking just outside the building.

"Hey, there's our good buddy. Need to wave good-bye to him." Joni said to Mary, who was just getting behind the wheel. Coming around to the side of the Lincoln, Joni raised her arm in the time-honored one-finger salute, then turned and got into the passenger seat. Inspired, Mary also got out and stood by the car to give the cop the finger. Giggling a little, they drove into the street, and in seconds were back on the interstate.

As the women were leaving, Gary Wedemeyer watched the whole scene from an office window in the courthouse, laughing aloud at their final defiant gestures. And feeling good about his role in freeing them with only one fine, the three hundred dollars for Joni's lapsed license.

The sheriff had worried. "What if those women get to Lincoln and look up an attorney, bring a lawsuit against us?"

"Can't guarantee it, sheriff," Gary said. "But I really doubt it. They're just happy as hell to leave North Platte behind as a bad memory. Probably won't draw a deep breath until they're out of Nebraska, never to return."

God, Gary thought, those were some tough women. He wondered what his wife would have done in the same circumstances. He was pretty sure she too would've stood her ground, and somehow ended up embarrassing whatever foolish police officers bothered her.

Taking little sips from his afternoon coffee, Gary thought again that, in general, women were really much more resilient than men, and usually much more interesting. The public defender's thoughts would have been much appreciated by Mary and Joni as they resumed their journey. In fact, his ears should have been ringing, because they were talking about him. The nice-looking little guy with a twinkle of good in his eye who'd calmed them down, and most importantly, got them the hell out of there.

"You know," Mary opined as she set the Dreadnaught's cruise control on seventy-one miles per, "you can almost tell right away if a man likes women. Likes us for who we are, and not because he wants to get in our pants, or need some other kind of favor. Right, Mike?" she said over her shoulder to her floppy companion. Turning to Joni she offered with a smile, "I gotta get used to him being back there now, I guess!"

"Yeah, I think you're right. But Mary, about Mike, if we get stopped again?"

"That's not going to happen," Mary assured her. "Because we're the two most careful women in the world until we get to my sister's place. Right?"

"Sure. But how do we do that?"

"Simple. We drive only one mile per hour over the speed limit, never any more than that. We check the lights every time we stop for gas. It was fixed, you know."

"Really? How, who?" Joni asked.

"I don't know. I just know that the lawyer Gary said not to worry about it, it had been taken care of."

"Great, so what else?" Joni asked.

Mary laid out the plan: "OK, speed limit, working taillights, also no more night driving. It's late enough now that we're going to have to stop in either Lincoln or Omaha tonight. Look at the map and figure it out, will you? And hey, don't worry about cost. I've got plenty of money. You and I are now joined at the hip as jailmates, so I'll cover expenses from here on out. Besides, that fine must have tapped you out, right?"

"Yeah, pretty much. I had four bills, more or less, when I left Geeville. I spent some on gas and food until I got to Wamsutter, then Sam, the too-friendly trucker, gave me one-fifty cash for my dead Honda."

"What about the stuff in your car you couldn't bring with you? That you left there," Mary asked as she glanced over at Joni, thinking again how pretty she was.

"I'll see what happens. I have their phone number, so I'll call when we get to your sister's. Patti, the dude's wife? I liked her a lot. Liked him too, for that matter, until he started feeling me up."

"Unbelievable," Mary spat out. "Men like him always have that stupid argument. 'Sorry, but we have needs you know, and sometimes we can't help ourselves.' I mean, even rapists make excuses like that!"

"I know. From your first date in high school, when the guy starts begging you."

The two drove in silence for a while, still in a bit of a shock over their ordeal.

"Listen, Mary," Joni broke the silence. "Thanks for spotting me on expenses."

"Don't worry about it, we're not talking a fortune here, are we?" Mary assured her. "Besides, if you feel you owe me, I'm sure we can have you help with some chores at Theresa's."

"Think she's worried about you?" Joni asked.

Noting the eighteen-wheeler passing her, Mary replied, "Of course. One, I really am overdue, and two, she's a natural-born worrier. I'll call her tonight. When I talked to Emma from jail on Saturday morning, I lied and told her the car broke down and couldn't be fixed until Monday. So I asked her to call Tee and let her know."

"So besides being a worrier, what's she like? Theresa."

"God, did you see how fast that truck was going?"

"Yeah, probably racing to see his girlfriend."

"It's been a while since I've seen Theresa. She came to Mike's memorial, but we had hardly any time together before she had to go back. And that kind of bothered me, but I've gotten over it. I suppose because we're really close, despite the distance and the relatively few times I've seen her since we each got married. But what's she like? Let me see, first, she's small, like me. Maybe she's gained some weight—who hasn't?—but her frame is really too small to hang many pounds on. Both of our folks were short, my mom was about my height. And Dad? Heck, he couldn't have been more than, say five five or five six. He did get heavy as he aged, mostly in his chest, it seemed."

"Did you like them, your parents?" Joni asked.

"Yes, we loved each other. Not that we ever showed much affection back then. My dad, Ernst, was actually more affectionate than my mother. He'd pat me on the head, the shoulder, at least when I was little. But hugs, hardly ever. Hugging my folks was just about like hugging Mike the Mannequin back there. It didn't mean they didn't love me, it just wasn't our way. Heck, Mike and I, the real Mike? We hardly ever hugged or kissed each other in front of other people. In front of Emma, of course, but the whole hugging everybody and saying 'I love you' on the phone, all that? I think that started in the '60s, when Mike and I were already who we were, you know."

"My grandma, Eunice, was an old hippie, and she told me she loved me all the time," Joni said. "Thing was, she really did! I knew it. And my dad always said he loved me, but he was just a little too huggy, if you know what I mean." Joni looked over at Mary.

"Did he, uh . . . ? Mary asked delicately, concern filling her voice.

"No," Joni quickly clarified. "Just holding you a little too long, hugging you too tight." Joni actually hugged herself, feeling silly. "Just not cool about the boundaries, you know, especially after I was a teenager. And he's still like that."

"Have you talked to him about it?"

"Talk to Chet? Never happen! He'll listen all day long to some asshole on the radio talking about conspiracy this, conspiracy that, but personal stuff, like 'hey, Dad, why don't you bathe more often?' Can't do it. Remember, I'm on this mission because he's afraid the lawyers who sent the letter might be federal agents, trying to get him to Minnesota and send him to Guantanamo or something."

"Hey, Joni," Mary changed the subject. "There's some trail mix in that bag behind my seat if the cops didn't take it. Can you reach back there and get it? I'm snackish."

"Here it is. The cops didn't get it." Joni opened the plastic bag and put it between them in the cupholder.

Taking a handful, Mary said, "Take some. We're jailmates, remember? So share and share alike."

After several mouthfuls and with her eyes firmly on the car she was about to pass, Mary said, "My dad, Ernst? I just remembered a funny story about him. Care to hear?"

"Sure, shoot," Joni settled in to listen.

"OK. Well, neither of my parents were much on clothes. Didn't have any money, and I think, didn't really care about it either. *Vogue* wasn't exactly a household word for us, you know? So anyway, when I was still at home and Theresa was coming home from her first year of college for Christmas? Dad left early to go to the train station, Union Station in downtown Chicago, to pick up Tee. We found out later why he left early. He went to Marshall Field's, the big department store, to buy himself a new pair of pants. He went there because my uncle worked at Field's—he sold shoes, and could get us a break on stuff. So Dad meets Tee at the station and she almost loses her teeth, she's so shocked."

"What happened?" Joni grabbed another welcome handful of the trail mix, spilling some seeds on her T-shirt as she stuffed it into her mouth.

"It was pretty funny, at least to us. Dad had bought a pair of pants, on my uncle's advice, that looked like part of a clown suit—big black and white checks! They looked ridiculous, and even more so on a man who always, I mean always, wore either black or dark blue pants and a white shirt. Of course, neither Tee nor Dad said anything about them. He's just strutting beside her all proud of both her, his college girl, *and* his pants. Mr. Cool!" She smiled at the memory.

"Anyway," Mary continued. "They come home, I'm there, our mother is there, but not our brother, Konrad, who was in seminary. And we greet Tee, some actual hugs, if I remember. And it's Merry Christmas all around, you know. But Mom is going crazy—and this is a very reserved, very quiet lady—about Dad's pants. Especially because she's worried he plans to wear them to Midnight Mass on Christmas Eve, which was the next day. I mean, both of my folks cared a lot about what other people thought and said about them, so to my mother those pants of Dad's were a scandal waiting to happen. Heck, he might as well have showed up at church in his underwear, for God's sake!"

"Wow, all that drama for a pair of ugly pants?" Joni wondered.

"Yeah, I know, but it was a different time. Pay attention, Mary!" she said suddenly, realizing she'd been driving in the passing lane since she pulled around that semi some miles back and now someone in a large black and very threatening SUV was right behind her. "Anyway, it became clear that our dad was for sure going to wear those horrible pants to church, because he hung them on the outside of his closet, a clear sign. So Mother was beside herself."

"Why didn't she just tell him not to wear them?" Joni asked. "Was she scared of him?"

"Not a bit, he was the least scary man in all Chicago. No, just as he would never, I mean *never*, have said anything critical about any of her outfits, all three of them—likewise, what he wore was his business. That's just how things were between them, and I bet between lots of people back then. More formal, you know. More respectful, you might say." Mary paused to grab some more trail mix.

"Was it that way between you and Mike?" Joni asked, and found herself glancing back at the mannequin.

"Are you kidding?" Mary laughed. "The dear man had the fashion sense of a garbage collector! If I didn't intervene, he'd wear the same thing day in, day out, year in, year out. He was clean, mind you. But clothes? He believed that men who showed an interest in clothes were probably homosexuals. Gay, you know? So I often just bought things for him, he didn't mind so much if they came from a thrift store, so they were cheap. He thought buying clothes was an extravagance."

"So you didn't have trouble telling him he needed new clothes?"

"Not a bit. Things changed I think, between men and women, between different levels of people, even between blacks and whites, after the war. World War II, I mean. You might say my parents were old school, while Mike and I? We thought we were hipsters. Well, we *were* hipsters, hip before the hippies were even born."

"Y'mean, like—what were they called, the pre-hippies?"

"Beatniks. Not that we sat around playing bongo drums in coffeehouses. We were too busy working, but we listened to jazz, bebop mostly. We went to clubs when we could afford it. Drank wine, drank gin—heck, Mike and I probably drank more in a year than my parents did in their entire lives. Heck, we started smoking Mary Jane back in the '50s!"

"Mary Jane?" Joni had never heard the term.

"Oh, I mean marijuana. That's what we used to call it," Mary explained. "Stuff wasn't very good, we called it headache weed, but it was the *idea* of it. Giving the finger to the authorities. Like we did to that cop back there!"

"So, like *On the Road*, huh? I had to read that in high school. I actually liked it! What was that guy's name?"

"Kerouac, Jack Kerouac. There was a whole school of those guys that kind of swam together. Neal Cassaday, not a writer but some kind of hero to them. Ferlinghetti, Burroughs—but the best one?—we thought anyway, was Allen Ginsberg, the poet. We saw him read right here in Pasadena. Whoops, I mean *there* in Pasadena. A couple of times. One time he and his boyfriend—Ginsberg was gay—stripped down to their underwear while they were doing the reading! Some people got pissed off and left, but most of us stayed. It was funny, and cool, of course." Mary chuckled with delight at the memory.

"Why was he your favorite?"

"Well," Mary gave a long pause. "Mike was a very political guy, he couldn't blow his nose without it having some political meaning. I think he was born that way, probably started arguing with the doctor the moment he left his mom's womb! I wasn't so much, and I'm still not terribly political, but I did become more and more so. Both because Mike was right, and because of what he taught me."

"Which was?"

"One, don't take shit, and I mean *shit*, from anybody. And two, whenever you can, help those getting crapped on. The poor, minorities, you know. So Mike's criticism of the Beats—the writers, painters, and so on—was that while they had the right idea about authority, which was to call it into question, most of them didn't do a damn thing to help anybody else. Many of them, Kerouac being the prime example, led totally irresponsible personal lives. Mr. On-the-Road really screwed up his only daughter, for example. That was the exact opposite of Mike," Mary recalled fondly. "He was always Mr. Responsibility—to me, to our daughter, and to his coworkers in the grocery biz."

"He was really a good guy, huh?" Joni sounded a little dubious.

"Yes, one of the best. He was a political anarchist, and the Beats were just personal anarchists, if that's a distinction! But you know? If I keep on yakking about him I'm going to get real sad, so I'll have some more trail mix and leave it at that." Taking a handful of nuts, seeds and raisins sprinkled with tiny bits of dark chocolate, she sighed deeply.

Both of the women were silent for a while, Joni looking at the map and Mary noting the landscape, still pretty bleak by her standards but much better than the deserts in Nevada, Utah, and Wyoming. Here, at least, there were cows, most of them black and spread out in vast numbers along the roadside. And grass and trees, small ones but for clumps of cottonwoods here and there. Windmills, the occasional tractor and buildings, not lots of them but enough that you knew the area was occupied. Thank God, Mary thought, remembering with a shiver the empty area where that skinny SOB had attacked her, something she still hadn't told Joni about. Why, she wondered?

"OK." Joni looked up from the map. "Lincoln is about 225 miles from North Platte, and we're coming into Kearney, which is about halfway there. How do you feel? Getting tired?"

"Not a bit," Mary replied. "Those two days in jail, remember what I was doing most of the time?"

"Yeah, you were sacked out asleep."

"Right. And believe it or not, I actually slept well. I'm lucky that way. I can sleep anywhere, anytime—and sleep well, so I'm plenty rested. We'll gas up at Kearney, get a Subway sandwich, if that's OK with you, then drive to Lincoln. I don't care if it gets a little dark, then we'll get a motel right off the freeway. We'll go have a drink, and then get up in the morning and flee this godforsaken state!"

"Fine, but . . . ."

"What?" Mary asked.

"You never finished the story about your dad's pants."

"Oh, right," Mary chuckled as she wheeled past another giant RV, a Cougar. "Did you see that Joni? Cougar? The stupid names they give those monsters—it's about as much a cougar as I am, for God's sake!"

"Yeah, I know," Joni said. "They used to come to the Worst Western, that was my name for the motel I worked at in Geeville. I always wondered why. Like why would you have a mobile camper, bigger than a lot of people's apartments, including mine, and then stay in a motel?"

"Who knows," Mary said. "But, back to my father's trousers. So it's Christmas Eve morning and Dad has to go meet one of his hamsters, that's what the ham radio guys called themselves. This guy was having a problem with his rig and the club my dad was in was getting ready to broadcast a Christmas message to our troops overseas, I think. Anyway, my sister, the good little Catholic girl, actually had the nerve to tell Mother she should just get rid of the pants. Give them away, whatever. Coming from Theresa, this was startling. What had half a semester in a Catholic women's college done to her, we wondered? Mom at first rejected the idea out of hand. 'Who knows,' she said, 'what the man paid for them?' Bold little me, I told her whatever it was, it was too much!"

Mary, clearly enjoying her memory of the story, continued. "So that seemed to end it, those awful pants hanging there on Dad's closet, the time before Midnight Mass just ticking away. And my mother's stomach, always subject to her nerves, was getting more and more upset. I remember asking Tee if we should hide the pants, but she said no, that Mom would find them and know we did it. But Tee had one more great idea, which she said would have to wait until our Mother took her afternoon nap." Mary paused, laughing quietly to herself.

Joni, now caught up in the story, nudged Mary to continue. "So, the pants?"

"Right, *the rest of the story*, like some news guy used to say. So, Mother takes her nap, right there in the bedroom, next to the pants. We wait until she's snoring, sound asleep, then sneak in and take the pants and the fancy Marshall Field's wooden hanger and head outside. In the backyard there's a little snow on the ground but we don't even take time to put on coats or boots. And now I understand Tee's plan—she's got a box of stick matches and the pants, and we go over to our incinerator. Every house had one in the alley for burning garbage. We take some old newspaper from a can next to it, wrap it around the pants, stick them in, and light it.

"We had to do it twice to get them going. Now, I'm not sure what those pants were made of, but they went up in a blaze. A short blaze luckily, because about twenty minutes later our dad came home. We were safely in the living room, reading or playing some game or whatever. A little while later, Mom woke up and Dad goes up to their room. We hear some low-key talking—my parents *never* raised their voices, never! Then they come down and Mother asks us if we've seen our father's trousers, 'the new ones,' she said. We said no, of course. And that's the end of it. Dad wore his old blue serge suit to Mass that night."

"Mary, you gotta be kidding, right? That was the end of it?" Joni exclaimed, finding it hard to believe.

"I kid you not," Mary said. "Nothing further was ever said. But every once in a great while, Dad would kind of mutter, 'I wonder what ever happened to those pants of mine?' You know, I'm going to remind Tee about that when we get there. See if she remembers. And what else she remembers!"

Chapter 32

While Theresa spent an anxious weekend fretting about her sister, Luther had a far more anxious time dealing with one of his recurring Nam-mares, as he called them. Arriving home on Saturday evening after his day at the farmers' market, he had immediately popped open a beer and poured a shot of brandy. The rush of alcohol got him into the mood for making his meal, a veggie stir-fry. Another shot of the brandy further clarified one of his favorite tasks, chopping garlic, onion, ginger, broccoli, bok choy, Napa cabbage, eggplant, and his elegant Red Noodle pole beans.

As he chopped, he admired his very sharp Japanese cook's knife, bought recently with the money from his father. Wondering, as he did with so many things, why Americans couldn't make knives like that? Wait a minute. He remembered the Leatherman multi-tool that was omnipresent on his hip, American designed and made. A very good knife! Turning on the gas under his ancient, funky wok, he waited until it began to smoke, then added a little cooking and sesame oil. Next he put water on to boil for the rice noodles he'd mix in with the veggies once they were cooked.

First into the wok were the onions, letting them cook a bit, then the ginger and garlic, taking care not to burn the garlic. Then he dumped all the rest of the veggies in at once, turned the heat down just a bit, and added fish sauce, some mushroom soy, and finally a couple of hits of the ubiquitous sriracha hot chili sauce. Finally, he stirred it all up with a great maple spoon Rusty had made for him.

While opening another beer, Luther thought, as he had many times, that the only good thing that had come out of the war against the Vietnamese was the arrival of their cuisine in America. As for what good had come for the Vietnamese, nothing! Not a goddamn thing but pain and suffering and death on an unthinkable scale. Dropping a packet of the rice noodles neatly tied with a tiny bit of string into the boiling water, he turned the gas under the wok way down and put a lid on it, wondering if someone had tied that string by hand.

Put a lid on it, Lute, he told himself. All this gloomy shit you keep bouncing around in your tiny brain! As he drained the beer, he knew the wok, the noodles, the fish sauce would just bring back a rush of memories of his time over there. But stir-fry was his favorite meal, easy to cook and super tasty. What was he going to start doing instead, eating cold cereal and watching *Rockford* reruns for supper, like John Moe? Lute remembered the last time he'd stopped at John's house in the evening, the old man so wrapped up in his TV show he barely acknowledged Lute's presence.

Nope, no cold cereal for Luther Rasmussen. Draining the ultra-thin noodles over the sink, then running cold water over them until he was sure all the scum was rinsed off, Luther picked up several batches of them by hand. He put them into the wok, stirring it all together, this time using a fork. He let the whole mess heat for just a bit while he got out a large bowl, its edges chipped, and put it in the sink to let hot water run over it. No use making good hot food then dumping it into a cold dish! He admired the bowl, his favorite, which was blue and white and covered entirely with words and characters in various languages that all meant peace. It was something the U.N. had put out in the 1960s or '70s, probably when he was over there.

"Peace," he thought as he scooped most of the contents of the wok into his bowl, opened another beer and poured another shot of brandy.

He sat down at his kitchen table and cleared a space amidst all the books and magazines piled on the table. "What bullshit!" Hell, the world was just as violent as it was when this bowl was made, maybe more so.

The U.S. government, it seemed to Luther, was intent on putting its military in every little niche in the entire world. There would probably be a base in Winona soon, he thought, his mind then veering as the booze started to seriously kick in. He lit on the memory of that asshole with the big new truck in the stall next to him at the market. Was *that* why the U.S. was trying to dominate the world? To make sure dudes like that had all the fucking toys they could possibly have? The dually, the Harley, the this, the that?

Christ, Lute could hardly stand to look at the marinas up and down the river, including in Winona, filled with monster boats that properly should have been in some seaport, not on the Mississippi, for God's sake. Who owned all those boats? How often did they use them? How could they afford to buy and maintain them, wrapping them in miles of blue plastic every winter to protect them, and from what?

These and similar disquieting thoughts occupied Luther as he deftly used his chopsticks. God, he loved this meal, so simple, so tasty, so different than the food he ate growing up. Meat and potatoes, gravy aplenty, green beans, and a salad of iceberg lettuce. The sole spice he remembered was black pepper.

Luther thought about Rusty as he rinsed off the handmade wooden spoon he'd used to cook. He went out on the kitchen porch to smoke a cigarette, trying to enjoy the autumn evening and thinking that Rusty was a guy who seemed genuinely at peace with himself. Your own peace was one thing, but being at peace with everyone else, that was even more difficult to imagine. Doing that—being at peace with pretty much everyone he met—certainly explained why the kid, not really a kid, was able to stay married to the beautiful but mercurial Carmen.

Funny thing was, Rusty shared almost all of Luther's political views—the fascistic connections between corporations, the government, and the military; the unceasing assault on people of color in the rest of the world; the absolute inability of American leadership to address the climate-change threats. Truth told, Luther took a deep hit off his smoke, Rusty knew more than him about a lot of these issues. He was like his mother, a voracious reader, and spent a lot of time on the Internet too. Many of the books Luther was currently reading, he remembered as the alcohol mixed with the tobacco to work a pleasant haze, Rusty had either recommended or procured for him. But why wasn't he, like Luther, angry about the situation?

"He's a sweet man," Theresa often said fondly and by way of explanation to Lute's questions about her son.

But how in the hell do you become sweet? And does a person even want to be that way? Feeling sorry for himself, he'd once or twice wondered if he hadn't gone to war, would he too have been as peaceful as Rusty? But he knew as soon as he posed the question that the answer was a resounding no! Not just because of his weird upbringing, it was also who he was. From the get-go. It could have been detected probably moments after Luther was born. The doc might have said, "This is a troubled baby, and he's going to be a troubled man. Let's just hope he doesn't hurt anybody!"

But then he had hurt people, over there, in the free-fire zones, which was another way of saying the whole fucking country outside of Saigon. And the body count, reporting dead little kids and old mama- and papa-sans as VC, helping the officer class advance their careers. The fucking harassment and interdiction shit, when they shelled villages and rice paddies and whole forests into craters.

He now field-stripped his cigarette, something he'd learned way back in boot camp, about the only useful thing the bastards taught him, he thought, throwing the tiny bits of tobacco into the breeze that was stirring in his yard.

He knew who should have been harassed and interdicted, fucking Westmoreland, and what was that asshole civilian's name? Bunker, perfect name for a war zone, Ellsworth Bunker! Where did those cocksuckers come up with those names, William Westmoreland, Ellsworth fucking

Bunker? Remembering the time Westmoreland, all starched and shiny, emerged from that deadly assault the VC had made on Saigon, right in the heart of the American fortress, to tell the TV media heads that everything was A-OK, all under control. Lies, lies, lies, he told himself as he opened another beer and poured another shot. Then he rolled a monster J and toked up. He took hit after bomber hit until he was thoroughly wasted and heading right back, while sitting on his porch in the dark, into his tour. A story he'd gone over and over again, sometimes in full daylight and sometimes wasted in the dark, always with the same miserable outcome.

His tour began after finishing his biology degree at Luther College in 1963. Bio-lite, he termed it. Luther thought his expensive education really hadn't taught him much, and after graduation he continued working on the small dairy farm just outside of Decorah where he'd helped out during college. The elderly couple who owned it, Jim and Elvira McNab, treated him like the son they'd never had. And he was far more comfortable with them than he'd ever been with his own parents.

After getting into a big fight with his father about his "future," Lute bought an old Airstream trailer and moved it onto the McNab farm, where he took over the milking chores for the small herd of Jerseys. Jim's knees had given out in the many years he'd been bending over, morning and night, to hook up the milking machines to the cows' udders. The task was even difficult for Lute, as his great height wasn't especially suited to bending over. For those twelve cows he put the machine on and took it off twice a day, so that was forty-eight bends at least. And there was always some problem with a machine that required more than one intervention.

No wonder Jim, who carried quite a bit of weight, had finally been unable to do it. But since he was young and fit, Lute just learned the easiest way to milk the cows, feed and water them, then usher them out of the barn into the pasture, and he loved every moment of it. This, he used to think, is real biology. Hands on with living, breathing, eating, shitting—and, boy, did cattle shit. Just the memory of how warm and quiet, how utterly peaceful, it had been milking those cows soothed him now as he dragged on his smoke and shivered a little in the autumn night air.

He'd ended up doing almost all of the farm work once Jim's legs left him almost crippled, needing to either be on a tractor, in his pickup, or in a chair most of the time. And Lute loved all of it. The pigs and chickens, of course, and a few scroungy turkeys. There was even a small, very noisy flock of ducks. Talk about shitting! Those ducks sprayed a steady stream of soup out of their asses everywhere they waddled!

And maybe four months into his being on the farm, months during which he never bothered to make the short drive up to Rochester to see his parents, or even call them, Jim and Elvira invited him to sit down after supper one night and asked if he was interested in taking over the farm. Not right away they said, but sometime in a to-be-determined future. He'd protested that he was just a college greenhorn, and they'd protested back that he was proving a quick learner and Jim would be here quite a bit longer to give him needed guidance. Jesus, they were good people, he thought, slapping his knee and slamming down another gulp of beer.

But it turned out Jim wasn't around a bit longer. One day that fall, he tipped over his old John Deere B, with its dangerously narrow front, on a too-steep slope in the woods and broke his neck. For which Lute blamed himself, of course—why in hell hadn't he been there?—and still did today. And right after the funeral, the McNab's daughter, another Luther grad who had some fancy job up in the Cities, sat down with her mother and Luther and made it very clear that she intended to sell the farm right away and move her mother into a suitable apartment up in Minneapolis. End of story. No discussion. No chance for Lute to persuade her to sell him the place on a contract for deed, let him pay them off over the years.

No, she wanted cash, and right away. And so by Christmas, he'd moved his trailer up to Winona, a place chosen more or less at random, into a low-rent park and taken a job in the early spring with one of the companies that towed the massive barges filled with grain or coal up and down the Mississippi. Not a bad gig—good pay, but boring. Still, he got great food and a coworker turned him on to the benefits of smoking weed. Dangerous sometimes, going through the locks, walking carefully all the way to the end of a tow to check on stuff. But mostly just boring, and he really missed the farm, especially those cows, for whatever reason. Off the tows, he'd gone once or twice to see his parents in Rochester, and each time it took less than an hour for him and the old man to be yelling at each other, his mother sitting quietly crying in her chair.

"Don't you dare swear in my house, you hear me?" his father would yell, all righteous and prim, like some old Lutheran minister.

"Fuck you, fuck you, and triple fuck you!" Luther would toss back, taking some strange delight in simply saying those words aloud in that house, to that man, and not realizing at the time that the F word was going to be the single most important term in his Marine vocabulary.

By the following December, he'd signed up to join his majesty's military. The ice had put an end to the towing season, and he was getting drunk and into bar fights every night. He sold the Airstream to a woman who'd been living on a leaky houseboat on the river. She gave him a hundred bucks and promised to send the rest to whatever address he forwarded, which he never did.

He spent that Christmas at Parris Island, getting more shit than anyone else in his platoon because he was so tall—and worse, because he'd gone to college but refused to consider going to Officer Candidate School.

He survived the weeks of boot camp, then it was off to Camp Lejeune in North Carolina for advanced training. At both camps, it was hard to believe he was in the same country as Iowa and Minnesota. Finally, it was June, and there he was deplaning at Da Nang. Getting all the gear, boots, pack, the M14 and finally reaching Quang Tín.

And that's where the shit really started to hit the fucking fan. The chopper blades like huge fans, spreading shit all over that tiny country with its tough, tiny people. Tough motherfuckers, kicked our big American asses all over the map—the map being their country, which was the big difference between them and us. Their land, their families, their history, and him just a freakin' hired gun. Lute recalled how he couldn't understand any of it from the beginning, even back in boot camp where the drill instructors constantly talked shit about the "gooks" and how backward they were, what punks they'd be in battle.

Really, he brooded now, then how come we left with our fucking tails between our legs after killing about five million of them? *Punks.* Hardly. The real punks were the upper echelons of the American officer corps, the ones who stayed in Saigon and other safe havens and issued orders while they played tennis, went swimming, ate the best chow, and slept with the prettiest women. They were the fucking punks. Not that some of them didn't pay as the war wore on. Christ.

He took another hit of brandy, which was tasting like shit now, and he put his head between his legs to ease the dizziness. He closed his eyes only to see that fateful July day, right after he'd arrived in country, when his company hit the island of Ký Hòa in an effort to dislodge the VC base they were told was there. One hell of a scary firefight. And when it was all over—Lute began to shake at the memory—three Marines were dead, none from his platoon, and they counted six confirmed enemy dead. But, Luther raised his head and looked into the dark in despair, the big and awful *but* of the whole terrible war, at least one hundred women, children, and old men—clearly not combatants—lay dead as well. Just lying all over the fucking place, with him wondering out loud if this was all right, killing all these civilians, and being told by the shit-ass sergeant in another platoon to forget about it. *Collateral damage, dude!*

Maybe it was a mistake, he and a few of the other new guys said to each other. But it wasn't. "It fucking wasn't!" Lute shouted out loud now at the increasingly cold and very dark night. "Every fucking place we went, we murdered people, man. Every fucking murderous goddamn—fuck America—place," he continued to shout, half-sobbing, as he stumbled out onto what passed for a lawn in his yard.

He fell down, remembering frightening, Technicolor bits and pieces of his last foray, just before his time was up. It was in a tiny village he couldn't remember the name of. But he did remember, always would, coming across the remains of several huts that had been blown to bits, along with the people in them. "Looks like a goddamn gook stew, man," one asshole bragged just before Lute sucker-punched him.

Chapter 33

Stopped for the night in an old motel just off the interstate in Lincoln, Joni finally heard about Mary's ordeal with the kidnapper.

"It *was* kidnapping, wasn't it?" Mary puzzled as she shook her head and sipped her second gin and tonic in the small, shabby bar attached to the motel.

"Of course it was!" Joni exclaimed as she nursed a beer, not enjoying it but trying to be sociable. "I'd like to find that son of a bitch and run him over, Mary! Jesus! I still can't believe it."

"Me either. I can't believe I was lucky enough to get away!"

"Lucky? *Plucky* is more like it. Here you are, eighty years old, a woman. And not a big woman either. Shit, people can barely tell there's someone behind the wheel when you're driving, and you had what it took to beat that shit bird. Too bad you didn't run him over."

"Yuck!" Mary grimaced. "Perish the thought, that body under the car, me driving over him, then getting out of there. If that had happened, I probably would have driven back into Cheyenne and told the police."

"Well, *that* would've been a mistake." Joni shook her head. "Heck, they'd still have you there, you know."

"I suppose," Mary began, draining her drink, and then taking out the lime and sucking on it. "One thing's for sure, it's been a heckuva trip, and I may tell no one but you what really happened. God, I wish Mike were still alive, he'd love this story."

"Yeah, but if he were alive, he'd of been with you . . . ."

"Right, a whole different trip, I guess, if he'd been with. That guy probably wouldn't have gotten in the car."

"How long were you married?"

"Fifty-nine years and a few weeks."

"I know this sounds like a talk-show question, but," Joni paused to sip from her beer, "what was your secret? I mean like most people I know either just split, ran away like my mom, or got divorced."

"No secret, honey. People often asked that, and we—well, I—always told them it was just luck. Just a lot of good luck, and the right person at the right time. Both of us had a lot of rough edges, could have just as easily gone the other way. Besides, and I'm not a bit superstitious, but I've always thought taking credit, bragging if you will, for dicey things like marriage or raising kids, is just courting trouble. Know what I mean?"

"You mean like the moment I was patting myself on the ass for my old Civic lasting so long, it conked out on me?" Joni smiled ruefully.

"Right. Pride goeth before a fall, and that sort of thing."

"Sure. My grandma? She totally believed that, she never took credit for getting sober 'cause she was always looking over her shoulder for the dope dealer to come knocking. But I'm going to take credit for getting up my nerve to ask you for a ride!"

"Yes, and I'm glad you did. The cop thing, just a story for us to share. No serious harm but for those stupid two days in jail. Can you believe it? I'm now officially a jailbird. Mike would be proud! Does your arm hurt where that goon grabbed you?"

Joni rubbed a hand over the arm in question. "No big deal. I've had much worse falling off a bicycle. You ever get hurt—bodily injury, I mean?"

"Yup," Mary called to the bartender, who was busy watching some game on TV, for another G and T. "I'm having just one more, to celebrate getting out of Dodge, you know. These are pretty weak anyway.

And, yes, I've been hurt a few times; I don't think a person could live this long and not."

"S'pose not." the girl agreed.

"So when I was—I'm not sure—four, I think. I was riding my sister's trike in the house. Not something we were supposed to do. The basement door was open and—I don't have a clue why—I just rode the thing right down the stairs. Lucky, I guess, because all that broke was my nose. See how it's a little crooked to the left?"

Joni peered across the booth at Mary's face. "Yeah, I see. Bet that hurt!"

"Holy Mary, Mother of Someone, it did! But what hurt worse was the spanking I got from my mother. That I remember very clearly, not the pain so much, which was probably no big deal, but the insult! Me, her precious daughter, could have been badly hurt or crippled even, and what did she do? Spanked me, for God's sake!" They laughed. "My first taste of injustice, Mike said when I told him the story. Set me on my ornery path."

"Was there other stuff?" Joni asked Mary as the bartender, a very tall man with a tonsure-like haircut and a dirty white shirt, leered at her as he set Mary's drink down.

"'Nother beer?" he asked.

"No thanks, but a bag of those corn chips would be great, please."

The man turned to the bar and with his simian arms grabbed the chips off a rack and handed them to Joni, continuing to stare at her and lingering as if waiting to join the conversation. He finally gave up since neither woman even looked up at him.

"Well, nothing much else, I guess. Injury-wise, I mean. Just the usual kid stuff, scrapes and bruises on the playground. Pushed off my bike by my brother, who almost got his head handed to him by our dad for doing it. But once we moved to Pasadena and I started landscaping, getting hurt was just part of the job. Nothing terrible, but you don't handle roses, for instance, without getting thorns, literally! And cactuses? I was a regular pincushion, still am. Clipped the end of a finger off with my pruning shears once too," she said, holding up the index finger of her right hand to show its missing corner.

"Ouch! That must have hurt like hell!"

"My pride, mostly," Mary smiled. "What a klutzy thing to do, and me a supposed professional. And my back, of course. Always lifting stuff the wrong way, too heavy, whatever. I have to be a lot more careful now, shoot I could have added that to the list of my woes for that lawyer, the cop grabbing an old lady with a bum back! How about you?"

"Nothing drastic," Joni answered, slowly removing the label from her beer bottle. "Same kid stuff as you, minus the brother, but plenty of neighborhood punks who thought pushing a girl off a bike was cool. Only happened a couple of times, though, since my dad threatened to kill them if they touched me again."

"Is he a violent guy?"

"Well, we're not talking serial killer," Joni grinned. "But he has his moments, usually when he's juiced. When I got older, I usually didn't even tell him about stuff that happened, it was just more trouble than it was worth. Mostly, though, I was left alone just because everyone knew his rep."

"Yeah," Mary noted. "Men can be useful that way. Wonder if women can get a reputation like that?"

"My grandma? I told you she was an ex-junkie, so she'd seen it all. I mean *all*! Been a hooker, stole stuff, dealt drugs, rode with a biker gang for a few years. She had plenty of jail time, lots of cops messing with her. So nothing scared her. But where my dad was like a match, just waiting for somebody to strike him into a hot flame, Eunice was a slow burn, letting shit build up until boom, the big explosion." Joni took the last sip of her beer and leaned back in the booth.

"What happened?"

"Well, once we had this neighbor, a nasty guy with a really nasty dog. It's funny how they usually go together. So the dog got out all the time and terrorized us kids. Bit a few kids and scared the hell out of me. Chet wasn't living with us then, for whatever reason, and Eunice didn't want him to get involved. She was afraid he'd beat the guy up and we'd get sued, he'd go to jail, whatever. So one summer, when there was no school and I was about eight, that dog chased me into our yard and I came screaming into the house. Eunice got me calmed down, then told me to stay in the house and watch TV while she went over and talked to the guy with the pup."

"And?"

"Well, of course I didn't stay in the house. I crept along behind her while she walked real slow. She wasn't great on her feet. She went up our alley to the dude's place, by his backyard. And there he was, messing around with something and that dog right by him. So Eunice just leans on his fence and tells him she needs to talk to him. Well, he knew, or thought he knew, what was coming. Thought she was going to complain about his stupid dog, so he gets all smartass and says something like: 'Just say what you gotta say, and creep back to your cave, old lady.' So my grandma pauses, like she's thinking this over, then says in a very loud voice I could even hear over the barking of the crazy dog, 'Listen, you little lump of dog shit, here's the skinny! Next time your miserable mutt chases my granddaughter, or any kid, he's dead. I will shoot that little effer so full of holes, you'll be able to see through him. You dig?"

"Whoa, bad granny," Mary said admiringly.

"Right. Totally bad. So the guy can't believe his ears, this old woman yelling at him, cussing him out, threatening his pup. He leaps up, he was a little dude, and comes charging over to the fence, yelling at the dog to shut up the whole time. Gets right in Eunice's face, starts swearing at her, telling her to back off or she'll get hurt, blah, blah. She lets him rant, then reaches over the fence and—this was great—pushes him in the chest. Then she says something like 'You'd best get the eff away from me, little man, and shut your stinking trap.' Well, he's totally surprised by this, an old woman having the chops to push him! So now he's beyond pissed off, and starts to come at Eunice again—the fence is between them, mind you—and I was kind of hiding behind a bush in the alley. But guess what she did then?"

"I haven't a clue."

"She pulled out a piece from her apron and pointed it right at him! Can you imagine?" Joni saying this so loud the bartender looked over and the only other patron in the bar turned and looked at them too.

"A piece—you mean a gun?" Mary asked, eyes wide.

"Right, a little black pistol, but big enough to set that guy on his butt. Which literally happened 'cause he fell back, scared shitless, and tripped over his miserable mutt. And the best part?"

What?"

"All the yelling brought a small group of neighbors, and they all hated the guy and his dog too. So there were people in the alley and people on the fence on both sides of his yard. They all saw the whole thing, which made him look like the little turkey he was!" Joni grinned at the memory.

"And then what?"

"Nothing much. Eunice pocketed the gun and strolled down the alley. I mean strolled, while he's yelling he's gonna call the cops and send her old ass to jail. But everybody knew he wasn't going to do it. If the cops would come to the house, she'd just say he was lying and all the neighbors would back her up, he knew that. Fact is, he and the mutt and his wife, who he beat on, left soon after. Their house was just a rental anyway."

"Wow, but where'd she get the gun?"

"I never had the nerve to ask her about it until some years later. Told me she'd taken it off some biker who owed her money from when she was dealing. He was wasted. She took the gun, then split."

"Was it loaded?"

"I don't know. Maybe not. Then maybe so. That's the whole Russian-roulette thing with guns, right? You never know, so why take a chance?"

"Right. Mike hated guns. So what happened to Eunice's gun?"

"I'm not sure," Joni said, shaking her head slowly. "Guess Chet probably sold it right after Eunice died. As crazy as he is, he never owned a gun, or used one as far as I know. Good thing too, as quick to flare up as he is!"

"Carlos, my son-in-law, he wanted me to have a gun with me on this trip, but I told him no. I have no idea how to use one, so what would be the point?"

"Was he in a gang or something?"

"Carlos? No, not a bit of it, he's a teacher like my daughter. Speaking of whom, I better call her right now," Mary said, getting up. She left money and a tip for the drinks on the table. "Go ahead to the room. I'll be there in few minutes," she said to Joni as she started toward the hallway. Then she flipped open her phone, squinted at her contacts list, scrolled down to Emma, and pressed the green call button.

Chapter 34

THERESA WAS STILL WORRIED ABOUT HER SISTER, even though she'd heard, briefly, from her the night before. Mary was in Lincoln, Nebraska, then and might even make it to the farm today, Tuesday, depending on weather and other variables, including simply getting tired.

"Whatever you do," Mary had said, "don't wait up late for me."

OK, but then what? Theresa couldn't just hang around her own place all day, drinking coffee and worrying, so she decided to do something she'd been avoiding—visit Tony's sister Magdalena in the nursing home. Usually she went once a month, but it had been over a month now, so it was time. OK, she told herself, just go and get it over with!

Still a little light rain, so she wore a jacket over her warm Norwegian sweater, and a jaunty red beret fashioned after a French sailor's cap, with two leather tassels hanging down in back. Taking a quick peek in the hall mirror, she told herself, "Not bad, old girl." With that, she patted Mose on his old doggy head on her way out the door. She headed off to Winona in the Subaru, noting again that her wonderful Legacy—it really *was* a legacy, a gift—was just about to turn 270,000 miles.

The car was made in Indiana, by Americans, just like that classic Hoosier cupboard her mother had all those years ago. Smiling at the memory of her mother's delight, Theresa remembered when that thing got delivered to their house. The neighbor ladies coming by to exclaim over the flour bin, the sifter, the white metal counter that pulled out for rolling out piecrusts or kneading bread. She had almost bought one at an auction a few years back, but there was no room for it in her kitchen or elsewhere.

As she shifted the Subaru into third gear—she wouldn't consider a car with an automatic transmission—she remembered fondly how her father would always, in his vast impatience, shift directly from first into third with his three-speed column shifts. The result was burned-out clutches and poorly running engines. More than once when he was teaching her how to drive, they'd had to stop so he could lift the hood and fiddle with the steering linkage so she could actually shift.

Accelerating—she also liked to drive fast—she smiled as she recalled that her driving used to actually scare Tony. Her otherwise-well-behaved dad could be a monster behind the wheel too, running yellow caution lights, tailgating, using his horn far too often. Her mother would do anything to avoid riding with him, preferring the bus, or even walking. Walking? Ernst never walked, ever. The corner store a block and a half from the house? He drove there. Ernst was a driving fool, for sure.

We all have our eccentricities, she told herself as she shifted into fifth, then quickly down to fourth again as she sailed into one of the wonderful corners the road going down into Winona offered, fully confident that her old all-wheel-drive wagon was as capable as any sports car.

In Winona, it was a gray day, perfect for visiting a nursing home. Theresa drove right to the east, or Polish, end of town, where Magdalena lived. Or, more accurately, was imprisoned.

Theresa pulled into the small parking lot of St. Candida Care Center. Candida was an obscure woman murdered by the Romans before Augustine turned the church into the Roman Empire. Among many local women, the joke was that the bishop who named the care center hadn't a clue about the yeast infection, Candida, that many women are periodically burdened with throughout their lives. Hence the nickname for the institution, Holy Yeast Care Center. Not terribly clever. Wonder what

Garrison Keillor would do with it on Lake Wobegon, Theresa thought as she entered the small one-story building, the heavy heat inside almost stopping her in the doorway.

"Hi. Can I help you?" the young woman behind the foyer desk greeted her. "Oh, it's you Theresa. Come to see Magda, I bet?"

"Hi, Mindy. How are you? How's Magdalena?"

"Fine, me. Magda, the same I guess. Have to ask the staff for sure. Still raining?"

"It is. I know we need it, but I'm getting tired of this weather."

"Yeah, Eldon is having a heck of a time getting his beans in," she said, referring to her husband, a man who not only put in many acres of row crops, but drove truck for the creamery too. Which meant he was home just long enough to get his wife pregnant almost every year, much to the delight of their priest.

"Is she in her room?" Theresa asked.

"Not sure. Let me get one of the aides up here," Mindy said, calling on an intercom twice before another young woman arrived, her haphazard hair dyed a violent red.

"Hi, I'm Henrietta. Just call me Henry. Who did you want to see?"

"Magdalena."

"Oh sure, Maggie. Some of us call her that because it's easier to remember than Magda," the woman explained, smiling.

"Well, actually, it's neither. It's Magdalena," Theresa said firmly, already feeling herself getting annoyed.

"Well, she's in the rec room. It's therapy day. Are you staying for lunch?"

Perish the thought, Theresa thought. "Yes, I guess I will." She had to stay. Part of the scourging she needed to undergo for being eighty-two, still fit, and not in one of these places.

Following the woman's truly enormous waddle down the dark hall, passing by the usual three or four sorrowful figures of uncertain gender drooling in wheelchairs along the way, Theresa chided herself for her repugnance at the whole scene. It always reminded her of some obscure medieval painting of souls in purgatory. Well, if this wasn't purgatory, what was?

"Here we are, rec time! And there's Maggie, whoops Magda, right over there." She wheeled the woman's wheelchair away from whatever she was doing and pushed her toward Theresa.

"Hi, Magdalena. How are you?" Theresa asked as she put a hand on her sister-in-law's shoulder, noting her shiny hair—unwashed for sure. A thin green blanket was draped over her shapeless pink-and-white flowered shift, and she was wearing overlarge fuzzy pink slippers on her feet. Egads, Theresa thought.

"Pretty crappy, Tee, now you ask," Magdalena answered. "How in hell else would I be in here?" The bitter words emerging from a small pinched mouth in what had once been, centuries ago, a pretty face, now crumpled inward with the absence of her teeth, which no doubt were resting in a glass by her bedside.

"Where are your teeth? Can somebody get her teeth, please?" Theresa asked, raising her voice so the aide in charge of "therapy" might notice.

The woman did, coming toward them, replying in an overly singsong voice, "I'm sorry, did you have a question? I'm Miss Nelson, the nurse in charge of therapy. Magdalena is working on her household skills this morning."

"Right," Magdalena screeched. "Had me opening cans with a can opener. Then I got to boil water, put the spoons in the spoon drawer, fold napkins, great stuff. Like I hadn't already spent years doing that crap in my own house. When I came here, I thought it was so I could rest!"

"Well, Magda," the nurse responded. "These are the things you have to be able to do if you're ever going to be on your own again, you know." She looked up, offering Theresa an icy smile.

"Well, I'm just wondering why Magdalena doesn't have her teeth in. Isn't that part of dressing her?" Theresa was unable to control her anger.

"Well," the woman said, maintaining the forced smile. "She's really supposed to be responsible for doing that herself. Aren't you, Magda?"

"I hate to insist—" Theresa raised her voice, "but her name, the one she always went by before she came in here, was Magdalena. *Is* Magdalena, not Maggie, not Magda, which, incidentally, sounds like a Japanese automobile."

"Teeth, teeth, maybe a thief, a thief in the night, not very bright, took 'em. Hah, hah!" Apparently Magdalena had slipped into a state of rhyming. The last time Theresa was here, she'd talked with the head nurse, who had explained this new development to her. Well, Theresa thought, it was one heck of a lot better than drooling.

"All right, she doesn't seem to mind," the nurse said. "But if you think it's important, I think we can work on the name issue. You're her sister I take it?"

"No, her sister-in-law. She is my late husband's sister. They, Tony and Magdalena, grew up just a few blocks from here."

"Oh, how interesting," the nurse replied, clearly not interested, and offering that awful smile. Why did the woman keep doing that? The smile was frightening. "Are you staying for lunch?" she asked pointedly.

"Yes, I wouldn't miss it," Theresa said grimly. "And I already informed the aide who brought me back here."

"Henry? *That* girl's likely to forget. She's not the brightest bulb." Theresa wondered if this nitwit considered herself the smart one in the bunch.

Hey, Theresa thought, how about some Christly intervention here? Maybe strike this awful person with lightning or something, or burn the place down—without actually hurting any of the residents?

"So," Theresa declared firmly, "I think Magdalena and I will just go to her room, if that's all right?" Her tone making it clear she wasn't actually asking for permission.

"Certainly, you'll probably find her teeth there," the rude woman quipped. "Lunch, by the way, is at eleven."

Barely into the hall, Magdalena said in a voice loud enough to be heard back in the rec room, "God, I hate that little bitch, cold as an ice-box cucumber. Making me open goddamn cans! What's next? Buttering a cracker? Know what, Tee? I'm gonna smack her!"

Theresa couldn't help herself, she laughed out loud in agreement with Magdalena's assessment of the woman. She wheeled her charge down one of the several halls that led off the common area, heading for Magdalena's room.

"Twenty-seven. There it is, Tee. My goddamn cage. Cage, cage, please page me in my cage." Theresa pushed her sister-in-law to a corner of the tiny, dark room where a small window looked out on a depressing yard, used mostly for smoking by the women on staff.

"No, not in that stinkin' bed, put me in the chair," Magdalena demanded, nodding to a very worn armchair covered in faded brown cloth next to the bed.

"Sure," Theresa untied the belt that held Magdalena secure in her wheelchair. "Here we go, one, two, three. Up we go and into the chair."

"Jesus, Tee. 'Here we go, upsy daisy into the chair?' You're starting to sound like these assholes around here," Magdalena spat out at her.

"Sorry. That was stupid of me. I was saying it to myself more than you. Comfortable?"

"Course not, whaddya think? That's the deal with this place—it's a freakin' torture chamber. Tie you in the wheelchair. Teach you to open cans. Always telling me not to swear. Fuck them!" Magdalena saying the last bit loud enough to reach the hallway.

"OK, OK," seating herself on the edge of the bed, Theresa asked her sister-in-law, "You know, last time I was here, the nurse told me you'd hit some people. Any more of that going on?"

"Which nurse told you that? Oh, you mean Mother Superior? She's not a nun, but she sure as shit acts like one. Yeah, I hit somebody, that stupid old bitch who started calling me names, Baggie Maggie and such. You'd hit her too!"

"Who called you that?"

"One of the newbies, not even in a wheelchair, sitting there in the TV room, calm as you please and giving me shit. So I rolled over there and gave her a smack. A smack attack, rat-a-tat-tat, smack that. Give you one too, Tee, if you give me any," she chortled.

"Any what?"

"Shit, of course." Magdalena chuckled.

"Right, like I've always done. Tony and I always took good care of you," Theresa reminded her, trying not to get defensive, remembering the state of the woman she was talking to.

"Ah, Tony. Tony baloney. Hey, that's what that mean broad needs, a slap of baloney. Right in her face, know what I mean?" the old woman said gleefully.

"Magdalena, calm down, will you? No wonder they're mad at you. Where will you go if they kick you out of here?"

"Come live with you and Tony baloney," she replied, smiling wickedly. "Peek in your room and steal your teeth at night when you're sleeping!"

"Well, you can't." Theresa reminded her, already exhausted by the visit. "You can't move in with me. We talked about that before, remember? I'm up there all alone and just too old to help you. What if you fell out of your chair? Doubt I could get you up off the floor."

"Bet Tony could get it up, huh, Tee?" she opened her toothless mouth, laughing.

"Hey, Magdalena, stop it now," Theresa told her firmly. "Tony's dead remember? It's been over twenty years."

"Dead? Better red than dead, remember? He was a strong son of a bitch, wasn't he?" She asked with her head down, possibly a bit more in tune with reality for a moment.

"He was indeed, strong that is. But he's gone, and I can't have you up at the farm. It would be too dangerous for both of us." Theresa explained kindly, thinking of her woodstove and how quickly Magdalena would burn the house down. Like in *Jane Eyre*, the crazy woman in the attic setting the house on fire.

"So . . . stuck here till I croak," Magdalena said petulantly. "The food sucks, you know."

"What do they serve?" Theresa asked, lighting on a safe topic of conversation.

"Slop. Plain, old slop. Cook has less brains than the droolers out there in the hall. We still get fish on Fridays, like when we were kids."

"Fish, what kind?" Theresa prodded.

"Who in the hell knows? Probably catching it right out of the river downtown. Like me and Tony when we were kids."

"Did you? I don't remember him talking about that."

"Well, we did. Catfish mostly. Son of a bitch to clean, all slimy. Had to skin 'em with a pliers. Dad loved 'em, though. Man, he could eat a mound o' them things," she reminisced.

"What else did you and Tony do when you were kids?" Theresa knew such an open-ended question could be dangerous—but, gosh, she had to entertain Magdalena somehow.

"Who cares? You don't really want to talk to me, anyway," Magdalena tossed at her guest. "You just want to get out of this damn place as soon as you can! Soon, soon, you old prune! Prune? The month of June? Anybody got a spoon? Wanna spoon in June, at noon? With a goon? Or a loon? Hey, you didn't know I was a poet did you? You with your snotty college education? Miss Tee, Miss Tee with her college degree, thinks she's better than you, and a whole bunch better'n me! I know you, Miss Tee, your nose in the fucking air, same air we all breathe." Her voice had risen now, and she looked at Theresa like an angry child.

Theresa knew that Magdalena couldn't control herself, that she really wanted her to stay and talk. But today she was making it harder than ever. "Well, I'm sorry if I ever gave you that impression."

"Well, Miss Tight Ass, you did, and you still do. All nicey-nice, should get you a job in this joint, everybody treating us like goddamn babies. And they smoke, all of 'em. You can smell it on 'em. Drives me crazy! Won't let me have a ciggie, but they're all out there yukking it up, smokin' their tiny brains out right outside my window!" she declared angrily.

"Hey, how about I talk to Mother Superior about it, OK?" Theresa offered. "Can't see any problem with your smoking at your age."

"Right," Magdalena agreed. "You're not a bad egg, Tee, even if you are a college snoot. You a teacher, while I'm working in that goddamn laundry my whole life, and now here in this shithole. Not fair!"

"I agree, not fair. But what in life is?"

"Well, you ain't had such a bad life," Magdalena pointed out grumpily. "Teacher, pretty farm up in the hills, kids."

"Kids?"

"Yeah, I don't remember their names. There's the boy comes to see me once in a while. They're both red heads, him and her."

"Rusty? He's my only child," Theresa reminded.

"Come on, Tee. Must be another one, she comes sometimes too," Magdalena insisted.

"Oh, you mean Carmen. She's Rusty's wife. She's a redhead too."

"Well, they're married. So she's your kid too, right?" the old woman declared.

"I suppose," Theresa sighed.

"Hey, Tee, you're named after a saint, did you know that?"

"Yes, I know, so are you."

"Yeah, the hooker! That's what I should a done," Magdalena laughed.

"What?" Theresa asked, lost in her own thoughts for a minute.

"Been a hooker, made some real money, partied a lot. Get to go out on the river in those big yachts," Magdalena grinned at the notion.

"Right," Theresa disagreed. "And probably end up dumped over the side into the river some day. Laundry life wasn't great, but you're still alive."

"Alive?" Magdalena grabbed Theresa's arm. "You gotta be kiddin', and you so educated. If this is alive, stick me in the ground, please. Next to the folks, but not next to Paulie, that bastard."

"Yes, I know, not next to Paulie," Theresa reassured her, referring to Magdalena's dead but not-much-missed husband. "There was a St. Paul, but your Paulie sure didn't qualify."

"Got that right, that asshole. Spent all his time at the bars, too drunk most of the time to even have sex with me!"

"Uh, well . . . ," Theresa began, but was saved by the arrival of a staff person.

"Lunchtime, ladies. Let's eat." This one was so thin her green uniform hung on her. Probably a smoker, Theresa thought, immediately regretting the entirely judgmental state she got into whenever she came here.

"OK, Tee. Lunch. Munch, munch, munch. Punch, punch, punch." Magdalena reached out for her wheelchair and almost fell. Theresa caught her, then slid her over into it. And *not* belting her in, for God's sake.

Wheeling Magdalena down the dull-green corridor toward the dining room, Theresa almost gagged at the smell of food combined with the complex odor of the place—a musty, medicinal, diapery, old-people smell. She hoped that smell was nowhere in evidence at her own home. Well, Mary would let her know, for sure.

In the lunchroom, Theresa was directed to a small alcove at the far end of the space, a spot with more light than the rest thanks to a large skylight donated by some Polish family, of course, according to the plaque prominently attached to its base. Pilsudski, in memory of, she couldn't quite make that out, and who cared anyway?

Seated at the round table were two others in addition to herself and Magdalena. A man, a rare gender here, and a very fat woman whose overall appearance made Magdalena look like a movie star. She had matted grey hair that someone had tried, badly, to dye black and a face like spoiled, caved-in squash, Theresa couldn't help thinking. Her eyes were totally blank—nobody there, it seemed. Her hands were in her lap, ceaselessly gripping one another. Anxious hands, Theresa's mother would have called them.

The man was the first to speak. He was short, of indeterminate age, and had all his still-somewhat-dark hair as well as a nice face. He was wearing a checked shirt under a pair of very clean dungaree overalls.

"Hi, I'm Walter. You Magdalena's sister? Hello, Magdalena, by the way."

"Hi, Walter. Don't you alter, a thing about yourself 'cause I like you just the way you are. Wanna party later?" Magdalena gave him a broad wink.

"No thanks, Magdalena," he replied. "My party days are over, not that I had that many."

"I'm not her sister," Theresa said as she reached across the table to shake his hand. "Sister-in-law. She's my husband's sister."

"Widow?" he asked in reply.

"Yes, I am. Tony, my late husband, Magdalena's brother, has been gone a long time now."

Nodding his head slowly, the man said, "Sorry to hear that. Lost my wife just last year. Married almost sixty years, we were."

"I'm very sorry to hear that. But how nice to be married that long," Theresa said, and meant it.

"Yeah, they had plenty of time to poke each other. Know what I mean, know what I mean," Magdalena giggled, poking Theresa's shoulder with her ancient finger.

"Yes, I think we know what you mean, but Magdalena we're not interested, OK? Can you just sit quietly for a minute until the meal comes?" Theresa suggested as she tried to give Magdalena a hard stare.

"OK, Miss Tee. You and me, it's just you and me. And him, and us, but don't make a fuss. Not me!" was the silly reply.

Turning to the man, Theresa apologized.

"That's all right. I know what Miss M. is like. Kinda enjoy her once I got over the shock you know. Pretty boring around here, and she sparks it up." He smiled.

"I bet. You must be new, I've not seen you here before."

"Yup, after my wife, Mildred, passed I was on my own, on the homeplace, and thought I was doing OK. But the kids said otherwise, kept pushing me to come here. Kinda sad though," he said with a frown.

"Why?" Theresa asked.

"Well, heck, I barely got my coat off 'fore they sold the whole place to some mining corporation that wants to mine sand on the place. It was a century farm, and they didn't care a bit. Broke my heart to lose my wife, then the farm."

"What?" Theresa asked shocked, "That's awful. Couldn't you get a lawyer or something?"

"Too late. Signed it over to them some years back, so the nursing home wouldn't take it all when we came in here. Guess we were lucky they didn't just put us out on the street. Just put me out to pasture, in this place."

"Pasture. Rapture. Angel's a-comin', crossing the Jordan for to carry you home. You, Tee!" Magdalena pointed at Theresa. "You!"

"Thanks, Magdalena. You're in top form today, my dear," Theresa pronounced.

"She's always in top form," Walter said. "Less they've got her too medicated."

"Really, what with?"

"Beats me. They gave me some stuff, said to take it if I was having trouble adjusting you know. But I never took it, don't intend to either. Don't wanna be a zombie," Walter said, nodding in the direction of the other woman at the table, busy wringing her hands.

Lunch soon came, delivered by an overly cheery—"Eat up now, folks!"—woman, also of considerable girth.

As if reading Theresa's thoughts, Walter noted, "Got some big ladies in here, all right. Bad as the meals are, I gotta guess they're eatin' elsewhere. If you don't mind, may I say a little grace?"

"Sure," Theresa agreed, bowing her head and motioning to Magdalena to do the same, and she surprisingly did so.

"Bless us, oh Lord, and these thy gifts, and bless us all inside and outside this place. Amen," he said, looking up to see both Theresa and Magdalena crossing themselves.

"Oh, so you're Catholic ladies then?" Walter noted.

"Born and raised. Both of us were members of St. Stanislaus right up the street." Theresa smiled as she made a game effort to cut the very dry piece of chicken on her plate, shoving the soggy French fries off to one side.

"Really? My mother went there as a young person," Walter said as he put a bite of food into his mouth.

"Polish?"

"Yup. Kielbasa, stuffed peppers—the whole of it," Walter said, smiling. "Dad was German. I'm a Rohl. I darn near got into trouble marrying a Polack gal like my mom. Sorry, I meant Polish!"

"But your father was Catholic too, no?" Theresa asked.

"Catholic, Catholic, beat me with a big stick! Terrible food, isn't it?" Magdalena said as she simply pushed the food around on her plate.

"Thank you, Magdalena. Nice addition to our conversation. But I agree about the food. Does it really have to be this awful?" Theresa wondered aloud.

"Yeah. You wonder. Still . . . ," taking a large forkful of fries he went on, "person's gotta eat. And yes, my dad's family, the Rohls, they were Catholics. But they were *German* Catholics, the right kind, you know—not heathens like those darn Poles, with all their saints."

"Don't we all have the same number of saints?" Theresa suggested.

"Not sure," Walter pondered. "But the Polish always seemed to have more, don't know why. Anyways, my parents hitched up, big ruckus in the family. But my mother was so sweet and such a good cook, which is very important to the Germans, they just had to accept her."

A sweet mother? How nice of him to use that expression, and how unusual, Theresa thought. What a man! "And your wife, what was she?"

"Well, that's a tall order," he replied, smiling. "Smart, organized—which I ain't—always told the truth, no matter what—"

"No, sorry," Theresa explained, "I meant her people, her ethnicity?"

"Well, I don't know about any 'nissities,' but her people were from Luxembourg," he answered. "You know the group around here, got that little museum open once every ten years?"

"I do," Theresa nodded. "It's in Rollingstone, the museum, but they settled all over this region."

"Well, her folks spoke French. That's all I know."

"French? *Parlez-vous*, here's to me, here's to you. Wish I were French, Paris and all that," Magdalena grinned and started to eat.

"Well, who knows, Magdalena," Theresa smiled at her sister-in-law. "Maybe some Frenchman stopped off in Poland when Napoleon was attacking Russia. You could be French. But, Walter, how much do you know about Luxembourg?"

"Nothing. It's a little place in Europe, I guess," he admitted.

"Not that I know a lot," Theresa said, "but it is small, only about half a million people. And it has three official languages, French, German and their own tongue, Luxembourgish. Now there's a mouthful."

"Hey, Tee. I know something," Magdalena volunteered.

"What?" Mary replied, wary.

"There's a Luxemburg in Wisconsin, right across the river," came her surprisingly safe answer.

Agreeing, Walter said, "Yeah, there's one over there, but ain't it on the east side of the state?"

"I think so. Never been there, have you?" Theresa asked.

"Nope, too busy farming," he said. "About the only time off we took was for the State Fair, up in St. Paul."

"Yes, my husband and I always went," Theresa said. "Then I went a few times with my son and his kids when they were small. Haven't been in years, though. I don't even go to our fair here in Winona County."

"I *always* went to the Winona fair," Magdalena said as she rubbed her hands together. "Loved it. 'Specially the rides, I loved the rides. Dad would take us when we were little, not Mom, though. She hated them rides, scared of 'em."

"That's me too," Theresa agreed. "I love to drive fast, but that's OK because I'm in control. But I can't stand the rides, watching those men with all the tattoos running the machines. Not sure about them."

"I married one of those guys—Paulie. Remember, Tee? He sure wasn't no saint, I tell you." Magdalena hit the table for emphasis.

"Indeed," Theresa said. "And tattooed he was, and like we agreed earlier, poor Paulie was no saint."

"Shit, Paulie had more tats than teeth." Magdalena took out her uppers and held them aloft, making her point.

Looking around the table, Theresa noted that while Walter had eaten all of his food, the silent drooling woman across from her hadn't even touched her plate. Magdalena was still nibbling. And she herself had tried the chicken, and eaten just a bit of the fruit cocktail in a heavy syrup. So much for dining at St. Candida!

Soon the cheery aide came and dismissed their table. Theresa shook Walter's hand once more, saying they'd surely talk again, then pushed an unusually quiet Magdalena out to a cleared area to participate in after-lunch bingo, apparently a daily routine. Within minutes, it was clear that Magdalena wasn't going to play—or rather, wasn't going to play quietly—so Theresa took her back to the room.

"I hate that silly-ass game, Tee. It's for old people."

"Well, rumor has it that both you and I *are* old, Magdalena. But I sympathize about bingo. It's a boring game no matter how old you are. Do you want to watch some television?"

"OK, see what's on," her charge agreed.

TV at noon was even worse than TV in the evening, Theresa soon saw, wondering once again how on earth people could abide watching the silly thing. She had grown up without it. Her parents got their first set some years after she, Konrad, and Mary had left home. She and Tony bought a TV sometime in the '50s. He'd climbed to the top of their old windmill tower to put up an antenna, but because of the hills and coulees where they lived, reception was always spotty. So basically, they rarely tried to watch it.

Some neighbors eventually got those enormous ugly dishes to get cable reception, but the thought of one of those Martian devices in her garden set her teeth on edge. So there she was in this modern American age, no TV!

Tuning through the channels, Theresa finally found a program to Magdalena's liking, some game show with words and numbers. She didn't pause, just turned the remote over to her sister-in-law and bid her an awkward, as always, good-bye.

"Magdalena, sorry, but I've got to go."

"Oh . . . and I suppose I can't go with?"

"I'm sorry, my dear, but you can't. You know that, don't you?" Theresa asked.

"Donchoo? Donchoo? Choo, choo, now I'm blue, really blue, 'cause you won't let me go with you!"

"I know, but I promise I won't be as long coming next time, and maybe I'll bring my sister Mary with me next time," Theresa suggested.

"Mary, Mary, quite contrary, how does your garden grow? Big like a dick? A buffalo prick? Is that how your garden grows?" Magdalena spun out gleefully.

"Bye, Magdalena. Good-bye."

Easing out of the room, she stopped at the front desk, asking if she could talk to the woman in charge.

"She's not here today, Theresa," Mindy told her. "You'll have to make an appointment."

"OK, why don't I do it now? I need to talk with her about Magdalena's medications."

She settled on a date two weeks hence, at nine in the morning, and took a slip of paper with the info to remind her to put it on her calendar.

"You need one of those smartphones, the kind that has a calendar and you can get on the Internet. You can play games. It's amusing when you're bored," Mindy suggested.

"I, my dear, am already amused and never bored. Thanks anyway," Theresa tossed back at her.

Nice going, Tee, she thought as she headed out the door, being snotty to that poor woman. But a smartphone? I'm plenty smart enough, thanks and no thanks. No question about it, she thought as she drove out of the parking lot, that place brings out the worst in me!

Chapter 35

Luther awoke in his yard at three a.m., shivering and having to piss very badly. Barely able to stand while trying to take a leak, he realized he had just pissed on his boots. Nice move, motherfucker. In the house, which was also very cold, he stripped off his clothes and took his sodden self to bed. Lying down, he thought, for the one-hundredth time at least, that he should have come back from Vietnam and done the right thing by hunting down the war's architects. He should have found them—McNamara, Kissinger, Rostow, Bunker, Westmoreland—and assassinated all of them. Instead, he pulled the covers over his head at the thought, he'd punked out and hidden here on the farm, growing veggies and cutting wood for the bourgeois jerks with fireplaces.

"I really like the cherry, Luther, it has such a nice glow in the fireplace."

"You know, Luther, people like to brag up their oak fires, but I tell you nothing beats a maple log. Don't you think?"

"Now, Luther, the way I start a fire is with a few old wood shingles. I get them from the Amish, then add something light like poplar or box elder, you know? Only then do you add the real wood."

Blah, blah, blah, fucking blah. He put his head further under his pillow, but it did nothing to ease his miserable headache. The pounding persisted with vigor until he fell into a fitful sleep, dreaming for once not of the horrors of Vietnam nor the fireplaces of Winona.

Instead this night's dreams floated in and out of some post–climate change world where winter never ended, and he had to wear his worn-out coveralls year round. Crocodiles were popping up through the ice on the river, and huge eagles were preying on people in cars on the highway. The giant birds smashed windshields with their monstrous beaks, swallowing small children in several vicious gulps. Old women were fleeing their stalled cars, screaming. Then Theresa, oh shit! Luther woke suddenly, shivering under the covers, half asleep but too wired to get back to sleep.

Feeling like shit, he got up, made some coffee and went to let Azteca out until he remembered with a pang that she was gone. He hadn't made a move to replace her either. Theresa actually threatened to simply show up with some pup and force him to take it. No, he needed to find his own dog.

But he'd have to start with some breakfast in the meantime, just boil water and throw in some oatmeal and raisins. He smelled the milk in the refrigerator, it was just going but he used it anyway. He'd give the rest to the outdoor cats later. He wrote milk on the shopping list hanging on the kitchen door. Rubbing his hands together, he realized the house was freezing. There wasn't a fire going, what did he expect?

He got a fire started as he ate the oatmeal and drank coffee. He got it going with some box elder, but he'd have to go out and get some harder stuff later to really heat the place. Feeling like shit, he really had no idea about what to do today. No more booze, that was for sure. But he did take his coffee outside to have a smoke on the porch after putting on his ancient down vest that leaked feathers.

The scene of last night's lunacy. Raging Moon Farm, all right, he grimaced, putting out the cigarette after only two drags. It tasted like crap. Back in the house, he knew he couldn't read and he didn't want to listen to music, but he couldn't just mope around all day. That was a sure path to getting fucked up again later.

Then it hit him, an actual good idea. He should go see the only two local guys he could stand who'd also been in Vietnam, although not with Lute, Terry Holst and Rich Wearmouth. He'd ask them about dogs, did they know of any, then come home and get on the Internet to continue the search for a new pup. A new pup was necessary; dogs had always been part of Lute's long attempt to maintain some sort of sanity.

In his pickup he didn't even bother to turn on the heat. There wasn't any! He'd pulled the leaky heater radiator out last spring and hadn't replaced it. The outdoor temp wasn't that cold, but he couldn't get warm with this hangover. The wages of sin and all that. Along the three-or-so-mile drive to the Holst farm, he noted several new monster grain bins erected since he'd last been this way. Of course, there was a new one at Terry's when he drove in the yard, a bin the size of a goddamn church. But he stopped himself from getting worked up, remembering that he came to see this man, not shit on him.

Terry's cute wife greeted him warmly, her permed hair a mix of blonde and gray. "Haven't seen you in ages, Luther. Where've you been keeping yourself? You should come to dinner sometime," an offer she'd made many times over the years but never actually followed up on. Well, Lute thought, neither had he.

"Oh, just busy, Linda. You know, I'm as busy as you guys are. Is Terry around?"

"Yup, he's out in one of the buildings. I can call on his cell," she offered.

"No, don't bother. I'll find him. Nice to see you, Linda."

"You too, Luther," she said, turning back to the house. "Come more often, won't you?"

No, I won't, he thought as he strolled across the farmyard. Linda and Terry and their many kids, now grown with kids of their own, were just too relentlessly upbeat for Luther. Always smiling, everybody blonde and cute—the women and kids anyway. Burgers and fries and Fourth of July here every day it seemed.

Luther pulled open the door on one building, pausing as he remembered his series of bad dreams. "Hey, Terry, you there?" Luther called. But he got no response from the gloom inside the huge old building filled with all kinds of farm junk that was hard to figure in the dark. Luther headed into another building, a modern pole shed. It was enormous, probably forty feet wide and eighty feet long, one of several of similar size on the place. Terry farmed on a large scale, making Luther and his gardens look like child's play.

"Terry! Hey, Terry," Luther called into the shed.

"Yo, Luther, come in out of the rain, man," came the reply from inside. Terry's big voice boomed off the steel walls and roof of the building.

"Hey, you're right, it's raining. I didn't even notice," Luther answered into the dark building as he tried in vain to locate the man. Luther hated not being able to see him right away as his eyes adjusted to the light, some more shit lingering from his overseas adventures.

"Right behind you, man, right here," Terry loomed suddenly next to Luther, who did everything he could not to punch his neighbor. Or was this guy his friend? Well, sort of, he guessed. In a matter of sorts.

"Man, you still scare easy, don't you, Lute? Just like the Nam, ain't it?" Terry said understandingly. He was as tall as Luther but much bigger, with shoulders as wide as a barn door. Right now he grinned his lopsided smile at Luther, one half of his face basically one big scar. That was a little present from the VC when they blew up his tank just outside of Saigon, getting Terry sent home on full disability after less than thirty days in country.

"Nah," Luther demurred. "Just been especially jumpy lately. Not sure why."

"Well, good to see you, Luther," Terry said, enfolding Lute's hand in a giant paw missing its thumb and index finger, and shaking vigorously. "Bet you came to see my new tractor."

"Well, yeah, I guess. What'd you get?"

"You gotta be kiddin', man, a Deere, of course. You know what they say, nothing runs like a Deere!" This was followed by a big guffaw. "Wait, lemme turn the lights on and open that door." Terry turned to the wall and hit the switch to raise one of the huge doors on the building's north side.

"Like they say in church, Luther. Let there be light, huh? Over here," he gestured for Luther to follow him. They moved past an array of what Lute considered very large machines over to a corner where a shiny, new, bright-green, four-wheel-drive tractor glistened. The ladder leading up to the cab was a solid eight feet in length.

"She's a beaut, ain't she? Go ahead, climb up there," Terry said, pushing Lute gently toward the ladder. Luther climbed reluctantly but dutifully up into the sparkling-clean cab, big enough to house a Hmong family, he thought. Terry followed him and leaned in.

"Just what you need at your place, huh? Get 'er done"—Lute hated that phrase—"in no time. GPS, CD player. But you can also plug in your smartphone over there in that little slot. This goddamn thing is smarter than I am, tell you that!" Terry said, beaming with pride. "Spendy as hell, you know, but worth every penny, like they say."

"Planting a lot of corn and beans, huh?" Lute queried, moving his hands over the steering wheel. Hell, at least it still had one of those.

"That's what it's all about. Freeing Uncle Sam from those goddamn ragheads and their oil, right? See the new bin I just put up?"

"I did. It's a monster," Luther replied, truthfully.

"Yup, that's the biggest one in the county on a private farm. Not as big as the co-op's in Moeville, of course, but they've got the goddamn rail line right there, so they need one that big. Come on, I gotta show you a couple other new toys," Terry said, heading down the ladder. Lute looked down at the top of Terry's engineer's cap made entirely out of American flag material, his usual garb.

Walking a few paces further into the center of the machinery-crowded shed, Terry stopped at a large mass covered with a tarp.

"Guess what's under this then, Luther?" he asked proudly.

"Can't do it. Buy yourself a Harley?"

"Nope, no time for that folderol. Look," Terry swept the tarp away with a flourish and revealed a new four-wheeler that was almost the size of a small pickup. It had both front and back seats, a roof, lots of ground clearance, lights and a big winch on the front. And all camo paint, of course.

"Like her?" Terry gave another big grin. "Go on, get in."

Luther obliged. He couldn't say no, of course, so he got in, sitting behind the wheel.

"All the bells and whistles, man. First class. Wasn't crazy about buying Jap stuff, but they tell me the Kawasaki's the best there is. GPS, just in case I get lost out on the acreage," Terry said with big laugh. "A radio, and even a place to charge my goddamn cell phone. How about that?" Terry asked as he moved his great bulk into the seat next to Lute, the machine pitching a little as he did so. "We can take it out if you want. Don't mind the rain. We got a roof." He reached up and tapped it.

"Nah, that's OK. Some other time, Terry. Nice rig, though. Actually, nice rigs!"

"Yeah, they sure are. Hell, I could take this goddamn thing to Winona if I put the slow-mover sign on the back. Take awhile, but you never know."

"So what's it for?"

"What's it for? You gotta be kiddin', man," Terry exclaimed. "I'm out late, real late, fall plowing and need my supper? Linda just hops in this—and bingo, it's there. I need to fix some fence between me and that silly-ass lawyer who bought the Harris place out from under me, with his goddamn llamas or whatever they are. Bingo, throw in some tools and there I am. Maybe next year me and Shawn," mentioning one of his sons, "wanna finally go elk hunting like we been talking about for years, just throw this on the trailer and hook 'er up to the pickup. There we are in Wyoming, hunting elk in solid comfort. A few beers and bottle of Jack right there in that built-in cooler. I was kiddin' about the tractor, of course, but hey you really could use one of these at your place."

"I don't know. I just bought a new tractor, you know. Little New Holland three-cylinder diesel. Nine speeds. I love it."

"Yeah, I heard," Terry said. "You won the lotto, somebody said."

"Not exactly, a relative kicked off and left me some money. I got lucky," Luther scratched himself.

"Well, you can come borrow this thing anytime, see if you like it," Terry said patting the seat. "You might just decide to get one. Never know until you try."

"Thanks, I might do that," Luther said, knowing he wouldn't. "But hey, Terry, mostly I came over because my dog died. Wondered if you knew anybody with a litter of big dogs. Shepherds or Rotties, something like that?"

"Well, you know that crazy woman? The one with the sheep? I stopped over there last week to try to get her to rent to me. The usual thing, she won't do it, hates big machinery, blah, blah. Anyway, she has them big dogs for guarding sheep. Huge white things, forget the name. Think she said something about a litter. Pyrenees, that's their name, Great Pyrenees. Molly something or other, that's the woman."

"I know her," Luther acknowledged. He also had no intention of going over there.

"Yeah, well, to know her is to not love her, lemme tell you. Not a bad-looking woman, but crazier than a loon, if you ask me," Terry shook his large head.

"Sure you aren't just pissed at her because she won't rent to you?" Luther teased. "Hell, she's only got about fifteen or so open acres anyway, right?"

"Hey, these days with corn and bean prices, every square inch counts, lemme tell you," Terry proclaimed. "And, yes, I'd like that land, but that ain't why I call her nuts, ask Linda what she thinks about her. But c'mere, let's look over there in that the far corner."

Following Terry, Lute was treated to a description of every bit of the huge machinery they passed as they moved from the north to the south side of the building. A new sixteen-row corn planter, a disc harrow big enough to level Winona into the Mississippi in a day, several round balers capable of making bales weighing well over a ton. And a strange device, about fifteen feet high, mounted on a large trailer that also held a series of large, black plastic cases.

"Every one of them cases holds fifty bushels of corn," Terry said in answer to Lute's question. "See that feeder tube, just hook it up to the planter, it fills it up automatic. No more bull with dumping bags of seed. Straight from Land O'Lakes, the seed, in the cases. Hell of a good idea." Terry patted the trailer as they moved on.

"OK, here she is. Feast your eyes on that, Luther." No tarp this time, but still a flourish of Terry's arms, the left one of which moved quite awkwardly, another remnant of his war injury.

"What, some kind of dozer?" Luther asked as he walked over to more closely examine the very old machine.

"You bet," Terry acknowledged with pride. "They took a B John Deere, put some treads on her, and bingo—a dozer. Got it at auction down in Florida, of all places, last spring near this place Linda and I go. Lots of farmers go there for the winter, so they hold auctions, big ones. Anyways, got this beauty shipped up. It was spendy, but worth every penny. And see that," Terry said, pointing to a multihued fire hydrant, "know what that is?"

"Looks like a fire hydrant to me—from a city? Funny colors though."

"That's right. Someplace down there in the South got funny ideas and painted all their hydrants that way. Replaced them, so I bought one. Like it?" Terry asked.

"Yeah, I guess. But what do you do with it?" Luther asked as he scratched his still-aching head and felt a small shiver of cold go through him, hangover payback.

"I don't know, just wanted it. Like the dozer. It can't do much work, the B never had much power anyway. Maybe plow a little snow if you like, but had to have it, you know how it is."

Luther didn't know, having rarely been subject to a "had to have it" impulse, but he nodded politely anyway.

"Well, I got to get going on that combine I was working on when you came. But on the way back, lemme show you what I done to my truck. Come on," Terry urged.

Out of the building finally, standing in the light rain, the two men stood looking at Terry's F-250 three-quarter-ton Ford pickup. It seemed as long as a house, with its four-door cab and full-sized bed. New last winter, Luther had seen it once or twice in Moeville. And one day Terry had actually stopped by Lute's place, something he rarely did—mostly, Lute thought, to show off the truck.

It was black with some kind of green-and-white flares painted on the front fenders and running back into the front doors. Cost a penny or two extra, Terry had proudly noted. Now, however, they were looking at two newly painted panels. One on each side of the truck's bed, just before the wheel wells, they depicted on one side Terry's new 4WD John Deere tractor in all its immensity against a backdrop of a bright yellow cornfield. And on the other side, with a background of a dusky-brown fall bean field, was one of Terry's combines, also the size of a small building.

Beaming while the rain dripped off his cap and onto his heavily scarred features, Terry told Lute about a man he'd found to do the painting, just across the river in La Crosse. "Just takes a goddamn picture, does some computer stuff with it, and bingo, there you have it. Hell, men put their favorite dogs on their trucks, their Harleys, you name it."

"And their wives?" Luther couldn't resist.

"Uh, no. Don't imagine Linda would be too happy to see her face all full of mud and cow shit from the barnyard," Terry admitted.

"Yeah, probably not a good idea. It looks great, Terry. Never saw anything like it. Listen, man, thanks for the tour. You got some great stuff. If I don't see you, I hope you have a great harvest."

"Thanks, looks good so far. As long as the weather holds, no snow, we'll be in clover, hey, I mean corn, I tell you," Terry predicted. "See you around, Luther, and don't be such a stranger."

"I won't," Luther promised. "See you." He climbed into his truck and drove out of the yard, colder than hell and wishing he had a heater.

Literally a mile down the road from Terry's farm, Lute pulled into the driveway, such as it was, of Rich Wearmouth's place. The place was the one-hundred-eighty-degree opposite of where he'd just been and what he'd just seen.

Not really a farm, per se, Rich's place was an amazing jumble of things, among them a trailer house attached to an decrepit old farmhouse, three or four, maybe more, semi trailers propped up on a variety of cement blocks and decaying railroad ties, none of them remotely level, and a whole junkyard of rusted-out vehicles.

The light was on over the mobile home's entrance, which was a set of cement steps. If Lute remembered right, the light was always on, day or night, winter or summer. The wires to what had been a doorbell hung from a hole uselessly, so Luther knocked as hard as he could. The rain had strengthened, making it harder to hear the knock indoors, and Rich's hearing was lousy, probably since Nam.

But someone, who else could it be but Rich, Luther thought, opened the door and actually yanked him into the dwelling. Peering at him in the dim light, Rich began a slow, lazy, gap-toothed smile, genuinely glad to see Luther.

"Hey, bro, glad you're here, man," Rich welcomed him. "You won't believe this, but I had a funny feelin' it might be you. You know?"

Smiling back at his friend, and this guy *was* his friend, Lute answered, "You know I never set much stock in that shit, but now that I'm getting older, stuff happens. I do get these feelings sometimes, dreams, some daytime shit. It's spooky."

"Got the cure for that, my man. Let's burn one," Rich suggested, turning in a very small space to sit on a couch even more untidy than Luther's and picking up a long wood-handled pipe with a tiny clay bowl in which he placed a nice pinch of weed.

"Don't know if I should, bro. I got totally fucked up last night. Booze, smoke, I'm still sufferin'." Luther ran a hand through his wet hair.

"Hey, dude, booze? That shit'll kill you, rot your friggin' liver, shrink your tiny brain. But this shit? They don't call it *medical* for nothing." Rich lit the pipe and taking a monster hit, handed it to Lute.

"Tiny is right—my brain, I mean. Suppose I should quit the sauce, huh?"

"Fucking A, tweety bird. Look at my kid!"

"Andy? What's going on with him?"

"Fucker's in jail, again. DWI, it's like the fourth or fifth one, man. But he won't give it up, so off to silver city he goes."

"Shit," Luther relit the pipe and took his own long hit. "Sorry to hear it. But me, I never get behind the wheel when I'm wasted. I used to do it all the time. I'm just lucky I didn't kill anybody."

"Right, me too. You weren't around, but when I was just back from Nam, I was crazy like a motherfucker. I couldn't drink enough hooch—beer, wine, and the hard stuff. I was getting into fights. And I *did* almost kill somebody—me! Long story short, you've heard it, the old lady leaves me and takes the kid. Then I had that serious encounter with the bridge abutment? I've been sober ever since! Dope, o' course, but this don't count!"

They both smoked a bit, then Luther broke the silence.

"So I just came from Terry's." Luther watched Rich refill the pipe. "I don't see a lot of him, he's Mister America with the flags and shit. But funny thing is, I like him, always have. You know the assholes like him—Vietnam Vet plates, join the Legion, VF fucking W. But 90 percent of 'em never even saw any more combat than a bar fight. I hate those fuckers. I see their cars I think about setting them on fire. But for some reason, I haven't a clue, I've always liked Terry. And he and I are day and night, man. Day and friggin' night. But Jesus H. Christ, has he got the stuff. You know how he is, like a kid with his first bike, so happy about the new tractor, the new four-wheeler, the whacked-out pictures he's got painted on his pickup. And he's not faking it, man. He's really like that."

"I know. Course me being down the road here so close, it's easier for me to be pissed at him. All that shit, he's always braggin' it up."

"Corn prices are way high, I know, but how in the fuck does he afford it? Linda works at the nursing home, no big bread there. So how?"

"Come on, man. If you had Uncle Sam paying you about thirty-five hundred every month for your whole life? He's got total disability remember? You'd be fat too. Instead, you and me, we got our heads fucked with over there, but came out with all our fingers, you dig? Sorry, friends, too bad about your fried wires, there is no payout for that, man."

"But he's been working his ass off the whole time I've been here. Gotta give him that, the man's a working fool. So where's the disability?"

"I don't fucking know, ask the VA. His face is fucked, missing some fingers and his left arm don't work too good. I don't know," Rich said as he got off the couch and put a piece of wood from a nearby cardboard box into an ancient woodstove too large for the tiny room. The fire was burning sharp and bright through tattered mica windows.

"Jesus, buddy, more wood? I came in cold but now . . . ," Lute had already removed his jacket, and now he pulled his ragged old sweater over his head too. "Say, I lost Azteca, my pup. I miss her like crazy, and I gotta get a new one to help me stay afloat. Anybody got pups that you know of?"

"Well, not me. Tyler," he gestured to a very large dog sleeping by the stove, "ain't got it up recently any more than I have. So no pups from his large butt. But remember that hippie chick, the one with the sheep? I heard she's got pups from those big dogs she has, some Spanish breed I think."

"They're Pyrenees, the breed. Terry told me that too. But I certainly . . . ," Luther shook his head and paused. "Not a friggin' chance. I am *not* going over there."

"Oh, that's right. She about moved in on you, I remember!" He flashed a lopsided grin.

"That's right. She did, or almost did. She moved here what, ten years or so ago? Nice-looking, short shorts out in the garden and legs all the way up to her pretty neck. Seemed kinda cool, a little older, she'd been around some. So she comes over and checks the place, and me, out. We smoke a little weed and bingo, we're in the sack. She was hot."

"Christ, man, shut up," Rich laughed. "You're just reminding me of all I've been missing lately, dude."

"Sorry," Luther pretended to apologize. "I was at the market on Saturday, more young nooky there than you can shake your stick at. Anyway, that woman? We got together a couple more times, and then she shows up with her suitcase, suitcases actually. Like she plans to move in."

"I kinda remember that now, it didn't go so well right?"

"Nope." Luther shook his head. "I told her I didn't want a roommate, but she figured 'cause we got it on, we should pair up. Big mistake, she starts screaming, calling me every name in the book, throwing my shit around. I don't know what the fuck to do, so I go out in the woods, and me and the dog hide out. We came back late at night, and she was gone. She left a long note about what an asshole I am, which I am, I guess. But, shit, I do all I can to avoid her."

"Man, those are tough waters to navigate. Say, rain's lettin' up, one more serious toke and let me show you my animals." Filling the small pipe, Rich handed it to Lute, who took his hit and gave it back.

Rich's place was small and crowded. Besides the couch, there were a couple of armchairs both heaped with books and magazines, and an old kitchen chair also piled high with reading material. Next to that a ragged and sagging cardboard wood box held a huge stack of newspaper for fire starting. The two men exited the tiny, cluttered home into the gray afternoon and indeed the rain had stopped. Luther followed Rich, thinking once again of the irony that probably the least well-off person he knew was named Rich.

They headed into the maze of animal shelters. The first was one of the cantilevered semi trailers just outside the mobile home, an Emerald Dairy logo faint on one side. It was Rich's chicken coop. Entering the rear of the trailer by a slippery ramp made from wooden pallets, Rich shooed the chickens away from the door and closed it behind them. A small amount of light entered the coop from the far end, which led permanently into a small, fenced outdoor run.

In the poor light, Lute could discern the standard five-gallon zinc waterer, a four-foot-long wooden feed tray with a rotating bar across the top to prevent the chickens from roosting on and shitting in it. And on one wall, a linked set of six metal nests for laying eggs, a device dating probably from before World War II.

"Whoa, Rich. Where'd you get those nests?" Luther asked, impressed. "Last time I was here you just had some plywood boxes."

Rich grinned. "You dig 'em, huh? I got 'em at an Amish auction. Real vintage shit, man. Don't rust, and check out the little holes in the bottom so I can just stick the hose in there once in a while to clean 'em out. Man, if they made one big enough to house me and Tyler," referring to his dog, "I'd settle right in. Just hose the SOB out once a month or so."

"You mean once a year or so, don't you?"

"Fuck you, Mr. Clean!" Rich laughed. "Last time I was at your crib, bro, I didn't see nobody from *Better Homes and Gardens* taking pics."

"*Battered Homes and Gardens*, more like it. Just shitting you. How many eggs you getting?"

"Dozen, more or less. Starting to slow down now the light's getting shorter."

"A dozen—what the hell do you do with them?"

"Well, maybe you didn't notice, friend, but me and Tyler got this kind of yellowish cast to our skin. Heavy on the eggs for chow around here, lemme tell you, dude," Rich joked.

"And?" Lute persisted.

"Well, let's see. I give some away, trade some to Quint Schumacher for his butter and cottage cheese. I tried to sell some to Terry and his old lady, but she's too finicky, prob'ly thinks the eggs are dirty or something. If I just got too many, I give 'em to the pigs. You need some?" Rich offered.

"Nah, I get mine from Theresa. I trade her for veggies, but thanks. Didn't know you had hogs."

As they slipped down the ramp from the coop, Tyler the giant shaggy dog, his hair thoroughly matted with burrs, joined them.

"Hey, how'd he get here?" Luther wondered.

"Yo, Tyler, tell the man how fuckin' clever you are. How you open the trailer door all by yourself. How you just push up the handle with your nose, and out you go," Rich said as he rubbed the dog's head with affection.

Their next stop was a structure Luther had trouble actually understanding was a building. It had a steel roof, or actually roofs, over it. It was a series of pens of varying sizes set off from one another with a random assortment of pallets, wire fencing, boards and sheets of roofing steel. The whole thing was so totally without form as to be almost . . . art.

"Wow, Rich, this is like some crazy fencing you got here, man."

"Yeah, I know. But remember my name for the place, Anarchy Farm? Well this is anarchy fencing, dude. But look at my pigs, man. Check out these beauties." Pointing to a pen knee deep in straw and manure with about a half dozen small pigs in it.

"Feeders. Where'd you get 'em?"

"Lanesboro, at the auction. Calves too," Rich said, nodding toward an adjoining pen that was equally manure filled and home to three Holstein calves. The white parts of their coats were dark with mud and manure.

"Steers? What'll you do with them?"

"Oh, I'll raise 'em for a bit, then keep one to butcher and sell the other two. Same with the hogs. Feed 'em out, sell 'em, and keep one for the freezer."

"Jesus, man, that's a lot of fucking meat."

"Yeah, well, me and Tyler will eat that bridge when we come to it. But, man, corn is so high people can't afford to feed animals out like they used to, so I got all of these for almost nothing. I mean, I hear guys are just throwing bull calves on the dump. Not worth the expense to raise 'em."

Turning to another pen that opened into a small fenced yard, Lute noticed probably the most forlorn donkey, or maybe a mule, he'd ever seen. Not that he'd seen that many, anyway.

"What, or who, is that?"

"That's Sorrowful Sam. Former icon of the now lost Democratic Party, you dig?" Rich said, smiling as he reached over and patted the animal on its head.

"Yeah, I dig," Luther laughed. "Good name for the critter and for the party. But where'd you get him or her—and what is it, a mule, a donkey, or a burro?"

"Burro. He was one of those wild ones they round up out west every couple years. Some farm lady got him, had him a while, then her old man told her to dump him. It's a him, see," Rich said, pointing to the creature. "Look at the size of his unit, he must be excited to see you, man. Anyway, I got him out of the *Shopper*. It was a rescue deal, so I didn't have to pay a dime. Just stuck him in the horse trailer and here he is, since last spring."

"Whaddya do with him?"

"Feed him and try to pet him. He's not crazy about being handled," Rich said with a smile. "We hang out, talk politics and shit. He's smarter than he looks."

"But is he really as sad as he looks?" Luther asked as he tried in vain to pet the burro.

"Hey, how would you feel if you'd been running around out in Montana some place with all the senorita burros, fighting off the wolves and coyotes, then some fuckers with a chopper show up and shoot a dart into you?" Rich imagined. "The next thing you know, you belong to some lady who wants to make you her personal plaything. Is he sad? You fucking bet!"

"So what's the difference between you and the lady who had him before?"

"Well, if I had the bread, I'd just load him up and haul him back out west and let him go out in some desert," Rich sighed. "But my truck is lucky to get into Winona. And gas, shit I'd have to rob a bank. So, I got plans to get him outta this crappy pen and take that three-acre piece that's all weeds and scrap trees now and put up a decent fence. Turn him loose. Meanwhile, I'm just keeping him alive, you know."

Knowing that the likelihood of Rich actually building that fence was very low, Lute offered, "Tell you what, brother, I'm too busy now closing down the gardens, cutting wood. But next spring? I promise I'll be here as soon as the snow goes, and we'll get that fence up."

"Really? If you're serious, man, that'd be great," Rich said in earnest.

"When was I ever not serious? That's my problem, so they tell me."

Rich nodded. "You're like that mythological dude. Can't remember his name, but he carries a heavy load up the hill, it rolls down, and he just carries it back up again."

"Sisyphus. It was a boulder he pushed up and down forever. Yup, that's me, all right. What's that noise?"

"My geese, man. Over here." Leading Luther to another pen with a sizable yard where three horses stood eating from an enormous round bale of hay just laying in the mud. A covey of geese, all neck and noise, strutted around in the mud too. "Those are my guard geese. Ol' Tyler's hearing is just about shot, so he wouldn't know if a pack of coyotes came into the house. But these dudes? They're all about keeping a weather eye on the place."

"Can you eat them?" He thought it unlikely, but it seemed a reasonable question.

"I suppose. Maybe do one at Christmas. But that's not why I got 'em. They guard the place and I just like them, like watching them. I think of them as some kind of cops, you know, from some foreign country where the fuzz wears white. Marching around all silly, givin' orders, making a lot of noise. Peter Sellers kind of shit, y'know?"

"Maybe I should borrow them to protect me at the farmers' market," Luther suggested. "Did I tell you about the most recent guy who made a stink about one of my signs? Some man from City Hall, checking on permits or something. He strolls through the market one day and stops to look at my signs, reading that one from Le Guin about the revolution? You know, it's inside you or nowhere?"

"Right, I got all her stuff. Anarchy Farm, remember?"

"Well, the other sign is about the rich, what will the poor eat when there's nothing left?"

"The rich, right?" Rich nodded.

"That's it. So the dude asks me what my problem with the rich is, and I tell him they're bloodsuckers. He gets pissed and tells me to take the sign down, and I tell him to fuck off. I think he was getting ready to seriously try to force me to take it down, but he thought better about it. So he warned me he's keeping an eye on me, then hustles off to find the dude who kind of runs the market." Luther grabbed hold of the fence.

"George something or other, isn't it?"

"Right, George. He's OK. He used to be a social worker or something, one of your typical bourgeois liberals whose whole goal is not to offend anyone. So he comes to tell me he's had a complaint about my signage. He won't say who, but I know it's the city guy, and he says maybe I should take down the rich-poor sign."

"Serious?" Rich says, shaking his head. "Say, friend, while we're chatting and all, got any ciggies?"

"Oh, sure," Luther says, taking out his pack of home-rolled and offering Rich one, then taking one for himself. He lit Rich's, then his own, and took a big drag. "Sorry, man, I thought you gave it up."

"I did, but then I think—shit, I'm getting seriously old. I gotta die sometime and I love the smokes, so why not? Spendy as hell, though, so I don't always have them."

"Spendy is right! Which is why I roll my own. Amsterdam Shag. The tobacco. Get it on the Internet. So anyway, I told the guy at the market that the sign wasn't coming down, and he should stop getting his panties in a twist about offending some lousy bureaucrat. Dude just shakes his head and says it'll have to go to the market board. The decision about my sign, I mean."

"And?"

"I guess they talked about it and voted, it was a close vote I heard, 'cause I didn't fucking go to the meeting. But they let me keep the sign. Another vendor told me later that several people spoke up for me. Since I'm one of the oldest, I mean long-time, members, blah, blah."

Both men leaned on the haphazard horse fence, some of it hurricane fence from a suburban backyard, plus more sheets of steel roofing.

Some of the fence was red, some green, and most of it was twisted and rusty. There were steel posts here, wooden posts there, and many crooked railroad ties stuck in between. Lute asked if Rich rode the horses, and if not, what were they for?

"Nah, I don't ride 'em. I never did. I had some cowboy notion about it way back when, after the old lady took Andy. I thought it might be cool to have a pony for him when he came here, so I got one. That smaller black one? That's McCabe, like that great movie with Warren Beatty. But when I tried to get Andy to ride him, the kid was scared shitless. He cried like hell, so that didn't work. But hey, I've told you this before."

"I guess you're right. I seem to remember that now. But what about the other two?"

"The big guy, that's Berkman. He's named after the anarchist who almost killed that son-of-a-bitch U.S. Steel guy Frick. And the mare, she's named after Emma Goldman. She came over here from Russia and lectured against capitalism and kept going to jail. Anyway she and Berkman were lovers, and these two horses get it on once in a while, so . . . ."

"Any offspring?"

"No, fortunately. I think Berkman's shooting blanks or whatever. Anyway, no foals, no colts. Just three old ponies I couldn't stand to send to the dog-food factory."

"You *are* a sentimental SOB, aren't you, Rich?" Luther said, smiling.

"That I am, and no fucking apologies. I love my critters. Whatever the hell's going on in their heads, I haven't a clue. Even Tyler. I talk to him all the time and he pretends to listen. But I know he's just hanging around for a pet and some chow. Although I do think he's really into some old Chet Baker LPs I've been spinning. You wanna hear?"

So the men and the dog went back inside the trailer, done with their tour. It had started to rain again anyway. They smoked another pipe of weed, and listened to a couple of Chet Baker sides, talking about what a thorough asshole the dude had been even though his music was so mellow. They ate three cans of sardines, the kind in hot sauce, with crackers and onions. And then Luther finally left, feeling better, in both his body and his head, than he had in a long while.

Was it just the weed, he wondered as he drove home? No, it was good to see both Terry and even more so, Rich. Comrades from Nam, even though it was something he never talked about with Terry, and only in passing with Rich. The weed helped, of course, especially if he wasn't drinking at the same time. Smiling to think of how, in his way, Rich was as proud of his crappy little place with its jerry-rigged animal shelters as Terry was of his massive operation and its gargantuan machinery. Well, Luther acknowledged, whenever people came to look at his gardens, he felt the same way.

Chapter 36

Mary and Joni left their Lincoln motel quite early on Tuesday morning, settling for the bad coffee in the motel room rather than spending time searching for the good stuff.

"My daughter, Emma?" Mary said as she pulled back onto the interstate. "She's got one of those new smartphones where you can just ask it to find something, like a Starbucks, and it tells you. That would be handy on a trip like this!"

"Yeah. Especially if it told us where the cops and the bad guys were! Half the women I worked with at the Worst Western had a smartphone, never mind how much they cost. They were always texting somebody—boyfriends, girlfriends, kids. And looking up shit on the Internet too."

"Mike here," Mary gestured to the figure seat-belted between them, "he and I always did crosswords on long trips. He did most of the driving, and I ran the crossword. One of those phones would have been handy for looking stuff up."

"I suppose. Eunice used to do them. She had crossword books all over the house. Her favorites, if I remember right, were from the *New York Times*."

"Speaking of my late lamented, are you spooked by having him here between us?" Mary asked Joni about the mannequin, which she'd reinstalled into the front seat.

"It's a little weird," Joni said. "But I get your point about him feeling neglected there in the back. It seems like half the shows on TV now are about zombies, people returning from the dead, or vampires. So having him here is kinda like that, I guess."

"Well, he's neither a zombie nor vampire. Just a crazy old lady's whim, I guess, because believe me I know that he's not alive or returned from the dead, or whatever. And when I started out on this trip, it—he—was just a good idea to help keep me safe. But I guess he didn't, did he?"

"What do you mean?"

"He didn't keep me safe. That crazy bastard that jumped me, then all that stuff in Nebraska. But your being here," Mary paused, "that's good."

"Amen to that."

"And there's something, I don't know if I can explain it, about having him here. A comfort, I guess. And I know that's strange." Mary turned to Joni and smiled tentatively.

"Well, no harm. But what's your sister gonna say?"

"Theresa? I haven't a clue, really I don't. She's always been basically a polite woman and kind, so if she disapproved, or thought I was nuts, it'd be some time before I found out. Minnesota nice, y'know. Lake Wobegon and all that."

"What's that?"

"Hey, it's raining." Mary turned on the windshield wipers, setting them at a slow speed, as the rain was inconstant. "'Minnesota nice' is just a notion, as my mother would have said, an idea. One that describes how people in Minnesota act polite and avoid saying negative things."

"They're hypocrites, you mean?" Joni asked.

"That depends, I guess," Mary answered. "Tee isn't a hypocrite, but I also know she's loathe to hurt your feelings too. I've never lived there, so I couldn't say, but I think the way we were raised was pretty similar to the way things are there now."

"And what does that mean?"

"Well, avoiding conflict was a priority. That's why I was often in trouble—I'm conflict prone. I swear I never heard my parents raise their voices to one another, but Mike and I yelled a lot."

"They didn't fight?"

"Not that I saw," Mary answered. "Maybe behind the bedroom door, but I know for certain they never, I mean never, got into it with other people, especially the neighbors. Heck, we had a nasty old man across the alley who was too cheap to buy an extra trash can, so he'd put some of his trash in our bins. And his incinerator, the little burners we had behind each house for burning stuff, his didn't work so he just used ours without asking. My folks would grumble about it, but never say a word to the old guy. Not a peep!"

"Wow. My gram would have scalped him!"

"And across the street from us was an elderly couple, retired I think, who my mother felt sorry for. I'm not sure why exactly, but we gave them our *Sun-Times* newspaper when we were done with it. The trouble was, Mother was so worried about them getting it that same morning that often Dad wouldn't get to read all of it. He'd mumble a little about it, but always gave it up so Mom could race across the street with it. That, my dear Joni, is the essence of 'nice.'"

Both women were suddenly silenced as a semi roared past them, too close really, showering water over the Lincoln as if they had driven it into a creek.

"Jesus, Mary, and Giuseppe!" Mary exclaimed, putting the wipers on full speed. "That scared the heck out of me."

"Me too. Did you see the big cross on the back of the truck? I guess he thought the Lord would forgive him if he ran us over!"

"My sister still goes to church."

"Is she gonna be laying a whole Jesus trip on us?" Joni asked warily.

"Oh no, not a bit of it. We were raised Catholic, went to Catholic schools, and then she even went on to a Catholic woman's college, St. Teresa's, just like her name. But she knows I'm not a churchgoer now, so we haven't really talked about it much. And don't forget,

'Minnesota nice,' means she would never bug anyone about religion, that wouldn't be polite."

"That's good," Joni said, relieved. "But what about that lake you were talking about?"

"Oh yeah, Lake Wobegon, it's from a popular show on public radio, it's been on the air for years. It's not a real lake or town, but this guy has a radio show where he has created all of these characters and he tells stories centered around their lives in this little town in Minnesota called Lake Wobegon," Mary explained.

"Does that mean something?" Joni asked.

"*Woebegone* means like gloomy, down-in-the-mouth, every day's a rainy day, that sort of thing."

"Why's it been popular for so long?"

"I never thought about it much. I've always just liked it, I guess. The guy pokes a gentle kind of fun at people in the town, people that someone my age can recognize even way out in Pasadena. He tells stories about little stuff that happens to people. Like a kid goes off to college and comes home totally changed, his parents don't get it, and awkward stuff happens."

"Wow, like, really exciting. Sorry I've missed it!" Joni said, not impressed.

"Right," Mary agreed with a laugh. "It's pretty low-key, wry kind of stuff. Anyway, because the show comes from Minnesota and it's set there, some people see the whole state that way. Didn't your grandma ever talk about it, being from there and all?"

"Some, but not much really. I always had the sense her life didn't really start until she left home, left Minnesota. I guess like I hope mine will now that I'm going to Minnesota. Kind of a strange twist of fate, huh? So is Theresa whatever you call it, *woebegone*?"

"I really don't think so, but you'll have to decide for yourself when we get there. Meanwhile, look at the atlas will you? See if there's a way to get around Omaha."

Joni did and found 680, which sweeps up and over the city and its Iowa neighbor, Council Bluffs, joining 80 once more north of the two cities. The two women drove in silence but for passing traffic and the rain, now heavier on the windshield, until Joni spotted a sign noting the turnoff several miles ahead.

Leaving 80, they soon found themselves in a rural area of slightly rolling hills filled with not only the usual cornfields, but also large areas given over to grazing cattle, most of them black.

"What's with all the black cows do you think, Mary?" Joni asked, breaking the silence.

"I bet they're Angus, Black Angus. Anyway, I'm pretty sure that's what they are. If so, they're for meat, beef, not to milk."

"I didn't know there was a difference. I just thought cows were cows, but I remember the menu at the motel always featured Black Angus steaks and stuff, and one time some fast-food place was advertising Angus burgers. Now here they are, and they are really black. Go figure."

"They're supposed to be the premier beef," Mary said. "Unless you go for that fancy Japanese stuff, Kobe, but you really don't hear as much about that anymore."

"Never heard of it."

"Well, I never ate any. It's way too expensive. They used to have some of it at the place in Pasadena where I bought fish. I asked the clerk once why the Kobe was so pricey, and he said it had to do with how and what they were fed, including beer."

"Beer, no lie?"

"Yep, or so he said. If we had one of those phones we could look it up. But oh shit, forget the beer, look at that!" Mary exclaimed, suddenly pointing at the dash.

"What, what's the matter?" Joni asked, alarmed.

"My aging brain, that's what's the matter," Mary fretted. "Look at the gas gauge!"

"Whoa, uh-oh," Joni agreed. "Guess we gotta find a station quick." Joni looked out the window, but all she could see was cattle and cornfields.

"Right, except look where we are. In the middle of nowhere. There's no station around here, nothing but farms," Mary bemoaned, slowing the Dreadnaught.

"So don't they use gas?"

"Sure, but do we just show up and ask to buy some?" Mary suggested, dubious.

"What else can we do?" Joni replied. "Doubt there's any roadside assistance here like on the L.A. freeways."

"OK, we can give it a shot, I guess." Mary sounded very tentative.

Driving quietly for another ten minutes or so, Joni finally saw a place to exit and just beyond, sort of below the highway, a farm with a house, barn, and outbuildings. A light was on in the house, so Joni jumped out to knock on the door. As she was knocking, she noticed that it wasn't really a very old house, not like from some farm calendar or something. It was just a rather plain place that appeared to be well kept, if she was any judge, which she really wasn't. And nobody was answering.

Back in the car, the two women conferred about what to do, agreeing they should go together into the other buildings to try to find someone. Together because who knew what they might find, given their luck so far.

The large building closest to the house was the oldest one, a barn that looked like it *was* straight out of a farm calendar with its high steel-covered roof, and two cupolas with weathervanes that looked like roosters. The stone walls on the lower portion were painted a bright white and there were very large red doors on each end of the building, one of them inset with a smaller door.

Gingerly opening the small door, the two women stepped just inside, adjusting their eyes to the low light offered by a series of windows along each side of the building. The floor was cement, with some sort of well or channel right in its middle and there were two rows of steel structures down each side that kind of looked like cages. It was a bit creepy.

"What are those for?" Joni wondered.

Going over to one for a closer look, Mary answered, "I'm not sure, but I think they were for the cows when they milked them. To hold them in place maybe?" She had no idea where she would have picked up that tidbit.

"Weird, it's like some kind of cow jail. There's nobody here, let's go," Joni suggested, her discomfort apparent.

No lights were on in either of the next two buildings, but then there were no windows either. Both of these were made of red steel, with white roofs, and one was quite a bit larger than the other.

They cautiously opened the service door of the smaller building, which was closest to the barn, again encountering darkness. It was even darker in here because there were no windows, just some panels in the roof that let in a tiny amount of light.

"Hello?" Joni called out, not really expecting a reply, and not getting one.

"OK," Mary said, "Let's try that last one and then the house again one more time. Then let's get out of here. A big place like this, in the middle of nowhere is just a little spooky!" Mary took Joni's shoulder and gave it a squeeze as they exited and moved to the final building, the largest one on the place by far, set somewhat into a small hillside dotted with a few trees.

Tentatively opening the final door, the women were almost blinded by very bright light that seemed to be coming from the entire ceiling. They noticed right away that it was warm and comfortable inside too.

Before they could say anything, a voice hailed them from a far corner of the place. "Hullo there, can I help you ladies?" an elderly man called to them, a slight quaver in his voice.

"Yes, please," Mary answered. "We actually ran out of gas. Could we possibly get some from you?"

"Oh, OK," the man said as he came closer through what appeared to an enormous cluster of tractors. "Whatcha drivin', gas or diesel?"

"Gas, it's a Lincoln," Mary answered, having no idea why she added that. Lincoln, Blynken, and Nod, so help me God, she thought.

"Got 'em both, even some kerosene," he replied. "Some of these old machines used to run on kerosene, you know." The man was now finally visible, having come almost the entire length of the enormous building to meet them. He was small, slightly bent, wearing dungaree coveralls and an engineer's cap, and wiping his hands on a very dirty rag.

"Great. We'll pay you, of course," Mary said. And why had she added that, Mary wondered? Silly woman.

Up close, the man had a mottled, red-and-white sort of face, with great wrinkles creating valleys across it. And he was clean-shaven, causing Joni to wonder how he could possibly shave such skin without seriously injuring himself.

Putting out his hand, now reasonably clean, the man said, "I'm Willem, pleased to meet you."

"Mary," she replied, shaking the offered hand.

"And I'm Joni." She also shook his hand.

Squinting at them, Willem asked Mary where they were from. She replied briefly with the details about coming from California, and going to Minnesota to visit her sister.

"Never been there, to California. Always wanted to see it. The ocean, the palm trees, but never got there. Now Minnesota, been there prob'ly twice for farm auctions. Good ones too, I got some of these over there," he explained, gesturing to the sea of tractors.

"Oh," was the best Mary could come up with.

Undaunted, the man asked, "Know what these are, the tractors?"

"Other than that they're tractors, I have to admit I don't. But I see John Deere on them, so I guess they have that in common." Mary smiled at the man.

He laughed kindly and elaborated. "Lot more than that ma'am, lot more than that. Come here a moment, if you'd be so kind," he offered, gesturing to the nearest machine. "See this letter B? Well that's the model they are, John Deere Bs, every blessed one of them."

"Wow, you sure have a lot of them," Joni said. "They seem to be in pretty good shape."

"You betcha, tip-top, if I do say so myself," he replied. "Restored every single one, every one. And did it almost all myself, still doing it.

That's what I was working on when you came in, come take a look." He led them down an open space between the machines to an even more brightly lit corner where one of the tractors stood, kind of half undressed, on a concrete pad with tools scattered all around it. "Got some engine work to do on this one, just got her in August, went all the way down to Tennessee. Ever been there?"

Both women shook their heads no.

Torn between wanting to get her gas and move on, and being polite to this old guy, Mary asked, "How many do you have of these tractors?"

"Fully restored, ready for the parade or whatever? Thirty!" he told them proudly. "Then another fifteen or so in bits and pieces out in that other building. Parts tractors, I pick 'em up cheap, haul 'em here to get stuff off that's good. Then I clean it, paint it, and so on."

"What are they for though?" Joni couldn't help asking.

"Keep me from going crazy, the most important." He grinned. "A man's got to keep busy, can't spend too much time watching television and all that foolishness. Even the news is junk, I say. But, just come over here and let me show you one of these old Bs."

Reluctant—but what could they do?—the women followed the old man over to a nearby vibrantly green machine.

"Not gonna bore with you too many details, us collectors can get pretty long-winded, even bore each other. So I'll make it quick," Willem promised. "Now see those two narrow wheels up front?"

They both nodded.

"OK, well they make this what we call a row-crop tractor. That narrow front allows the tractor to go down the middle of a row of corn, and the rear wheels can be moved to adjust to the row width. They were made starting before the war, the one I was in, in '35. And Deere quit making them in 1952. The company made exactly 111,340—not give or take, exactly that many. All made right here in Iowa," Willem explained.

"Iowa?" Mary exclaimed. "I thought this was still Nebraska?"

"Nope, you're in Iowa," he answered firmly. "S'pose you're headed back onto the interstate, I-80?"

"Yes, we are," Mary replied.

"Well, that junction is about thirty miles from here, and you're lucky you stopped for gas. There ain't none until you get there," he informed them.

Still looking at the tractors, Joni asked, "So they were made here?"

"In Iowa, yes," Willem continued. "But way over toward the other side of the state, in Waterloo."

"Waterloo, like Napoleon?" Mary asked.

"I suppose so, but I don't really know why it's named that," he pondered. "Nearest place to here is called Beebeetown—don't ask me where that came from either!"

Mary asked how powerful the tractors were, noting that as a landscape worker, John Deere equipment was not uncommon in her field.

"Twelve horse, give or take. Now I know that don't sound like much, with lawnmowers now claiming sixteen or twenty horse, but these little machines did one heck of a lot of work. Don't know exactly how they measure horsepower these days, but this tractor can outpull many of the modern small tractors with twice or more claimed horsepower. Note that I said *claimed.* Say," he said, taking Joni's elbow, "go ahead and climb up on it, take a seat in American history."

Though she wasn't inclined to do so, Joni nonetheless did as asked, grabbing the steering wheel to haul herself up to the seat.

"See that lever to your left, that's the clutch." Willem pointed out. "Didn't have a foot clutch like most, which surprised some folks when they first drove one, but you soon got used to it. Knew a fella lost his legs in a train accident, just a kid when it happened. Still, he farmed all his life with one of these because of the hand clutch, you see?"

Joni and Mary didn't quite see, but Joni dutifully fingered the lever, thanking Honda for insuring that the clutch was on the floor in her old Civic.

"Well, I'd like to start it up for you ladies, so you could listen to that great old chugga-chugga two cylinders. There's no mistakin' 'em, I tell you. But then you'd leave smelling all smoky, so let's go get your gas," he said turning back toward the front of the building.

Outside, Willem pointed to a red tank sitting atop a steel trellis over near the old barn. "Just drive over there, keep your fill side toward the tank, and we'll get you going."

"OK," both women said, and started to walk away. But then Joni hesitated, feeling rude, and rejoined the old man en route to the tank.

"So, that your grandma?" Willem asked her as they walked.

"No, just a friend. We're going to Minnesota together."

"Oh, got family there?"

"She, Mary, does. Me, I'm not sure." Grateful when the old man ceased his questioning. As little as she was required to say about what she was up to, the better, she thought.

Unlimbering the heavy black hose from a stirrup on the tank's trellis, Willem opened the gas cap on the Lincoln, inserting the hose.

"This is a mighty nice machine. Town Car, huh? What year is it?"

"It's an '89," Mary answered. "We've, I mean, I've had it for about four years."

"Like it?"

"I really do," Mary acknowledged. "Never owned a big car before, but it's real comfortable and gets good mileage, or so I'm told, for being so big. Kind of a land yacht, I guess." Mary put a hand on the car's faux-leather roof.

"Well, nothing wrong with comfortable. Me, I drive a big Dodge pickup. Three-quarter-ton gas-guzzler, but gotta have it to tow my tractors to fairs and whatnot," Willem said.

"Oh, that's plenty," Mary said, reaching out and touching the man's arm. "You don't have to put all that gas in there, and I'm going to pay you for it."

"Yup, I do recall you saying that, but I only put about five gallons in there, and I don't need the money," he pulled out the hose and recoiled it on the fuel stand. "But you can repay me by honoring this old man and staying for lunch. How's that?"

Looking helplessly at each other, Mary and Joni knew immediately what they had to do. Go listen to more tractor tales from this sweet, lonely man, and then hit the road.

"Sure, sure, that'd be great," Mary answered. "But I'd still like to pay you." Mary reached for her purse.

"Nope, won't hear of it," Willem said, waving his hand. "Look at it this way, sometime somebody's gonna need some help from you and you'll do it, won't you? So please put your purse away, drive up by the house, and let's eat something."

Inside the house, Willem told the women to put their rain-damp jackets on hooks in a tiny entryway to the kitchen, which was a very large room lit with a round overhead fluorescent light, buzzing slightly. A stainless-steel sink looked out over a curtained double window onto the farmyard. Next to it was a 1970s-era fridge, notable for its avocado green color. Then all the way around the room were cupboards, tops separated from bottoms by laminate counters. Next to a door leading further into the house, however, the cabinets ended and were replaced by an antique Hoosier cabinet, with storage space underneath its white enamel tin counter, and above that a cupboard with three doors.

"Hey," Mary said with delight as she walked over the old cabinet. "A Hoosier!" Turning to face a smiling Willem, she reminisced, "We had one of these when I was a kid, in Chicago in the thirties. Does it have the flour bin, the one with a sifter and the bread drawer?"

"It does indeed," Willem replied. "Go ahead and open it up."

Mary did, joined by Joni looking over her shoulder.

"See, Joni. This tin can holds the flour, and when you pull this little cover off the bottom and turn the crank, voila! Sifted flour." And as she turned it, a tiny amount of flour fell out.

"I don't use it anymore," Willem declared. "Not a baker. Never was and too old to learn. You can't teach an old dog how to bake, y'know. That Hoosier cupboard was my folks', I still remember my mother when it came. We had to take a horse and cart to the train station to pick it up. She ordered it from Sears, of course. Man, she was so excited, so proud! I couldn't part with it when we built this new place. My wife, Mary, same name as you," he added, nodding to Mary, "wasn't keen on it, but she humored me, God keep her."

Walking to the sideboard where Willem had assembled lunch materials, sliced turkey, lettuce, American cheese, mayo, mustard, and bread—as white as the paint on the bottom of the old barn—Joni took up a knife and began to help him.

"Coffee?" Willem asked.

"Yes," they both replied.

"Mary, would you mind doing the honors then, the pot's over there on the stove," Willem pointed.

Mary nodded, noting that the stove was an older electric. She hated electric stoves, too hard to control the heat. But wow, she thought, he had a percolator coffeemaker, when on earth was the last time she'd used one of these? She put cold water in from the sink, added coffee from a can by the stove, filling the basket to the top, then pressed the grounds down so she could add more.

Silence ensued for several moments, the only sounds the slight buzzing of the overhead and a loud ticking from a 1950s-era electric clock over the Hoosier, bright red with a rooster in its center.

"What's the name of that cupboard again?" Joni asked, breaking the silence.

"Hoosier!" Both Mary and Willem answered at the same time, then laughed.

"It's from Indiana is all I know, and you could order them from the Sears catalog," Mary responded.

"Yup," Willem agreed. "From Indiana, I think *Hoosier* was the name of the company that made them too, but I'm not sure. They were popular in the turn of the last century 'cause kitchens didn't have any cupboards. Houses didn't have any closets, for that matter, so folks had wardrobes. Remember them, Mary?"

"Sure thing," she said, turning to Joni. "Great, big wooden portable clothes closets, really. They came in all shapes and sizes. We had 'em in each bedroom growing up, we kids would hide in 'em for fun—hide and seek, y'know?"

"Why were there no closets and no cabinets?" Joni queried.

"Too expensive," Willem responded. "Heck, folks were just glad to have a roof over their heads back then. Just bare walls inside, with wallpaper in the living room if they got a little money. Say, this ain't much lunch, how about some soup? Campbell's cream of tomato maybe?"

"No, thanks," Mary replied as she was hovering over the percolator, recalling that the coffee was done when it perked up into the small glass on top of the lid.

"OK, let's eat then." Willem said as he and Joni put the sandwiches on small plates and placed them on the table. Mary and Joni sat down, while Willem went to the Hoosier and withdrew a pint bottle of Canadian Club Whisky. Then he went to the fridge where he retrieved a large plastic bottle of ginger ale, setting them both on the table while he got three small glasses out of another cupboard.

"I almost forgot, a toast. I don't have much company these days, so this is a big celebration for me, you know." He poured the glasses almost full with the soda then added a splash, only a splash, of the whiskey to each. Joni and Mary exchanged dubious glances.

They were seated at the small green-and-white table with shiny metal legs. An item, Mary recalled, popular after the war in many households stepping gingerly into the new age of American consumption.

Willem lifted his glass and proposed a toast to the two women and their journey. "Lucky me, you runnin' out of gas. Company's rare these days since most people my age are long gone." Peering at Joni, he added, "Drink up, girl, not enough liquor in there to hurt a fly. Not a drinking man myself. It'll take me a month or more to finish that little bottle. Course, my folks never touched the stuff, and Mary either. My mother'd have a fit if she knew I was keeping booze in her Hoosier, and that's for sure!"

"How long have you lived here?" Joni asked, her interest growing more genuine. She took a quick bite of her sandwich to kill the awful taste of the soda and its alcohol charge.

"My whole life. I was born here. This is a century farm. Maybe you missed the plaque out front? It means my family has been here over a hundred years," Willem said proudly. "That's unusual these days when everyone's on the move. Make more money someplace else, farm work is too hard, too dirty. Course, I get around a lot since I got into restoring those tractors, stay overnight in motels and whatnot, but only time I really was gone was for the war."

"World War II?" Mary asked, spreading more mustard on her sandwich.

"Yup, the big one."

"Where were you?" Mary continued.

"Middle of nowhere out in the Pacific Theater. Why they called it that—*theater*—I'll never know, like it was some kind of show. It was a show, all right. But I was lucky, never saw combat. I was stationed on a big island called New Caledonia. Don't suppose you ever heard of it?" he asked his guests.

Both women shook their heads. Joni asked what he'd done there.

"Mechanic. They figured out I was good with machinery, so they sent me there to fix stuff. Jeeps mostly, but the occasional tank, trucks, dozers, even a few motorcycles. Huge setup, as I remember. We lived in tents, hundreds of them. Rained like the dickens there, mud everywhere, so the tents were set up on pallets, supposed to keep 'em dry. Didn't though, it was always wet—your tent, your boots, your clothes. The machine shops, though, were made out of steel, nice and dry there where we worked. And I'd rather be in the shop than in my tent, tell the truth. Food was pretty terrible, and you'd go kinda crazy to have something to do. Men gambled, drank, got into fights, lots of sickness from the tropics, that type of thing."

"Did you get sick?" Mary wondered.

"Nope. More luck, I guess. Got homesick, though. Wrote a lot of letters, got quite a few back from here, mostly from my mother. Dad wasn't much of a writer." He paused and smiled. "Funny thing was, Army didn't want the Japs to know where we were, afraid they'd find out, so they read all our mail, what went out to the States. So we couldn't tell our people where we were. But soldier I worked with was from Minnesota, told me there was a place had the same name in Minnesota. So I told my parents that, and they got ahold of an atlas and figured it out."

"There's a New Caledonia in Minnesota?" Mary asked.

"Yup, just *Caledonia* though, not *New*. They never let on in the letters, but when I got home, they told me they'd found it right away tucked into the southeast corner of the state. No idea why it's called that. Where are you going in Minnesota?"

"Winona," Mary answered. "A town on the Mississippi, in the southeast corner. My sister lives there, and we're going to see her." Joni noted and was pleased by Mary's *we*.

"So how long were you there, in that place I mean?" Joni asked.

"Two years, give or take. Know what we did when we left?" He got up then, taking Mary's coffee off the stove and setting out cups. "Cream, sugar?"

"No, black's good for me," Mary answered.

"And for me," Joni added.

Sipping his coffee, Willem noted, "Hey, this ain't too bad, little stronger than I usually take it, but not bad. And what we did when we left? We took some dozers and dug enormous pits. You could have buried barns in them. We pushed all that machinery—jeeps, trucks, motorcycles, generators—right into those pits. Covered them with dirt, trees, and rocks. Make a man weep. And those people who lived there, the native people, they went crazy digging into that mess to try and rescue some of that stuff. Didn't have a blessed thing them people, so only natural they wanted it. Who wouldn't?"

Grimacing over her too-hot coffee, Mary said, "Well, apparently the Army didn't want the stuff. Why not?"

"Exactly what we wondered. Back home here, when it was all over, we was still farming mostly with horses. Dad had the one John Deere, a

B, of course. That's how I got started collecting them, the first tractor we had on the farm. And I'm thinking how we could have used those jeeps—easy enough to turn one into a tractor, you know—those trucks, all of it, back here. But no, the muckety-mucks told us that the folks who made the stuff, Ford, GM, Chrysler, told the government they didn't want that stuff to be used 'cause it would compete with the new stuff they wanted to sell to folks. So we just dumped it, all over the Pacific, into holes or into the ocean. Millions of dollars worth of perfectly good machines, a crying shame, and I still think so today."

"But why not leave it then for the people on the island?" Joni was perplexed.

"Beats me, never could figure it. Came home and told my folks and the neighbors, they couldn't hardly credit it. Some of course said it was Roosevelt, in tight with the money-grubbers on Wall Street, but I don't think that was it. Tell you one thing, though. I never trusted the federal folks after that. Come around wanting to get me into one or another farm program, gonna make me rich, sign up for this, for that. Not me, no siree, not me."

"You said your wife was named Mary," Joni changed the subject.

"Yes, know it sounds corny, but she was the love of my life," he said with a smile. "Only woman I was ever interested in. She was a town girl, from Beebeetown, like I mentioned. Courted her a long time, she had to take care of her parents and I had to help out here and then take over the farm. We barely had time to go to a movie, but we finally did the deed and got hitched. Being from town, she was a more modern person. Never much liked the old farmhouse, so after my folks passed I tore the old place down. Saved some of the lumber, of course, then built her this house back in the '60s. Got the money from raising pigs, something you could do then."

"Children?" Mary asked.

"Nope, time we got married, we were too old. Only got to live here for twelve years, then Mary died. Cancer, heck of a thing. She took sick and only lived for maybe six months. I nursed her here until the end. Broke my heart, like they say."

"Oh, I'm sorry to hear that, Willem," Mary offered kindly. "I lost my husband just two years ago. It's part of the reason I'm taking this trip. I needed to get out of our house, too many memories. I found myself talking to him, like he was still there, you know?"

"Yep, I know about that. I did the same. Less now after all these years, but once in a while I'll just pretend she's in there sitting in my mother's old rocker, doing her embroidery and asking me about the farm."

Getting up, Joni went over to one of the counters, which held several framed photographs. "Is this her?" she asked, holding up a picture in an elaborate gilt frame that showed a rather stern young woman with short brown hair and a labored smile. Clearly uncomfortable with the photo or the photographer.

"Yes, that's my Mary," Willem replied. "Hated to have her picture taken, just hated it. 'This isn't Hollywood,' she'd say, 'it's a farm in Iowa!' I never even tried to take one, but a friend of hers took that one, just before we got married."

"But you must have wedding pictures," Mary said.

"Nope," he said, shaking his head. "Mary wouldn't hear of wasting money on such. I couldn't persuade her, and I was just glad she finally agreed to marry me. I don't miss 'em, I'd just take 'em out and get all sad."

"And who are these men?" Joni asked, gesturing to the two other photos next to Mary's, each showing a young man in uniform.

"Sad story for them too. Don't know why I keep 'em there, in fact. One on the right is, was, my brother. Younger'n me, so he missed WW Two, but they got him for Korea. Big, strong farm boy, so they put him in the infantry. He made it out of that hellhole—what we were doing there I still don't know—but he came back changed, badly changed. Shell-shocked, that's what they said. Never quite right in his head. Married his high-school sweetheart, had a kid, that's the other picture there. But she had to leave him, divorce, 'cause he just wasn't fit to live with. I know, because after she went, he and his boy came here to live and he had these nightmares, sometimes even had 'em in the daytime. Sometimes he'd just sit in a chair, on a tractor, wherever, shaking like a tree in a bad storm. Well, finally the storm took him, one January he just left the house late at night, had a bottle of booze. I found him the next day froze to death by a big, old oak on the other end of the property. Not sure, of course, but I think he did it on purpose. Too many ghosts rattling around in his head."

"Well, I'm very sorry again," Mary said. "To lose your brother that way. Was he the only sibling you had?"

"Yup. Just Jimmy and me. Me the lucky one, him darn unlucky."

"And the other one here, your nephew?" Joni asked.

"Yes, that's him. Or *was* him. Great kid, even with all the trouble with his dad and his mom finally just taking off to who knows where. For Mary and me, he was like our son, the one we never had. Good grades in school, working fool here on the farm. But Uncle Sam took him, got called up for another war I can never figure out, Vietnam. Didn't even get a letter from him before he got killed. They didn't want to tell us, but some of his buddies wrote us later, told us it was what they called 'friendly fire,' meaning he got killed by our own troops, a mistake. Read up on it some later, turns out maybe a third of them that got killed over there, in that godforsaken place, were killed that way, by our own people. Hard to believe, ain't it?" The old farmer shook his head sadly.

Mary agreed, "It *is* hard to imagine, being killed by your comrades. Awful, just awful!"

Continuing, Willem pointed to the photo of his nephew. "He and my folks, my brother, Mary, they're all buried in the little Lutheran cemetery near here. You'll think it's strange, but I go over once in a while, talk some to them. Not much of a believer myself, heaven and hell and all that, but if there is one, my people belong there, in heaven. Good people."

Looking at both of them, Willem apologized for his outburst, such as it was. "Sorry, ladies, I just get sad, you know?"

"Don't apologize. We know what you mean," Mary said, including Joni once again. "I hate to say this, Willem, but we've got to go. I'm already way overdue, and I'm sure my sister is worried sick, not to mention my daughter back in California. Can we do the dishes first?"

"Not a bit of it," he protested. "I can't tell you what a treat it was to have you two lovely ladies visit with me. We got on to some sad stuff, but that's life, I guess. And I did get to show you my tractors. Now you can go to Minnesota and tell 'em you met this crazy old coot who collects John Deere Bs, has a big, shiny mess of them," Willem grinned.

"Crazy, I don't think so," Mary promised. "My sister lives on a farm, and I bet she'll be impressed. You know, I always wondered why so many little towns in our country have some kind of military thing in their parks. A cannon, some kind of machine gun, a tank, and even sometimes an airplane. Why in the heck don't they have tractors, or other old farm stuff instead? Those machines made this country, not the guns. Don't you think?"

"I couldn't agree more!" Willem stated. "Your friend has got a good head on her, young lady," he said to Joni as the women put their now dry coats on. Neither of them were huggers, but they each gave Willem an awkward squeeze as they left the house. Seeing him standing in the door waving, they motored the Dreadnaught out of the driveway.

"Jesus, what a guy, what a story," Joni finally said, breaking the silence once they'd gotten up to speed on the highway.

"Yes, definitely. I can't say anything about the other stuff—the creep who jumped me or the cops—to Theresa. But I can sure tell her what happened when we ran out of gas in Iowa when we thought we were still in Nebraska!"

Both laughed, then lapsed into rain-driven reveries until they reached the connection with the interstate, where they stopped to gas up, pee, and buy some corn chips.

"Corn chips? Of course," Mary chuckled. "It's Iowa."

Chapter 37

Joni and Mary realized that after their long lunch with Willem, they wouldn't be able to make it to Theresa's until very late that evening. They reluctantly decided to stop for the night at Ames, home of the University of Iowa.

"Did you ever think of going to college, Joni?" Mary asked as she set the cruise control on the Dreadnaught to just over seventy.

"Yes and no," she replied thoughtfully. "I had a couple teachers in high school who insisted I was smarter than I thought I was, and so I should go to college to find out. Trouble was, I had no idea what I wanted to study, and I didn't want to borrow a shitload of money to just wander around scratching my head thinking 'hey, what am I doing here?'"

"Yeah, I know what you mean. A friend teaches at a local community college in L.A. and has all kinds of horror stories about students being there who shouldn't be. Lost souls thinking that somehow college was going to save them, get them a great job, deliver a great life, and so on. He actually believes that probably half of the students there shouldn't be."

"How about you? Did you ever go to college?"

"Nope. When I was a teenager, all that really mattered to a woman from my social class was to get married—and try like hell not to have a baby before you did. Besides, I was a lousy student, couldn't sit still, hated taking direction. So spending four more years in a classroom wasn't for me!"

"But you said your sis went."

"Yes, she liked school and was very good at it. She was a great reader. She became an English teacher. Think I mentioned it."

"Did she like it?" Joni asked.

"As far as I know she did," Mary. "We can get the down and dirty when we get there, but I've never heard to the contrary. She was always more mainstream than me, likes kids, dogs, people, the whole thing, I guess."

"You're not crazy about kids or dogs?"

"Kids, not especially, and dogs, absolutely not! I was a landscaper, remember. Dogs were my enemy. They crap all over the yard, make big holes, and dig up plants. And kids? I loved my daughter, of course, but I was never crazy about the little tykes. Mike wanted to have more children, but I nixed it. My folks were horrified, a Catholic girl with only one child."

Not sure what else to say on the topic, Mary turned to the old standby, the weather. "Can you believe the rain hasn't stopped?" she said as an enormous pickup blasted by them, covering the windshield with water.

"Dude's in a real hurry," Joni observed. "That old guy Willem didn't seem in any hurry, did he?"

"Not a bit. He struck me as the kind of man who takes his time. How else could he be, fixing all those old tractors?"

"Yeah, they were something. But don't you think it was kind of strange that he never mentioned Mike here? He must have seen him."

"Probably, but maybe not. He was just at the back putting in the gas," Mary remembered. "Still, he comes from a time and a place out here, where people tend to be very careful. Look right at you and see a booger in your nose and never say a word. Being polite, I guess. In fact, I was surprised he told us as much about his life as he did."

"Right. And most of it really sad. Jesus, those stupid wars took practically his entire family! Was Mike in the army?"

"Yes, he was, right after the big war, luckily. He was in the Army Air Corps, kind of an early version of the Air Force. They made him a cook. I'm not sure why, but that's what got him into being a grocer."

"Grocer?" Joni asked.

"Yes, he was a greengrocer, which is an old-fashioned name for somebody who takes care of the produce section. The lettuce, carrots, cabbage, and all that. He was always active in union stuff, though, so he finally went to work for the union. The UFCW, or United Food and Commercial Workers. He did mostly organizing and he was good at it, except for his big mouth. He wasn't the most diplomatic of men. He finally quit when they pulled some stunt on a union in Minnesota. It was in a place called Austin, I think we'll drive right by there. There is a meat plant there called Hormel, where they make Spam. You've heard of Spam, right?"

"Oh yeah, my dad eats that crap. Loves it with eggs for breakfast," Joni said, making a face.

"I'm no Spam fan either. Especially after the company screwed its employees."

"But I thought a union protected the workers?"

"Well, in theory they do. And at Hormel they did at first, but the longer the strike went on, the more unhelpful the union got. So the national office of the union, where Mike worked, finally took responsibility away from the local union and cut a deal with management. It was a clear case of the big union screwing the little union. So anyway, Mike quit after that. He went in and yelled at the big wigs, really told them off. A real diplomat weren't you, Mike," Mary said to the mannequin.

"What'd he do then?"

"He just went back into produce. He was real experienced, so he didn't have any trouble getting a job. Stayed there until he retired. He was a great guy, even with all the noise he made."

"We aren't much on being told what to do, are we, Mike?" Joni said laughing.

"See," Mary said with a grin. "Now you're talking to him too. He was that kind of guy."

"He did kind of creep me out a little at first. But now I think it's kind of cool, us and him."

"Right, wherever you are, Mike," Mary raised her voice, "I bet you're digging it, aren't you? Your old lady and a cute young woman riding shotgun with you."

"'Old lady,' you sound like a biker chick!" Joni laughed.

"Not that I know of, it's just what I am, an old lady," Mary laughed as well.

"You know, Mary, you just don't seem old to me. You know, like all bent over, hard of hearing, and full of stories about the good old days."

"Thanks, I guess. Wish I could take credit for not seeming old, but I flat can't. I smoked plenty of ciggies back in the day. Drank my share of booze, and I still drink a bit. Lucky genes, that's what I've got. Just a toss of the Darwinian dice, my dear, it's that simple!"

"Darwinian, what's that?" Joni was perplexed.

"Darwin was the scientist who discovered evolution. You know, how we come from our ancestors adapting to stuff—weather, food, whatever. But, you know, some people exercise, eat all the right stuff, don't smoke or drink, and then bang, they're dead at fifty. Others, like me, eat whatever we want, smoke, and drink—and we sail into old age."

"But your work must have helped, don't you think the landscaping kept you in good shape?"

"Probably, for two reasons. I worked in an office for a couple of years when we first got married and hated every minute of it. It wasn't the people. Even the bosses weren't bad. It was just being cooped up inside. So I'd have been done for years ago if I'd had to stay in an office. And you're right, the physical part of landscaping work was good for me too. Actually, I don't think we humans are supposed to spend most of our lives indoors sitting on our butts. We're supposed to be outside chasing animals and gathering wild greens. I mean it!"

"No kidding. I hated being in the Worst Western, cleaning up after other people, changing the nasty sheets, vacuuming until I wanted to throw the goddamn machine over a balcony. I'll never do that again. But I don't know how I'd do working outdoors, I've never tried it."

"Well, maybe you can get a little practice at my sister's. See how it fits. Meanwhile, how about a little music on this rainy day. Look through those tapes and pick something. Actually no, don't pick something. Play some Ella."

"OK," Joni agreed, reaching for the box. "OK. Wait a minute, where'd you get all these?"

"My grandson Andres back in L.A. made them for me, mostly from records Mike and I have had for years," Mary said. "Great stuff from our jazz glory days."

"Glory days?"

"Well," Mary paused, "everybody today thinks listening to live music has to either be in a concert hall or in some giant stadium. But the jazz scene, with some exceptions, was mostly in small clubs. Places that held fifty to a hundred people, often fewer, most of them diehards who would travel a hundred miles or more just to hear, say, Ella. Now Mike and I never had lots of money, but we went to clubs a lot. Mostly around L.A., but up to San Francisco a few times, or Oakland and other places up and down the coast. Martinis and smoke so thick you had to squint to see the stage, not to mention crappy food if you wanted to eat at all. It was glorious!"

"Sounds great, actually. OK, here's some Ella Fitzgerald."

"Great, put her in the player, please."

And Ella sang Cole Porter's "My Heart Belongs to Daddy" to them in that wonderfully light, always-upbeat voice, while the Dreadnaught's wipers scraped a background accompaniment.

"She must have been pretty young when she sang this," Joni commented.

"Not necessarily. She started out really young. This is a good story: She went to a talent contest at a famous club, the Apollo, in Harlem, intending to tap dance, but she didn't because the people before her were so good. She gave it up and decided to sing instead, and she was an instant hit. But her voice? You know it never really changed, even as she got older. She got a little heavy, but it never showed in her voice."

"She was black, right?"

"Yup, and not real pretty like, say, Lena Horne. But she doesn't sound black, necessarily, does she?"

"No, actually, I can't tell just listening to her."

"That's why she was so successful, with whites I mean, in a time when racism was routine as apple pie. I'm sure there were people who heard her on the radio, and had no idea she was a big, old black woman. We saw her once, you know."

"Really, where?"

"Back in the early '60s, real early, pre-hippie for sure," Mary reminisced. "She did a ten- or twelve-night gig in L.A., at a little club right on Sunset called the Crescendo. She'd just come back from some big tour in Europe. They loved her over there. Black American jazz musicians were a hot item in Paris. Mike scored these tickets, maybe a lot of lettuce changed hands, I don't know. Anyway, we got to go two nights; it was just Ella and a little quartet backing her. She was just like she sounds too, or sounded, relaxed, easy-going. If she forgot the words, which she did once in a while, she'd just say so and make stuff up. And scat! Man, that woman could make the Martians sit up and dig!"

"Scat, what's that?"

"That is a funny word, I guess," Mary laughed. "It's a kind of singing, you'll hear some on this tape. She's one of the best. Maybe *the* best. It's sounds and made-up stuff instead of words. It's mostly a black thing, although there was this little Jewish guy, Mel Tormé, who was real good at it too. There . . . listen."

They listened to "Perdido," almost all of which Ella sang in scat.

"Wow. It had almost no words at all. Drugs?"

"Drugs? Do you mean was she using them? No, not a bit. It's just her, straight up. And never a hint of gossip about her life either, kind of at the opposite end from, say, Billie Holiday."

"Her I know about. Eunice played her all the time. She was a junkie, right?"

"Not really. Smoked a lot of Mary Jane, I heard. But she didn't use heroin, which was the drug of choice for jazz heads back in the day. Everyone assumed it because of her sound, real slow, low-key, and little bit slurry. Totally the opposite of Ella."

The two women remained silent for a time, listening to Ella, and looking out at the hazy countryside, until Joni asked about silos. "What are those towers they have on the farms?"

"Silos. Farmers store feed in them, grain and hay, and it ferments like sauerkraut, which helps preserve it. Kind of like a big thermos bottle, or a huge canning jar, I guess. They're also, you could say, a symbol of success. The more silos, the more successful you are. Supposedly." Mary smiled over at Joni.

"Like, say, skyscrapers?"

"Right, monuments for the achievements of anxious men. Like pyramids and cathedrals, mosques and so on. Have you ever heard about Stonehenge?"

"The place in England?"

"Right, another giant monument of men, kind of an early skyscraper thing. Scientists spend their lives writing funky articles trying to figure out places like Stonehenge and they still have no clue what it was for."

"Scientists?"

"Yes. Anthropologists, mostly. Or archaeologists. People who study ancient ruins, and uncivilized tribes of people, like American Indians."

"I guess I remember some of that, from social studies in high school maybe. But you're not saying the Indians were, like, 'uncivilized,' are you? I mean that's not cool, is it?"

"I am, actually. 'Civilization'—I've read some about this—is actually about one small group of people managing the lives of huge numbers of other people, the worker-bees, slaves, soldiers, and so on. And it's kind of a new idea—compared to what most humans did and some still do, which is to not have 'bosses' and 'kings' and so on, share everything, no huge buildings like pyramids, churches, skyscrapers. So when I say 'uncivilized,' it's a compliment."

Joni looked skeptical.

"A compliment, really?" Looking at Joni, Mary was glad she got it, and they both laughed.

"So how come you know this stuff?"

"I took a night course years ago at Pasadena City College. And I liked it, actually. A crazy guy taught it. He'd spent years in India studying holy men called sadhus, men who sleep on nails and hang stones from their testicles."

"From their balls—whoops—testicles, for real?" Joni challenged.

"Oh yes, he had photos and slides, lots of them. Guys with huge beards, the kind the Harley guys wish they could grow. They live by begging, a little rice here, a banana there, so they're mostly really skinny. They believe in something called rejection of the body."

"Rejection of the body?"

"They have it in all kinds of religions," Mary explained. "The belief that your body is just a hindrance to getting saved, meeting your maker and so on. No sex, little food, little or no clothing, no friends or family. All that stuff just gets in the way of your spiritual nature. That's the God-crazy part."

"No thanks. I actually like my body!"

"I like mine too," Mary smiled, "one of the main things I liked about my work in landscaping was being able to use my body to do actual stuff. I planted trees, built walls, dug ponds, I even loved getting dirty. Something my sister and I were never allowed to do as little girls. And I still like to dig in the dirt. I can't wait to do some work on Theresa's farm." Mary actually thumped the steering wheel in anticipation.

The Ella tape had run out, and both women remained quiet for what seemed like a long time, the only sounds being the swish-swish of the car's wipers and the roar and splash of a car or semi passing them. They finally stopped in Ames—at a Best Western, of all places. Mary paid for a room with two beds and a television the size of a garden shed. They watched TV, eating chips and salsa and a bag of cheese curds, until Mary fell asleep gently snoring. Joni turned the tube off, thanking her lucky stars once more that she'd asked this great old lady for a ride to Minnesota.

Next morning as they drove away in bright sunshine, Joni said, "God, I can't believe it. I actually stayed at a Worst Western!"

"You should have seen some of the places Mike and I stayed in when we were young. Tiny little cabins with no bathrooms. Maybe some heat, maybe not. Musty bedding with roaches big as rats. One low-watt bulb hanging over the bed, now those were the worst kinds of places, believe me!"

"You know, Mary," Joni laughed, "you're a real wiseass. How does that go with being raised a good Catholic girl in Chicago? Everything you've told me so far about when you were a kid? Totally doesn't go with the woman driving this car with the mock hubby in the front seat." Joni pulled one of her knees up to her chest, to stretch.

"Well, we all change. Believe it or not, you have big changes ahead of you, most of them good, I hope. Me? There wasn't anything wrong when I was a kid, none of the crap you hear about where parents beat their kids, lock 'em up, or even the horror stories you keep hearing about going to Catholic school. With nuns rapping knuckles, pedophile priests, and that sort of stuff. Some of the nuns weren't great, but some were just fine. And none of them ever did more than grab some silly boy by his ear and haul him out of the room."

Mary held up her right hand for inspection. "See these knuckles all knobby and bent? None of that's from nuns, it's from landscaping. Banging up your hands is just part of the job. My dad never hit me, ever. My mom spanked us once or twice. Like after my tricycle ride down the stairs. Yelled at us when we were snotty little kids, pushed me once when I was a very snotty teen. Both of us were so surprised at that, we actually started laughing. But, and here it is in an eggshell, it was all very, very boring. It was stiflingly boring, at least to me. My folks were fearful people living in fearful times, the Depression bracketed by two world wars. They were the children of immigrants, people who were always waiting for someone to knock on the door and hurt them or their children, send them back to the shithole in Germany they escaped from. Just like the Latinos and Asians now in L.A."

Joni nodded. "I worked with a couple of Mexican women, they worked their butts off and never complained, never. It drove me crazy!"

"Do you think they were here illegally, scared of getting caught by the INS?" Mary asked. "My daughter's husband's parents are Mexican immigrants. I think they're actually citizens now, but you never know. And in a way, they're always sitting on the edge of their chairs waiting for someone to kick their door in and send them back, even when they're here legally."

"But back to you," Joni reminded Mary.

"You mean this me versus the girl in Chicago lo these many years past?"

"Yes."

"I was bored, that was it. I was simply bored. Now this was pre-TV mind you, so it wasn't like I saw all these other worlds I could be part of. We didn't go to the movies much either, it was too expensive. So I wasn't star struck, hoping to become a famous actress. I just had a worm inside of me, gnawing away, trying to reach the light, or something."

"A worm?" Joni didn't get it.

"Yeah, great metaphor, isn't it?" Mary laughed. "But my parents, bless their anxious hearts, just hoped I'd find the right guy, marry him, and have a bunch of kids for them to enjoy in their old age. It scared the dickens out of them when I left for California the summer after I graduated. I had no money and no plan. I just went."

"All by yourself?"

"Nope, the older sister of a friend of mine, a nurse, wanted to go out there and needed somebody to ride along. She had a car, an old Ford, and I knew how to drive and wanted to go. My folks were furious at her, but once we were on the road it didn't matter. 'I don't know about you, Mary,' she told me, 'but I'm never going back to Shitcago. Never!' I was impressed, believe me. It seemed to take forever, but we drove right to Pasadena, she'd read about the Rose Bowl, the orange groves and all that. We rented a small place, and we both got work right away. Me in a typing pool in a big insurance place, and her in a local hospital."

"And?"

"We didn't share a place long, she had guys coming over almost every night. And little Catholic me was appalled, or maybe not appalled, just uncertain. Anyway, we went our different ways, me to another apartment with a girl in the typing pool, and I don't remember where the nurse went."

"And how did you meet Mike?"

"Dancing, that's how I met him, the little Irish hoofer," Mary laughed. "Hey, that man could dance. My roommate hauled me to some local place that held dances, contests and so on, every night even on Sundays. They sold beer and junky food too."

"Were there DJs?" Joni asked.

"No, there was no such thing," Mary said. "It was all live bands back then, and some were great, especially the Latin ones. God, those guys could cook! So I went there a couple of times. I wasn't a dancer, but that was OK because most of the guys weren't either. You know how it is, they were all anxious about women, horny as toads, so they'd drink a couple gallons of beer and then get the nerve to ask you, 'Wanna dance, honey?' And you're there to try to have a good time, meet a decent guy, so you say yes. And you're not really having a good time. Until I met Mike that is. Do you like to dance?"

"Not especially. Things haven't changed much, I guess. We had dances at school with dopey dudes standing around giggling, afraid of looking like the fools they were. Eventually they'd go out in the parking lot and get wasted, and then stagger back in and ask you to dance. You can't dance, and then they can't either. One guy in my class *could* dance his ass off, but I never danced with him. That was about it until I started barhopping after high school when I met a few guys who could really dance, much better than me. What was the point?"

"The point, my dear, is that it's a great thing to do," Mary declared. "Hey, maybe you'll get lucky in Winona and somebody will grab your dance card. Somebody like Mike. Everybody said he was a natural. He and his buddies used to sneak off to some clubs in Queens where they played Latin music and jazz, where people did dance. Mike and his pals were underage, but that didn't matter back then. So they'd go in, or sometimes sneak in, and hang out in the background. They couldn't believe their little Irish Catholic eyes, or ears!"

"What do you mean?"

"You ever hear of that old TV show *I Love Lucy*, real popular in the 1950s? There was a ditzy redhead, Lucille Ball, with the Cuban husband?"

"Eunice loved that show," Joni smiled. "She watched the reruns night and day. Old hippie smack addict, rock-and-roller from way back, and she loved that show. I could never figure out why."

"So you saw it?" Mary asked, laughing.

"Yep, too many times actually."

"So the husband, Ricky, in the show, he was a bandleader. He was Cuban, so they played Latin music. Well, in real life he was named Desi Arnaz, and he really did have a band. And Mike actually saw that band, along with many others like Xavier Cugat and Tito Puente, in different places in the city, including Queens. And what really got to him wasn't the musicians—Mike couldn't play a note on a kazoo—but the dancing. The beautiful women, I imagine they all looked beautiful to him then, in tight dresses and high heels. And more important, the tough, macho, little Cuban and Puerto Rican guys doing all kinds of fabulous dance steps. Cha-cha, tango, whatever passed for salsa back then. So he got the bug, like the jitterbug, get it?" Mary teased Joni.

"The jitterbug, is that a dance, or some kind of insect?"

"A bug like ants in your pants, maybe. Makes you dance your little heinie off. It was a black thing at first, of course. *Jitter* meant the jitters, like when you get jumpy from drinking too much. So booze and dancing, there's nothing new there. But bored white people like me and Mike picked up on it, and by the time we met, it was a hot thing in the dance halls. I can't really describe it except to say you used your whole body, all of it, and just got down. Real down! So when Mike was stationed in Mississippi after the war, he and his friends would go to clubs in town there in Biloxi and dance like fools. He met some women who showed him some of the cool Latin stuff he'd seen in Queens, and he turned out to be a quick study. I remember the first time I saw him at the club we went to in Pasadena, the whole place stopped still to watch him swing some chickie around the dance floor, and you know what?"

"What?"

"Something in my little German Catholic soul just clicked, *snap*, and I told myself that not only was I going to dance with that little man, I was going to marry him. And I did, me and that dancing fool. Isn't that right, Mike?" Mary asked, reaching over and patting the mannequin's knee.

"And hey, here we are at Albert Lea," Mary announced. "We'll go east on I-90, and should be at Theresa's in a little over an hour. Look at the map, will you? I think we take the exit to St. Charles, then head into the boonies to her place. I've got directions in the glove box," she said, waiting while Joni dug them out. "Right, there they are."

Joni looked at the directions and verified the St. Charles exit, feeling herself getting excited. What was Theresa like? What was her farm like? How would the meeting with the lawyers in Rochester go? Who freaking knew?

"So what's rattling around in *your* head?" Mary asked Joni, smiling at the thoughtful girl next to her.

"Me?" Joni asked, turning to her new friend. "I'm actually getting excited. I want the driving to be done, want to meet Theresa, relax a little. And I'm a little uncertain. About what's going to happen."

"Uncertain is fine," Mary reassured her. "Worried is not. I'm sure you can stay with Tee as long as you need to. She'll take to you, I know. Look at it this way, you've got the whole rest of your life ahead of you, and it's not going to be in Garberville changing sheets."

"You're right about that. No more stupid hospital corners!"

"That's funny, Mike learned how to do that in the Army and made a big deal about me doing it that way," Mary laughed. "So hospital corners it was, and still is to this day."

Watching the fields they drove past, Joni asked, "What's that really tall crop we've been seeing since Nebraska? Like right there," she said pointing.

"That's corn, the all-American crop if there ever was one," Mary said. "They grow a heck of a lot of it here." She picked up the bag of corn chips and shook it for emphasis.

"It's kinda pretty, actually."

"Yes, Tee says that fall here in the Midwest is a really colorful time. See those trees, how colorful they are? And that field over there to the left, what a pretty brown it is? I think those are soybeans, probably ready to harvest."

"How come you know all this stuff about farming? Is it pretty much like landscaping?"

"Well, there's plenty of corn and beans back in sunny Cal, you know. And, being a landscaper, guess it's just natural that I'd be interested in farming. I told you, I'd rather hang out in a crowd of trees, or a field of corn, than with a crowd of people."

"I feel the same way about crowds actually," Joni said.

"Well, take heart, my dear. There will be no crowds at Theresa's," Mary promised.

The women drove in silence for quite some time until Mary spotted a sign for the city of Austin. "Hey, here's Austin, where the Spam plant I told you about yesterday is?"

By now Mary was driving on the interstate right through Austin, but very slow, at about twenty-five miles an hour, peering at the signs. "There it is," she exclaimed, "a Spam museum, can you imagine?

"Hey, Mary," Joni said pointedly. "Maybe you should drive a little faster. Fuzz and all, you know?" Joni wasn't anxious to encounter any more cops.

But Mary slowed down even more, and told Joni to lower her window. "OK, there's the museum," Mary said with excitement. "Grab Mike's arm and help him give Hormel the finger will you, he would have loved to have done that!" Joni reluctantly did as Mary asked, and as she stuck the mannequin's hand out the window, the Lincoln crawled almost to a halt and Mary yelled: "Screw you, Hormel, and your Spam too!"

Joni couldn't help herself but laugh out loud as she pulled the plastic arm back in the car, thankful that Mary had once again put her foot on the gas. "A museum for Spam, huh? What's next, toilet paper and nail clippers?"

"Oh God, in this country we like to build museums to everything. They aren't even actually museums in the real sense of the word, anyway," Mary pointed out. "A kind of worship that takes a new and even nastier turn. And speaking of turns, keep an eye out for that St. Charles exit will you?"

"It will be on your left, and then we'll go right back over the freeway when we get there," Joni added.

And suddenly Mary started to sing, "And to Theresa's farm we'll go, to Theresa's farm we'll go, hey ho the dairy oh, to Granny Tee's farm we'll go!" Making Joni laugh all over again.

An hour later, with only one wrong turn, they pulled into Theresa's yard, horn blaring. Mary flung open her door and headed straight for her sister. After they hugged, Theresa greeted Joni with a warm handshake, and then a hug too. There were lots of tears, and lots of laughter.

"I can't believe you're actually here Mary. Just can't believe it!" Theresa must have said it a dozen times over.

"I am, sweet sister Tee, I am. Or actually, we are. Right as rain and all that other stuff, right, Joni?" Mary said with a wink at her young companion.

Feeling awkward and certainly a bit out of place, Joni still smiled in agreement as they headed into the house to relax for a bit before they unloaded the car. What a wonderful place, she couldn't help thinking as she looked around the farm. It did look like it came right off a calendar!

After they'd shared lunch, as the two sisters continued talking non-stop, Joni slipped away and wandered around outside. The barn with its goats, the white dog named Mose, and the chickens. Joni didn't think she'd ever seen real ones. The huge gardens with all the lovely flowers and real cows right in the field across the road. Best of all, nobody else was around at all, she couldn't even see any neighbors. Maybe two or three cars had driven by out on the road the whole time they'd been there. Talk about peaceful!

Back inside, Mary answered her sister's questions about her young passenger. "Yes, I picked her up in Nebraska. Her car broke down and she was headed, is headed, to Rochester to find out about some kind of an inheritance her father got. He sent her, I'm not exactly sure why."

Not sure why this story sounded familiar, Theresa merely said, "Well, she's welcome to stay as long as she likes. She seems like a nice young woman, and God knows it won't hurt me to have some youth around here. But tell me—Emma, Carlos, Andres?"

And so the sisters caught up deep into the evening through chicken stew for supper, with squash and blue potatoes from Tee's garden, and continuing as a bottle of red wine disappeared into their glasses. That and some large slices of lemon meringue pie left them feeling more than happy.

That night in bed, slightly tipsy, Mary sang quietly to herself. "Mikey, oh, Mikey, our fearful trip is done. Came half way cross the continent to have a bit of fun. Wish you were here, lovely buddy. Wish you were here."

And he was of course. Along with Tony, Theresa's husband. And Eunice, Luther's sister and Joni's grandmother. Luther's buddies in Nam, long-gone. The Tofte twins and their father. Their mother. Some miscreants too—Luther's angry dad and Magdalena's Paulie. Then too were the men who'd built the barn and the house and the chicken coop. And the women who'd fed them. A few Native peoples lingering in the fall air. A passing shoemaker who'd stopped at the farm a hundred years ago to make somebody some boots . . . .

The End

Acknowledgments

I would like to thank the following people for their encouragement and assistance in completing *Riding Shotgun*. Tom 'Geezer' Day, Dan 'Dreadnaught' Donnelly, Randy Freeman, Gary Fridell, Brenda Jokisalo, Michael Orange, Bronwyn Schaefer Pope, David Rhodes, Josh Schaefer, Trudi Schaefer, and Jeanne Swope.

About the Author

Born in a military family, Paul Schaefer was raised everywhere from the quaint English countryside to New York City.

After a stint in the Air Force, Paul took his own family to a remote Pacific island where he completed a PhD in anthropology. Drawn by happy memories of visiting his grandparents' farm, Paul and his young family finally put down roots in Wisconsin. In true woods hippie fashion, they bought an abandoned nineteenth century farm. No electricity, no heat, no running water, no problem. Homesteading required nothing more than a lifetime of sweat equity.

Off the farm, Paul shared his talents as an organizer, instigator, and adjunct professor, keeping the counterculture alive while raising a family. Now grandparents, Paul and his wife Trudi still go full tilt, filling their days with barn animals, gardens, grandchildren, and a steadfast desire to raise their voices against the establishment.

A lover of books, music, and art, this is Paul's first work of fiction but likely not his last.